FIC   Cokal, Susann
COKAL   Mirabili

I0437578

DATE DUE

MAR 3 1 2001		
AUG 2 4 2001		
SEP 08 2001		
NOV 2 0 2001		
SEP 0 1 2005		
FEB 1 8 2006		
NOV 0 2 2		
APR 0 9 2016		
APR 2 6 2016		

Gilpin County Public Library
Box 551   15131 Hwy 119
Black Hawk, CO 80422

DEMCO

MIRABILIS

MIRABILIS

SUSANN COKAL

BLUEHEN BOOKS

A MEMBER OF

PENGUIN PUTNAM INC.

NEW YORK

2001

BlueHen Books
a member of
Penguin Putnam Inc.
375 Hudson Street
New York, NY 10014

Library of Congress Cataloging-in-Publication Data

Cokal, Susann.
Mirabilis / Susann Cokal.
p. cm.
ISBN 0-399-14753-5
1. France—History—14th century—Fiction.
2. Black death—Fiction.
3. Wet-nurses—Fiction.   4. Miracles—Fiction.   I. Title.
PS3553.O43657 M57   2001   00-068048
813'.6—dc21

Printed in the United States of America

1   3   5   7   9   10   8   6   4   2

This book is printed on acid-free paper. ∞

Book design by Marysarah Quinn

Au Nid, tout ce que je ne suis pas,

and in memory of
Edward Joseph Cokal (1935–1996)
and
Hanne Agnethe Rasmussen Cokal (1940–2000)

ASSUMPTION

AUGUST 15, ANNO DOMINI 1349—THIS IS
Villeneuve's desperate time, and its time of
miracles. In the heart of the city, in the
church of Saint-Porchaire, a virgin stands on
the edge of a labyrinth. She is fifteen and her
parents' every treasure, the only child of
theirs who lived. And she is good.

Stone walls and a lead roof cup this girl's
body in coolness, blow it full of incense, kiss it
with the petals of dying flowers. The virgin
barely notices. She is listening to the music of
a bell; her father made three for the tower and
she is called after one of them. In its peals she
hears her name—*Blanche. Blanche.*

Blanche is full of hope. For though these
two summers past the townsfolk have been
dying a strange Black Death, her own limbs
are strong, her skin is unbroken, and she is
prepared for Communion. The streets may be
paved with corpses, but her small sins have
been confessed and she is here, in the church
to which her mother dedicates both alms and
prayers.

Her mother looks at her now and, with
a wave of her rosary, indicates that Blanche

should raise her eyes to pray. The bells have stopped, the censers are swinging, and the nave is full of people; their heavy feet have hidden the labyrinth's tiled lobes. In the sanctuary, priests hum like dancing beetles.

Over the shoulders ahead, Blanche sees a golden Lady set up on the altar. A virgin gazes at a Virgin, at long golden arms curving round the crystal globe of a womb in which the Eucharist sits like a promise. This is the town's finest monstrance, made to house the bread of God and deliver his son's body for special feast days; a thousand mouths water for that comforting dryness. Blanche is hungry, too.

Virgo serena . . .

A young priest with the yellow eyes of a hart takes the heavy Virgin in his hands. He murmurs the Gloriosa while sunlight streams through the colored windows and stains the rock-crystal belly. At last he raises Her. Blanche's body colors, too; her face turns blue, her hands red, and she smiles to herself as she prays. And as she does this, she feels her limbs lighten and tingle. She grows lighter, and lighter still, while the feeling becomes a sort of *sparkle* behind her eyes . . .

Beside her, a gasp. Within her, a lurch. Blanche is floating upward. Before she knows it, her feet have left the floor. Her mouth tastes of dust, and her left shoe falls off. Unseen hands continue to lift her until she rests high above the heads of her parents.

Blanche Mirabilis.

Blanche's mother and father fall to their knees. To them and to the others she appears to be mounting thin air—perhaps, they think, she's climbing a stair no one else can see. The people around them kneel, too, until only the yellow-eyed priest remains standing, looking dazedly up her skirt at two clean legs.

The people shout, "Grâce à Dieu—un miracle! Deo gratias!"

Silent and still as a griffin, hovering in the air, Blanche closes her eyes and prays for calm. Like a damp fog it comes over her. Then the invisible hands sweep her slowly round the nave, while the shoe comes off her right foot and crowns a baker, who cries out in gratitude.

Three times Blanche makes the sacred circuit, still too astonished to speak. Her heart beats so loudly she thinks it will burst through her ears. The people are now prostrate, faces down and arms out, their prayers booming through Saint-Porchaire. When slowly, gently, she is set down again, this time in the middle of the maze, no one dares to stand. But when she can finally bear to look through the scented air, her gaze finds the priest's. Two pairs of light eyes glitter, meeting over this miracle.

Nine months later, Blanche will lie in a heap of straw—her father dead, her mother gone, and an unholy flood about to wash her child into the world.

BOOK I

ROSARY

F THERE IS A SOUND OR A SMELL TO HOLI-
ness, I would say they are here, in silence and
the faint smell of smoke. In this district of
shadows, a white mist blankets shapes and
sounds, muffling sensation till, just above
ground, it winds around the feet like rope. I
stumble through the narrow streets, home to
soothsayers and charlatans, mages and fillettes de joie—people every town spurns but
somehow can't do without. They come here to
disappear, if they aren't mad enough to try
living in the forest.

But even sinners and madmen fear what
lies at the very heart of the shadow district:
the blackened church of Saint-Porchaire. A
decade ago, a great fire burned its center hollow, and the sinners inside it died; since then I
have been its only parishioner. And its welcome twines into the maze of silence—
"Beware, beware . . . of the demons that live
in the air!"

Marie, the anchoress walled against the
north transept, always rhymes gloom with
doom. She is the voice of Saint-Porchaire,
having lived here more than twenty years. By
a small miracle, she alone survived the fire, so
she has seen real air-demons here, orange

tongues licking and gray bodies twirling over the walls. She wails her rhymes in the voice of a traveling preacher—"Woman, have shame, lest the air take your name . . ."

By this I know she's heard me coming.

I break open the mist, jump a tumbledown boundary, and land in the atrium between the burnt church and the abandoned priests' house. Saint-Porchaire's walls close in, black with memory, and as I draw close Marie moans again, "Beware . . ."

People have said that this place is a sign of both God's great wrath and his infinite mercy—because when the fire raged, it lasted only as long as it was needed to purify the town's collective soul. The sinners died and the just survived.

I was across the river that day when I saw a vivid yellow sunburst and black clouds purling over Villeneuve. My twelve-year-old heart burst, too—I knew these meant fire, and I was sure my mother was inside. My mother, who sent me into the country to play, though I was already too old for that.

We were in the midst of a season of peste. Already nine people had died, and twice as many lay in a makeshift hospital in Saint-Porchaire's atrium. The townsfolk feared a pandemic like the one so long ago. So in secret council the town fathers—merchants, priests, citizens—decided the city must be cleansed of sin and sinners. That afternoon the most prominent wrongdoers were herded inside the church that Blanche Mirabilis had dishonored. The doors swung shut on Jews, adulterers, and people who'd congressed their own sex. Outside, the virtuous waited and watched; some even cheered as the council processed from the Palais de Justice, holding candles, and set fire to the straw before the great wooden doors.

The fire bloomed instantly, in a ball of light. Then it disappeared, worming its way into the church's wooden skeleton, jumping from doors to beams, from one level to another, causing stones to explode with heat, making the church an oven. The people inside pounded against the doors until smoke overcame them and they collapsed. One by one, on top of one another, they died. Meanwhile the flames reached the network of beams crisscrossing inside the roof, and all at once they, too, caught fire.

This is what the master builders said must have happened, when they tried to explain the miracle of the fire: The roof was composed of lead slabs. The flames heated the lead and destroyed the rafters beneath, and in the same instant the roof melted and the beams disappeared. The lead began to boil as it plummeted, and then it poured itself over the nave below, over the altar and ornaments and bodies. And this was the miracle—the collapse kept the flames from spreading, for the lead doused them and then froze solid. So the fire never claimed the bell tower or the deserted priests' residence, not even the little stone cell where Marie still wails her lyric prophecies.

But this remains a fact: That fire killed my mother, Blanche, along with two priests suspected of engendering me, and the women who said they had to cut her hymen to let me through.

For a few months after her elevation, my mother was Blanche Mirabilis, Blanche the Astonishing—her surname one of the few bits of Latin most people ever learned. After that August 15, not one soul in Villeneuve was lost to peste. People traveled miles to see her; the town fathers talked of building her a chapel, and their wives saw her face when they prayed. A young priest taught her to write so she could share her story with the world. And then I arrived, the daughter who, simply in being born, sinned unforgivably—and yet Blanche forgave and named me Good. The rest of the town called me Tardieu, God's Bastard.

On that July afternoon, as I stood on that riverbank and watched my mother burn, ashes blew over me like gray kisses. I felt my heart breaking, and I knew that if I put my hand between my legs it would come out covered in blood.

Perhaps God was watching that day at my side, and perhaps he felt as I did. Or maybe the Virgin whispered her own idea of justice to him. For even while Saint-Porchaire's rocks smoked and popped, peste broke out over the rest of the city. The victims who'd escaped the fire in the atrium died early, and the nuns who'd been tending them ran away. People fell, writhing, in their homes and the streets and the fields, one after another, hundreds of them, even as they tried to flee.

Perversely, those who survived still blamed the peste on Saint-Porchaire—said the burning sinners had put a curse on it. They let falling ash bury the atrium bodies, and let the melted roof cover the church corpses, and no one breathed here again. Except Marie, this creaky dove of the north transept; and myself, who for a time even slept in the funebral atrium, when I had no other home.

"...you may call and call," Marie says now, "but into air you will fall."

I pause to pull a thorn from my shoe, noting that an early toad has set to croaking. His voice rivals Marie's for direness.

"In the year's second month, thunder's malign. Rain, hail, and lightning are dangerous signs. People will die," Marie concludes; then, "*rich people* will die—"

"No one is dying today, Marie," I say loudly. Though I don't generally set much store by Marie's pronouncements, I am a little relieved that this one concerns the rich rather than myself. "And there's no thunder, either. Centre-ville is packed for a marché—this is the first year they've had one for the Virgin's Purification, and people are very happy."

Marie falls silent, as I knew she would. The voice of Saint-Porchaire has never spoken directly to me and never will, no more than will the Virgin herself or, now, my own mother, from whom I inherited the duty of coming here. Marie doesn't like me. But I finish my journey as if we are equals in conversation. "Already we've had three days of festival," I say, though I haven't attended a single event myself. "There are beadmakers and spice merchants, jongleurs and a play every day. Today it's the life of Saint Agathe ... Are you hungry?" I ask as I pass the bread and cheese through the slit that is all Marie has to see by, or to get food and exchange words by. "If you were walled against the *new* church, the one they're still building at centre-ville, you could listen to the story of her life. Remember what she said to the Roman who ordered her breasts cut off: 'Cruel one,'" I declaim in a voice much like Marie's, "'have you forgotten your mother and the breast that fed you, that you would thus dismember me?' It's one of my favorite stories."

Marie does not respond. The hand that accepts the food is twisted with rheumatism and gray from mildew; it is a painful hand, though its owner will never tell me so. Nor will she comment on the herbs I steep in her water to soothe that pain. She may well taste the herbs and know what they're for, but she'll resent the relative easement that she thinks distances her from God.

"Of course the magistrate took Agathe's breasts anyway," I continue as I hand over a flagon of that water, "and he served them to her on a platter, before stripping off the rest of her clothes and rolling her on a bed of hot coals. But then God sent an earthquake to scare the magistrate away before lifting Agathe into heaven."

There is a scraping sound. Wordlessly Marie passes me her chamberpot, an earthenware basin sticky on the outside with the mist's humidity. I catch the wet gleam of Marie's eyes in the darkness and think that if she were capable of making a joke, this would be it. She's saying, *This is what I give for your notions of holiness, Bonne Tardieu.*

Almost laughing, I finish my story: "Now the blessed Agathe, virgin martyr, protects women who breast-feed—none of whom, I promise you, can lay claim to *her* chastity." It is my own way of jesting, a joke on myself.

I look into the basin. Three days' excretion amounts to a splash in the bottom, nothing more. This shallow chamberpot, as my mother once explained, is the measure of Marie's sin. When the recluse was first sitting in her cell, watching the walls grow around her, she told the crowd that when she's clean in spirit God will stop moving her bowels. She expects, perhaps, that then her basin will brim over with roses, as another bowl did for a Hungarian queen who was later sainted. But Saint Elisabeth was giving table scraps to the poor—offering what might enter the body rather than what surely leaves it.

In silence Marie puts her hand to the slit, and I lean forward. Then suddenly there's a great *splash!* in the bowl, and the front of my dress is soaked.

"Pox!" I can't help but shout. These are my best clothes.

Marie has tossed me a toad, the one I heard croaking just now. His long legs thrash the mucky water, but he can't do any worse. Holding my breath, I fish him out.

"You've given us both a bath," I say to Marie, quite calm; and then, to the toad now quietly trembling in my hand, "You called and called, but what you fell into was somewhat less pleasant than air."

Marie offers nothing further. I set the toad down and watch him hop flail-limbed away.

I have to empty the basin off holy ground, so back through the atrium I tiptoe with it, feeling frozen earth through the new hole in my

7

shoe. Before me, on the walls of the old priests' residence, images of pain and death mock my careful journey. The patients of ten years ago carved a danse macabre wherever there was wood—a line of staring skulls and twisted bones that cover the cross-timbers and lintels and sills. Perhaps each man who could hold a knife hoped his work would trick fate— postpone the buboes' bursting, the brain's burning, the helpless convulsions that were the model for carving. The bones of those long-ago patients sometimes reach up through the soil, and when they do I sort them into piles; but there are none today. Beneath my feet I feel the bones instead pull back in resentment of me, the bastard. They ask who I am to be walking here on two healthy legs with my bowl of sin.

Now that I'm safely far away, Marie speaks again. "When God grows tired of winter's sheath, he grinds the ice between his teeth. He breaks it down and in his pain he sends it forth in pouring rain . . ." From somewhere, the toad croaks again.

Then comes a *crack!* that shakes the earth. Suddenly I'm on my knees. The sky is tearing itself open, white light slashing from side to side, crackling, burning, while thunder roars like Judgment Day. There's a taste of blood in my mouth—I must have bitten my tongue—and I realize I've dropped Marie's basin to cover my head with my arms.

I shout, "Holy Virgin!" and the air shimmers silver.

Cold and shining, at the cross between ice and water, the white rain pelts me drop after drop; glints over cloak and skirt, bounces on hard earth before melting a path inside. It drips off the bone piles like sweat. It drips from the walls like tears. The thunder meanwhile shakes into my marrow and lifts me onto my feet.

So I break into a run. The old bell tower looms ahead, offering shelter, black against the crisscross of lightning. My skirts tangle and I trip again and again. A tree behind me cracks and breaks.

What a way to die! Like that poor old prostitute last year, struck down as she sheltered under an oak.

The sky explodes again with a long, almost human roar. This time my body (so often a traitor to me, as I've been a traitor to it) hears the noise as the cry of a child. Milk springs to my breasts and I scream, "Holy *mother!*"

Ave Maria, gratia plena, Dominus tecum. Benedicta tu in mulieribus, et benedictus fructus ventris tui . . .

This tower is my sanctuary, where I'll find a roof for my head and quiet for my ears. A safe place, a black place—for though the paint used to be bright on the carvings outside, when the church burned the colors drank in soot.

I grope my way in to where the walls are cold, damp, roughly hewn because the masons thought none but God and his priests would see. There are no windows but there is a stair. I feel for the bottom step with my foot, and then I begin to climb, palms on stone, feet numb in the darkness. I haven't been inside in months, but my body knows the way and the lure is irresistible, even in a lightning storm. I spiral with the stair until, at the top, a gray light grows and the tower gives into the lofty quadrangle that used to house the three great bells of Saint-Porchaire. I emerge into the dark light.

Gray sky fills half the room; the rest is shadow, partly roofed. There's some fluttering of pigeons in a sheltered corner. If not for them, the tower would now be mute—the famous bells, Anne, Aliénore, and Blanche, have been moved to the new church rising in the new center of Villeneuve. The virgins of Saint-Porchaire, as the bells were known then, had been untouched by the fire, and new bells are costly. In any case no artisan now alive can duplicate those three. They are known throughout France, and brought their maker fame and a small fortune in gold, enough to hope life would offer his daughter something better than a dubious miracle and a fiery death.

The rain falls gentler now, plashing against the rock. I'm tired from the climb, and my foolish breasts still ache. So I lean against a wall and fold my arms over my heart to make the pain subside; thus can a woman sometimes cheat her own body. While I wait I count the beats of my heart until I run out of numbers. Then I say a prayer for the maker of Anne, Aliénore, and Blanche. And then one for Blanche herself, alone.

"Dear holy Virgin, shining lamp who enlargeth humankind in their time of misfortune, pray for me and for my departed mother . . ."

If you fear the Father, Blanche said to me once, *go to the Son. If you fear the Son, go to the Mother*. This is what I've done all my life—prayed to the Virgin, the Mother we can cry to even past the age of calling *maman*.

The one time I asked about my father was the one time Blanche spoke to me harshly:

You have no father.

When I wept she softened a little and added, *God gave you to me, and nobody else.*

". . . and grant our souls full life in the presence of God, though my petition is unworthy and myself undeserving."

There, I've finished. The prayer worked; the milk has withdrawn toward my heart, and my pulse is slow. I have only a chill settling into my bones.

And a morbid temptation. I tiptoe to the church side of the tower and look down into the nave, into my mother's tomb.

With rain dripping gently on the head it's soaked already, I grab on to the broken wall. Gray space pulls at my body. The distance to the floor— now the roof—is vast and I am afraid of heights, particularly this one; I fear I might plummet through that gray light, through the ruined air. *Beware, beware . . .*

Instead I blink slowly and look again. Somewhere below lie my mother and, perhaps, my father—one sleeping cozy by another under their blanket of rubbled lead. In the sound of the rain I think I hear them groan: *This is a cold place.*

Now I do find myself falling, dropping like the rain; but not down, not forward. I fall back, into the shadows. To where the floor is rough with decades' dust and I am pricked by splinters of broken beams. I roll over, feeling for a place to lie quiet.

One hand touches cloth—and, underneath, feels a body stirring.

I jump back. What is this thing? An animal brought here as a sacrifice? Peasants from the forest have been known to desecrate churches this way, misunderstanding true faith. I sit up, find a wood splinter, and poke at the thing. It moves—but does not yowl or grunt or whimper. Then I think this might be a baby left by foolish parents who don't realize that Saint-Porchaire is deserted, that no priest will find and care for the child they don't want.

Slowly, by touch, I begin to peel away the cloth. The long-damp wool crumbles under my fingers, and I feel, somewhere inside, a small round arm, a fragile hand.

As I touch that hand, a whisper stops me. It is eerie, high and quiet, and it disturbs the pigeons. "You are like Christ," it says.

I sit back on my heels. The name of Christ frightens me, here in this burnt house of God.

"What did you say?" I whisper back.

"Christ, being God incarnate and thus all-knowing, possessed the same wits at birth as he did when slain. And you, my lord, being a man, possess only the same wit today as you did at birth."

I wait a moment; there is nothing further. "I'm not a lord, and I'm not a man," I whisper into the bundle. "My name is Bonne, sometimes called Tardieu."

"You are *like* Christ our Lord—you are *not* our Lord," the voice says sharply. Its tone is high-pitched; the words have cost an effort. They are, however, clearly formed and tell me I have found an older child, perhaps aged six or ten. "Will you be my lord?"

"You are raving," I say in a normal voice, and continue to dig down through the cloths. The smells of mildew, wet fur, sweat, not so uncommon in winter—this creature hasn't washed in weeks and his reek rivals Marie's basin. Again I touch flesh, soft but damp and chilly.

"Holy septum!" the creature swears. "That hurt!"

"I barely touched you." But more carefully, I pull the child into my arms. "How long have you lain here?"

The child trembles; its body is slight and it fits me, chin on my shoulder, legs against my belly. My breasts ache again.

"I don't know," the child says. "I've watched the light change many times. I've had a fever. My heart aches."

"Where are you from? Shall I take you home?" I want to feed it, to nurse it, but the creature is so prickly.

It sags against me, neither agrees nor refuses.

"I mean," I say slowly, clearly, "I can take you home *with me . . .*"

There is still no answer. But the body seems to grow lighter in my arms, and I stand up as if carrying no burden at all.

Outside, heavy drops are lancing gray-brown puddles, one prick after another. As I leave the tower a muddy bone grabs my foot, and I trip—strike some ceramic shards and send them flying against the cell wall. I hear Marie cry out. The sky speaks, too. But I land with the child on top of me, and I have it wrapped inside my cloak. Soon I am running again—this time, for home.

THE CHILD

> *Hot as a coal, wet as a snail. Falling, falling, falling.*
>
> *But I know these are warm arms around me. And the smell of blood from human lips . . .*
>
> *O Lord, heal me, for my bones are vexed. And whoever you are, don't begrudge me this journey. You'll know what I am soon enough.*

I have a child, a charge, in my arms. What do I care if my shoe fills with water? If my mantle is sopping? If shutters slam as I pass—I run. And soon we are home.

The stair that leads from the alley to my little room is as narrow as Saint-Porchaire's, but straight. We enter by the bakery, climb past the bakers' domus, up to my door at the top. There we find Godfridus sitting on the uppermost step. His wispy red hair is hidden in a hood, his thin shoulders wrapped in a cloak, his big hands folded in his lap. He is a journeyman sculptor and needs to keep them warm.

"You must have finished early," I say as, all over town, church bells start ringing vespers. I shift the child's weight to one hip and reach for the key at my belt; the creature doesn't stir, has apparently fallen asleep.

"The master told us to go." Godfridus stands; the tools slung from his belt chime chaotically. "There's some kind of celebration in the barracks."

Unlike the other journeymen who are working on the new church—the unnamed structure that has already replaced old unlucky Saint-Porchaire—Godfridus has found his own quarters in a district somewhat removed from the chantier. He won't live at the site because he has projects of his own design to work on, for Godfridus calls himself an artist, not an artisan, and insists there is a difference between the two. He speaks with an accent of the south and learned his trade in Florence; he claims to experiment with a new style that Villeneuve as yet finds too strange, too ugly, to adopt. The town fathers who've approved the new church design still favor the thick bodies and round eyes of centuries past—the same as those they burned in Saint-Porchaire. So they have him climbing ladders in order to carve leaves and fruits on capitals that, in the town's haste to build a new center of worship, were set into place as bare squares. This is the only work Godfridus is allowed; other hands are carving the Nativities, Last Suppers, and Crucifixions that will earn the church its reputation and, perhaps someday, a bishop's throne. Yet Godfridus cherishes his hopes: At night he works buckets of river clay into tall and painful shapes, with a strange look of the real. Some remind me of the atrium's danse; all are destroyed in light of day, because they fail to match the pictures in his mind.

Godfridus is my one true friend.

"What is this you're carrying?" he asks, as we step into the murky warmth of my attic room. Before I can answer, he sighs—meeting warmth, my one luxury.

Today was a baking day, and the ovens at the back of the building are still heating the insides. The center of the room is toasty, and the child stirs in my arms as we cross it. Never mind that along the walls this could be a different room entirely; there a cold wind blows through cracks in the shutters, billowing the patchwork of wool and linen I have hung by way of insulation, and rain rattles along the roof to drip through in one corner. Before the fireplace and its supply of wood, I lay my burden down. I must stoke the coals.

Briefly I explain to Godfridus, grunting slightly as I work. "That is a child. I found it in Saint-Porchaire's bell tower." A little afraid of what my friend might say, I blow on the careful arrangement of kindling and coals. "It's very cold, perhaps ill."

Godfridus is excited, and troubled. "A child? Is it a boy or a girl? How old?"

"I don't know. It has the size and weight of a six-year-old, but its voice is strange, and it said strange things, and now it's fallen asleep."

I blow again and an orange light grows around us. The child lies motionless.

"Ahh." Brow wrinkled, Godfridus holds his hands out toward the fire. He has little interest in children, except in a general Christian sense.

"Sleep may be the best thing for it. Did you know there is blood on your teeth?"

Tentatively, I touch them with my tongue, taste the blood, then use a finger to scrub at it. "I fell down in the churchyard. I was carrying Marie's bowl." Outside, the bells have stopped ringing.

Godfridus studies my face, flicks a smut from my lip. "You're clean." We smile at each other. I often feel I am my best self when I am with Godfridus. But before I can say anything further, he asks, "And are you ... ready for me?"

I feel my breasts leak again, but nonetheless I say, "First I have to wrap this child up warmly, and then re-dress myself. I can't risk catching a chill now, especially with a sick child here."

"A sick foundling," Godfridus says. "Who will only cost you money ..."

"One of its garments is trimmed with fur," I whisper back, though I know he is right. Perhaps I should take my foundling to the orphanage right now, slip it into the secret box and out of my life ... But not like this, not wet; I owe this child some kindness, having perhaps saved its life already. I kneel and begin to undress it.

Godfridus tries to help me, but I brush him away: This is work that my hands know. He begins to ask me about my day. "Did you visit the wine seller's wife?"

The child's wrappings have become complicated, all fallen apart and tangled; I feel my face settle into a frown as I unpuzzle them. "Yes, I went this afternoon. Though I suspect she only wanted to get a look at me ... you know, Bonne, daughter of Blanche ..." Underneath the various cloaks, the child wears a long dress and hose; these disintegrate when I tug at them. It clutches a fat bundle in its arms, and I lay this aside. "She inspected me as she would a horse—rubbed my hair and picked at my teeth. Then she pinched my nipple and licked the milk off her hand."

"She must have liked it," he says. "It's very sweet."

"Yes, she said so. But she also said she'd heard that two boys died while under my care." I feel a twinge of sadness for them—Charles, son of a weaver, and Germain, a jeweler's third son. "She seemed unimpressed that I'd raised a boy and a girl, and she thinks she might prefer to hire a nurse from the country."

"Those two boys were sick when they arrived. The others are doing well now."

We both look down at the sodden lump I've been unwrapping.

"No one can preserve every child," Godfridus finishes dubiously.

"No." I sigh and get back to work. I have reached the undergarment now, a fine linen chemise, well embroidered. "Look," I whisper to Godfridus. "It *must* come from a rich family."

Suddenly the lump moves. It speaks. "A rich house, at least."

Godfridus and I jump back. "You're awake," I say.

"I am." The child struggles to sit up, shrugging away the hand I offer in help. It is too weak and falls back upon the hearth.

"Can you tell us your name?" asks Godfridus.

"When I give you my name, I give you myself," the child says. The orange firelight has left its face in shadow. "But I am called Hercule."

So it is a boy child I have found. "Don't try to talk," I say, feeling his brow. It's too warm. "Do you think you can eat something?"

"Yes."

He is such a small child that I am tempted to give him the breast. That is, after all, the best food, a form of blood that nourishes directly. But until I know more about this Hercule, I decide, I will give him some of my landlords' coarse brown bread.

Godfridus is already cutting the loaf. "Do you have any drink?"

"There's a little ale in that jug." I point. Meanwhile I try to tug the boy's chemise over his head.

"No." Hercule stops me. "Let me keep it on."

"It's wet and dirty."

"And I'll dry faster if you stop dripping on me," he says, as Godfridus hands him a hunk of bread and a mug of the ale. "In any event, I'm not the only one who's dirty."

This reminds me that I also need to get out of my wet and splashed-on clothes. Saying nothing, I go to fetch my brown everyday dress from the chest, and Godfridus thoughtfully turns his back while I change. The light gray surcoat and underdress, the rough chemise and breast bands— I hang them by the fire and set my good shoes underneath. I'll wash Marie's stains out tomorrow, if I can get a bit of lye. Then I reach for my dry things.

"Ready," I say, and Godfridus knows to turn. The old brown dress is draped at my waist; the upper part is left unfastened, for my breasts have grown rock-solid.

This is why my friend has come. He kneels on the floor.

As I lean toward Godfridus, I find the boy is staring at us. His eyes are round and white. Unconsciously my hands move to cover myself, overcome with shame—my breasts are ugly, the nipples so flattened from suckling that they hang like panting tongues. And from our postures, little Hercule must be thinking the worst.

"I'm a wet nurse," I say to the boy. "I raise children like you. But I don't have a baby to board right now, and I must rely on this friend to keep a flow of milk." I don't add that there is nothing more than kindness between Godfridus and me. He has vowed to live like Christ, and if there were anything even slightly carnal in our relationship he would, literally, be mortified. He whips himself with a scourge every month, in case of sins he might not remember. Each night and morning, he takes my nipple reluctantly.

But we both know this is good work. Before my milk came in, I was a laundress, and before that I picked nits from people's hair to earn a few crusts.

"Go ahead, eat," I tell both of them. Hercule puts the bread in his mouth and Godfridus begins to suck.

With that, I feel a pull all through my body. My friend's mouth frees me from the weight and ache of milk that I feel constantly pushing at my skin and stretching me tighter, tenser, bigger. Godfridus opens a good emptiness in me, an emptiness I feel all the way down to that part which the poets call a sad paradise. I feel myself starting to unfurl.

Outside, the wind blows; rain drums light, then hard, on the roof. The fire smokes. My good feeling mounts, spreading warmth and anticipation. Unknown to Godfridus, I perform certain movements, all inside, that promote the sense of bliss and relaxation. I am coming to a moment of perfection.

Then a knock on the door. We all startle: Hercule drops his bread, Godfridus's lips fall away, and I begin to shake. Only priests and town guardsmen go out in this weather and at this hour—the first to tend the dying, the others to provoke death.

I pull up my dress and open the door. Standing there in the black hallway, lit by a dish of fish oil with a linen wick, are a man and a woman. They are plump and look much alike, even lack the same teeth; they could be brother and sister or husband and wife. Their brown garments wear a liberal dusting of flour, and their hands and faces are lined with virtuous toil. The bakers.

I begin to relax again—but only to a point. "Master and mistress, please come in."

"Ah, you have a guest." The baker hands the lamp to his wife and rubs his hands together. He isn't meeting my eyes.

"Two, actually—" I start to say, but then I realize I can't see Hercule anymore, so I just gesture toward Godfridus. "You remember my uncle from the south." This is a necessary fiction; of course I have no uncle, no family, but we both need clean reputations. And with a significant look, I remind Godfridus who these visitors are: "The bakers who own this building." I don't bother to mention that strange little boy but say to them instead, "Would you like to sit?"

They look around and take the only chest. It sags and squeaks under their weight.

"So, you are Bonne's uncle . . . from the mother's family or the father's?" asks the sly bakerwoman. In the early days, she was one of Blanche's most ardent followers.

"From my mother's," I say before Godfridus can speak, and with every appearance of calm. "Godfridus was the only son—much younger than Blanche—and his name has been lost in the stories that surround her. He was apprenticed to a stone carver just before the troubles began."

The baker and his wife nod wisely, and the man looks at Godfridus with interest. He still has some feeling for Blanche, some small reverence; it was on his head that her right shoe landed during the assumption. This is why he has allowed me to rent this domus, and why he forbids his wife to treat me as she feels I deserve—I've heard that on the day of the fire, *she* stood outside the church and clapped her hands.

"I've been living in Villeneuve for two years now," Godfridus volunteers. "I am a journeyman at the new church—Fathers Thomas, Pierre, and Paul know me." He always makes a point of telling some strict truth such as this when I introduce him. He protects himself and me this way, as he has ever since I and a squalling charge (the boy who lived) tripped over his tools in the new church. That day he washed our scraped elbows and bruised feet, and in the months that followed he has been most kind.

Now Godfridus finishes, somewhat lamely, "Of course, we are all related in Christ."

But the bakers haven't come to discuss theology, and they've already lost interest in a possible uncle. "Mistress Bonne . . ." says the man, embarrassed, and I know exactly why they are here.

"Thank you for the bread this morning," I cut in, my voice low to keep the panic out. "It was still warm when your apprentice brought it up."

"Three loaves a week are due you as part of the agreement," my landlady says. "But aren't you forgetting something due us?"

I wish for more smoke from the fireplace, to hide in.

"We're sure you've simply forgotten," says the baker.

"Of course," says his wife. In the silence the chest they're sitting on makes a noise: *squeak, squeak.*

Godfridus leans over to whisper in my ear. "Bonne?"

"I'm a few weeks late with the rent," I confess into his ear.

I feel my friend's body tense. "I wish I—but I just bought a new chisel. I have nothing left, literally nothing." I think irrelevantly that at times like this, without a sou, he must be glad for the nourishment my milk gives him.

"Mistress Tardieu?" prompts the baker's wife.

"It's not exactly that I've forgotten," I say, and knit my hands together beneath my apron. "You see, my last client—a healthy boy—left me a few weeks ago, and this is not the season God has chosen for giving birth . . ." The chest squeaks again, which makes this as good a place to stop as any; I let my words trail off, then bring my hands out from the apron in a gesture of supplication.

"There are children on the way," says the baker, helpfully. "Just yesterday I heard of a widow, four months pregnant and very rich, who is looking—"

"And there's always the Hôtel-Dieu, the charity orphanage," puts in his wife. "They are in constant need of nurses. You might even live on the premises."

SQUEAK! SQUEAK!

"What is this?" The bakerwoman jumps up and raps the chest with her fist. "Do you have mice?"

"Doesn't sound like mice," Godfridus says. I nudge him.

"I don't think so," I say out loud, but the bakerwoman has already pushed her husband off the chest and is prying open the lid, which I left unlocked.

"We can't have mice anywhere around the place," she says severely. "Even with five cats in the yard, once vermin get into a bakery——" She digs around inside, tossing out linens and a lightweight dress I keep for summer.

Suddenly she screams, and her husband is so startled the fish-oil light goes out.

Godfridus is at their side in a flash.

"A baby—a dead little boy," she gasps, clutching her heart.

"Not quite a baby," says Hercule's voice, and his head pops up. "And I was just taking a nap. This chest is lovely for someone my size."

Dumbfounded, Godfridus gives him a hand, and the boy climbs out. What a strange child! "This is Hercule," I say.

"An orphan of the storm." He makes a bow, overly polite. Then he coughs, loud and long, and turns to spit into the fire.

The bakers stare.

"Hercule has had a fever," I fabricate, "but he's— Well now, sit down, all of you." Depleted, I drop myself on the hearth.

The bakerwoman ignores me and takes a fold of Hercule's chemise, which is now dry, between her fingers. She works it back and forth to test the quality. Her husband closes the chest and pulls her down on it, then Godfridus and Hercule sit on either side of me, backs to the fire.

"Is he really an orphan?" asks the woman. "What is he doing here?"

"I am indeed parentless," Hercule says.

Outside, thunder crashes; the storm has moved directly overhead.

"I take it this boy is your new client," the baker says hopefully. "Will he be staying long?"

"His shirt is filthy," says the wife. She is speaking plainly now. "How can a poor orphan pay you? And how can you pay us?"

As the rain crashes overhead, I choose to address her questions about my guest. "He isn't——"

But Hercule coughs roundly. "There are those with the means to support me," he says in his reedy voice. "But just now I suffer from lack of vitality. I will be staying with Mistress Bonne while my chest and my bones grow strong."

Now Godfridus and I go stiff as pikes.

"Excellent! Excellent! The air of Villeneuve is good for the bones," my landlord tells him. I can read relief in his voice; he is a kind man. "You will be staying a long time, I hope—for the maximum cure."

Hercule is not looking at me. "If you will find the bundle I brought with me," he says stagily, "I would like to pay these good people."

I hesitate a moment, confused and unsure. Then he coughs again, and seemingly with great pain.

"Of course," I capitulate. I fetch the sack and hand it to him.

Hercule rummages briefly and finds a leather purse. The coin that he fishes out of it is large and round and gleaming, even through the curtain of smoke.

The proprietors gasp. The woman jumps up; as soon as the coin is in her hand, she bites it. "Gold!"

"That will pay for a good year's rent, and more," says the baker.

"Then maybe you'd like to make change," I suggest.

Their disappointment is palpable. Few of us have ever even seen a coin of such value—and it seems the child carries several.

"No need for that," Hercule says. The effort it takes to hold himself straight is visible now. "I sense I may be staying here long."

"If that is what your *guardians* wish," I say. I don't add that I haven't been consulted about this arrangement, or that a child with a wallet full of gold coins isn't likely to stay long in my humble domus, not after he learns who I am. For the moment, I accept that one of my troubles is over.

"Well, then." The baker stands, holding on to the coin. "It all works out. I must say I'm very glad. Now, if you could give us a light from your fire, Mistress Bonne, we won't keep you any longer."

Godfridus and I relight their wick and see them smiling out the door. The bakers are happy; Godfridus seems pleased; and I am relieved, because I still have a place to live.

"What a strange child this is," I whisper to Godfridus; and out loud I ask Hercule, "Why did you hide from my visitors? Have you truly been sick? Why were you in Saint-Porchaire?"

But as if he relinquished his pain with his coin, Hercule has fallen asleep. He lies in the center of my bed, his body curled into the shape it took inside the mother who lost him.

GODFRIDUS

Now we are alone, at close to curfew time. Bonne drowses by her fire, having given up her bed to the child and his purse of gold. Having given up her milk to my belly, having tried to detain me in talk.

Outside, the clouds have rained themselves out and departed. The air is clear and crisp and the sky a white swath of stars, a glittering robe for the Queen of Heaven. In each twinkle of starlight I imagine the face of my muse. She is a real woman, with a face that shows the beauty of pain and the transcendence of suffering. A face I will form out of clay or marble, if only I can make my hands see it. Clara.

I spend my days among laborers and priests and unchaste women, carving leaves on stone capitals. My nights trying to capture that one perfect face, the face of beauty, of love, of the Virgin. Working in soft river clay, material like that which God used to fashion Adam in His image.

Perhaps we all seek some such reflection. Mostly of ourselves.

"Godfridus," Bonne asked me once, "what color are my eyes?"

Nor could she tell if her cheekbones were cut high or low, or if others could see when her breasts were full. She knew the color of her hair, brown, because it was long enough to wrap around her; but she was and is the only person in Villeneuve who cannot describe the face of Bonne the wet nurse.

Only the rich know their own faces. They gaze at themselves in plates of polished metal or glass. The rest of us see ourselves blurred, indistinct, in water or the blade of a knife.

I know I am ugly. I am grateful for it.

Bonne, I think, would like to be beautiful. But I could tell her only this—there are lines in her cheeks, a point to her nose; her mouth is thickish and wide. Yet for all that, it is not an ugly face.

Did she want to hear it? She gazed at me with eyes of watery gray, then ran wordless toward the recluse.

ODFRIDUS IS GONE AND I AM IN BED, HOT
with the child's body beside me, still aching
inside. I cannot sleep, but I doze. And as I
doze, I dream—perhaps I should say remember:

"Remember to breathe," said my lover.
So I drew down all the wind my chest could
hold.

My body, inflated, was nothing but a
shell, I thought with a strange detachment, a
shell to hold the air that God lets even sinners
suck. My breath was coming shallowly.

His tongue was an arrow, a tiny point
licking my lips, tickling me. Was this the perfect kiss? A proper kiss? Then the arrow flattened, licked across the slash my mouth made
as it gulped for air. I hurt. There was a pain,
sharp, down in my so-called paradise.

Love in a haystack, as hard as a needle to
find, and much more ticklish. Tickles all over,
and prickles, and sweat. I felt my flesh redden
with sun. His hands on my breasts, my hips,
were finding me, and where was I in all this?

I was somewhere above, floating, looking
down on two bodies writhing in a luff of dead
grass. The figure who was me, her arms were
at her sides, her hands pressing into the

scratch. These were hands that, in other times, back among the buildings, had picked lice and fleas from this man's hair, had crushed his vermin between two moon-clean fingernails, had rinsed his linens and scrubbed them harder than even her own monthly cloths. Because that's how she earned her bread.

Laurent. A master weaver with aspirations to becoming a merchant. Who had a wife, five sons, and an urge to churn within the bastard child of miracles. But I knew and know no regret—I prayed for a child as I lay there in the sun, with my eyes closed and the lids become glass stained red. A child would change my monthly blood to milk, give me a new life. For a wet nurse leads an easier existence than a laundress, and despite baby dirt and vomit and tears, it is a life more clean, more perfect.

"Wrap your legs around my waist," he said, and under the burning sky I did it.

I WAKE IN PANIC. The chemise is stuck to me like skin, and my heart's pounding in my ears. I wait for it to settle.

I may have brought this heart away from Laurent and the haystack intact, but I still remember, deep in my body, the feel of another heart growing inside. The tiny, frangible beats, the birdlike kicks. Finally, the emptiness.

To my side now there is a *crack*. The foundling. He is asleep but his sounds fill the room—creaking bones and rasping lungs. His body makes a lump of desperate, pain-wracked warmth. I inch closer. When I wrap my arms around his waist, he settles into me, bottom snug in the curve of my pelvis, head secure beneath my chin. I count his breaths. I pray.

"Ave Maria, gratia plena . . ." Over and over again, the magic formula: "Ora pro nobis peccatoribus, nunc et in hora mortis nostrae . . . Pray for us sinners, now and at the hour of our death."

When the second heart was full-grown inside me, it slid out into hay again. Then mine beat once more alone.

Slowly, dreamily, the boy Hercule relaxes.

 WAKE IN SHUTTER-STRIPED LIGHT, MY body curled around the child's. The roof is silent: No rain, and we are both warm.

What peace.

Then, unpleasantly, I remember Marie's basin and the way it looked, broken, when I fell. So I jump out of bed, shivering in the cold—this, the fifth day of the market for the Virgin's Purification, is not a baking day—and rush to pull on my clothes. But how will I replace the basin? I have one thin coin left, and a hole in my good pair of shoes.

I look at the boy whom I rescued and who has rescued me. He's already given a whole year's rent—I can't ask him for more, especially when he's alone and defenseless. It would be so easy to take advantage of a child with a heavy purse. If I hadn't found him, he might have been robbed and dumped at the orphanage, or worse.

Feeling the absence of my body, Hercule is waking. "Hungry," he mumbles with eyes still closed. Along the walls, the patchwork tapestry ripples.

I tell him I'm going to the marché. "I'll

bring back something good for you. Something to strengthen your bones."

He opens his eyes all the way and looks at my chest. "I've heard *that's* the best food," he says, pointing for good measure. "They give it to invalids and sick people . . . Close to where I come from, there was once an abbess who'd drink nothing else, and never took solid food. She tried not to move much either. She sat in a tower and drank her milk through a reed that a lover cut for her before she took the veil."

I stare. "Why would she do that?"

"She thought if she never used her muscles and never ate grown-up food, she'd never get older. One day her lover would come and rescue her, and she'd have the face of a girl of fourteen."

"And did it work? Did she stay young?"

"Well, she died in the tower one winter. People say the nuns who served under her got tired of milking the village women and carrying the buckets up the stairs, so they stopped. She was too weak to get downstairs herself, and in the springtime they found her, skin and bones, perfectly preserved but looking about sixty-eight, which is how old she was."

"Oh." The story makes me sad, though of course the vain abbess got what she deserved.

Hercule's eyes sparkle at me. "Still, she was never sick a day in her life. Maybe there is some power in mother's milk."

I tighten the laces over my bosom, over the wet stains already spreading there. I tell myself Hercule will have none of me; he hasn't paid for that. Wordless I go to my money chest and get out the last coin, no heavier than a dried pea; I wrap it carefully in a scrap of cloth and tuck it in the pocket tied round my waist. Only then do I speak. "I'll bring you something from the market," I say again.

"Meat?" Distracted, Hercule makes a show of licking his lips. "Beef?"

"Cheese, more likely. Or some nourishing lentils." There must be some way I can bargain for those.

He subsides, coughing piteously. But I go out and shut the door, still uncomfortable at hearing such a young child tell a story like that, and so well.

OUTSIDE IN THE COLD, a white sun glitters on frozen rain. Rooftops, trees, and gutters offer diamonds to the poor. My spirits lift, and I feel a new kindness for poor Hercule, whose young mind is surely confused with his fever. Thinking about this, and about how I can get more money for his food, I walk to Godfridus's domus on the west side of town.

This is a day of leisure for my friend; the new church chantier is closed to honor the end of the Virgin's Purification festival and the day sacred to Saint Amand the pilgrim, who was born near Villeneuve and is being considered for the name saint of the new church. Nonetheless Godfridus's shutters are open, and he's vigorously at work. Buckets of clay squat all over the room with bulbous shapes draped in muddy linen. He doesn't like me to see what he's fashioning; I think it is some sort of head. But he empties my breasts, and I convince him he must take me to market. Godfridus is careful that all his shapes are draped and his door locked before we go down.

My putative uncle lives in a busy part of the city. Even this far from the marketplace, every shopkeeper has his counter down, and they all vie for our attention as we pass. "Cloves from Araby," a spice seller cries. "Sugar against a toothache—"

"Pies for sale!" calls a strolling vendor. "Pigeon or pork!" Two orange cats fight over a piece he has dropped.

In the unaccustomed sunlight, I can observe my friend's face for the first time in many months; the long, dark winter with its smoky fires and gray days has kept him hidden from me. His hair, I notice, has grown longer and thinner; the ends graze his shoulders, but there is a circle like a tonsure at the back. His skin, as is natural this time of year, is shiny and very pale, and though he lives carefully, his brown wool cotte is spotted with grease and could use its spring washing. His hose fit baggy at the ankles and are white at the knees with dust; his teeth, however, are a strong, clean yellow. The muscles of his arms and shoulders and even his jaw ripple as he muses, unconsciously rehearsing the gestures he uses to sculpt.

I suppose it would be unnatural if, seeing him so clearly, and so very much mine, I did not feel the thrill of which romance singers speak. My friend and protector, knighted with chisel instead of sword. I would not be alone in loving him; his strength and the light in his blue eyes make him attractive to many women. Perhaps even more so because, at the slightest provocation, he is quick to say that he lives like Christ: humble, poor, and chaste. Few women can resist a saint.

And no saint can suffer a woman who makes a living from her body, whether she sells her sex or her milk. I know what Godfridus thinks of me: a fine object of charity, a substitute niece, a fallen woman trying to do better—but never a wife.

Godfridus and I walk in silence down the Grand' Rue, thinking our own separate thoughts. I keep seeing the child, Hercule, half-sitting in bed and telling his impish story, with eyes slitted in pain.

"Water for sale!" calls a man with a bucket. "Fresh from the spring!"

The marketplace is in the new-church square. When we get there it is full; people who have been here all morning are milling about, faces flushed with ale or wine or fermented honey, according to what they can afford. They hide the scars along the walls where houses were torn down to clear space for the new centre-ville. We pass through cold shadows cast by the church towers, unfinished, that loom above the booths and tents; these shadows reach nearly down to the Palace of Justice and the prison entrance. The courts, like the church worksite, are closed today.

Godfridus and I look for the stall held by his friend the potter. We pass families and couples, lovers and fillettes de joie, a man with a cock he wants to pit in a fight. Boys have claimed a corner where they can throw some balls around; two little girls are teasing a dog with a stick; a fine lady haggles with a perfume seller. We're surrounded by human noise, and cart wheels creak slowly behind us.

Suddenly a deep voice booms at our backs. "Villeneuve, beware!"

The crowd's motion stops for a moment. In the silence, there's only the bark of the dog.

Then the same voice fills the space: "Villeneuve, repent!"

Godfridus and I turn around. We look into the eyes of God.

He is pointing straight at us, and at no one in particular. He wears a mask of silver and long curls of gold; his robe is engulfing white. After a moment he pivots slowly and points that finger at a man in red who is crouching beside him on the stage cart.

So this is a play of our Lord and a sinner. The two actors stand on a wooden stage on wheels, which trembles under the Lord's footsteps—but then it also trembles for the sinner. Behind them yawns a great green hell-mouth, sharp teeth pointing the way to damnation, a backdrop painted with a terrifying orange uvula.

The words have stricken the crowd silent. Even the ball game has stopped, and all eyes are staring. In the reverent hush, the donkey who has been pulling the cart begins to make water, and the cart with God and the sinner sways.

The man in red takes up a stone from the stage floor and cradles it under his chin. "'Tis true," he says, in a voice no less booming than God's. "I arrived here by my own power, having chosen ill at every crossroads on life's path. But along the way I paved my steps with good intentions."

He turns the stone to the crowd; on one side is painted a clutch of gold coins. "I meant to give to my poor brothers . . ."

God points sternly into the mouth of hell. "Instead you took for yourself."

The sinner lays the stone back down. Crying "Forgive me!" he leaps into hell, forcing his way through a slit in the backdrop. Immediately afterward, a thin stream of real flame bursts from the painted lips, and there is an anguished scream.

Now God turns to the audience. "Repent! Repent! The moment is more close and more final than you can know, and much easier is it for a camel to pass through the eye of a needle than—"

No one needs to hear the end. Around me everyone's fumbling for a purse or some trinket of value. While the sinner continues to scream, God descends to weave among the crowd, his white robe held up slack in his hands to form a pocket.

Godfridus and I do not give—we're saving our coin to buy Marie's pot. But we watch. Tears of panic stream down the faces all around, whether commoners' or nobles'.

"Forgive me, Lord," a woman sobs as she drops a cheap bracelet into God's apron.

"Jesus, have mercy!" cries a young girl, throwing in her hair ribbon.

"Let my wife's baby be a boy," a shrewder man says as he tosses in a grimy coin. "We've got three girls already."

When everyone's given all they can and the pockets are drawn shut again, God climbs back onstage. The sinner reappears and takes the donkey's bridle, and the cart moves on to its next station. One or two members of the audience follow, as if in a trance.

Godfridus's lips curl—recalling perhaps the wrath of Jesus at the temple. I grab his arm to call him back to this world.

"It's an art," I say soothingly. "The priests encourage it." I see one of them now, Father Pierre of the new church, gazing after the actors with a thoughtful expression, as if he might take the subject of a sermon from them. Of course, a drama seems different when the roles are played by guildsmen in a religious festival. "Yesterday this troupe presented the life of Saint Agathe," I say slowly, thinking how much time seems to have passed since then.

I shiver, because I see that Father Pierre has seen me looking at him. His face is covered with knobs and his eyes are like mud; when I was a child, I feared him and the frequent visits during which he tried to worm my mother's secrets from her. Now, when our eyes meet, I cross myself and turn away.

The market has taken up its business again. The shoppers, the jugglers, the more stolid merchants with their booths. Soon this part of the square is once more bustling with people bent on pleasure, just as if no one here had repented a few moments before. And I for one am glad the mood of penitence has passed.

Godfridus and I move from stall to stall, looking for the potter and a plain earthenware bowl. This shouldn't be a complicated transaction. But it becomes so, because there is still so much to see: the jugglers, the dancing dwarfs, the Negro whose owner will show him naked for a few deniers. Not to mention the piles of bright things for sale, and the people all dressed in their best and on display. I see rich men and women wearing wool and velvet and brocade, in shades from scarlet to saffron to blue. For someone who steps into a crowd only for church (and then hides herself in the shadows), it is a fierce and wonderful hour.

Godfridus tugs my sleeve. "Look, there is Jacques. He'll give you a good price on a bowl."

With a parting look for the sad Negro, I go—Marie is my duty. I am glad to find that Jacques is not a good potter, so his wares are misshapen and cheap. We choose a suitable flat bowl, bubbled on one side.

"It's for a recluse," Godfridus explains as I lay down my coin and get one back, the weight of a fingernail-paring. Perhaps enough for a few lentils or an egg.

"I couldn't sell that bowl to anybody else," Jacques says cheerfully. "It is an ugly thing, certes." I smell strong ale on his breath.

With our purchase made, we turn back. But we go slowly, linger, still looking at those who are here to work, play, or entertain. On the market's south side, a man thrusts a sword down his throat; removes it, swallows again. An aging fillette displays her legs, while under a flying buttress two toddlers start a fight and a yellow-starred Jew rubs a bruised arm. The light is changing at the approach of noon, but cold air continues to circulate. The Negro has a runny nose.

Then comes an explosion of sound. Dogs bark; a woman screams. The people push first away from and then toward the noise, as a large animal bellows and the word spreads: *A child is caught in the bear-baiting ring.*

Why do Godfridus and I follow? We have no choice—the bodies have become a tide sucked down to the ring, and we can't fight out of the current. There is a carnival urge to witness bloody death, human death, and we are borne along.

I'm appalled—but I also feel the need to see. "The poor child," I say, as if in excuse. But I, too, watched the sinner jump into hell.

We stop, flush up against still bodies, people craning their necks to catch a glimpse. Then more bodies arrive behind, and we're wedged even tighter together, nudged forward even though there seems no more room. My nostrils are full of human odors, hot breath and eager sweat.

A whisper rustles back from the edge of the ring: "... *stranger* ..."

Godfridus bends down. He has caught a glimpse over the crowd's heads. "You don't want to see this," he says loudly into my ear.

I demand, "Pick me up."

He makes an uncertain sound.

"I have to see—pick me up!" So he puts his hands in my armpits— the basin goes on his head—and he lifts me high enough to see.

I see. First the four dogs with teeth bared, mouths slavering; then a huge hairy body and a little, light childish one. Which I recognize.

"Hercule!" I've never seen him in the light, but yesterday I carried that body and now I know it instantly. It lay curled in my bed all night;

now it is curled again, in pale dress and hood and hose against which a gash in his leg shows bloody red.

From mouth to mouth, the name spreads: *Hercule . . . Hercule . . . Hercule . . .*

"Let me pass!" I wiggle down to the ground, push against the bulk of a couple in front of me. Their bodies part for a heartbeat and I squeeze in between. They close after me, muttering, solid.

"Bonne!" Godfridus is right behind me, but his desire to detain me can't equal my desire to go forward. I worm my way between bodies, wiggling and shoving. Somewhere on the way, the veil and barbette slip from my head.

The child in the ring echoes, "Bonne!"

And now it is my name that circulates. *Bonne Bonne Bonne Bonne . . .*

I don't know what I can do. I just have to be there. I can't leave the little boy alone to die walled in by a blood-lusty crowd. He said my name. "I'm coming!"

And there I am, ringside, butted up against the makeshift wooden fence. What I see first is the bear, short and skinny for its kind, huddling in its chains. Its fur is matted with its own blood, and it has no claws. It keeps falling to all fours, then standing up on its hind legs and shifting from side to side like a scared man. Each time it stands, it seems to have grown smaller.

But it has nothing to fear now. The dogs—four of them, scarred, brown, and ugly—are now clubbed around a figure on the dirt. They snarl. I hear a pair of yellow jaws snap. Their thick hairy bodies hide Hercule.

Slowly, with my eyes on all five animals, I haul myself up and swing a leg over the rail. The dogs do not notice; the bear fidgets. So I slide over and fall to the ground in a tangle of skirts.

Now nothing in the ring moves. I stand up, brush my hands off by reflex. All around the circle, my own name is blowing louder—*Bonne Bonne Bonne Bonne . . .* as the crowd recognizes me. I feel their pulses lurch: The spectacle has become more complicated, more interesting. Blanche's bastard has arrived.

"I'm here!" I call to Hercule. "Can you move?"

One dog raises its gnarled head and growls at me. Its nose nudges at the lump on the ground.

The bear is crying now, human sobs of fright. Before its master condemned it to the ring, he taught it to dance, and in this moment, as I step toward the dogs, it rises on its toes and cuts a caper—its trained response to menace. Then I realize it is no longer afraid of the dogs (they'd only kill it, anyway): It fears me and Hercule. Because we're humans, even if one of us is small and defenseless.

"Throw the dogs something to eat!" calls a voice in the crowd. I recognize Godfridus. "Or throw a rock!"

"That's right—throw a rock," the townspeople echo.

"Pray to the Lord," says a voice I think may be my landlady's. "Let God protect the child!"

I have to ignore the voices. I make my feet carry me so close I can feel the dogs' warmth through my skirts. Then my body has an idea: In my breasts there's the same wet tingle the dogs must feel under their tongues. Feeding time.

I fall to my knees. "Virgin, save us!" I rip the front of my dress open.

The fabric doesn't want to tear—two layers of wool—but I yank on the lacing and rip the neck. Somehow I manage. Then I claw the bandeau open, and out fall my breasts—ugly, sagging, with nipples like tongues, and veins like the marbling in old cheese: a mother's breasts.

The dogs are so startled that they break apart, sit back on their squat legs for a moment. Hercule curls tighter into his ball. Then the dogs come to sniff. I feel a wet nose on the white of my left breast. A red tongue licks a pair of hairy jaws.

I think my heart will burst from my chest.

Beyond, Hercule lies with blood running down his leg. He's hiding his face. "Get up!" I whisper loudly. All four dogs are sniffing at me. "Run away!"

"Run away!" Godfridus shouts far off.

But the boy is paralyzed. So I keep kneeling there, waiting for the dogs to fall on me.

When the first wet tongue touches my nipple I feel a thrill of fear, then a trill of the unconquerable pleasure I feel whenever I'm suckled. The milk gushes out suddenly in twin fountains, every pore open. I stand, holding my breasts up and squeezing them so the liquid arcs outward.

The crowd gets very quiet. Even the bear stops crying.

The milk has no time to reach the ground. The dogs catch it. They nudge one another's heads, gently, to take their turns. I point the streams from one to the other.

There seems no end to what my breasts hold. They fill four stomachs. Five—the bear is kneeling, mouth open, and I point a stream at her, too.

Gradually all the animals are satiated and they settle, bellies down, and sit panting.

There's no point in closing my dress. With milk still dripping down my ribs, I cross the ring to Hercule, and I run my hands down his spine, then over his limbs, checking for injuries. He is fever-hot and shaking, but unbroken.

The dogs are still; the bear is frozen. No creature moves but Bonne.

I slide both hands to the in-curve of Hercule's waist and pick him up with a pinch. His body's slippery with sweat. I lift him above the dogs' heads and hand him over the rail to Godfridus, who accepts the child silently. Then I heave myself up to straddle the fence. And I commit a sin.

It's a sin of pride. As I look out over the mass of people watching me, it seems I can read their thoughts: *A miracle!* those minds shout at me. They think I've miracled the dogs, as the Eucharist miracled my mother. That I, Bonne, am pulsing with holy spirit.

I look at these people looking at me, and my face flushes and shines. I sit there on the rail, my dress open, my head held up, breasts dripping, proud. The crowd roars. I look around, smiling at each one of them.

Then suddenly, in that sea of faces, I feel a tug.

The poets tell us to look at the eyes—windows to the soul (windows to hell, some say, in the case of a beautiful woman). *These* eyes are like crystals that glow with every possible color, blue-gray-green-gold-black, like sunspots, set in a face the color of dusk, under hair the color of midnight. A gleam of gold and jewels all around the head, but no brighter than the eyes themselves.

They seem to know me. And they're beautiful.

I falter, sag; I am tumbling over the side, into the crowd, but I can't look away. Two red lips part, and a head turns away, and I can't hold myself any longer—I'm falling at last, through shapeless, soundless air. As wind combs my hair with its fingers, blows softly up my dress. And white light shines in my eyes.

I'M CAUGHT.

Godfridus catches me, and he sets me on my feet. The townspeople have moved back to give us space; Hercule sits on the ground before us, breathing heavily.

I think I hear a whisper: "Sorcière." *Witch.* Or maybe "Sa mère"— *her mother.* Some people are already walking away: broad backs and hats turned to me.

But something wonderful has happened. I've just rescued a child. And there's a tight little throng around me now, saying my name out loud and in praise. Gentle fingers probe my body and Hercule's, checking us for breaks or bruises. The boy keeps his arms across his face, as if he's still afraid. Somebody wraps an almost-clean cloth around his wound.

My head, dizzy. Burning. I feel as though I've seen a vision—the Virgin, maybe, or Eve, our first mother. Those eyes, that hair, that mouth.

So many bodies. I cannot breathe.

"You shouldn't take such risks," scolds Godfridus. "You shouldn't expose yourself." He tries to step between me and the throng, tries to cover me with the mantle I discarded on the fence.

"Godfridus . . ." I wonder if I'm babbling. "Do you know a woman, beautiful, with dark hair and strange eyes . . ."

He grabs my shoulder and shakes me, even while he enfolds me in my wrap. "Speak up. Are you all right? I am this woman's uncle," he says out loud. The crowd seems to press in closer. Hercule sits up and reaches for my hand.

Then the little throng ripples. It's as if a ghost is passing through; people fall back from it, from me. They open up a pathway.

I turn and face—that face. The one that is already haunting me. The sharp features and everycolor eyes, the lips like red cushions. They are smiling at me from the other end of the human tunnel. She pauses a moment and hands something to another woman, a servant; then nods at me.

Through the open pathway, a skinny breathless maid runs up to me. "Here." She pushes something soft into my hand. "It's from her. Hello, Godfridus."

Godfridus says hello, too, before the maid runs away. My hand is tightly clenched, holding this thing inside.

"See what it is," says the child. And his little paw starts to pull at my fingers.

I lift my hand above his head. A rich woman gave me a gift—what a boon—perhaps there's a coin. I look down the tunnel, but she's gone. I open my hand and see.

A square of linen, wonderfully fine. It has been hemmed and embroidered with spring lilies, white threads on white.

"That's pretty," says Godfridus.

I hold it to my nose and sniff. It smells of money, of spice and perfume . . . the East, maybe, someplace I have never been. "Do you know the name of the woman who gave it to me?"

"Yes. I did some work for her last autumn—decorating her husband's sarcophagus, a very—"

"Tell us who she is!" Hercule cries impatiently.

A woman leans in from the crowd, speaking in a hushed voice: "Her name," she says, "is Radegonde Putemonnoie."

HERCULE

This is how it was: A bark and a howl, and all those mouths around me— terror in my loins.

It was the dim call of a joint that had ruined my sleep and brought me outdoors. Pork, pigeon, beef—I didn't care. There was nothing in the domus but old bread to eat, and Bonne had said today would be a market day. After weeks of fever, lying starving in that church tower—just to bite into roast flesh and suck the sweet juice out . . .

I thought I had the strength. I pulled the hood close around my face and hid from myself. I went abroad.

Down the lane of the spice sellers, around the corner into the leather district, where the streets reek of rotten skins and the piss used to cure them. I followed my nose, my stomach. On to the marketplace.

Here are food sellers and wine sellers and a great hairy beast, a bear, a monster. It is in a ring, though, and chained to the earth. The people are lining up to see it.

Some dogs. Some children. With my hood up and my plain clothes on, I am one of them. A water seller kicks me out of his way, but he can do this. I'm used to a beating—all fools are.

Little girls fighting over a doll. Little boys tossing balls in a clear patch of earth.

No child just stands around.

Want to see what I can do? I grab the boys' balls and toss them in the air—one, two, three, we all lose count. Brown with mud, they spin in a dull circle, dazzling in dullness. They sing as they fly, of spinning and springing and the joy of flight, the joy of light.

The beast roars. The dogs bark. A crowd gathers to see me spin.

One of the boys begins to cry. "Mes jouets! That boy stole my toys!"

I ignore him and toss the balls higher, toss them in interlocking circles, in rings pierced with arrows.

"Those are mine!" the little lump screams, beating his chest. "Papa!"

A man starts toward me, rubbing his hands. He's looking not at my hands but at my face. And so I drop the balls and run, run anywhere. Duck through the crowd, between pairs of legs, under a railing.

The animals close around me.

The rest is unclear. I was so weak. My body hunched into itself, and I think I began to cry. "Anne!" I may have sobbed. "Anne!"—for at such a time it's natural to think of a ladylove, and this may have been her death, too, out in the forest. Then I called to the Lord: "Seigneur!" But what right did I have to beseech the one who made me this way?

Faces furred, faces smooth, animals and people. They were hungry— all of them—hungry with all their being, consumed by appetite for spectacle.

Until she stepped forward and caught me again in her round arms, against her round breasts, and all spun round around us as she carried me. The mouths closed, sated, and let her pass.

Once we pass out of the market's immediate circle, people start to ignore us again; the news hasn't spread this far. We choose the quiet streets to go home by, having had enough of excitement.

Godfridus carries Hercule in his arms; I'm clutching my mantle over my chest with one hand, holding Marie's new basin in the other. The precious linen square, the gift of a mistress named Radegonde Putemonnoie, is in my pocket.

We take the child severely to task.

"What were you doing in the marketplace?" I ask. "You who are so unwell?"

"I was hungry," he says in a small voice, head hanging low.

I feel a twinge. "How did you fall into the bear-baiting ring?"

"I was—it was an accident. Some boys chased me."

We have reached one of the misty lanes around the shadow district, and it isn't necessary to ask any further. Godfridus grunts and sets Hercule down on a doorstep. "You're a small thing," he says, stretching, "but uncommonly heavy. Just a moment."

We all catch our breath. The air creeps through my mantle, like chilly hands on my flesh. I look up, seeking warmth; as it is nearly noon, the sun's moving directly overhead.

Hercule's hood has been pushed awry, and he happens to be looking up, too, just as the sun pokes its finger straight down into this street. It illuminates his face.

"Hercule!" I gasp. "Godfridus—look."

The child stands up as if to run, but with his hurt leg he can't get far. He falls back into Godfridus's arms, and mercilessly I push the hood away.

The face of Hercule, the boy I nestled in my body all night, is not the face of a child. It is lined—puffing slightly around the eyes, sagging a little away from the nose. There is a scar on one cheek. Experience is written on that face, experience it took more than six or even ten years to win.

Godfridus sees it, too. "Who—and what—are you?" he demands. I am speechless.

"I told you my name," the creature says sullenly, having decided not to struggle. "I am Hercule Legrand—"

Hercule the Great. Hercule the Big.

"—lately of the Château Coussin."

"Where is that?" Godfridus looks around as if to find a castle suddenly sprung up on this narrow street of houses. I see, across the way, a face peering out the top floor of a house that juts over the street. An old woman in a white cap who quickly vanishes.

"Coussin is on the other side of the great forest." Hercule squirms, sitting, and lets the hood settle around his shoulders. "It is the principal seat of Lord Robert de Souligny."

I am fascinated by this face; his eyes are green, his lashes long, his features well cut—but, still, not the features of a child.

"How"—I swallow; I must ask—"do you come to have the body of a child and the face of a thirty-year-old man?"

"Can't you guess it? You *have* guessed it. I'm a dwarf." He says, with a bitter tone, "A prodigy, a genius, a sport. A freak. A marvel." Halfheartedly he thumps himself on the chest, then winces. "Thirty-two years old."

"You look perfect," I whisper. "If it weren't for the sunlight, I never would have known . . ." In the dark, I held him in my arms.

Godfridus adds, "You are no regular dwarf. Dwarfs are like those in the marketplace, bent and big-headed and awkward."

"True," says Hercule. "But I'm told I'm one of the lucky ones. Perfectly formed in the image of humankind, malformed only in my stature. A natural freak. Or maybe not so natural—there's said to be such a thing as a *made dwarf,* sealed into an earthenware jar so the growth is stunted, and I might be one of those. It would explain why I am as you, just smaller of body, madder of mind. Which makes me a perfect fool."

"How could you eat?" Godfridus asks, distracted.

"Oh, naturally one would leave the head free, at the neck of the jar. And tip the vessel to one side to let dirt flow out. But as regards me, this is only a rumor, you understand—I have no memory of it. In fact I don't remember much from my childhood. I just know I was abandoned young and raised by monks who nursed me on honey and water . . ."

I say resolutely, "So you are a dwarf. Then you have been trained to do tricks?"

"Tricks," Hercule repeats, again with that bitter voice; then it changes to a jovial mocking. "I work miracles! I can turn a white rose red and raise flames from a bowl of water. I can turn a man black when he bathes. I can write with an ink invisible to the eye, which only fire will coax out of secrecy—"

"I can do that too," I interrupt, "with the juice of an onion. And I have heard of a red wine whose fumes will change a flower's color. Don't waste your breath." Now my shock is finished, I'm starting to feel angry at the trick he played on me. Asking for my milk!

"You were Lord Robert's fool," Godfridus emphasizes.

Hercule sighs. "Yes. But I was one of many. He had us all sleep together in an old henhouse, which he liked to visit with huntsmen. He tried to breed us, to produce a race of tiny people. He had us mate for his sport."

"Is that why you left him?"

Hercule pauses before answering. "That is part of it. That, and the pain. A dwarf, even one who looks well, lives a life of constant torture from within. These little bones hurt. My skin hurts. My lungs are weak, and my heart is sore from beating at Lord Robert's beck and call. I ran away to get some peace."

Peace. What I thought we had achieved just moments ago, before the sun came out and showed me this. That sun, now, has moved indifferently on, and we are in shadow.

I shiver. "What do you want, Hercule Legrand? With your hidden identity and your stolen coins—"

"Not stolen," he interrupts fiercely. "They were given to me, along with my clothes and other gifts, by Lord Robert's wife, Lady Anne. *She* was my benefactress."

"And now you want me to be that for you."

"I paid for a year's lodging with you," Hercule says. "And if I'm not mistaken, the only money around your domus is mine."

His speech is punctuated with a loud crack from his pelvic region; it sounds painful, but too well timed to be genuine. Still, it reminds me of the creaks and groans I listened to in bed, and the possibility that the leg wound will go septic. How very real is the dwarf's need of protection—as real as my need of a patron and of money.

I tiptoe up to Godfridus's ear. "What do you think?" I whisper.

His blue eyes have gone dark. He whispers back to me: "Scriptures say that dwarfs are born when a woman conceives in evil—during her monthly flux, or before weaning another child, or when there's a baby already in her belly. Dwarfs are children of sin, and their bodies are the sign."

I ponder that phrase, *children of sin*, and say slowly, "This one seems perfect."

"Dwarfs are prey to superhuman lusts."

"But he says he did not like mating for Lord Robert."

Godfridus leans in so close his breath tickles the inside of my head. "Be careful. Remember who you are."

Bonne, the bastard daughter of Blanche. Who has a recluse to care for and only one friend in the world; who is herself a child of sin.

"Hercule Legrand," I say out loud, and his little head rises. I can't meet his eyes. "You may stay with me—but *as a child*. I won't have anyone know there's a dwarf living with Bonne the wet nurse."

Hercule claps his hands and prances a little—a reflex ingrained by years of fooling, I think. "I'm glad," he says simply, then pulls a coin from my ear and presents it to me.

I take it, wondering what all I am in for. I had thought lords' fools were supposed to be witty, but this one seems just daft, a fool indeed. "Pull up your hood," I say. "We'll go home."

HERCULE

Now begin the happiest days I have known. For in spite of the cracking bones and the heavy heart and the blood that never cools, I have a home.

Not the henhouse at Coussin, where Lord Robert's dwarfs perched half-asleep on narrow shelves. Not the pallet at the monastery, where orphans crowded three to a bed. I have my own straw mattress, and my own linen sheets (bought with my own money), a poultice and linen bandage on my leg, and at mealtimes I get my own portions, just as big as Bonne's.

In the morning it's bread, sometimes fresh from the bakers' ovens. In the dark early hours, I fetch it. The bakerwoman likes me, since the miracle at the bear-baiting ring has brought more business to her. Bonne and I eat this bread with lentils. Then she might take up some sewing, while I go back to bed and rest. She goes for a walk, to visit the sculptor, feed the recluse, or do the marketing. For dinner we might have a pie or more bread and lentils, peas, cheese, maybe sausage. I sleep in the afternoon—strengthening sleep, not won with a tiresome backflip or somersault. Then the sculptor comes for his dinner, and the two of them talk—gossip of the town, nothing much. I pretend to keep sleeping, watching him suck at those breasts that once saved me. Their white glow in the firelight, the quiet sound of his lips, the look on her face like I've seen on church virgins . . . By curfew he's gone, and I wake. There's more bread for her and me, and some legumes, and I tell her the tales of my life. About courtly games in which I tumbled half a dozen girly dwarfs, or flew from the ceiling on a wire. About games of love with the big ladies, receiving their gloves or a laughing kiss.

She wants to know how rich people live.

"It was a grand house?" she might ask me, her eyes round over their bowl of mush.

"A castle," I correct her, "with woven rushes underfoot and velvet on all the walls. Even the chairs were made of gold."

"And the ladies?" she asks. "How do the ladies live?" I know she is thinking that in her pocket, closed tight with its drawstring and tied to her belt, lies that linen scrap the rich woman gave her.

"They live well, Lady Bonne"—that's what I call her, as that's what she is to me. "They wear silken dresses and sit on turf benches in Lord Robert's gardens, playing lutes and singing songs of love. They wash their hair and dry it in the sun, enticing lovers to them like mermaids . . ."

I tell her what she wants to know. I say what she wants to hear. I repay her for the peace and the comfort and the talk.

But one tale I will never tell her. It is the true tale of how I came to be lying half-dead in a church tower and then found this space of peace with her.

I will tell it here.

Let us pray, said the bald priest, and who were we to resist? A passel of celebrants hungry for whatever could be coaxed to lie on our earthly altar, our appetites whetted by work—for some do consider the hunt to be that; after all, one must keep one's balance, even after the third barrel of ale has been drained, and it's no easy feat controlling a horse who bolts at a slaughter's first scream.

It was Lord Robert's annual fête de la chasse, and this was the grandest feast ever. Dishes of every deception around, and the tables, as it is said, groaning—in this case quite literally, for by a whim of the lord his meal had been laid on the nude bodies of virgins. The girls had all they could do to keep from writhing in offended modesty—but one good writhe would destroy the cooks' real work, knock over the joints and spill the sauces, and that was one thing Lord Robert would not tolerate. So while lords and ladies, dwarfs and dancers gave thanks to the Lord above and asked for goodwill and good hunting, unhappy virgins kept the food warm with their blushes.

"Be grateful," I told them, "for your bath and the butter"—each girl would take a pound of the stuff home to her family—"and imagine the meal you'll make off yourselves later."

I was in the corner, poised to sing and strut for my supper. A fool must be ever at the ready. At one end of the trestle, a ruddy monk was nibbling a virgin's toes, declaring them sweet. The noble lady beside him tittered behind one hand before joining the final "Amen."

We asked for grace and thought we'd received it. Lady Anne—table center, eyes downcast—ladled the first morsel onto her husband's trencher.

Anne. Only a fool would love his lord's lady, and I was that fool. Because she treated me like a big person, a man, with the power of a man to think and converse. Because she respected me and wouldn't join in the kissing games. Because her husband was deceiving her with a vavasour's daughter. She told me once she was a bigger fool than I, and she accepted a tiny glove from me.

It was her duty to serve her husband at the feast. She took a slice of the boar's head, spooned out the stuffing inside, and even gave him a tusk. Very properly done.

And I as chief jester, chiefly a fool, made a joke. On sanglier and sanglots, boar's head and woman's tears. On stuffing and tusks. On—indeed on; I mounted the nearest serving dish—wise and foolish virgins. I was rewarded with gales of bawdy laughter and a fat capon tossed right to my pocket.

I stuffed it inside. "An impotent male"—for even this crowd knew about castrating birds—"still knows his way to the dark place." I swaggered around the table, swinging the sack at my waist.

They laughed at me through faces shining in grease. All but my dear Lady Anne, my love, who continued to gaze at her trencher.

What could be wrong? I'd observed no amours of her husband that day, and the vavasour's girl wasn't here. It seemed Lady Anne should be glad. Perhaps she was tired, or her monthly curse was at hand; she had a quite terrible time with it, as her maids told me.

I resolved to distract her, conceived of a trick. My joke would make her laugh at last, give her delight in the day and her life. Or at least make this feast a little less loathsome. So I ran to the kitchens to plan, and I traded my capon for what suited me more.

The result was a pie, a wonderful thing: the crust cobbled together from what was around, the innards—to be revealed later. I had it carried, top crumbling, steamy-delicious, into the feast hall, where the trumpeters blasted an envoy, the diners grew silent, and I recited a verse of my own composition:

> Love is a hunt for what's lasting and true,
> Which is why it is death that true lovers pursue—
> For a heart imparts pleasure whose lifetime is fleet,
> While a corpse transforms love into just so much meat.
> Leaving the lover to hunt for his pleasure
> With a heart once imprisoned now his own in full measure.
> So take heart, Lady Anne, from the love you are gave,
> And be grateful for hearts that now beat in the grave.

With this I plunged my fat little hand into the pie, proclaiming—

> Love is contained in this poem's art,
> As the crust of this pie holds an enemy's heart!

though I believe these words were lost in the uproar that followed revelation of the pie's insides. Lord Robert staggered drunkenly to his feet and waved his sword around, bellowing he'd have revenge on the dog who betrayed him. The virgin platters jumped up from the table screaming and dripping food. The guests at first thought this was a planned entertainment and chased the virgins to deflower them, or at the very least to lick them clean. One of Robert's knights blubbered under the table, crying that he hadn't told anyone, hadn't breathed a word about the murder...And there was I, standing like a fool holding the bloody heart of a hart over my head.

How was I to know the vavasour's daughter had that very day been run through with her master's noble sword? Lord Robert had found her in bed with a beater he'd hired, at her request, to get game from the bush. Whereon he butchered them himself and threw their entrails to the hounds.

When the story was told that night, Lady Anne left Coussin. She would return to her parents at Artois; the marriage would be annulled. But Anne, my love, never reached her parents' house—she disappeared somewhere in the forest, murdered in her turn by bandits or wolves.

Thus did I kill my love—though I did not come to destroy, I was in danger of the judgment. I could not stay at Coussin. So I wandered from town to town, chased by my own drunken demons, my joints cracking, sores weeping, seeking a change. Love, peace, magic.

I would kiss the very devil's arse, if he'd transform the stuff of me. So why not the bosom of Bonne Tardieu?

Radegonde Putemonnoie: That is the name of the most beautiful woman I have seen, and probably the richest; she of the soft linen square, embroidered and scented. She is a rich woman who saw something good in me and gave me a gift. And when she turned to walk away, I could see she walked with a pregnant woman's heavy hips.

Each morning I slip into the town, combing the streets for information. Godfridus can tell me a little, for he carved her husband's sarcophagus some months ago; but he is reticent, says only that she seems a good woman. I wonder if he is in love with her.

Deo gratias, since the great market day some people are willing to speak to me; I ask at every spice dealer's and pie shop, strike up conversations around the great well, listen to gossip in front of the Palais de Justice. I learn that Radegonde Putemonnoie has everything. She *is* everything.

I hear she is almost nobility; she moves more gracefully than any lady, her body bending like silk under water.

I hear she bathes in rosewater, in asses' milk, in the first blood of virgin girls. I hear that a dozen maids shuttle buckets of hot water up and down the stairs to her bedroom all day, that she sits in the bath all day long, that she is part mermaid.

I hear she doesn't bathe at all, just wipes herself with a piece of silk at night.

I hear her mother was a Negresse.

I hear she is the true heroine of a fairy tale, the one in which the cursed princess pricks her finger on a needle and falls asleep for a hundred years; only that instead of a princess she is the daughter of a Moorish merchant, instead of a needle it was a golden brooch that slipped while her maid was dressing her, and instead of a century she slept four days. When her father put the clumsy maid to death, he watered his garden with her blood, and the roses grew so fast and thick they pulled down the walls of his house. It was then, the story goes, that her husband-to-be found her, reading a romance in the wilding garden, and took her away to marry him.

Or her parents died of the peste twenty years ago, and she married her father's business partner. Or she had no parents, was raised in a nunnery to which her beauty drew men like a star, and the nuns married her off to save her virtue.

It is known that she and her husband moved here almost two decades hence and built their house from the ground up. Some say the walls are hung with golden tissue and the floors are paved with silver tiles. Half the town has at one time or another been in their employ.

I hear, also—and this I believe—that her husband's will specifies this: If she fails to produce a male heir, she will be given to a convent, to live out her days praying for Henri's soul; in that event, her brother-in-law in Paris will inherit the Putemonnoie wealth. But if she does give birth to a boy, she will be the child's guardian and oversee his fortune until he reaches maturity, at which time she may do as she likes. This arrangement shocks me at first, but I am told it is fairly common among the better classes. By law a woman can inherit nothing of value anyway.

Radegonde Putemonnoie glides through the town like a cat, in her hand a pierced ivory box holding balls of musk and crushed amber, whose smells balance and smooth her humors. On her bosom, between her breasts, she wears a heavy enameled pendant: On one side, two lovers kiss; on the other, Death grins. She is thirty-eight years old and expecting her first baby, conceived on her husband's deathbed.

In a cage under her bed Radegonde Putemonnoie is said to keep a toad who wards away what evils might infect her overnight. She owns an enormous emerald worn oval and smooth from the motion of her tongue, because she sleeps sucking on it to preserve her youth.

She cooks, by herself, over a brazier, special unguents and cremes that she rubs into her skin or swallows.

She killed her husband.

She is a virgin.

She is a witch.

I STAND BEFORE HER HOUSE, a great mass of squared walls and wings with a needle-thin eight-sided tower in the center. Her embroidered square is in my hands, but I do not ring the bell. My hands stroke the cloth with its careful laying on of threads.

I realize I've stood here before without knowing who was inside. Once or twice while passing through the heart of town, where the rich merchants live, I would stop, gaze around me at the looming stone edifices, not a horse hair or speck of cow dung padding out their walls; false columns flush against the facades and around the windows, their tops blooming capitals with laurel leaves, sheep and shepherds, monsters, or women in fine clothing, all as suits the owners and their businesses. I have wondered at the riches these houses hold, in dwelling space or in cellar warehouse: ells of golden cloth, bushels of saffron, heaps of rubies, perfume by the barrel. I imagine these in the bowels of every large and coldly solid staring edifice.

And last summer when I stood here, with green vines creeping over garden walls, and trees rustling leaves above swollen fruit, and the smell of roses weighting the air, I watched a bent man in a brown jaquette leave through a front door and hobble downstreet toward the river.

"He doesn't have long to live," a gossip whispered behind me. "He's the master of that house, but a witch has enchanted him."

I turned to hear more, and the gossip—a fuller's wife who knows my landlady—recognized me. "Bonne," she said, and hurried off.

As I, now, speed away.

FEAST OF
SAINT STEPHEN
OF LYONS

[FEBRUARY 13]

GODFRIDUS

It's the night before Saint Valentine's Sunday,
and a light snow is falling from the stars. Bonne
has opened her shutters. As I approach, gritty
and weary from the chantier, I see her head
and the dwarf's silhouetted against the orange
light within. And when I come inside, I find an
icy chill from wall to wall instead of the usual
warmth.

"Tomorrow the birds will be mating,"
Bonne says, as if by way of explanation. "We're
watching them pair off now." She seems giddy—
usually she stays away from windows.

"So far, only pigeons," says the dwarf. "Or
doves, if you prefer to call a dungheap a mid-
den. We were hoping for falcons or hawks or
nightingales."

Slowly I remove my hood, thinking, I do
not like that dwarf. He is prone to superstitions
such as that birds mate on Valentine's feast, but
that is not his worst. At night, sometimes, when
I am helping Bonne, I see his little eyes slit
open, and I know he is watching us but I don't
know what he's thinking. Sometimes his speech
is pure rave—though he says it's his body that
suffers, I suspect his mind's unbalance.

For her part, Bonne does not seem to notice the dwarf's misdoings. She is often preoccupied, staring into space when she could be sewing or listening to my reports from the new church. I have heard she's been taking long walks through the city, dreaming her days away rather than looking for work. Perhaps the dwarf has given her too much.

I brush the snow from my hood and shoulders. It does not melt. "Saint Valentine," I say in a teaching tone, "cured a blind girl, converted her family, and was decapitated."

The dwarf has a quick rejoinder. "The true saints are always the martyred ones. Killed for—or even in—the church." He weights his voice with importance.

Bonne turns to him. In her face I think I see suspicion and desire—desire to believe he has spoken sincerely. She wants to like him and to think he likes her and thinks well of her unfortunate mother.

"Martyred, yes," I say, and sit stiffly down on a chest. "But only after doing deeds to help their fellow men."

It is late. Bonne's breasts must be full, but she makes no move toward me. She's staring out into the black air, her head on her arms on the windowsill. I decide I will wait for her only until the next bell. Meanwhile I have some little news to give: "There is to be a spire on the apse of the new church, sixty feet high. The town fathers approved it today in council."

The other two exclaim in amazement, but not for me. A pair of pigeons—doves—is thrashing by in a tangle of beaks and feathers. "Look," Bonne says, "their wings are covered in blood . . ." It is good that she sees lust is savage.

Only the dwarf remembers me. "A spire that tall will tickle the angels," he says. "And raise taxes all over town."

I tell him, "You are sounding too much like Lord Robert's fool. With your jokes that aren't funny and your stories of lust."

He says, "Lust is funny."

"Lust is a sin."

There is silence. I have silenced the dwarf! Then Bonne stands up and gives herself a shake, which cannot disguise that she is trembling. Perhaps she is cold at last, or has been thinking more of the unfortunate Blanche and the way desire brought her down. Bonne closes the shutters. "Enough! Both of you. Whatever lust is, the birds can indulge theirs without us. I'm going to clean my best dress and surcoat for tomorrow. Godfridus, give me yours, too. Oh, don't worry," she adds, when she sees me look askance, "I won't use urine and ashes this time. I bought fuller's earth and lye. The best. They drink the grease right out of wool, and you'll be all serene for the martyr's feast."

I hesitate, nonplussed. "But you've sworn you won't do laundry anymore."

"It's springtime," she says, "or almost. We both need a change. And it so happens that tomorrow, after Mass, I may ask you to do a favor in return."

"What about me?" the dwarf asks. "Don't you want to wash my clothes?"

"Yours are all clean," she says.

I hand over my surcoat, feeling cold.

THE FEAST OF SAINT VALENTINE

[FEBRUARY 14]

 STAND BEFORE THE HOUSE AGAIN. THE house of Radegonde Putemonnoie, where the richest woman in town lives with her emerald, her toad, her gold. And her unborn child.

I am cleanly dressed, in my light gray, with the old blackish mantle thrown back so it won't be too noticeable. Through the iron gate I see a wide, empty courtyard and a house wall with open shutters. There are grilles over the window openings.

Godfridus, in his freshly de-spotted surcoat, nudges me. "Go on," he says, with the simplicity of one who is never afraid or ashamed and who is eager now. He seemed pleased out of proportion when I asked him to bring me here, and thus far I haven't asked why. "Ring the bell."

While I hesitate, a gentleman rides by on a black horse, both their heads held high. The horse's hooves splatter us with the slush of last night's snow. This would seem to be a reason to leave; how can I show myself muddy here? But as the sound of hooves fades away, I pull the cord that rings a bell in the courtyard and, presumably, in the house.

In a few moments, the maid from the marché comes to the gate. She is skinny but she has a dimple, which shows when she sees Godfridus. She is one of those who can recognize his beauty. She looks squint-eyed at my skirt, then into my face.

"So you are here." She has a Paris accent.

"I—I'd like to speak to the mistress."

"Mistress Putemonnoie is much occupied. And she doesn't play hostess to tradespeople, especially on Sunday." She says this last while looking at me.

Something about the maid's resistance makes me stubborn. "She gave me a gift. I want to thank her for it."

Godfridus adds, "Mistress Putemonnoie sought Bonne out at the marketplace, Agnès. Please let us in."

So, to please him, Agnès stands aside. She locks the gate behind us, then leads us to a thick wooden door strengthened with iron whorls, the main door of the Putemonnoie house. Again I hesitate, and Godfridus fairly pushes me in.

The air inside the house is strange. It smells wonderful, for one thing, and I can't decide if it's cool or warm. These are the middle days of February (but the weather has been peculiar), and we are in a vast room where footsteps echo brushily against a stone floor. I know the stone must be cold, and in a moment I feel it through the hole in my shoe. Carpets hang on all the walls, but there is nothing standing but a bench.

"You can wait for her in the solar," Agnès says, and there is something in the way she says "her"—a reverence that goes beyond respect for the person you work for. I think she is showing me how to behave when I meet the woman. "You remember the way," she adds to Godfridus.

"It has been a long time," he says. "And this house is an easy one to get lost in."

"Then follow me." She shows him every sign of pleasure; she has probably been waiting for this day—and perhaps Godfridus has been waiting, too, for an excuse to come.

We climb a flight of stairs and go in and out of a series of rooms. The air gets noticeably warmer, and the fragrance grows stronger—I think it is musk, maybe, or amber—or perhaps I haven't smelled it before. Maybe it's something newly shipped from the East. To me it is the smell of beauty and money and a house all one's own that one never has to leave.

At the end of a wide hall, Agnès pulls back a red tapestry panel. The door beneath it is open, and a wave of heat billows out.

"*She* keeps two braziers going, as well as the fireplace," Agnès tells us. "It's for health—the baby's, of course."

"Yes, the baby's," I murmur, the first words I've spoken inside this house. I am hardly conscious of having opened my mouth to talk; I am looking around eagerly, greedily.

I notice first that Radegonde Putemonnoie isn't there. Swallowing a lump of anxiety and disappointment, I turn my face away from the others. The two braziers Agnès mentioned are blazing, fiercely orange, on the floor, which is covered first in many-colored tile and then, in the far half, with a patterned red carpet. More carpet hangs on the walls. A number of deeply carved chests and benches, and some x-shaped chairs, account for the remaining space.

What amazes me most about the room is its light. Warm light: The shutters are swung all the way open, but where you'd expect the empty gray of winter sky, there are thin panes of utterly clear, greenish glass, arrayed in diamonds and crisscrossed with lead. Nearly all the sun's light enters this way, though the room stays toasty.

Agnès sees me staring. "Those come from Paris," she says. "You won't see many—they're very expensive."

Godfridus walks over to the window and touches the glass. "They weren't here in the summer."

"But then you'd want the air in the summer, wouldn't you?" says Agnès. "Mistress bought them last year. See, they're mounted on these frames so we can move them from room to room. She already has a set for the baby's chamber—yes, the baby will have his own place to sleep. And next year we are going to install glass permanently in all the private rooms."

Here I have been so vain of my little home's dark warmth, which comes only secondhand from my landlords' ovens.

"Ingenious." Godfridus knocks against the windowpanes with the calluses on his fingertips. Though he's a craftsman and has worked riches with his own hands, he hasn't seen such wonders of technology in a private home before. Until now, glass has been only for God.

Agnès is watching him inscrutably. "I'll look for Mistress," she says abruptly, and disappears behind the tapestry flap.

I continue to stare around me, still holding on to the linen square that la Putemonnoie gave me. It feels damp in my palm. Such richness here! I inspect the heavily carved benches with their embroidered cushions, marvel at the scenes of courtly love on the storage chests. Every surface is cluttered; I see ivory and gold boxes, an elaborate candleholder, a broderie frame.

I walk over to study Radegonde Putemonnoie's fancywork. One corner of the linen has flopped over the frame, obscuring the pattern; I want to set it straight and see what design she's working, but I am timid. This back side is a snarl of bright threads, and her thread basket's a tangle. A bone needle is stuck carelessly in the middle of it all.

"This house is a marvel," Godfridus informs me, leaving the window as I leave the frame. "There are privies upstairs and down, and the late master was known for his collection of saintly relics. I haven't seen them, but . . ."

I imagine the beautiful woman of the marketplace, skirts bundled around her middle, sitting over a hole in a bench while her waste drops into a pot or a pit or the street far below. It's a comforting vision; her excrement may disappear immediately, but she still produces it.

"... and a vial of the Virgin's blood," Godfridus concludes. I barely hear him.

Just then the atmosphere in the room shifts. We hear the soft brushbrush of leather slippers in the hall, and a tinkle as of bells. The tapestry flap is lifted; Godfridus stiffens and smiles; and I turn to face Radegonde Putemonnoie.

She is here, entering with her head high and her back straight. Her heavy black velvet skirts drag on the floor as she walks with eyes focused forward. Agnès follows closely, with a tray, and the panel swishes shut behind her.

Radegonde Putemonnoie does not look at me. She goes immediately to a brazier and holds out her hands, head bent. Her hands are cold and she is heating them. She is absorbed in herself.

And so am I, absorbed in her. When she stopped walking, the music stopped, too; and this is how I know it came from the keys at her belt, the keys that unlock all the secrets of this great house. They shine against the black of her overdress, almost as bright as her famous enamel pendant.

53

Her gown is cut low and tight, with buttoned sleeves that show the curves of her arms; the overdress is sleeveless and finds a way to cling. Her bosom, small for the moment, will swell in the coming months; now it cradles the pendant's lovers' faces, which means Death must be pressed against her heart. Her waist is slightly thick.

Though Radegonde Putemonoie's form generally gives an impression of smallness, the hands that so hold her interest are large; they are bony and well shaped, with nails pale and oval, kept long either from vanity or to signal she is in mourning. Her skin there and about her face and neck is murky, with a good red color to the cheeks. She wears no veil, despite her widowhood. A multitude of braids wrap her head unusually, in the manner of a crown, and like a crown they are studded with jewels; the face below is mostly cheekbones, with black half-circles cut by down-focused eyelashes, arcs of eyebrow, a long straight nose, and those full red lips that smiled at me in the marketplace. Now she's set them in a line, serene—with the way she's holding her hands, I think she could be the loveliest saint in a tympanum, her arms just about to move in some holy act: Martha serving a supper; Veronica wiping Jesus' face with her veil; Elizabeth receiving the infant Jesus.

But Elizabeth was old, and this woman looks younger than I do. Though I am told she is sixteen years older.

Yes, she's as beautiful as a statue, and nearly as still; even more perfect, though it is a perfection unexpected, because it contradicts every poetic convention.

When at last la Putemonnoie's head lifts, she looks not at me, but first at Godfridus, to whom she nods (jewels flashing); then at Agnès, who hands her a cup of wine; and then at the broderie frame. She flips the upturned corner down and starts the air moving around the room.

"So here you are," she says, turning to me at last. "Bonne Tardieu, the bastard daughter of Blanche Mirabilis." Her voice is surprisingly deep and soft, as if she has been sleeping long or singing.

Agnès gives a cup to Godfridus, then one to me. Godfridus gazes rapt at la Putemonnoie—of course it is not the maid he has come to see. Does my face also wear that look of obvious dazzlement?

"I—yes, my name is Bonne." I don't protest the surname now. "I've come to thank you for your generous gift in the marketplace. It is beautiful."

I see that, even as I have been examining her, even as she has scrutinized her hands, so is she now studying me. The everycolor eyes flicker from my brow to my mouth to my bosom. "I'm glad you think so," she says. "I worked the square myself."

I feel myself go hot all over, and my hand crumples the already damp bit of cloth. "I'm doubly honored."

Her weird eyes stay on me. "That was an amazing scene in the bear-baiting ring. You have wonderful breasts—wondrous, it seems."

"I—I am a wet nurse, mistress."

"I know." I see the faintest beginning of a line form between her brows. "I've made inquiries about you. You're quite famous in this town, especially since Saint Agathe's market."

I flush again—not for my unsought fame, but because she has been asking about me. Or she's had her servants ask; either way, it's the same. Carefully, I take a sip of the hot, heady wine.

La Putemonnoie seats herself on a bench heaped with cushions. "But you have no infant to care for now?"

I think of Hercule. "No, mistress. I am looking for work."

"And so you have come here."

I say boldly, "I came only to thank you. Although it was clear to me at the market that you are going to have a child."

She purses her lips as if I've displeased her. She looks down at her thread basket and plucks at the end of a length of green silk.

Godfridus clears his throat. "Bonne is a good, pious woman, mistress," he says. "She is my niece."

"Yes, I've heard that," la Putemonnoie murmurs. "And she should be pious, being the daughter of a holy woman and a priest." Her eyes dart up then, to see how I've taken her barb.

I stare ahead. I won't deny or dispute. La Putemonnoie pulls her thread free from the tangle.

Godfridus continues earnestly, "Bonne works hard, and her milk is good."

She lifts her needle, a delicate gesture. "Brunettes give the best milk," she says. "Blondes are anemic, redheads too choleric."

Quickly I pull off my veil and barbette and bow my head, showing her the part down the middle of my hair.

There is a long silence. I feel la Putemonnoie has won some victory, has made me reveal myself. She knows now how much I want her patronage. And I do want it—although at this moment, playing the lady with me, she seems very far removed from the lovely woman who sent me a gift through a crowd. Even if she is just as beautiful as that one was, she is giving nothing away.

When I look up again, her needle is threaded and she is sewing. "So tell me," she says, her own head glittering, "what you have to offer as a wet nurse, besides brown hair and milk that your uncle says is good."

I anchor the veil and begin to tuck my hair underneath again. "I have raised two children to the age of four, mistress—exclusively on my milk. I taught them to talk and to walk and to use the privy on their own. I have a warm home to raise them in. I know a certain amount about practical medicines, having studied herb lore and the interactions of the body's four humors. I know how to swaddle so the moisture of the womb is preserved and the limbs grow in straight."

"All this any woman from the country could give me."

"Perhaps," I say, as the veil slides off again, "but I can do it better. I will love your child and care for it as if it were my own."

At my words, she drops her needle. I think I have pleased her—most wet nurses view infants as mere work, and this is to be her only child, and her salvation. I bend down to the carpet and pick up the sliver of bone and hand it to her. At the same time I stuff the veil into my pocket.

She licks the thread end and reinserts it. She resumes her sewing, and when she speaks, her voice is conversational in tone. "I understand you have also been a laundress." Pointedly, it seems, she is ignoring the mud now dry on my skirt.

"Yes." I hope she won't mention my years as a nitpicker.

"That can be a useful skill. Do you have any others?"

"I can read and write. My mother had me learn."

"How unusual."

"It isn't so unusual," I say modestly, "not for a great mistress such as yourself."

She pauses, needle in the air. The everycolor eyes focus on me. "You are no great woman. Neither was your mother."

Her rebuke stings. I was wrong to brag; no one needs a nurse who can read and write. Especially one who learned from a Jew (I'll keep that fact to myself for now). Still less does a woman need a nurse whose mother was Blanche the Astonishing.

I take a deep breath of air. "Mistress," I say, "my mother was the greatest woman she could be. She worked hard. It was not—"

I feel Godfridus touch my arm, urging discretion, but I continue nonetheless:

"It was not her choice to be elevated to a miracle—and she certainly didn't choose to bear a child some nine months later. You may think of her as a harlot, but she had no memory of conceiving me. There used to be many women in this town who would swear she was virgo intacta when brought to bed, and that the midwife had to cut her hymen with shears before my head could pass.

"She named me Bonne to show she did not resent that I'd brought her low. Other people called me Tardieu, short for 'God's bastard,' to mock her. Still she treated me with every kindness and tried to give me a better life than she herself had lived. After showing me the letters she knew, she found a clerk to teach me the rest. In any case, Blanche is dead now, as are the women who defended her. I can promise that my milk is wholesome, and that a baby will thrive on it."

Behind Radegonde Putemonnoie, I see Godfridus looking wide-eyed at me. Agnès is smiling in triumph. But Mistress Putemonnoie has let her face relax; some of the hard bones are softening, the eyes glowing with a different kind of light.

She puts down her tapestry. What comes next makes my knees go weak: She says, "I would like to try some of your milk."

MY MILK IS PLENTIFUL, as always. She must be pleased. And I, how I feel with those plump red lips on me—

Godfridus and Agnès, my companions, please observe: The great bourgeoise is bent before a common wet nurse. The soft dark hands are pressed to the bony bosom, holding the pendant that shows lovers backed with Death's ugly face; the chapped and wrinkled pale hands guide the sleek dark head. The red mouth is fastened on the blue-veined breast—a living tongue sucking at more life, teasing and tickling the node of a well-worn nipple.

The two of them watch us, Godfridus and Agnès, with bald and unabashed interest. I wonder if the maid smirked when she saw me undress, saw how ugly my breasts are; I was too ashamed to look around then, sure that if I saw her—or *her*—looking at me, my milk would freeze. I feel them watch a good long while, and they look down only when la Putemonnoie pulls away—as if that's the intimate moment, when her mouth leaves my body.

She took much more than a taste from me; my right breast is nearly empty. My whole body is unbalanced, and it's a dizzy moment before I can move. Then, lopsided, I lace up my underdress and surcoat. There won't be much for Godfridus tonight, but he won't mind; he's too good to cry over a little milk.

He's smiling at me again, showing his approval, and I can see the space in back where he lost two teeth. He thinks I have done well.

Now Mistress Putemonnoie does something fascinating. She reaches into her sleeve and pulls out a square of embroidered linen like the one she gave me; with this cloth she wipes her lips in a dainty gesture.

And as she does this, Agnès flutters like a mother bird—she smooths the lady's hair, lifts and settles the chain around her neck, puts her in order. She folds the linen square and sets it aside, then hands la Putemonnoie a fresh one from a basket sitting on a chest. The lady accepts her ministrations with an air of abstraction. I see her twitch, and I know she's just smothered a burp.

Then la Putemonnoie stands. She shakes out the velvet of her skirts, smiles fondly down at her feet.

Suddenly she turns to me. "From now on, you must come precisely at noon."

I feel myself sway. "Mistress?"

"I'm going to tell my cooks to prepare a basket for you every day. You may collect it at noontime. No no"—she holds up a hand to stifle any protest or question—"I must see to it that your milk is strong."

"Does that mean"—I hardly dare to hope it—"you want to engage me?"

The pillowy lips purse. "I'm considering it," she says slowly. "I think your milk is good now—only good. Let us see what happens when your diet is improved. I must have the best, you know . . . my baby must have the best. I'll give you meat and honey to eat, good blood-strengthening food. Then I will make a decision."

I bend deep, spreading my skirts as I've seen nice women do. It seems the whole world is opening up before me. "I am most grateful."

"I haven't made you any promises yet," she reminds me. "We will consider this a trial period. This baby—it's the only child my husband's house will ever have."

"God rest his soul," Godfridus says, crossing himself, and Agnès follows his motions.

La Putemonnoie seems not to notice them. She is looking thoughtfully at me. "I may also have some other bits of work for you from time to time. When you come for the basket—be sure you are prompt, and come every day—the scullery maid will let you know whether to step upstairs."

Perhaps she wants me to wash her dresses or linens—work I have forsworn. But I think I will do anything for a chance to come back to this glorious room; I would even pick out the lice from her hair, if she had any lice.

I say, "I will be prompt."

La Putemonnoie smiles. It seems to be a genuine smile, warm and frank, meeting my shy eyes. "And now I mean to give you a small gift," she says, "something to remind you of the promise of new life during a gray winter. I think you of all people should appreciate it."

"How kind." I am surprised. She is again acting the gracious lady of the marketplace. Perhaps she is going to give me another linen square— I can see myself wiping my lips with one, then pulling out the other . . .

"Shall I fetch this gift?" asks Agnès.

"No. All of you, wait here." Radegonde Putemonnoie sweeps out through the tapestry door.

We are stiff, waiting. Godfridus stares out the glassed windows, and Agnès and I, both flushed, size each other up from the corners of our eyes. Hers are sharp.

"Don't expect special privileges in this house," she says. "This gift will be a special token, not a daily habit. And she's testing other nurses."

"I expect nothing more."

Godfridus drums his fingers against the windowpanes, like rain. He waits as we wait.

Then there's that brushing step outside, and Radegonde Putemonnoie comes back in. She looks more like a bride than a widow; her skin is glowing, her eyes radiate, and in her hand she carries a rose.

A rose. Bright scarlet, flat petals spiked by pointy sepals; a dark green stem. When she hands it to me, my fingers leap to stroke the petals, anticipating the touch of dry fabric—how my hands tingle when they feel, instead, the moist livingness of a real flower!

Swiftly I turn to the window. Outside it is still cold February.

"What magic—" The flower has fallen from my hand. In my excitement, I feel the stem crush under my foot. "What magic is this?"

"No magic." She makes a gesture, opening her hands. "This rose bloomed last summer in my garden. What do you mean by trampling my gift?"

Godfridus kneels by me, pulling the rose from under my skirts. The blossom dangles on its bent stem, and he snaps it off just under the head. "See"—he passes it to me—"it's real, it breaks." I smell its juice.

Agnès clears her throat. "To preserve roses during wintertime," she recites, "collect the buds and pack them in a bottle made of Beauvais clay. Then fill the bottle with finest sand and stopper it tight; if you lay it in running water your roses will keep for a year. No magic," she concludes with satisfaction.

"Agnès," says the mistress, "once again you're speaking out of turn."

"But well," Godfridus, the man of peace, is quick to add. He asks la Putemonnoie, "It is an amazing trick, mistress. Do you have a running fountain in your garden? Or do you go down to the river to sink the bottles?"

But Radegonde Putemonnoie is annoyed. First I stepped on her gift, then Agnès gave away her secret. She sits down again and picks up her tapestry, acting as if we are not there. Her needle jabs the cloth.

Godfridus, confused, stammers an apology. "I meant no impertinence, mistress. Only that I'm very interested in your arts."

I keep my eyes on the woman during this speech. Her long fingers continue their fast, precise work, and her mouth (itself a rosebud) twitches. The pendant rolls along her breast.

"My arts," she says, and by her tone I am sure she's thinking of the rumors of witchcraft attached to her. She turns the tapestry frame to face us. "See this? The Garden of Earthly Delights. *This* will bloom forever."

We are dismissed.

"WHAT A FORTUNATE THING," Godfridus says as we walk home, "if indeed she does take you on. Your clientele will change—you'll be wet nurse to fine families. You won't need that dwarf . . . Mistress Putemonnoie herself will pay you well, I assure you. I earned more for a month's work on her husband's sarcophagus than I do in three at the new church site . . ."

This will bloom forever, she said. And she is timeless. With that perfect face, that smooth neck, that supple body whose only link to common time is the baby growing inside it—the baby who will emerge in July, leaving its mother no doubt barely changed.

Around us the common folk roil in their usual late-day mumble, some on errands of business, some purposeless for the moment. Dogs worry over something in a gutter. Two little girls comb each other's hair.

". . . what a surprise, that after you spoke to her so openly she was kindly disposed. Of course she must have liked the taste of your milk . . ."

I still feel her lips on my right breast. I feel the swelling in my left. I feel her rose cupped in my palm, her linen square folded in my pocket.

"Godfridus—" When I turn to him, I can't speak anymore; his kind, ugly face looms up before me, but I don't even see it. I reach down at his side and grasp his hand, clutch it hard.

"Bonne!" His face comes into focus now—startled, distant, his eyes shuttered off from me. He backs away.

But I won't let go. I can't; my heart is full. I press the hand to my chest and then to my lips. I am aware that I'm confusing him. But there's a tremendous welling-up in me, and I must kiss him, bony, stone-chipped Godfridus.

"I'm so grateful," I say incoherently, "I'm so grateful. That you came to the house, that you vouched for me, that you were with me . . ."

"Bonne, I—" He manages to disengage himself. "You are my *niece*." As if he believes the fiction.

We stand still for a moment, people all around, and then Godfridus takes a step away. "I'm going home," he says. "I have to work." And, forgetting my milk, he leaves me.

GODFRIDUS

Her hands, her body, her heat. Thank God I live alone, I am alone, with only the drunken cobbler to hear and God's eye to see me. I think I may be sobbing. I throw myself at my work. My best clay head, waiting under her wet veil—I dig, I push, I mold the clay, willing my fingers to be gentle, to make something good.

But what man can be unstirred when a woman takes his hand and kisses it with wet, open lips?

Yes, I have put my mouth to Bonne's breasts. I have seen her naked, or nearly so. But I have done these things from Christian charity.

And now my hands have trembled the Virgin's eyes into their sockets, squashed the Infant's nose. My hands are dirty, and they desire too much.

Humility, poverty, chastity.

The way the maid looks at me. La Putemonnoie's lips. Bonne's breast warming under my mouth.

I can't chase the images, I can't chase the longing away. My hands won't stop their trembling. So I go to my one battered chest and feel beneath my tools, take out the leather strap that's come with me all the way from Firenze. The one my father used on me when I was young. "For you, Lord!" I cry, and bring it down hard, making myself humble and chaste. "Clara!"

SAINT
GEORGETTE'S
DAY

Y THE NEXT MORNING THE BIRDS HAVE paired off for good, two by two in nests of twigs under eaves and along roof ridges. Their twittering fills even the noisy workday streets as, with Marie's basket empty on my arm, I go downstairs to collect the day's bread. A long line piles up behind me, and I even hear my name whispered. The bakers have been enjoying very good business since my "miracle" at the bear-baiting ring; they are even thinking of adding a second apprentice.

"Ah, Bonne!" The bakerwoman says it out loud, and loudly, when I reach the counter. She seems about to burst with the pleasure of seeing me—but not just because of the miracle, which is old news now. "I hear you have met la Putemonnoie!"

"Yes," I say, and stop there. I noticed the people in queue behind me all stood up straighter when they heard that name, and I'm afraid of displeasing the mistress, if news of gossiping reaches her.

But I am not allowed to stop. "You've been to her house?" the bakerwoman asks.

"Yes."

"And gone inside?"

The queue leans forward, all ears.

"Yes."

She looks at me slyly. "So you are going to be her wet nurse."

"Maybe." I squeeze the basket's handle hard.

"But you'll be going back. You're being considered."

"Yes."

"How lucky! Very lucky." The bakerwoman, excited, shoves not one but two loaves at me. "Here. Give one to la Putemonnoie. Tell her where to buy the best bread in Villeneuve. Will you do that?"

I look at the loaves, thick and round and brown. Coarse grains are sticking out of the crusts. I put both into my basket and turn to go, saying nothing.

"I'm told la Putemonnoie is very beautiful," the crone in line behind me says. "Though terribly young-looking for a woman her age."

"Yes, she is," I murmur, and I hear the same note of reverence in my voice I've detected in Agnès's. I will try to keep it out the next time I speak; no one, least of all la Putemonnoie, must think I feel differently about her than about any other patronne . . . And I don't, really, it's just she is so very wealthy and powerful, and can make such a difference to my future.

"She and I are of an age, you know," the bakerwoman gossips. "Both married in the same year, too—Father Pierre told me so, and it's in the record books at the Palais de Justice. Of course"—she looks down at herself deprecatingly—"you couldn't tell to look at us . . ."

"Well," someone says, "it's more than years that make for age."

The bakerwoman chooses to cross herself. As her purse has thickened, her body has grown thinner, and we've all heard her say that prosperity is wearing her down, now that she has to get up very early and stay on her feet all day.

"Deo gratias," she says.

MARDI GRAS
[FEBRUARY 23]

ATER THAT DAY IT BEGINS TO RAIN, AND
the weather holds steady for a week. It is re-
lentless and filthy, running off roofs and
flushing out balconies; it thaws the ground
and turns the streets to muddy soup. I present
myself at Radegonde Putemonnoie's house
every day, promptly at noon. She feeds me
well—every kind of meat I can think of, and
not too many vegetables; it is a rich person's
diet. Hercule and Godfridus gobble up the
scraps. On these visits I wear my good clothes,
which I sponge clean every night, even
though la Putemonnoie hasn't sent for me
once.

Fat Tuesday is the wettest day yet. Only
the most stubborn revelers, schoolboys and
off-duty apprentices, are in the streets tossing flour and sausages, celebrating the Lord's
largesse; the rain mixes the flour into beige
wafers that stick to clothing like leeches, and
the sausages lie drowned in puddles. On this,
the last day before enforced fast, I feed Marie,
who's splashing around her cell like a puppy
in a bucket and moaning, "March rains bring
summer pains, fruit to the bough and sweat to
the brow"—though as I have to remind her,
March is a few days away.

I am sweating already. With every step,

my feet sink to the ankles and disappear. I have to hold my skirts high to stay tidy, exposing my legs and drawing the workmen's whistles. By the time I've crossed town and reached home, I am panting with fatigue.

Hercule greets me from bed, where he is wrapped in a blanket and knitting prodigiously. He has learned this skill for the long, dull hours of his convalescence, and is fashioning black hose to replace those he arrived with. When his pains aren't too bad, the little fingers can fly through the darkest hours of evening; while the bone needles clack and scrape in his hands, he gazes into the fire or watches me. I do my own knitting or just dream awake.

"You're getting fat," Hercule says enviously.

"But I'm wet to the bone," I say, squeezing the water out of my skirts. "And in just an hour or so I'll have to go the other direction and collect my basket from la Putemonnoie . . . Ah." I ease into my one x-chair, satisfied that such is the extent of my problems. "Now earn your keep. Tell me a story."

"A story . . ." He is coy; this is our routine.

"Tell me something about the court at Coussin. About Lady Anne," I invite, and I settle back for a long winter's tale. A tale of Hercule's lovely lady and her depraved lord, I think cozily, or perhaps the secret of his own so-called bruised heart. A yarn.

But before Hercule can get started, we hear a tapping on the door. The visit and the visitor are unexpected—I open the door and stifle a shriek.

He stands on my threshold in dripping black robes, the bumps on his face glistening. He could be a gargoyle but is actually a priest from the new church: Father Pierre, who used to terrify me with his visits to Blanche.

"Doesn't that boy go to school?" he asks by way of greeting, as he lowers himself into the chair I just left. It's warm here, a baking day, and Pierre's body is too well padded with flesh for comfort—there's so much of it that matter oozes out of his skin in sweat and, more permanently, that series of bumps on his nose and cheeks. His hands, too, are ugly, covered with dark brown spots, and his eyes are a dull, pale brown. He is a short man and always makes me conscious of my height—as if that were sinful, too. "A boy from a good family needs some education."

"I am very weak," Hercule says in his little-boy voice. He has pulled the blanket up around his face.

"It's true," I say, and in a whisper, "His heart. Anyway, Father, I can teach him what he needs to know."

"It fills the hours with good work," says Hercule.

"For both of us," I add, with a warning look at him. Hercule tends to overplay his role. "But, Father Pierre, I'm sure you haven't come to talk about my client's schooling."

Pierre decides to sign the cross, then he tucks his hands inside his sleeves. "Blessings. You are right. Actually, it is your work I want to discuss—your *good* work."

I wonder at the way he stresses the word, but I don't change expression. "Would you like Hercule to leave for a moment?"

"No no. He might be of help. The innocence of a child . . ."

Hercule strains to look especially innocent.

Pierre continues, "We of the new church—which is, we hope, soon to be consecrated as a cathedral—have learned that your services have been engaged." He hesitates just a moment, then pronounces the name in a hushed voice: "By Mistress Radegonde Putemonnoie."

"That is true," I say calmly enough. "I hope to be her baby's wet nurse."

"You will live in her house, then?"

"Perhaps." I keep my face turned away from Hercule; I haven't told him of this possibility. "We haven't arranged our affairs completely. But in the past, as with this boy here, my clients have come to live with me."

"Hm." Pierre nods. "Do you know Madame Putemonnoie well?"

"Almost not at all." I notice I've put up a hand up to my heart, as if to settle it. "I've scarcely met her."

"You were introduced by a friend?"

"My uncle. Godfridus the stone carver, who works for you at the new church."

"He has done some work for her, too, I think?"

"Her husband's sarcophagus."

The priest pauses, thoughtful, laying one plump finger against a prickling chin. "I may speak to Godfridus as well . . ."

Hercule pipes up, "He lives like Christ."

"That's right," I say, shaking my head at the dwarf. My whole body is warning me that the priest wants something, and I must be careful. "Godfridus—my uncle—hardly eats or sleeps, and never drinks alcohol or blasphemes; he is chaste, and he mortifies his flesh every month." I take a breath. "My life, too, Father, has for years been blameless . . ."

"Very nearly so," he agrees, and gets to the point. "And now you have been given an opportunity to atone for the sins of your youth. And your birth. God has chosen you for a special task."

"Work?" My joints tremble. "You have a position for me to fill?" I feel both relief and regret; even if Pierre isn't here planning to hang, burn, or dismember me, I'll still be sorry if I have to quit before my work in the big house has started. And I do not want to suckle a horde of orphan babies at the hospital. "Father, I'm afraid I really am promised—fully promised—to a new patronne."

"Which is precisely how you will serve the Lord," he says with an easy smile. "You, sinner that you are, hold a rare opportunity within your grasp."

"So you have said, Father."

His voice sharpens. "For a long time we in the church have been concerned about your patronne's soul."

"Her soul?"

"She is a rich woman. And as you know, it is easier for a camel to pass through the eye of a needle than—"

Hercule says, almost in a whisper, "Who'd be fool enough to try slipping a camel through a needle?"

I don't respond to either remark.

Pierre continues smoothly, "And think how much more unreachable the Lord's kingdom must be for a wealthy *woman*, who by nature of her sex is created flawed and therefore must labor greatly to achieve her salvation."

I pause, considering my answer. "She has been generous with me."

"I'm sure that she has been, beyond your expectations or deserts."

I bow my head, ears burning.

"And yet, daughter, is this generosity not to her advantage, if you are to feed her heir?" Pierre, too, seems to be weighing his words. "I wonder—we wonder—if perhaps her activities are not as unselfish, not as pious, as they might be."

"I've never seen impiety in that house. Otherwise I wouldn't have promised myself there. As I've said, I know the mistress very little, but . . ."

"Certes, my child." He shifts on the chair. "We know your heart is willing to be good. We are simply reminding you that, in case you should notice something that could . . . pose a danger . . . to our virtuous community . . . well, you will know what to do with that information."

I clarify: "You want me to watch the mistress?"

"Only as you would watch her normally, being in her personal employ." He smiles again. "It is after all every Christian's duty to watch her neighbors that much. We haven't forgotten your mother, Blanche—"

I sign the cross, glad I can put a hand before my face for a moment.

"—the event visited on her, and the sad occurrences that followed," he continues in a mournful tone. "The direction her life took was unfortunate; it may well be that she once had a good soul. Perhaps you will undertake this task for her sake, to reflect honor upon her. As well as on yourself."

"I'm not trying to get any kind of reputation in Villeneuve," I say.

"But in heaven, daughter."

"Yes." I bow my head, just as the stone sinners do before Christ in the tympanum of the Last Judgment. "In heaven."

Father Pierre is gratified; he makes Hercule and me a quick blessing and departs, fumbling his way down the stairs.

If the new church is to become a cathedral, I think, Pierre will not rest until he is made its bishop. And what a coup it would be—a paving stone on his own path to holiness—if he could prove the richest woman in town to be a witch. If she were denounced and arrested, her wealth would be forfeit to the church. If she were not denounced, merely threatened—warned, rather—no doubt she would be glad to reward the church with money and endowments, perhaps on a monthly basis. There is no way the situation will not benefit Pierre.

And if she is staunchly proven not to be a witch, via willing testimony from one of her intimates . . . how grateful will la Putemonnoie be to that person?

A noise calls me back to my smoky little room. When Pierre left, Hercule took up his knitting again—but now, moving suddenly, he thrusts one needle and then the other into the brazier. A shower of sparks flies upward, and the room fills with the stink of scorched bone.

The dwarf stares at me with defiance, daring me to scold.

I know what is in his heart: Where would he go if this domus were closed? "I won't leave you," I say, and wonder if I'm lying. "I won't move to la Putemonnoie's house." The walls of my throat are sticking together.

HERCULE

The grim days of Lent are settling on us. No meat, no sweets, no white bread or wax candles for the common folk—as of today all is penitence and self-inspection, as gray ashes replace the handfuls of flour and strings of sausages tossed in the street yesterday.

Mardi Gras—Fat Tuesday—was a day of gorging and wasting. I wasted my knitting needles and a skein of black wool, then ate all the honey in the house. Now Bonne tells me that I, even I, must pray in church. I must leave my warm and cozy nest and venture forth, acknowledge my sins and be chastened—though she does not tell me to take part in confession, and there's little chance the priests will be welcoming her into their red-draped boxes. We have too many secrets, she and I, for that. But to keep up appearances, we collect the sculptor and make a trek to the new church.

The place seems a poor thing in the early light, rough and unfinished; the walls wait for friezes, the chapels for altars, some windows for glass. The cold air is pouring in, and I don't see why we had to walk all the way here, when Sainte-Marguerite is much closer. Bonne doesn't like crowds, and every soul in town must be within these walls, milling about and greeting one another with somber goodwill. Everyone's sincere in the first days of Lent, even through the aftertaste of wine and headache from overindulgence.

"God's collops," I mutter, for Bonne's ears alone, "it's cold in here. And so crowded your cunt must be shriveled up like a walnut, as the old woman said..."

Poor people, rich people, ladies, lords, and persons of the middle class. Bonne walks through them, peering into faces and holding my hand as if I'm a child who will run away. We circle the nave. Her hand is hot.

"At Coussin," I say, "we'd each have a metal ball, hollow, with a coal inside, to keep our hands warm." Some people here do have these spheres; the smell of heated metal mingles with the incense. I add, "Would you like to hear a story? One Presentation Day I collected these balls and filled them with hot droppings from Lord Robert's stables. The ladies took them gladly enough, but by the time the priest made his opening benediction..."

"Be quiet," says Bonne. "Remember you're only six years old." She pulls me to a dark corner behind a massive pillar. She—we—seem to hide behind it. Then she leans cautiously out, and I see her staring at a woman in black, a widow with black hat and barbette. The woman stands with two servants near the sanctuary, and many people are looking at her. She is so still, so calm, fingering a string of black rosary beads—she absorbs all the light in the place.

I prance a little at Bonne's side. "Who is that?" Though of course I know.

"Stand still," says Bonne, as a man in furs approaches the widow and speaks to her. Of course we cannot hear what they say.

A bell rings inside, and the people quiet down. Some of them sit, having ordered their servants to bring chairs from home for that purpose. The rest of us stand, watching the priests in their black robes and violet sashes—violet for the days of fast—process in haltfully, singing. They march down the center of the nave: the fat one with the bumps on his face, the bald one with the green veins, the ancient one with the perpetual tremor. Their voices quaver, unskilled and unpleasant. Then come the choir and the clerks, all in gray and all set to burst their skulls as they sing high and through their noses. The words are indistinguishable.

With a hey, and a ho, and a hey-nonny-no,
In springtime sinners praying go . . .

Lady Bonne nudges me. Apparently I was about to do something dwarfish.

The priests sit, then stand; they kneel, cross themselves, spin around, and tuck their feet behind their ears. Or if they did, I'd be better inclined to listen. They move through the opening rituals, then ponderously the fat one ascends the pulpit. All chins raise to look at him.

He announces the theme of his sermon, first in Latin, then in vulgar: "Honey and milk," he says, "are under thy tongue."

There is a general shifting and grimacing, as those who consumed too much honey and milk yesterday regret what it's done to them. Bonne tucks a wisp of hair under her wimple and pointedly does not look at me.

Then follows the text: Christ is the milk and the honey, and all the milk and honey we need—let us give thanks for the sweetness and sustenance. Let us savor our blessings as we chew our dry bread and drink our green water, for this is Lent and the proper time for such thoughts. Let us be grateful. Etc.

I notice the bakers, our plump landlord and his slightly more slender lady, trembling as they listen. Perhaps they have been guilty of pride in the mortal bread they fashion with their hands. Perhaps they have made it too fresh.

"...for Christ promises us His body and His blood, and we are to rejoice in them . . ."

While the fat father speaks, Bonne's face is dutifully pious, and her eyes are turned in the proper direction, but I sense her spirit is elsewhere. She is thinking of the widow. She is admiring the woman's clothes, perhaps— "Fine raiment offers no protection against the fires of hell." Or perhaps her beauty—"Nor shall a pretty face guard you against God's just anger, for we are all equal in the eyes of the Lord." For the woman is beautiful, in some strange way. Even beneath the heavy roll of hat and stiff barbette I can see that. Her bearing is regal, every bone of her bespeaks power and privilege. She compels people to bend to her, to fetch and carry for her. And she is used to being looked at. Her lips are plump, her eyes bright. And though one is *dark where the other was fair, there's something of Lady Anne about her eyebrows . . .*

I remember, suddenly, the fatal banquet at Coussin. The reek of wine, the clamor of jesters. That bloody, awful pie.

". . . Alas! How soon you grow tired of Christ, how soon you begin to swell with sin . . ."

It was a stupid trick I played, like filling the hand warmers with dung. Only, the dung won me a fur-trimmed jaquette, and the heart I presented to Lady Anne cost me everything.

". . . but He shall lay the banquet, and ye shall not eat of it . . ."

Cold no longer, I break into a sweat. The words are working, on me as on the people around. Others are crossing themselves unprompted, or clutching their cooling metal balls with white knuckles. As one body, we tremble and sigh.

Bonne is listening. Her gray bosom rises and falls—calm, quiet. She looks up and smiles. Because here is the sculptor, he whose stones lurk in the shadows and perch over our heads obscurely waiting. The one man who is sure he has never done any wrong, so sure that he gave himself a monk's name. Bonne looks up at him and smiles.

My palms itch. I rub them on my haunches—but it's as if they've blood still on them, I can't satisfy the itching. Redemption—vanity! One and the same. Feed the hungry, cure the sick, raise the dead . . . the so-called miracle of the loaves and fishes—a mere feat of duplication, any fool with a looking glass can do it, then convince a crowd their bellies are full. And what old man has not seemed to die a thousand times before his death, recalled by a lucky touch or draft of wind?

But Anne, vanished in the forest . . . no magic will bring her back.

There is no magic.

There must be.

I've had selfish hopes for so long. A mage at Lord Robert's court once promised that if I swallowed the horn of a unicorn the pains in my body would cease. I bought from him a horn, thick and bloody, matted with hairlike fibers; it belonged to a unicorn of Afric, he said, and I must grind it into a powder. The horn cost me a year's wages and took a month to grind, a week to eat. It did nothing for me. Nor did the love charms or spells worked with Anne's monthly cloths . . .

The sermon is concluding. "Pray for the blessings of Christ and of His father. Their wine is sweeter than honey, more nourishing than milk, and They will not pour it out for those who indulge in wine of a lesser sort.

"Now confess and take Communion."

I have heard that in Saint-Porchaire, after I was born, Blanche refused to look at the altar, gazing up at the deep blues and reds of the windows instead. She stood gazing while the Latin droned on and the baby on her arm soaked the swaddling clothes. She gazed while the recluse in the cell outside shrieked. And she steadfastly refused to give her seducer a name.

GODFRIDUS

"Dust thou art, and to dust shall return." The coldness of ash on the forehead—fronds from last year's Palm Sunday, carefully burned and ground and mixed with holy water, sketched in a cross on my brow. They dry in a thick paste, the clay of holiness.

There must be no work today. Only penitence. Let Bonne smile at me if she will—I shall only frown at her, and think on Christ.

We file out soberly, Bonne and I and the dwarf who passes as a child. We emerge into white sunshine, a hint of spring. And a crowd of sinners in plain clothes, registering tardy penitence. Each wears a cross on his forehead.

The bright sun is too much. The dwarf looks sick, my head aches, and Bonne's face wears a look of dazzlement. She appears confused, seeing all the people gathered on the square—confused and worn. She's pink around the nose, and her lips are chapped, her hands rubbed raw with washing. She loses a shoe and bends down to ease it on, and I catch a glimpse of her legs up to the calf. She has slim gray ankles, a hole in one legging showing gray skin beneath.

This shouldn't move me, but it does. She looks poor and cold and alone, even between me and the dwarf. She's so careful to be clean, and yet there's this hole in her garments. I think about the night, when I will kneel and drain her breasts—their heavy plumpness in my hands, the pucker of the nipples, the sweetness of the milk. That is the one thing about her that grows richer. Her hair will come unbraided, and it will slide across her shoulders and tickle my lips . . .

If she hadn't held my hand that day, I wouldn't be thinking of her in this way. I wouldn't notice her chapped lips or slim ankles or think much about the sweetness of milk melting into my mouth . . . She would just be Bonne.

"Why are you scowling, stoneman?" The dwarf cocks his wrinkled little face at me, deep in the shadows of his hood. "Is there a saint out of place in the facade?"

We all look toward the grand facade of the new church, where not a single one of my sculptures stands: The Last Judgment there was carved a decade ago by a so-called master from Poitiers . . . But I notice Bonne's gaze has frozen, fixed on a black figure near the sundial.

It is la Putemonnoie. She stands with her maids, Agnès and the little one whose name I don't know. This is a social and business occasion for her; merchants and men of business—seldom with their wives—approach and speak. We see her nod and gesture. Today, as every day, her wealth is the object of homage.

The sun beats down, lighting frosty plumes of our breath. A flock of doves starts up from a skeleton tree and wings noisily overhead.

La Putemonnoie glances over. We must be very visible, Bonne and I, both so much taller than the average. Bonne straightens up and her pale eyes open wide. The two women nod to each other. Only as an afterthought does la Putemonnoie nod to me. Meanwhile Agnès hops a little, up and down, trying to catch my attention.

She knows me as Bonne's uncle. I nod but do not smile at la Putemonnoie, then at Agnès, as echoes pour from the church: "Terra es, terram ibis . . ."

On Bonne's face—in the lines on her cheeks and around her eyes—I read the pinched look of longing. "It is nearly noon," she says. "I should go. I must see Mistress Putemonnoie today . . ."

"But you just saw her," I say, as the dwarf stiffens.

"That is your new patronne?" he asks, removing his hand from Bonne's. "The woman from the marché is my rival?"

"She's not your rival," Bonne says. "She's your benefactress. You eat her meat and drink her wine every day."

And I drink them, too, in the milk I drain from Bonne's breasts. Thus have I tasted blood cooked by both women.

"She's the one you're supposed to watch, then," the dwarf adds. "The one the priest says is a witch."

"Bonne?" I turn to her.

Bonne bites her lip, which is pink from her teeth when she speaks. "Pierre told me to test the purity of Mistress Putemonnoie's soul," she says. "He did not say she is a witch. And look at her—the whole town comes to her to pay court. How can such a woman have anything to fear?"

"You used to show better sense," I say. "If he suspects her of witchcraft, you and she are both in danger."

"Pierre has ordered me to go. I have no choice," she says, leaning away from me.

"But what about me?" The dwarf sulks. "If you go to her now, who will take care of your orphan?"

Bonne looks down at him, not unkindly. "You seem to be very good at taking care of yourself." She licks her lips, then smiles, as if testing her face. Finally she settles her apron and starts across the square.

We watch her go. La Putemonnoie's party watches her approach— everyone on the plaza watches her, including a cluster of rival wet nurses. Bonne Tardieu walking over to join Radegonde Putemonnoie, on Ash Wednesday.

Women of bodies and unique powers: They have both been given particularly large ash crosses.

Dust to dust, and God is love.

Radegonde Putemonnoie is glad to receive me, or at least she tolerates my coming to her. When I draw near she says my name, and then as if she has been waiting only for me we turn toward her house. Our progress becomes a procession: I am now among her entourage, following with her maids, preceding her footman, and as we walk, the town notables continue to approach and pay their respects to the mistress. If my presence gives them any pause, none show it; I am accepted as part of her charmed circle.

How can this woman have anything to fear from a mere priest? How can I, under her protection? I think how she and I will laugh over Pierre's suspicions, how perhaps she will make him pay for them by seeing the bishopry—if there is one—given to some other priest. I look forward to telling her about it, once I have assured Pierre and the other town fathers of her virtue.

Up streets and across plazas we servants walk with measured steps, following the mistress's swirling cloak. At the great house, where normally I would turn toward the kitchens, la Putemonnoie motions for me to accompany her into the main building. I feel the servants' eyes upon me as I trail her through perfumed rooms. In the solar, where the braziers are blazing (against church edicts that prohibit fire on the day of Ash), Agnès helps her remove her cloak and then discreetly, reluctantly—there must have been some sign from the mistress—withdraws.

La Putemonnoie approaches a table laid with cold meat and assorted dried fruits. This is a day of fast, when we are to eat only bread and water, and only after sundown; but she must have been given dispensation because of her pregnancy. I try not to let my mouth water as she lingers over the array. Some of those dainties I've never tried, and all look more delicious than anything I've ever eaten.

La Putemonnoie picks up an almond cake in jeweled fingers, bites into it hungrily, then puts it back on the table and sits down. Perhaps she's experiencing an all-too-common bout of nausea, as I often did during my time. But I can see she has been eating well; from her face to her fingertips she has grown thicker, as befits a woman growing an heir. Her black velvet houppelande accentuates her girth, with furred sleeves and hems and neck. Her pendant's lovers are facing outward.

"Bonne the wet nurse," she says in her low voice, "you may take off your mantle. Tell me of your health." She smooths a curl of hair away from her neck and into her crown of braid; even though she's sitting down, I have the sense of looking up at her.

I do as she says, then bow. "I am very well, mistress, thanks to the food you've been giving me."

"I hope it is strengthening your milk as well as your body."

"I'm sure it is," I say, although Godfridus hasn't commented on any change. "Would you like to try some?"

"Thank you." She swallows her last bit of cake. "I would."

So we go through the process again. This time when I have bared my breasts I lean over and put the nipple between her lips. After a few tugs from her mouth, surprisingly strong, I have to put a hand on the wall to brace myself. She seems to pull clear through me.

"You are flushed," she says when she comes away.

"You are fleshed," I reply. It's a joke Hercule might make.

She smiles politely, showing a double row of white teeth. "Did it feel nice?" she asks.

I gape. "Mistress?" Does she mean what I think she does?

"The suckling." She strokes her belly idly; if she is curious, it is idle curiosity. "I have heard some say it gives the nurse pleasure."

"*Beh* . . . Sometimes." If my face was flushed before, it flames now. "It—that depends."

As I begin to wind the bandeau, my fingers fumble. I lose the cloth, and it unfurls, dingy, across her carpet. I have to drop to my knees.

"On what does it depend?" I hear her ask from above, as I gather the bandeau together. "The size of the mouth? The age of the suckler? Is there some skill—"

"Mistress—" I stand at last, and miraculously I manage to cover myself. "I can't say. It's just different, it changes." To distract her, I point at the tapestry frame lying at her side. "I see you've been working your Garden of Earthly Delights. It's very pretty."

"Ah." Her eyes release me and she picks up the frame. "Thank you. I designed it myself." She holds it up for inspection while I quickly tie off the band. "I'm working on a tree that weeps honey. It will be surrounded by a cloud of bees."

"Very pretty," I repeat, lacing up the underdress bodice.

I feel la Putemonnoie watching me again. Maybe she's never seen a commoner dressing; servants never serve naked. I resist the urge to ask her what she is thinking, what she wants—such a question would be worse than insulting her cookery or broderie, worse than appearing naked before her.

"Your milk is getting richer," she says, "quite delicious. You must continue to eat well. And I believe some gentle exercise, to keep the humors flowing . . ."

How little she must know about a peasant's life! The daily rounds just to acquire food and get it cooked are more exertion than she sees in a week. But I am meek: "Yes, mistress," I promise, and tie the apron tight around my waist. I must prove myself to be a good eater, good exerciser, must keep my blood strong and clean—I don't know how many other nurses she is trying, but I must be the best. If she wants me to say I enjoy the suckling, I will do that, too. She holds—and is—my future.

I feel the ashes on my brow and remind myself I must also assess the purity of her soul for Pierre. I think I will not mention this broderie to him, or if I do I'll translate its delights to Eden.

"All right, then." She picks up her needle, pokes it firmly into the cloth, and draws it through with a *prick-suuucck*.

It is clear that I am to go. But I linger on and she doesn't send me away, not in so many words. So I watch the candle flames glow in her hair jewels, see her shake the baggy sleeve away from her wrist. The threads gleam as she weaves her embroidered web of honey and bees. I have time to gather my courage.

"Is there anything more you would like from me, mistress?" I ask at last. "Long ago, when you engaged me, you mentioned some extra duties I could perform. Maybe you'd like me to inspect the baby's layette. Or I could untangle your embroidery silks."

"I don't need anything like that." She studies me over the tapestry frame, drawing a gold thread through the cloth. She stops moving, and I resist the impulse to try smoothing my hair or adjusting my skirt. I just hold myself frozen as I was when last I spoke.

"But now that you mention it," she says, "there is something . . ."

Only my jaw moves. "Yes?"

"You say you can read."

"And write, and I know a little Latin."

She appears to come to some decision. "Then, since we have some time, and since the long Lenten afternoons must be filled in some way, I will show you something. Follow me."

She tosses her work onto the bench and lights a dish of fish oil with a linen wick. I think her hand may be trembling, but I must be mistaken. Then, the light wavering as she moves, she leads me out of the room and down a long passage. We turn several times, go up and then down a number of short flights of stairs, before finally, near the center of the house, we enter an empty, shuttered room.

The candle in my mistress's hand provides the only light here, making a hazy golden sphere around her body. She stops and presses her free hand into her side, breathing hard. "I have become so weak," she says.

"Babies can't help tiring their mothers," I reply. "Particularly on days of fast."

"Fast! *It* is eating—my strength," she says. Then she seems to shrug off her fatigue; she goes to a narrow door at the far end of the room and unlocks it. On the other side is yet another staircase.

We climb. The stair curls round and round upon itself. It is like exploring the interior of a snail. My breath is coming short, but Radegonde Putemonnoie mounts relentlessly upward, holding on to a rope anchored in the wall. She has become tireless.

"Almost there," she says after an eternity. Under her breath, the candle flame flickers, reflection dancing crazy on the walls. She stops to shield and let it recover.

She has forced me to stop, too. My head is at her knees, her skirts brush my face. That sweet musky smell pulses around us, filling the spiral shell. I am dizzy, and I'm afraid my legs will give way and plummet me into narrow darkness.

It seems we have been climbing forever. And soon it seems we have been stopped forever. I'm afraid to ask where we're going.

"Almost," she says again, and pulls herself upward.

WE COME INTO A TOWER. A small, nearly circular room with a peaked ceiling and shuttered windows. I stand catching my breath while Radegonde Putemonnoie goes from window to window, opening the shutters.

The light is first bluish, then gray. I see the room has eight broad angles and holds nothing but a chair, some shelves, and a slanted desk. The desk is positioned with one of its narrow ends against a wall, so whoever sits there can look out of several windows at once. Our candle burns uselessly on the floor in one corner.

Beyond the windows I see only white sky. It is so quiet I think I might faint.

"Come here," la Putemonnoie says from a window, beckoning to me. In the light, I can see the ash cross on her forehead; only the unpious would wash off a cross. "You'll see all of Villeneuve."

I don't want her to know of my fear—who would hire a timid nurse?

I step forward. But my throat's full of nausea, and it's not until she actually takes my hand and begins to drag me along that I really start to move. She makes me stand by the window.

"Look," she says. And I look.

The city is spread out below us, a tiling of gray roofs and brown streets. Those streets fan and circle the town's key structures—churches, squares, even this house where we stand in la Putemonnoie's stone needle. Here, at the center of Villeneuve, the street circles are concentric, ringing one another until they reach the wall by the River Boîse. The widest streets mark where the old city walls used to lie a hundred years ago; the narrowest, of course, belong to the district of shadows, where the buildings are so tight together it is impossible to see any lanes at all, except around the black bulk of Saint-Porchaire. In the newer sections the streets fall into tidy squares, crosshatching rather than circling. I follow one of these lines to an obscure corner, where even my little alley door is visible from this high roost.

Only the spire of the new church will reach higher into the sky than the tower where we now stand.

"It looks so dull," I say, sweating. Villeneuve is all brown and gray— brown and gray stone, brown and gray branches and twigs. Under ash-gray skies.

"Wait until spring," says la Putemonnoie. "Then at least the fields will be green, and my garden." She stands leaning against a lintel, arms crossed, breath blowing clouds of steam into the air outside. Her slightly rounded stomach rises and falls. Looking at her, I realize that spring really has begun; already sap is quickening, leaking upward from the earth into dry brown stems.

I wonder if my patronne would dismiss me for being sick on her shoes, for losing myself and my last meal while gazing into the vastness below.

La Putemonnoie continues to stare outside, absorbed in some private fantasy. "My husband," she says, "used to come up here to watch the roads into town."

"God rest his soul," I say automatically, swallowing hard.

"Yes, God rest his soul." She darts me a sideways glance, as if checking whether my blessing was sincere. I wonder, was hers? "On a clear day, you can see miles down the road, even to the forest. Master Putemonnoie used to watch for his agents riding into town. Now I watch for them."

Beyond the city walls the forest is a black blur, pierced by the river. That is the blackness into which lawbreakers and lovers disappear; I took refuge there myself after the fire. And it was just this side of the trees, in the haystack set in what is now an empty harrowed field, that I conceived my baby. I can see the exact spot from here. By showing me this, is Rade-gonde Putemonnoie telling me she knows about my past?

But now she's turning away from the window. She indicates the desk and pigeonhole shelves, and I turn gratefully to inspect them. "This was my husband's private office," she says. "Not where he did his accounts, but where he did his thinking. His private thinking."

Rolls of paper and parchment still sit, dusty, on the shelves, and a faded quill pen lies next to a pot that I guess contains a cake of dry ink. I imagine the bent man sitting here, gazing out the windows and scratching notes to himself. I even think I can hear the scratching.

Suddenly la Putemonnoie picks up a ruling stick and knocks it on the wooden ceiling beams. The scratching sound changes to a flutter and an outraged coo.

"Doves," she says. "They nest between the ceiling and the roof."

"You don't like them?"

"They cover the roof with droppings and clog the drainpipes."

But I don't feel she's telling me the whole truth; she simply dislikes the birds, I think, the way I dislike heights. I like knowing about this quirk; it makes her more real to me. "Doves are portents of hope," I say gently. "When the rains stopped, Noah sent a dove out to find land—"

She makes a face. "I didn't think you took those stories so seriously," she says, tapping the stick between her fingers.

"Ah." I realize I am staring at her. Her cheeks are bright with color, and the light from the windows hazes the wisps of hair over her compli-cated braid crown. "Do you ever wonder," I say on an impulse, "why we never see any baby doves? They always seem full-grown."

"The babies stay in the nest," she suggests, whacking halfheartedly at the ceiling again. "I don't know. If my husband were here, maybe you could ask him—I believe he made quite a study of these doves."

"Is that why he built this tower?"

"He had this tower built," she says, "in order to kill himself with work." She sits down in the chair, bored by her fruitless game with the birds. She tells me, "The room that gives onto the staircase was his bed-chamber. He climbed up here as soon as he woke, and he wrote until mid-day. Every day."

"Instructions to his agents?"

"No—not always. He was composing a book."

"A book!" I thought only monks made those, and most of them only copy what's been written before.

"A history book," she explains, "about himself, about his family, his travels in the East, and how he founded his spice empire. He called it a livre de raison, a book of reason. It was to include recipes, ways of using his spices in food, medicines, perfumes. Instructions to his children for advancing the business and status of the Putemonnoies . . . He spent all his life writing to sons that never came, and the effort of it killed him." She taps the ruling stick against her hand, *thwack, thwack*. The doves above are scratching and cooing.

All I can think to say is, again, "God rest his—"

She cuts me off. "No doubt you think I'm callous. That I don't respect my husband in death and probably didn't do so in life. You think I am a bad wife, a bad woman." Her eyes meet mine frankly.

"No, mistress." Though naturally I shall not be repeating her words at the new church.

"Yes, you do. I can hear it in your voice." She waves a jeweled hand. "And I know my reputation. The Putemonnoie woman is vain and selfish, caring for nothing but herself, neglecting her husband. Well, indeed I was glad he had the occupation of this book. At least he wasn't lazing around the house, drinking wine all day when he got too old to travel, as some husbands do. But I resented it, too. All this writing he did to prepare for his children, and I—who did not conceive a child until he lay dying—I never learned . . . to . . . read."

I hear the doves scratch.

"You can't read?" I ask stupidly. I'd thought all ladies learned their letters.

She waves again; I think she is embarrassed. "I know some numbers, and I can sign my name. But the book my husband was writing—it's just senseless marks to me."

She stares down at her hands now, perhaps thinking that though they can embroider a flower exquisitely, they are useless to her survival—she is said to be a smart businesswoman, but to save her life or her fortune, she couldn't write a page of instructions.

"Do you want me to show you?" I ask. I'm breathless with hope. "I could teach you how to read and write, as my mother taught me."

"No." She gets up abruptly and walks to the back of the desk, where the higher side rises up. "Well, perhaps you can teach me later; for now, it would take too long. No, I want you to read the book to me before the baby comes." She kneels and unlocks the cabinet door on that side. But before she reaches in, she fixes her enormous multicolored eyes on me. "I can trust you, can't I?"

"Mistress?"

She regains her self-assurance, makes her question into an order. "I mean, you are to read me the book as it is written. That is what I require. And first you must promise you won't make up any stories, put words in my husband's mouth to mislead me . . . Promise, Bonne."

"You can trust me, mistress."

"Good." She turns back to the desk and pulls out an enormous book, bound already in red leather, with rippling pages and a few extra leaves sticking out from top or sides. "This is it"—her lips curl again—"the history of Henri Putemonnoie. I want to know everything he wrote."

I take the volume out of her hands. It is even heavier than I expected. "This will take many hours, mistress."

"Fine." She brushes her hands lightly against each other and pulls herself to her feet using the edge of the desk. Once standing, ignoring the birds settling at the windows, she surprises me again: "Do you think my husband loved *me*?"

"Of course," I say in some confusion. "Of course he did. He must have! I have heard you were poor, mistress . . . no disrespect . . . and he married you for love—because you were—and are . . ."

"Because I'm beautiful?" She shakes her head, and a perfumed wind fans my face. "Beautiful," she repeats bitterly. "Maybe he did marry me for my beauty—but if so, he hated me for it, too. He never stopped reminding me of it, and of the fact—he even called it a fait accompli—that it would fade."

I notice she hasn't commented on the story of her origins, sketchy as I have made it. I also note that she shows no false modesty about her beauty; she accepts it as her possession and her right, like the dress she wears or the bench she sits on.

"If it has faded," I say, "I can't see."

She laughs. "Bonne, you sound like a courtier. Or a poet. Full of flattery, hoping to be invited to a School of Courtly Love."

"You are very beautiful," I insist, and she seems to soften. No one can dislike hearing it.

She takes the book from me and sets it once again on the desk, her hand resting lightly on top. "You know, of course, that if I don't produce an heir I am to spend the rest of my life in a nunnery?"

I nod.

"With Henri's sarcophagus in my cell, for me to plant my elbows on as I pray for his eternal salvation?"

I gape. "I didn't know that."

"It's true. He wrote it in his will," she says, almost with satisfaction. "He offers the good sisters of the Immaculate Heart a handsome dowry for taking me and seeing to my barest needs; I myself get nothing, and Henri's brother, everything. Was this the action of a man who loved his wife?"

"It is the letter of the law . . ." I murmur, but she pretends not to hear.

"Henri knew I can't read. He didn't want me to learn, and in the early years of our marriage I didn't have much desire to. There were other things to do—I was furnishing the house and planning the garden, creating the proper home for a wealthy merchant and his wife and children. Then, in recent years, with his agents trained and his fortune secure, my husband started retreating to his tower room for hours at a time. I found out he was writing in this book, and he promised he would read it to me when he finished. He tantalized me with that promise for years— 'Just a few more pages,' he'd say, just let him describe a few more events and he would be done. He wanted to get the tale of our lives together, and of his life as a merchant, exactly right, and then he'd read it all back to me. This autumn, as you know, he died, without finishing his account. All along, he must have planned it this way—he wanted never to finish, and he wanted me never to know what was inside."

"Mistress," I say, in what I hope is a mild, soothing voice—I don't need to point out that fits of temper are bad for the baby—"surely he did not plan to die when he did. As his first child was about to be born."

"Maybe not, but he was prepared for it," she says with an air of finality. "He planned for everything.

"Now, Bonne, I want you to start immediately. You will come every day to read to me, even Sunday. You may eat your dinner in the kitchen, then you'll come to the solar, where I will have the book locked in a special chest. No one but us must know of it. I'll pay you at the end of every week."

"You are generous," I say, running my fingers over the red leather. It is as thick and soft as velvet. A man's whole history written down in a book—it will be better than the Bible, whose story everyone knows without reading it. And that man is (was) the husband of Radegonde Putemonnoie.

87

"A reasonable sum," she amends. "I'll pay you a reasonable amount. I'm not educated, not formally, but I am acquainted with the principles of business. If we haven't finished the book by the time the baby comes, the fee for the reading will supplement what you get for the nursing."

"For the nursing?" I repeat, hardly daring to hope.

"Yes, Bonne Tardieu. I have decided you will be my wet nurse, if all goes well. And it must go well," she adds, almost under her breath.

This seems too good to be true. Afraid my delight will show too strong in my eyes, I gaze out a window, though I am now blind to the view and thus without terror. I allow myself to daydream for a few moments. To hold the Putemonnoie heir in my arms, to feed him from my body . . . and to read, and be paid to read.

Overcome by its own weight, the book slides toward the little ledge at the edge of the desk. La Putemonnoie catches it. Her fur sleeves are white with dust as she holds the book in place. "I will know if you lie," she says. "I am a good judge."

"I will not lie to you, mistress."

I must have reassured la Putemonnoie at last, for she spreads the book on the desktop and begins turning pages. I catch a word here and there: *spices . . . silks . . . forty thousand . . .* Maître Putemonnoie's writing is clear, though cramped and economical; it is exactly the writing of the bent man I saw last summer.

Mistress Putemonnoie picks up a loose leaf that has been folded and stuck between the bound pages. "What is this?"

I open it and read the lines that must be mere black squiggles to her. "A recipe for something called treed, a food made in the East."

She makes a face, inscrutable to me, and sticks the page in haphazardly. "What looks like a good place to start?" she asks, flipping rapidly through the leaves until she reaches a number of blank ones at the end.

"Well . . ." I hesitate. As far as I've been able to see, there isn't much order to the book; it has mixed accounts and recipes and long paragraphs of text with and without titles, all jumbled up any which way. "I can't tell, mistress."

"Then we'll have to begin at the beginning," she says, sitting heavily down on her husband's stool. "Read me the first page."

My fingers fumble and come away pink from the binding. "As you wish, mistress."

Surrounded by white sky and fluttering doves, on the first day of Lent, I start.

From Henri Putemonnoie's livre de raison
Ave Maria, Queen of Heaven and of Hope! I do humbly beg and beseech you, most shining and perfect of women, in whose mortal womb our Lord saw fit to plant His seed—that when death has sat upon my tongue and silenced my prayers, and when my feeble heart beats no more but in terror of the demons of Hell and the Master of the Underworld, you will deign to make of me the object of your infinite pity and mercy, and intercede with my holy Father and your own Son, He who through his death washed man free of sin. Let not my soul suffer the pains of eternal damnation, but let my death be as your Son's, a cleansing and an elevation. I raise my head that I may address you, Queen, in the Heaven of my Father and of yours, that you may most gently ask him to smile on me in death as in life, to preserve the works of a life long industrious and pious, and to preserve my soul from the

evils of punishment, even while my body undergoes its just and inevitable corruption. I pray that you might yourself offer my soul to your Son, that I might be granted eternal peace and, at your side, a joy that might never cease . . .

Radegonde Putemonnoie's pillowy lips twist. "'If you fear the Father,'" she quotes the church fathers, "'go to the Son. If you fear the Son, go to the mother.'" It is something Blanche used to say.

DAY OF
SAINT GERTRUDE
OF NIVELLES
[MARCH 17]

AM RELIEVED THAT HENRI PUTEMON-
noie's book begins with a prayer, for though
it was not till Ash Wednesday night that I
thought to worry what the church would think
of my reading, that worry persisted and kept
me awake. I comforted myself with reciting
his prayer, as much as I could, from memory.

"...*when my feeble heart beats no more
but in terror...*" In the light of morning,
some terrors become laughable. And so life
goes on.

Yes, the reading to Radegonde Putemonnoie continues, without fear now but also
without pleasure. Henri's livre de raison is a
book of dry facts, minuscule observations, and
pointless speculations. We take them in order:
the best way to disguise the taste of burnt
stew or to get salt out of butter; the best kind
of eel for frying (small head, glowing skin,
white belly—I thought at first he was describing his wife). How many angels might
stand comfortably on the head of a pin; how
many might dance there. The age-old questions. La Putemonnoie sews or simply sits
through it all, her mouth in a moue of dis-

pleasure, her temper flaring from time to time until finally she throws me out, as if I am responsible for what is written on those crackling leaves.

I find little opportunity for gauging the color of my mistress's soul; nothing to report to the priests. But then I've expected, and hoped, to have nothing for them. Just as I hope (futilely, perhaps) never to see Pierre's bumpy bulk on my threshold again. I attend services at the new church each Sunday and bring Hercule with me. We behave as we are expected to.

The readings take place in the solar, where la Putemonnoie's Garden of Earthly Delights grows and blooms. A cup of warm spiced wine sits always between us, and I am allowed to drink from it after she does. The wine and the warmth and the heavy book make me sleepy; sometimes I have to stare hard out the window at the sun to wake myself up. Sometimes la Putemonnoie leans over and shakes me or threatens to prick my arm with a needle.

"'The Culture of Basil,'" I might begin one day, or "'The Best Markets and Cities for Selection of Cinnamon, Stick or Powder,'" or even "'A Prayer for the Freshness of Meat.'" Sometimes, while la Putemonnoie speaks to a maid or sits on the privy, I turn to the blank pages at the back—what might have been written there, I wonder, if the Maître had had enough time? I long for a story about his life—or better yet, about his wife's: Where did she come from? What was she like when they were alone, the mistress with her master? Though certainly such intimacies would be guarded, even in these most private writings.

I think that if I were to write a book of reason, it would mostly concern her. Her beauty, her gestures, the wonders of her life. Though certain details of my own history might not be without interest as well.

La Putemonnoie is generous with me. The little store of coins in my chest is growing, one denier at a time. I no longer worry about feeding Marie or myself. La Putemonnoie has also given me an old blue belt to wear instead of an apron when I visit; it used to belong to her.

But she is a prickly woman! As she listens, her eyes and threads snap with annoyance. One corner of her embroidered Garden is a snarl of thorny thickets.

"My child won't get far on mere words," she says.

GODFRIDUS

Each night at home, each day in church, I beg—tapping my prayer in with my chisel, pounding it out with my hammer, smoothing it in again with my wet fingers. "Show me your face," I say. "Show me your face . . . I will make myself into your son, I will make myself your husband—but please show me . . ."

When I touch the clay it is her *face, always her face I feel; her breath that blows across my lips as I work the mouth; her skin growing moist and soft as my fingers sink, too deep, too fast, into it.* Clara.

How could I fashion any other?

And yet I cannot make it right.

Dried earth is brittle, smashes with a sound like bells when it's hurled against walls or floor. Smashes to dust. One after another the heads fall, and fall apart. The drunken cobbler below me groans and then slurps at his cup once more.

SAINT PIGMENIUS'S DAY

[MARCH 24]

HERCULE

It is a cozy morning near the end of a long month. I knit while Lady Bonne mends, with her big sloppy stitches: my little smock and braies, her own big chemise with its special neckline for easy access. When the brazier's embers go cold, neither of us budges—the season is that warm. La Bonne says she saw a crocus at Saint-Porchaire today, along with the tiny yellow skull of a newborn, laid bare by the recent rains. She is melancholy.

The absent sculptor, too—but him I'd call morose. His face hangs low as a monk's cowl, and sometimes we don't see him for days. Then I get to siphon Lady Bonne's bounty, and that's all the better for me. And for her—I've seen how her eyes slit in pleasure—

"Hercule," she says as she stitches, "I think you are getting plump."

"Plump!" I draw back in mock horror.

"Fat, even," she says soberly. "How else do you explain the way you keep ripping out the seams of your braies? You are getting as round as the bakerwoman is lean."

It is true, my health and my waist are im-

proving. Sometimes my bones don't crack all night. I credit milk in my case, meanness in the baker's wife's. Lady Bonne laughs, and as we debate, a smell of yeast creeps under the door.

It is not a baking day. La Bonne, puzzled, drops her much-loathed mending and opens the door. The bakerwoman herself tumbles in.

"I was on the point of knocking," she says with her perpetual whine. Since Bonne was engaged at the great house, the floury harpy has visited much—perhaps to get closer to la Putemonnoie, perhaps because the priests have asked her to put an eye on us, as Bonne has on her mistress.

"You are welcome," says Bonne, and adds nothing about eavesdroppers who might hear no good of themselves. She offers the woman the chair.

"So," I say as the bakeress sits, "why have you come?" She looks at me wide-eyed.

And then the door opens again, and here is Father Pierre, the ugly priest whose endless sermons Bonne drags me to each week. Clearly he should have the chair, but the bakerwoman doesn't offer. The priest must sit on the bed, next to me, which means that, as the straw crackles and mats under his bumptious behind, I have to claim a chill, wrap up in a blanket, and hide my wrinkles.

"Blessings," says the priest to us all. He seems nonetheless put out to find the bakerwoman here, as well he might, for even if he has set her to spy on us, while she is here he can't very well ask la Bonne what her *spying has accomplished. So instead he pretends to have come on churchly grounds.*

"I'd like to discuss your uncle," he says, and la Bonne jumps up from her seat on the old creaky chest.

"Spiced wine?" she offers both the guests. "As this is an occasion?" It is from la Putemonnoie, thus rather good—though not of the best. Bonne bustles, heating a beakerful over the embers. Blushing. Though why she should redden at the sculptor's mention, I couldn't say.

A good wine goes down sweetly, making the lips of sleepers to speak. Bonne hands the hot beaker to the priest, who coddles it in horny hands and says, "Godfridus has been working at the new church some years now . . ."

"Two years," says Bonne, as he seems inclined to lose himself in cup.

"Would you say he is ambitious?"

She licks her lips—what answer would do most good? "He aspires to bring glory to God."

"I've met this uncle," the bakerwoman puts in. Her beady eye is on the wine.

Pierre asks, "Does he plan to become a master?"

"I don't know. I know he wants to do good work. And he is very pious, as I have said before," Bonne throws in for good measure. She takes the beaker from Pierre's hand and gives it to the domus's owner.

I am busy holding my tongue. Though there is much I could say—about the work on the heads and the way he looks at Bonne, particularly as she undresses for him. When he has dove's eyes and waits for her to open to him—his niece, his love, his defiled—his head is filled with dew and his hair with the drops of the night. There is no man upon earth who doeth good and sinneth not. He is a fool indeed.

"Those who work well for the church, do well in the church," the priest hints obscurely.

"Are you thinking of advancing Godfridus to master?" the bakerwoman asks, happy to be in possession of the wine.

"Only the guild can do that," says Pierre. "But I have noticed him. He always looks tired."

"Oh"—the bakerwoman draws one hand across her whitened brow—"as to tired . . ."

"You are looking well, mistress," Pierre says politely. He reaches out and takes the beaker.

"Working my fingers to the bone!" she declares, spreading them. "Can you see how thin I've become? And these days it's been impossible to swallow anything—save the holy host," she adds hastily. "Of course I am grateful. Our busy season has been the Lord's doing, and we are glad for it. Soon we may buy another oven."

"Blessings," says Pierre. He drinks.

The woman begins to brag. "Even la Putemonnoie has tried our bread," she says. "Bonne brought her a loaf some weeks ago, and the mistress was most pleased. I've been supplying the Putemonnoie house out of the kindness of my heart."

Now la Bonne fetches her sewing, perhaps so she can bow her head. She told me she feeds the bakers' extra loaves to the pigeons at Saint-Porchaire—she can't present rough bread to the bourgeoise herself, and she'd feel silly giving it to the servants.

"I am sure your prosperity is inspiring you to many acts of Christian charity," Pierre says, sipping delicately. "We of the new church always welcome whatever the prosperous citizens can spare—"

"Yes, our guild is donating a window next Christmas," the woman breaks in. "We do our part for the church, my husband and I. We'll go on pilgrimage this summer and donate handsomely at Saint-Jacques."

"That is fine," the priest says, though he seems to consider it anything but. The money should stay at home, he'll think. "Such good works salve the soul. For we all must remember the wages of sin."

Death! I want to shout it, maybe cut a little caper—a macabre danse, to tear the stuffy sanctimony from the room. But then I think of the death I earned one undeserving lady, and I am quiet. For a moment I taste bitter blood and am a fool no longer . . .

When I come to myself again, the bakerwoman's speaking of a much-loved but rather common saint who has inspired many of her present habits. ". . . shabby clothes and uncombed hair. She ate practically nothing!" Her eyes gleam.

I'm happily the fool again. Be not righteous over much—else thou wilt destroy thyself. I think of a soul we might honor if we chose—Pigmenius the priest and scholar, patron saint of fools (or should be), the one who taught Roman emperor Julian, later the Apostate, the ways of the Lord. Once Julian recanted, he banished Pigmenius, who went blind in the wilderness. In darkness he wandered back to Rome, where gentle Julian said, "I'm glad to see you." Pigmenius replied, "I'm glad to be blind and not have to see you." Upon which Julian had him thrown into the Tiber.

But would a child know such things? Would speaking of them not jeapordize his benefactress's reputation? So I save Pigmenius for a winter's tale to Bonne, as I am saving my own story.

Father Pierre chuckles, holding his sides and dropping the empty beaker to the floor. He is proud of his own joke—"Where would bakers be if we all stopped eating?"

Lady Bonne sits quietly mending her chemise, not commenting.

THE FEAST
OF THE
ANNUNCIATION
[MARCH 25]

 ODAY GODFRIDUS IS GOING TO THE COUN-
tryside for clay. He's free because it is the day
the priests celebrate the Blessed Virgin's An-
nunciation (also the day special to ribbon
dealers, who are holding a market at the center of town)—an excellent day, he says, to
gather materials for the statue that will repre-
sent the holiest woman born.

I am going with him. I've insisted. It's
been long since I saw my false uncle, and the
day will make a change from duties that have
grown tedious and frustrating, performed for
a mistress as unpredictable as she is irresistible. This afternoon is my own, away from
Henri's words and wife and wonderful house,
and I am with my oldest friend. I feel a wave
of fondness for him as we clear the town gate
and bridge and Godfridus's flat feet *thud-thud*
against the dirt road as we half-walk, half-run
through the greening countryside.

Godfridus wants to gather the earth
quickly, then go home and work it up. He
thinks of nothing but his art these days,
though thus far he's been frustrated in his
quest to create beauty. The clay he collected
earlier does not please him, and the hours

spent shaping it are wasted. Every head he makes, he later destroys, because none comes close to the image he bears in his mind. So we're looking for a perfect bit of earth, a slash like a vein or a rib that holds an ideal form inside.

But he is talking now of another work, recently assigned—"No amount of artistry," he is telling me, "will raise this image above its subject."

This is Godfridus's opportunity for advancement, which I think Pierre would like me to believe has come about through his good office. This week, as Godfridus carves upon a capital in a murky corner of the apse, he is shaping not acanthus leaves but a demon biting a woman's genitals. He is doing the rough work of blocking out the scene; a more senior journeyman, one whose work the master likes better, will be brought in for finishing touches such as roundness of limb and curl of hair. The woman is an adulteress.

"But isn't the subject for the glory of God?" I ask, trying to help.

Godfridus doesn't answer my question. "Look around," he says instead. He is gloomy. "This river has flowed here since God created the world, and each tree in the forest takes the shape He's designed for it. The human figure is bound to be less perfect."

"That's precisely what the old stonemasons say," I remind him. "Which is why they think the devil must eat the woman you make. And why you break every clay figure you shape in secret."

His face tightens into sharp lines. "Perhaps I should stop," he says.

"Oh no!"

Godfridus says, harsh and resolute, "God made the world, and by imitating His creation we defile it."

"Was Christ any less perfect because he came here in the body of a mortal woman?" I ask.

He is momentarily stumped.

"God made the woman," I point out, "and he made you. And you are doing God's work. You will create some thing of perfect beauty." I squeeze his arm, the muscles taut from carrying the buckets and our lunch.

He says, "A perfect work is an end in itself. Like Christ, it doesn't reproduce itself."

My mind travels to my new mistress. If perfection is the highest possible achievement, something closed and finished, an end in itself, it seems to me noble that Radegonde Putemonnoie has let herself get pregnant. Because breeding distorts the body, accelerates its aging, and destroys its loveliness . . . I think that motherhood, though a natural phenomenon, actually breaks the cycle of nature—a new body begins before the old one has fully died; each baby born starts to murder its mother. Just as I did, however unintentionally.

"*Your* life won't end because you make one beautiful thing," I say out loud, thinking that la Putemonnoie's baby, too, will be beautiful—like herself, and like all the objects in her house, the stores of treasures blown and brewed and filigreed by master artisans.

I consider Henri Putemonnoie, who soaked in the cream of all his wealth when in his wife's embrace. How did he feel kissing those pillowy red lips, touching that satin flesh, drinking in the indescribable taste of her—I try to imagine it, the taste of perfume and spices and gold . . .

Just then Godfridus announces, "Here is a streak of clay."

We stand on a bank, near a thicket of naked bushes. The river below is brown and swollen, and in its rapid course it whistles like a lover blowing on a flute.

"See there, under the water." Gently, Godridus guides my head with one hand. "Will you dig first or shall I?"

"Oh." I feel dizzy but remember why we're here. "I will." My hands grasp the skirts' coarse cloth and pull—baring first ankles, then shins, knees, and thighs, preparing my body to join the elements in pursuit of what will bring greater glory not just to God and the rich men of the new church, but to a humble sculptor named Godfridus.

He is watching me. My kind uncle . . .

G ODFRIDUS

. . . *And now that face is belling up at me, and hands are pulling me toward the earth, down behind a black tangle of brambles, with the river running nearly silent at our feet. And lips—too wet—brush mine—too dry—and a tongue licks sloppily at my mouth.*

My heart has stopped.

I am a big man. God gave me strength to heft and shape great slabs of rock—all for His glory, for His glory. There is danger, and evil, in using strong hands to other purposes. Such as stroking breasts and thighs, and finding secret places like those that Bonne is guiding me to.

No. Stop.

*She pulls back and whispers—Does she whisper? Has she read my memories?—*But, dear, I am corrupt already.

I look into her eyes, trying also to read—and the eyes are gray; round, not almond; shining and moist, not clouded with decay.

I say to her, "I am corruption."

Twigs crackle under our bodies as we roll toward the hedge, our limbs locked together. My arms are around Godfridus, his leg trapped between both of mine, our bodies a confusion of elbows and knees and my loosened braids.

He struggles. But the harder he pushes against me, the closer I pull him to me.

"You know I'm not a virgin," I pant. "Please, I want this."

But he chokes out some words in a tongue I can't understand, and with a last heave he sends me flying into the bushes.

Godfridus sits up and backs away, disentangling himself from my hair. His chest is heaving. "What were you thinking?" he demands of me.

I curl my knees to my chest; the brambles snap beneath me. "I wasn't thinking," I say.

"You know the way I try to live."

"Christ." I am a ball of misery. "I'm sorry, Godfridus. It was—I don't know what happened."

"And remember," he says as if his mind is a little unhinged, "remember the Magdalene—clothed in hair, weeping in the desert . . ." He's silent a moment, as if he'd like to rehearse me the litany of my sins. But he says instead, "Don't think you have a rival. You must not think that! There is no other woman. I have given my chastity to God—to the work. I have to try."

"I know." I pull the skirts down over my legs. "I never did think you—had a woman." I can't look at Godfridus. "And I respect your work. I want you to succeed. Go ahead, live like Christ. For as long as you like."

He draws himself up. "The work is never finished. I'll be celibate even when I lie in my grave." He says this with relish, as if he enjoys thinking of the earth closed over him, his blood lying still in the veins.

"Enough. I was very selfish." I sit up, tuck my skirts in my belt, and jump in the river. The water licks my kneecaps. "So let's work," I say. "Throw me a shovel."

He does it, looking toward but not at me. Perhaps he wishes I weren't here now.

When I swivel to dig at the submerged claybank, I'm startled by the image of a woman's face—wavering green, framed in loose brown hair. In the instant before the blade meets the water, it seems to me that this is la Putemonnoie's face, as if she has been watching me—but of course she hasn't; it is only my reflection I've seen and that I now cut into.

A WOMAN MIGHT ERR for many reasons, I think as I plunge and lift clay for my dryly brooding uncle. Many of us, even the most perfect, can be said to have sinned in order to make a child. But not all of these couplings are wicked in themselves, not even if the woman breaks some laws—maybe she fornicates in a haystack; maybe she commits adultery. I've even heard it suggested that the Virgin was an adulteress. Whatever her reasons, it is true she cuckolded her husband, Joseph—but with the Holy Father, everyone's first husband—and thus her sin was not really a sin. I don't consider myself much of a sinner, either, despite that afternoon in the haystack. The important thing is the baby, and how a woman conducts herself once it is here. As, once mine came, I tried to be Good.

That afternoon with Laurent the weaver fell on September 8, the Nativity of the Blessed Virgin. By a gray and chilly first of November, I knew I was pregnant. Not only had my monthly blood stopped, but my back and breasts were aching, my stomach churned, and as I rinsed out the household linens of the widow Berthe Blangy, I fainted dead away. I would have toppled into the Boîse if a passing nun hadn't caught me; as it was, one of Berthe's chemises floated off and I had to pay her for it.

Berthe, living alone and in dubious virtue, nonetheless remonstrated with me over my condition. How could I have been so careless? Who was the father, and did I want a draught of a certain potion she knew of that would take away my problem?

I had to explain that I'd entered this state willingly, that I found the work of a wet nurse easier, more palatable, and more secure than that of a laundress. Berthe threw up her hands and dismissed me.

Once pregnant, I laundered as long as I could and then found a patronne—the expectant wife of a butcher and a former believer in Blanche—who took some pity on me. But not too much, as my only bed with her was a heap of dirty straw behind the pallets where her five oldest children slept. The stench of blood from the beef curing overhead was thick and chokesome, as were the flies. The plan as we set it was that when the babies came, if we all survived, I'd be given coin enough to buy lodging and swaddling clothes and would remove both messy infants (hers and mine) from her overcrowded home. Meanwhile I had enough to eat and to feed Marie, who was already murmuring, "Full moon above, and where is the love?" in her cell.

Conceived in straw, born into straw. With the children shrieking alternately in fascination and in horror, on the feast of the Ancyra virgins I started to give birth. First came the flood of salty waters, then the pains and blood. Many pains, much blood—it mingled with the smell of the beef until I couldn't tell the difference. I realized, truly and at last, that I had risked my life for this proposition, that I very well could die giving birth to the child I'd thought would save me. The sun came up; the sun went down. The butcher's wife came and went, and came again; this time she had a midwife with her, a sage-femme who knelt between my legs and felt my belly and told me the baby was being born wrong way round, leading with its feet. Even so, only one of its legs was near out; she could feel the little blue toes wiggling when she grabbed them.

"What should we do?" she asked the butcher's wife. She was not an unkind woman, but this was her work; she saw cases like mine every day. "We have to choose one or the other. Either I cut the baby out of the womb alive—and thusly kill the mother—or I cut it up inside, and save her." She had a sack of tools, and they rattled as she spoke.

Before my patronne could answer, I ground out between my teeth: "Try to move the child."

It was more trouble than they wanted to take, but for hours into the night they struggled. The midwife's hands were cold inside me, the butcheress's rough outside. I did my best to push and pull as well, but I had lost almost every sensation except that of searing, soaring pain. I was giddy as if standing at the top of a tall tower, and my head kept dipping into and out of knowledge of this world and the one beyond.

I heard the women—or were they angels—arguing again over me and my baby: Should they save the girl whose soul was already stained, or the baby who, though innocent, was no doubt doomed by what its forebears had done?

In the end, commerce must have won out: I was more valuable to the butchers than my motherless baby would be to the orphanage. I woke up feeling empty and weak, with blood and straw caked on my backside and a sticky sun shining through the cracks in the roof. I understood that I was alive, and that consequently there was no point in reaching beside me for the living, breathing bundle that had filled my womb. It had already been buried in unconsecrated earth outside the city walls, and my patronne was in labor.

I had no time to grieve. A maidservant helped me to wash and get ready, and soon the young one's wail filled the house and stable, and I was delivered.

Perhaps I was foolish to think I could have kept them both—my baby and the butcher's. Perhaps God was right to arrange things as he did. For though some nurses can feed four or five children at a time, and even give milk into their eighties, some have enough for only one child, and that would have been a terrible choice to make.

THAT HAPPENED on the feast of Saint Ives, patron of lawyers and orphans, six years ago. I am told my infant was—would have been—a boy. Since then I have lived as I've set it down here; but in the eyes of my neighbors I have had quite a different life. I have heard their whispers: Some think I killed my baby, others that I slipped him in at the Hôtel-Dieu's revolving door, which would have been the same as murdering him. Still others say I handed the boy over to Lucifer, his father; but they are in the minority. I even heard once that my little boy was born with doubled pupils and the pale skin and crippled toes of the Antichrist—but that is clearly a lie.

Over the years I have thought of a hundred names for him, and imagined the stages of his life as they might have been. I am sure his first word would have been *maman*.

No words pass as Godfridus and I walk home. There is only the squelch-squelch of feet and of mud settling into buckets as we pass haystack after haystack.

GODFRIDUS

How should I tell her? What would be the words? To say it is the absent face that matters, the quest after that which can be revealed only once every other mystery has ended. A woman long unseen, merely felt—mine being a perfect, bodiless love, like God's for His bride, Christ's for His mother.

I felt her first in church—or rather, stopped feeling her. There was one body less in the congregation, one atom less heat. I couldn't have guessed what it was that I missed. I'd never been conscious of noticing her. I only knew that in one moment I fell in love—with an absence.

In the master stonecutter's workshop, my fellow apprentices gossiped about a young girl of the quarter who'd been accepted into a convent. Was this not wonderful? Without a big dowry, born, it would seem, to a life in which the only certainty would be hard work, she had found a position of safety.

"I promessi sposi," a fat boy said. The betrothed couple—Christ and my love.

There was nothing more, it seemed, to say about her. She'd had no visions, brought about no cures or astonishing acts. She was just a good pious girl, a model of perhaps nothing but blandeur.

So what was the source of my fascination? I had never seen her and now she was invisible, locked behind walls on the edge of the city. Someone thought she had golden hair. Someone else said chestnut. While they bickered, I chiseled a block of granite into a round missile for a catapult.

They said her skin was milky white. Then they said it was the gold of cream, with cheeks like roses. The master shamed them into working, presenting me as a model of labor. I dreamed as I cut, and soon my companions forgot to argue.

But the idea of her stayed with me. At the age of fourteen, I found myself walking on Sundays and feast days to those convent walls, to twine a thread around a stick of shrubbery or to leave at the feet of a marble Virgin a ball of common rock worried smooth by my fingers. I would pray to that Virgin, asking for intercession, asking to be recognized. The white stone face gazed serenely forward. The blue-painted robes concealed nothing but more featureless white stone.

If the Virgin was absent from our earth, it was because she had married God. Thereby she became both sister and mother to all humankind. The mother of Christ. His brides' protector. Her physical absence translated into a spiritual presence.

I did not consider my love a sin. It was pure passion, a test, a suffering— I expected no consummation and surely never planned to sin incestfully or cuckold Christ.

And yet. I drew closer, if only indirectly. Made it my business to know her family—her father a water seller, her brothers variously apprenticed. I met the brothers. But even those boys, who'd grown up with her, could not describe my beloved for me. A younger sister, poor, vanished—it was as if she hadn't been born.

With a chisel in my hand, I grew into a man—hair where my limbs joined my body, a lump in my throat that deepened my voice. I grew tall, my bones pushed at my skin and then sank under muscle. I built strong stonecutter's arms. My hair reddened. And still I thought of her.

At eighteen I passed my exams and was made a journeyman. On the very first Monday that I presented myself at the quarter's main square, calling out that I was available for hire, I got a week's engagement. I was to help build a small chapel onto the apse of a convent church.

Handmaids of the Precious Blood. Her convent.

I worked all week, chipping out the shapes that, later, more skilled hands would refine into human figures and veined leafage. During this week I didn't see a single nun. They had been warned to stay away from the worksite, and even when their code dictated they enter the church for a service, thick cloth panels screened the chapel from their sight.

We workers held our tools silent till each office ended. The roar of my blood drowned out the words the priest was saying, the responses the sisters made. I felt her presence, one continuous shining pulse beyond the heavy veil. And yet I did not know her. Wouldn't one voice separate itself from the others for me? But none did.

The next week, I had work shaping blocks for a noble's new palazzo. As I cut, I thought only of how to catch the right master's eye the following Monday—I had to return to Precious Blood.

And so it went, that first year of my journeymanry. I worked intermittently at Precious Blood and at other chapels and palazzos and bank buildings, earning a reputation for respectable carving. Often I was assigned finer work such as finishing acanthus leaves or details in a background.

In the convent, I twice saw a gray-black skirt swish by the worksite—once, a foot. Impossible to tell even if they belonged to the same woman.

Her name, I decided (for in that year I'd begun to attach some name to every thing), was Clara. She would be small and plump and brown, of a size and shape to fit around my heart. Her eyes, beneath her white wimple and veil, must be luminous; her skin smooth, with a fragrance of incense and stone floors and velvet prayer cushions.

But I never imagined a consummation. I imagined only a meeting in which her face would be revealed to me. I wanted merely to see what I had always felt was there.

Summer. After a long day at Banco Ugnano, I sat spooning a supper of peas and lentils into a mouth too weary to grind its teeth. It was then that I felt a sudden lurch throughout my body, and I knew.

She was gone.

She was doubly gone.

I read this message in the pottage spilling across the barracks floor: The loss of something you never had does not seal up the hole that longing for it opens in you. All my blood puddled round this space, mourning over it even as it tried to harden against the loss. It couldn't harden.

When next I was able to work, and was engaged for the convent chapel, I saw a new mound of brown earth in the graveyard. Wet when first heaped over the corpse, the soil had dried in lumps as big as my fist, all clotted beneath a plain gray cross some other hands had carved.

The master saw me staring. "A peste carried off one of the young sisters." He crossed himself. "Three more are fighting it now in the infirmary—but not to worry, the air about this place is good, and no nun comes close enough to taint us with her humors." He gave what seemed to me a lewd chuckle. "Deo gratias."

"Deo gratias," I echoed, though there was nothing then that I coveted more than the death that might join me to this departed sister.

I learned that the convent employed a groundskeeper who had lodgings in town but also a key to the iron gate that kept the sisters' secrets. He was a kind man, old, with a wife and four children to feed. In short, I became his friend. And though I saw no evil in it at the time, one moony night found us bent over the grave, jumping with both feet on our shovels to hurry the deed along.

I would catch, if not a holy love, at least a holy death.

Our spades struck wood. She had been given a coffin to lessen the pestilential emanations. Leaving the box in its nest of earth, we prised away the lid with metal bars. Was my friend's heart as sick-thudding in his chest as mine? Was he as wet with perspiration? Did his fingers tremble as much about their work? I know only that, as I reached for the winding sheet, he fell back.

Layer by layer I unraveled her, cradling her gently in my arms as I lifted the fabric away. I exposed first a white arm and then a leg, two round breasts, a flower in a shroud of russet down, and finally a face.

"She is perfect," breathed the groundsman.

If not by some absolute plan, at least she was perfect in one sense—the grave had not decayed her. She lay in my arms as if asleep, the white skin moist, the long limbs yielding and pliant, the close-cropped hair aflame with color, the face composed and closed and even.

I had not imagined her beautiful.

But one last element still wanted revealing. The eyes, that feature always most difficult to carve. They had been sewn shut, and with my fingernails I picked away the stitches, one at a time. Behind me I heard the groundskeeper groan. All the while, I breathed deeply but smelled nothing—no miasma to carry her death to me.

It was done. A thumb on each lid, a deep breath, and I pushed.

To this day I do not know the color of Clara's eyes. For as I lifted her lids there sprang up a sudden breeze, a hot wind that carried on it the wet breath of corruption. Under my very hands her body fell apart. The flesh slipped from her bones, the blood puddled yellow-brown in the box, her skull snapped, and worms slid through the cracks.

My Clara.

Retching, weeping, my hands clumsy as if her blood were thick in my veins, too, I laid the winding sheet over her like a tatty blanket, dropped the lid back, and used all my body to push the dirt over it and raise that brown mound and gray cross over the signs of my wickedness.

After, I went a little mad. I lived many weeks in the forest, eating berries, drinking from streams, praying. I waited for death, wooed it with cold drafts and bad water and green meat, sought it among criminals and wolves. I glimpsed its face, gaunt and hollow-eyed, at every crossroads.

But it eluded me, and always has. My body resists disease and chill. My life, it seems, is charmed.

When snow covered the ground and hard living wore away my clothes, I realized I had been spared. I had to accept that I would live. And why had God preserved me, if not to increase His glory through works of my own sinning hands—works that He would watch decay through centuries, long after my eventual demise, when the humblest acanthus leaves that I had carved would blur into the semblance of human faces?

Io non mori, e non rimasi vivo. *I am still a journeyman.*

I AM GROWING SELF-INDULGENT, ACCUSTOMED to the ways of the rich, for whom every day is one of renewal. To prepare for Easter, I take a few of my precious coins to a cloth shop and buy two ells of light wool for a new cote-hardie. The shopkeeper waits on me himself, urging on me the finest weaves, the softest yarns, the richest colors. "These threads are spun from spring's first lambs," he tells me, "and bring good luck to the wearer."

My eyes dance over the rolls: scarlet, goldenrod, deep and costly blue. I try to think which would best suit my new position as wet nurse to the wealthy. In the end, however, I remember my mistress's pride and prickly nature; what I buy is sturdy, serviceable gray.

I think the new overdress will please la Putemonnoie, who has shown me her own new ensemble of black brocade over velvet. The cut of my cotte is modest, and I have taken pains with the sewing; my new garb will reflect well upon her. And according to tradition, now that I have new clothes, the crows won't soil me after church.

Easter Sunday is bright and clear. After Hercule and I hear Mass in the local parish, I send him home; I have a nice sliver of mutton to take Marie, and then I am due chez Putemonnoie. So I stroll through the shadow district's narrow streets, enjoying the day's warmth and the caress of mist on my feet. When I pass a ribaude outside a brothel, she melts away, as is proper; for once I don't think it's because she fears me, rather because in these new clothes I command respect. A Jew has planted an apple tree by his house, and a little bit of sun manages to shine through the branches—another sign of good luck, I think as I climb over the ruined wall and into the churchyard.

"Point at the sun, a death will come . . ." Marie must be able to see the bright blazing ball even in her cell. I wonder if she saw it dancing at sunrise, as it is said to do this one day a year. "Born at sunset, worse luck yet."

"Don't you know it's Easter, Marie? The day when death is defeated."

She falls silent, ignoring me; no doubt she disapproves of my sartorial extravagance, if she notices it. As I pass the bread and mutton through her stone slit, I say a private prayer that good deeds like this one, and overall good intentions, will find their reward.

"Give me an Easter prophecy," I say into the void. "What do the skies promise this year?"

Of course Marie doesn't reply. Instead she hands out her earthenware basin with its clouded, stinking contents.

"May the Virgin bless you likewise," I murmur, taking it. I carry the basin off the old church site and dump it in a most unholy gutter. Two mangy dogs bark at me, then jump into the ditch to inspect my leavings. It occurs to me again that the chamberpot of an ascetic is more foul, because more concentrated, than anyone else's. I call it therefore fitting that Marie's filth should run with the town's stale water, and offal, and rats, until whatever is holy about her excretions gets diluted and lost among the waste of the common humanity whose sins her martyrdom is designed in part to cleanse.

As I cross the atrium again, I pull a few pale new leaves from a plane tree to wipe out the bowl. There's a baby snail on one of them, and I set it down on the ground, well away from the wild rose that has started to send out thorns below Marie's window. Snails are symbols of the Resurrection, which must be in every pious person's mind on the day that commemorates the emptiness of Christ's own tomb.

As I scrub the basin, Saint-Porchaire lies silent and hot in its blanket of lead. The mist curls up from it like dragon's breath. But as the leaves tear, they send a fresh green smell to cover Marie's stench, and in the distance there's the sound of drums, such that the rhythm of my cleaning becomes like dancing.

Villeneuve has a particular way of celebrating Easter.

"They're sending the new-church relics away," I say as I slide the basin toward Marie. "Our gold and bones will make a grand tour of the countryside. How much would you pay for a look at Saint Vitus's knuckle?" Peasants in villages for leagues around will give a denier for the privilege, and the new church will grow richer.

As Marie stifles a belch, a wave of dank mutton reaches my nostrils. I wonder how many teeth she has left. "Well, a fine Easter to you," I say, and not unkindly, turning to leave. "Even though you can't go anywhere."

When I've taken a few steps but haven't passed out of hearing, I trip. Because Marie has spoken. And it must be to *me*.

"She rides through Scorpio and gives Mars a rise; this any can see with his own two eyes."

I pick myself up, toss aside a finger bone, and hurry back to the window slit. "What do you mean, Marie?"

But now she ignores me—I should have expected as much. Still, this is a start, and I am intrigued by her addressing me, however indirectly. Loudly, I walk off ten paces with heavy steps. While I wait, the far-off drumming grows loud, accompanied by piping and voices. Then I return on tiptoe.

"You may try and try, but many will die," Marie says, as if prophesying for no one but herself. I remember what she predicted in February, that the rich would die—and they haven't yet, at least no more of them than usual—but this prophecy makes me nervous. Someone who lives as bare as Marie has for so many years must know *something*.

So I wait. The pipes grow louder. I'm about to leave when Marie speaks for the last time:

"Venus doesn't need a whip," she says.

Then I hear the sound of chewing and I know she's finished.

HERCULE

Out the window and over the roofs, I catch bright colors: red and orange, harlots' green and priestly black—which is as bright in its way as any sunny shade. I hear, too, the crack of whips in flesh, a sound all too familiar from my days in Coussin. I see blood before my eyes.

All over town, mutton is being roasted, pies are being baked, flowers fried. The fast has ended. But I have better food in view—I am waiting for Bonne. An easy trick, but what magic! That a woman's body can produce food. My hungering bones itch and tingle . . .

While I stand here plotting to pull the bourgeoise's womb from her belly, the sculptor's fingers from his hand.

An infant has no morals, nor can any who have tasted that sweet substance, that extracted blood, a mother's milk. No wonder Christ was weaned before baptized. I cannot stand *that anyone else should claim my share!*

But I must stand, and stand tall, or I will see nothing. So I grab an apple and a ball of yarn and start to juggle, drawing bodies in air. I draw Anne, who was never a mother, and I draw Bonne.

I juggle my heart. It is melting . . .

Venus is the morning star and, to the poets, a guider of love. In the mornings, she brings forth dew to wet the animals' bellies and fill them with lust; she uses honey rather than force to coax her minions into action. She must be the one riding whipless through the stars of Scorpio—the scorpion, the animal of desire . . . and bringing death? To the wealthy?

Stumbling on bones, thinking only of this prophecy, I make my way out of the churchyard. I trust my feet to find the way through narrow misty streets and into wider ones.

I don't hear the noise till I'm in it—till I fall into it. Drums and a flute, a pipe and a lute, the streets of centre-ville ringing and singing as a glittering train winds through. The holy relics are on parade. Hundreds of feet, some bare, some leather-shod, tread the spongy spring earth after them.

Seated on a red velvet litter, Father Pierre holds up an enormous gold foot with jeweled nails. "The toe of Saint Mathurin!" he announces.

The people applaud, and a few cross themselves. "Saint Mathurin!" they echo.

"He was baptized at age twelve," Pierre continues, his bumps shaking with the volume of his voice. "After which he prayed God most earnestly to convert his pagan parents."

I try to push my way to the fringe of the crowd while Pierre and the other priests continue to extoll this and other relics. They are all in their best vestments, and the air is heavy with incense.

"The knucklebone of Saint Vitus!" cries another father, taller and thinner than Pierre, from his own litter. He holds up a large ivory hand. "A Holy Helper of the sick!"

A third priest, thinner still, has a hair from the beard of Saint Gomer in a chest of rock crystal. He declaims the details of Gomer's life and martyrdom: soldier to Pepin the Short, husband to a shrew.

The people cheer and cross themselves, cry "Deo gratias!" and swoon in ecstasy. They bear me along with them, one body in a press of hundreds.

The procession will lead to the town gates, where two of the priests will surrender their burdens to the last one. As I told Marie, this priest—the thin one? the tall one? Pierre?—will travel from town to town all summer, displaying the toe, the knucklebone, the hair, and lesser relics, all in their opulent cases, around our France.

I hear a round man, drunk perhaps on holy wine, shout to a neighbor, "It's true! I heard it from Father Thomas—that hair isn't from the jaws—!"

There are some citizens who, every year, protest this summer trip. They think it means bad luck to send the town's most precious possessions away. For this is Villeneuve's true wealth—not the spices and silks that come from the East, not the ells woven here from Scottish wool, but the fragments of holiness that are all our mortal world still knows of these exemplary spirits. These people come with whips to the procession, and against the Pope's dictates, they follow the priests and scourge their own flesh. Leather tongues bite into naked backs; blood pours down from the ragged gashes. Their leader carries a crucifix.

"Blessings!" cry the martyrs, and "Blessings!" roars the crowd. As if competing with them, the priests raise their shining vessels higher, and higher.

On every one of these faces I read passion. Passion that echoes the one grand Passion, that of Our Lord—suffering, joy, exaltation all at once. The whips hiss and the pious roar. The wounds bleed and the loincloths tear. Women break from their husbands to kiss holy relics—

Christ on his crucifix weeps and becomes one with God.

"DESIST!" Pierre has stopped the procession and points a trembling finger at the flagellants, who keep rubbing their backs with the butts of their whips. "Sinners! Our Lord doesn't want this—!"

Whatever else he might have said is drowned out as, at a sign from one of the town fathers, a troop of guardsmen surround the flagellants and aim iron-tipped pikes at their throats.

The crowd is howling. They like the flagellants, relish the spectacle of martyrdom—particularly on this day at the end of Lent, when most of us are still trying to keep our bodies from coming apart at the seams. They surge forward as if to fight the guardsmen.

"Pax!" calls ancient Father Thomas. "Peace! God is love!"

God is love, but Venus needs no whip. I break from the crowd, having seen enough.

GODFRIDUS

He moves within me.

My fellows stare. They know what is happening—they know the signs of inspiration, when God decides to move a mortal hand. They have placed soft wood in my hand, and here is my knife. It warms to my flesh, it cuts, it bites. Life spills out of—into—wood. Chips rain down like holy hail. The men pray.

Salve Regina, mater misericordiae . . .

My ears are ringing. Now Kings, Prophets, sinners sing to me, and colored light stains my hands. Before their eyes I shape a small hand with a cupped palm, the palm brimming with roses—roses clinging to a skirt, to the tip of a dainty foot, to the round rump of a laughing Baby.

I am carving life from wood—so much more yielding than stone, and warmer than clay.

I have been elevated.

Once again, I present myself at la Putemonnoie's house. The mistress has just had a bath, and Agnès is brushing out her hair. It hangs in black tendrils down her back, curling, swarming, melting, and dividing again.

Here she is, the woman I am supposed to watch for Jesus. So eerily beautiful, but so real to me. She gives me calm welcome, asks for news, and nods with polite interest as I describe the procession to her. Agnès braids her hair, discontent at my presence. She winds the braids around and around the mistress's head, then carefully inserts the long-shafted jewels that la Putemonnoie loves. Sapphires and emeralds that try to echo the colors in her eyes.

Looking at her, I forget—almost—the turmoil in the streets.

"—but that's not important," I say, interrupting my own story.

La Putemonnoie looks at me, swaying a little as Agnès slides the last jewels in.

My heart is beating very fast. "Shall I tell you something else?"

"If you like." Languid after the bath, she leans back on her cushioned bench and tucks a honey cake between her lips. Her stomach has grown to quite a respectable size; the heir is doing well in his sixth month. She dismisses Agnès with a wave of her hand. "Feel free to amuse me," she says then, and I am suddenly bold.

Until now I haven't had the courage to volunteer any news of my own, to tell of anything that bears only on my own life, not on hers or the town's. But now I want her to know something of *me*. As la Putemonnoie chews her cake, it all comes pouring out. I tell her about Marie.

I tell her about feeding the recluse, and about the rose slip that Blanche and I planted at the window so many years ago, so she'd have something pretty in her life whether she wanted it or not; I speak of the fire, and the terror Marie must have felt, and the amazing fact that she and her cell survived intact. I repeat the story of her ensealment, and how the reluctant priest—I think it might even have been Pierre—conducted the ceremony whereby she declared herself dead to the world, alive only in Christ, and shouted that when she is sinless she will be bodily lifted to heaven. I mention that Marie will not speak to me but nonetheless gave me a prophecy today, and I say what that prophecy was.

"Hm." La Putemonnoie takes another sweet; she has emptied almost an entire bowl. She seems uninterested in prophecies, gloomy or otherwise. "Tell me," she says, "why *do* you feed the recluse? Your mother is dead, and it must be some hardship for you. Why continue to do it?"

I blush, stare at my hands. This is the one gift I think I have to give, the one secret I know—what is a secret only because people have chosen to forget.

"Marie is my grandmother," I say.

"Ah!" La Putemonnoie sits up. "The mother of Blanche Mirabilis! She had herself walled in when you were born?"

Still blushing, I nod my head yes. "It was before my birth, actually, when Blanche's belly started to show."

"Here." Excited, la Putemonnoie gives her silver sweet bowl a little shove in my direction. "Have a honey cake. And sit down."

As I obey, she continues, "What an interesting family you have. So many holy women. And you, even you, performed your own miracle, saving that little boy from the bear at the market."

Giddy with success, I realize I have another secret to offer. "He is a dwarf, mistress."

"A dwarf!" She seems dumbfounded. "But I heard he lives with you."

"He does." Now, too late, I realize she may not like my sheltering Hercule. His kind do not have a good reputation; only noblemen tolerate dwarfs, and then only in menageries and cages. "No one else," I say, temporarily forgetting Godfridus, "knows what he really is. They think he's a six-year-old with a weak heart and bones. That last is true; he is ailing. He used to live at a lord's court."

She takes the last sweet and eats it slowly. Her lovely face wears the expression of deep thought. "Maybe," she says, "you can bring him when you come to live here. He might know a good trick or two."

My chest is about to crack open—I am to live here, she's asked me at last—and Hercule has been accepted. "You are—too good," I stammer.

"A recluse and a dwarf." She gazes at me, smiling faintly. "You surprise me, Bonne Tardieu. Next you'll tell me your pious uncle isn't what he seems."

I realize my confessions must stop here. "Oh, he is, mistress. He is very pious."

"Well." She gets to her feet, heaving to accommodate her belly. I dare to take her elbow and help. "After such stories, let's not have any of my husband's book today. I have an idea—we'll visit my warehouses below."

HERCULE

Three balls, six balls, nine balls, twelve. Two arcs in the air, a bow and its echo. A rain circle.

Two make tout, *two make a* trou—*everything comes down to a* hole . . .
Oh, not that tired joke again.

Spin, spin, spin until you (don't) fall down.

The rooms below are strongly scented, brimming over with the goods that Henri Putemonnoie collected. We are in the bowels of the labyrinthine house, stepping into the very center of the earth. La Putemonnoie unlocks one door after another until I can't say where we are.

By flickering candlelight, she shows me her fortune.

Spices—cinnamon, saffron, pepper, sugar, clove. Perfumes—musk, amber, rose water, plus distillates I have never smelled before; my nose burns. Slabs of precious stone, buckets of gold, copper, silver. Oils of various kinds, from olives, almonds, flowers, and lions. Furs from every animal under the sun; horn and bone. And cloth, much of it bought for her personal use. We pull apart the bales, and colors leap in the candlelight, more colors than I can name. The reds alone dazzle with variety—scarlet, cerise, rose, crimson, blood, wine, pourpre . . . At first hesitant, then greedy, I run my fingers through, drinking color like honey.

This length of dark samite is for la Putemonnoie's churching, when she reenters Christ after the contamination of childbed. These crisp linens will make a christening gown for the child; these will be his swaddling clothes. These colored velvets are for caps and coverlets. The heir must have the best.

I feel close to my mistress here—we could be just two housewives poring over market wares, planning a layette, rather than a rich woman and her hireling. At the same time I feel vaguely embarrassed about my new overdress, which only hours ago seemed so fine to me. It has no gold threads, no furbelows, no dagging. And of course such trims would not be proper to my station.

I think la Putemonnoie feels the closeness. "I never loved Henri," she confides, holding the candle low to stroke a brocade. "I've never been in love with anyone—except myself." She smiles, looking sideways at me.

I don't know what to say, what to do. It has been a day of confessions.

My fingers fumble and I limit myself, just follow her hand and stroke, after her, the soft fabric.

But she seems to expect no reply. She moves to another table, where she turns folds of velvet and satin and cloth-of-gold in her dusky hands; from her neck dangles that famous pendant, the two lovers backed with Death. Just now it is the single face that shows.

She looks up at me. "Here," she says, tugging at a length of forest-green velvet. "This will become you." Playing the gracious lady, because I have pleased her today, she takes me by the hand—hers is so soft, much younger than my own, the skin still as elastic as a child's—and begins to wrap me in the stuff. She makes me turn around and around as she wraps and drapes. She binds my arms to my body so I appear to have no arms, like a corpse or an infant in swaddling.

"Now look," she says.

I stop spinning. My back is to her. She holds a flat object in her hand and reaches it round in front me. The candle shows ivory in heavy relief; a hunting scene, I think—or no, an elegant woman, with her hair bejeweled and her lips parted. But before I can see her properly, la Putemonnoie presses a button and the carving falls to the floor, and la Putemonnoie lifts up a disk to me.

I see not a carving but what seems real. Another person has entered the room. A stranger, standing before me—a stranger wrapped in velvet. The mossy green flows over a pair of round shoulders, and round breasts, and a mound of stomach, and wide childbearing hips, before it falls in a river to the floor.

I have heard of these inventions, glass treated with silver so it will reflect like no other thing can, not even metal or water. This rare glass is showing me to myself for the first time.

It gives me new knowledge of my body—I could almost say I have been reshaped. I am slimmer than I thought, and my chest, though large, is not as big as it can seem to me.

Radegonde Putemonnoie has been following my gaze in the mirror. She sees that it will go no higher. So she puts her free hand on my head, palm on temple. "Don't be afraid," and she guides my head upward.

I see. My face.

Bonne's hair is light brown; I knew that. It straggles in thin tails out of its braids; I have felt them tickle before, on what I see now is a broad pale forehead that twenty-two years have touched with three lines above the eyebrows. Those brows are almost blond, nearly invisible, above pale gray eyes. I have freckles. My nose is small and there is a pimple on one side; my cheeks are round. Thank God I have no mustache. I like the mouth in the reflection; the lips are full and curved, and their outline is sharp. They are the one feature of my face that slightly resembles my mistress's.

In the glass, I can see a shadowy eye peering over my shoulder.

The lips curve up, curve down; they part (the teeth are mostly yellow, just one eyetooth is very gray)—and then a snail's track winds quickly over them and inside. More snails have crawled down my cheeks. Without realizing, I have begun to cry.

"Oh, Bonne." La Putemonnoie seems to understand. "But you're actually quite pretty. Even beautiful, in a way." She takes the necklace from her neck and slips it over my head. "In a dress of this fabric, with an ornament like this, you would look like a lady."

The pendant feels heavy, a fist knocking at my heart. In the glass, I see the image has turned itself around: The lovers kiss between my breasts. My tears stop.

Radegonde Putemonnoie's hand rests on my shoulder as she holds me there, looking at myself. Together we stare into the mirror's reflection, and a current runs hot from the pendant to my heart, up through my shoulder to her hand, her arms, the mirror, her heart.

If the lovers are looking out from my chest, then Death's leering head faces into me.

Death. The thought unleashes a wave of feeling. Quickly, before I can think, I turn around—clumsy, because I don't have my arms for balance. I startle her; her eyes are wide, the pupils tight black buds. Her lips part for a sharp breath.

I bend down fast, then pause a heartbeat. A dark, delicious smell is coming from her mouth.

She licks her lips. .

That ends it for me. Dizzy, amazed, I lick my lips, too. The velvet slides over my shoulders. *Then* suddenly brave, I lick at la Putemonnoie's mouth.

Virgin! I am kissing her. Or she is kissing me: I feel her warm, firm lips against mine. I kiss the way I've been kissed before, by Laurent—licking, dabbing at the outside of her mouth, leaving a wet trail around the rim.

Her lips open, suck at me. Surprised, I feel her teeth, her tongue. Down below I feel myself opening like a flower, petal by petal, fold by fold, while my tongue becomes a finger probing into her. Her tongue is soft, and the tip is cleft; I run mine along this hollow, as if in an embrace.

I have heard kisses sung of by poets and dancers, have read of them in the few pages of Scripture Blanche borrowed for our home. The perfect kiss is never described—unlike the perfect lips, the perfect breasts. So I do not know how to kiss. I do not know what the kiss I am giving means. But I keep on kissing.

I feel the velvet slipping off my body, replaced with coolness. Warmth piles upon my feet. The pendant lands again with a thump against my ribs and I wonder, with a small part of my mind, which side faces outward.

I can't breathe.

Common roses, wild roses, Rosae humiles—*they are flat and small, almost mean, but how they grow*

Falling. Dizzy. Faint, fainting.

Ora, the angels sing, *ora . . . pro nobis peccatoribus . . .*

My limbs go numb, and I start to black out

. . . nunc et in hora mortis nostrae.

BOOK II

LABYRINTH

UT SHE IS THE ONE WHO FALLS AWAY. Silently, with a soft warm breath, she collapses under me. I barely manage to catch her in my arms, ease her to the floor.

Radegonde Putemonnoie's lashes are dark new moons on her cheekbones. She lies like a sleeping princess.

The candle flickers, and my shadow menaces the walls. So I step out of the pooled velvet, kneel, and put my hand on Radegonde's bosom, making myself small. Her heart thuds against my palm, and I feel the ribs rise and fall. Deo gratias, she is still breathing.

Men kiss men to say hello; men kiss women; women kiss women. Simple greetings; why then has this one almost killed Madame Putemonnoie?

(And what would have happened to me if it had?)

I whisper against the dark whorl of her ear, "Mistress. Mistress." And I give her shoulders a little shake. "It isn't good for the baby, this lying on a cold floor."

GODFRIDUS
When the chisel slips, it's as if my thumb has been waiting. The pain is like morning light—color padding over my vision.

When I look down my apron is already scarlet. The rose I've been carving is painted with my blood.

They all see it, the guild journeymen and apprentices assembled with me for this celebration of relics. Even Maître Aubert. They gasp in wonder—but not the kind of wonder I'd hoped to evoke. Two moments ago they were watching me cut a little Lady in the space of a Salve Regina. Working in wood rather than stone, an exhibition in honor of the holy day and the relics leaving town. But this happened instead—in my pride, my strokes were too heavy, and I slipped.

It doesn't seem real to me yet. I'm giddy with the surprise.

My fellow journeyman Mathurin takes my hand and wipes at the blood. It stops just long enough to let us glimpse pinpricks of white fat pouting from the gash.

Seeing that, Maître Aubert pushes me to the floor. "Sit down. Don't let yourself faint and fall."

Yes, I am feeling sick. I who have never been sick.

"Put your head between your legs," says Martial, another journeyman. "Take deep breaths." To the others he adds, "I've never seen a man cut so far."

"It is as deep as any cut I've seen on a hand," Maître Aubert allows. "Better fetch a surgeon to sew it up."

It's true, then. I am going to lose my hand.

"No," I gasp through the nausea fog. "Bring my niece. Bonne Tardieu."

"Bonne?" The men look skeptical, but I insist. I won't risk my hand to some marketplace hack whose thread's been poisoned in the name of a miracle cure. Not when there is the vaguest chance of a real miracle, a real cure. "I will tell you the way. In the street of the bakers, over the sign of the loaf and the ring . . ."

Young Thierry, a first-year apprentice, takes off running. The others lay me out on my back with my thumb in the air, the stone cold soaking into my bones. So cold, so numb . . . though I can still hear the prayers echoing off the surface, prayers shouted (perhaps that's what distracted me) while my fingers flew through the wood. Mater misericordiae . . .

One by one the men move away, too polite to watch any longer. Or maybe they're bored. One of the apprentices can walk on his hands, and he flips down headfirst to do it.

Mathurin stays by me. He tears linen from my undershirt and tries to wrap my thumb in it. The blood leaps from my hand and makes a stain before the cloth can get close.

I force myself to speak, so I will not think. "My niece sews a neat seam, and she'll use a clean needle and thread, too."

"Yes," says Mathurin, looking at the bloody bundle he's making of my thumb, "women have a knack with wounds like this. Comes from sewing each other up after childbirth."

I wince. He knocked my thumb to the side as he tugged the linen into a knot. And already the bandage is slipping away like a rotten liver, my hand feels enormous, my head is swimming . . . Vita, dulcedo et spes . . . Bona. Did I say that out loud?

"Bonne . . ." I hear myself say again, though even I don't know what I can mean. Her beautiful face seems to waver before me and then disappear, as I catch a whiff of her warm milky smell.

Mathurin peers into my eyes. "You are dazed. I'll get some wine."

While he is away, the boy Thierry comes back saying he can't find my niece. At first I cannot understand this. "Bonne?" I say.

Then Mathurin is kneeling by me, tipping a cup toward my lips. Perhaps I have already swooned. "So get a midwife!" he curses at Thierry. "Get anybody—a surgeon!"

I feel the cold black bottom of my soul rushing up to meet me.

With a deep sigh, she wakes and opens her eyes. "I'm very tired suddenly," she says. "Shall we go upstairs?"

My own eyes blink and I say a quick prayer of thanks. She has recovered. "The baby . . . ?" I ask, feeling an impulse, still nervous, to chatter, even as I help her to sit up. "You are tired, of course, from the pregnancy, but the baby is all right? And you are all right? And not angry?"

"Yes." She tugs at the skirt upon her belly, then holds her hand out so I'll help her stand. I pull her to her feet. In the wavering light, she catches her own face in the mirror on the table, a reflection of dark shadows and of bones cut like a rosary bead. Perfection.

She smiles slightly at herself. "No," she says, "I'm not angry."

She turns suddenly and looks into my eyes. "I won't go to the convent, will I? You'll save me, won't you, Bonne?"

I can't tell if she's half teasing or deadly earnest. *I* save *her?* I feel my-self blushing in sudden darkness. For in the wind from her skirts, the can-dle has blown out.

HERCULE

When the stone-clothed boy comes for Bonne, my first hope is that the sculp-tor has died.

I'll bury him so deep his corpse can't swim up for Judgment Day. I'll bury him so even the worms won't find him. I'll bury him.

And how can I hope to do it? He is a big man, and I'm too small to hold a shovel upright.

"She isn't here." I slam the door, gladly, in the boy's face.

In extremis, like Christ, a man wants women around him. Christ had Mary and la Madeleine; the sculptor'll be lucky to get a sour-smelling squint-eye who performs abortions and buries afterbirth in her backyard. Still, a woman. To sew him up, a seamstress for his distress.

But not my Bonne!

I pull out my knitting needles and cast on. I work row after row, mut-tering as if I know the right magic to excise the sculptor from my own life. Maybe the thumb will go septic. He'll lose his hand, his job ... With each stitch I devise some new misery for him.

"May he have—boils!" I chant. "May he grow—warts! May his ears run with—blood!" I chuckle delightedly. There's noise outside, more festi-val shouting, so I shout the louder.

"May his foreskin close up—over—his—cock!"

Outside the golden light is waning, and we are in bed.

A body spends twenty years growing, fifty years dying. For perhaps a third of that time, we are in bed. Asleep or awake; with sore heads, stiff limbs, cracked bones—or soaring heart, throbbing flesh. Only infirmity or the prospect of pure jouissance can justify daylight hours spent in bed.

Radegonde Putemonnoie lies in hers now. Between snowy white sheets, under a lofty eiderdown, a sable-fur drape, and a red velvet coun-terpane. Her head and shoulders rest against more down and linen, em-broidered pillows holding her nearly vertical. She wears her necklace again.

She says she likes to nap at this time of day, and today, after our excursion deep into the house, she wants me with her. I've been reading aloud from her husband's book—the lore of toads, snakes, and salamanders—but now her breathing is even, and as the light starts to go gold and fade from the sky, it seems she is asleep. So I close the heavy covers and set the book on the bench beside me, that I may lean against that puff of feathers and fur and watch her.

This, I think, is the hour you can believe in magic, when outlines get hazy and the slant of a sunbeam falling thick on a counterpane can make your heart ache. When the scents of rose water and a loved one's hair make the blood prickle in your veins.

Her face lies still, as if chiseled in peachy marble. Veinless but full of color, full of light. As if she could float right up to the stars . . .

Inexorably the dark deepens; night falls and I lose my ability to see. Soon there are no freckles, no hair, no limbs—the white glint of eyes, maybe, if they were looking. They aren't.

My eyes give me so much pleasure. When will the maid come with a candle? (The maid, who will interrupt this peace.)

Radegonde breathes softly. One, two. Out, in.

And here is the advantage to nighttime: In the dark, you can't see the difference between a rich woman and a peasant. In the dark, you can't tell how a body has been used.

IN THE BLUE DARK, I flirt with dreams . . . I remember such an hour in the tiny room I shared with Blanche. She was sewing, I burying a stick in the rushes—my favorite game. Once it was hidden, I would turn myself around and then search for it. (I was a very small child.) I found it once, twice. The third time I hid my stick, the third time I spun around, I fell over myself, fell into Blanche; and when I sat up, wailing over some little imagined hurt, I saw the bone needle stuck clear through her finger.

The howl died in my throat. Even in the blue, Blanche looked pale. We were silent a long moment—in the street a dog barked—and then Blanche, always calm, pulled the needle out.

She did it slowly, she said, so the bone wouldn't break off inside. She joked that she had plenty of bone in her finger already (and really, it was hardly anything but; all the best food went to baby Bonne). As the needle emerged, a drop welled up on each side of the wound, shining black in the firelight; and then the drops lengthened, and wavered, and fell. I saw blood pour from my mother.

Hush, she said as I started to shriek. *See, it's nothing.* And she took a slice of stale bread (the linen had to stay clean for her customer) and wrapped it round her finger. She said, *We never run out of blood, because God fills our hearts full of it every night while we sleep. This is why you must always keep your heart open to Him.*

When she unwrapped her finger, the wound had closed. I begged to eat the bread but she wouldn't let me. Perhaps she ate that piece herself, or saved it for her mother.

After that, we called my stick game Needle-in-a-Haystack. And I still lie awake some nights with the covers pushed down off my chest, waiting.

I MUST HAVE FALLEN ASLEEP. Because suddenly a terrible clanging and tolling of church bells, and shouting of men and women, jolts me back into my body—my ordinary body, the body of fear and trepidation and caution.

"Is that the couvre-feu?" Radegonde mumbles sleepily.

"I think it's too early." I stumble, dashing to the windows. If I have missed curfew, I'll have to spend the night here. I fling open the shutters. "See, the sky is still orange to the east."

"The east?" Her words are almost lost in the sound of the bells.

"You're right," I say. "This can't be the dawn." I hang my head over the sill; in the street, a man is shouting for others to follow him with buckets and cloth sacking.

"It must be a fire." I pull back in and fasten the shutters, moving fast. "A big one."

"To the east—then it's the butchers' quarter." She stretches, lazy. "There'll be roast joints and fried sausages tonight—but what are you do-ing? Bonne, come here." She holds out a hand to me.

My eyes have adjusted to the darkness by now. But my mind cannot reconcile the cozy, fragrant nest to my one side, and the fierce danger rag-ing perhaps toward my own neighborhood. "I have to go home," I say, looking back to the window, where an orange nimbus outlines the shutters. "Hercule—the little boy—" I mean, the dwarf, but she doesn't correct me.

She sits up in bed. "I know you live to the north, not the east. Agnès told me so. You can stay, and let the townsmen stop the fire." She sounds imperious. "Come read to me. I'll send a manservant if you like."

I imagine for a moment what it would be like to spend all night here, even night after night. I am on the point of staying, of sinking down next to her, but in the end—"I can't leave Hercule alone. I apologize, mistress." And I fairly flee the room, away from her beckoning arms and commanding voice.

Down a smoky passage—for a moment I think the fire is here, too, but it's only the oil candles and braziers burning—to a stairway. I get lost, turn around; I have to ask a servant for the way outside.

He lets me out in the garden. A cool breeze from the west—no hint of smoke—kisses my cheeks. Even with the bells and the shouting beyond, the walls keep this place so quiet I can hear the herbs and flowers pushing at the earth. There is light to see by—fire and the moon; I see again the crocuses, a few spears of iris leaves, and a night-blooming vine whose heavy white flowers scent the air. It would be easy to linger here, fall into a drugged sleep and just stay here.

I stamp my foot. "The street!"

Radegonde's man smirks; he knows me for another servant like himself, in la Putemonnoie's employ. Who am I to be giving him orders? He takes me by the elbow and half-drags me back through the house and to the courtyard gate.

"Where are you going so fast?" he asks as he unlocks the gate for me. He must think his mistress has dismissed me, maybe that I'm running off with a stolen coin or silver spoon. Maybe he is flirting with me; I still feel the print of his hand on my elbow. He holds the gate closed.

I stare coldly at him. Beyond the iron bars, dark shapes flit by, and men shout.

"I have to get home." I push past, and the servingman's fingers clutch at my braid; but I yank it away and the gate clangs shut again.

Outside I stand alone, confused. A crowd runs by me in clumps, mostly men in groups of two or three. Everyone carries a bucket of water or sand, and the ground is dark where the buckets have spilled. I see a brown dog, given a fatal kick in the mayhem, breathe its last in a doorway. I see Radegonde's servant watching me through the bars.

I turn and weave my way to the north. Through the marketplace, past the new church. Anne, Aliénore, and Blanche ring out a dizzying thunder. I clap my hands over my ears, run awkwardly, so my breasts bounce heavy and hurtful.

Suddenly I feel a shift in the flow of bodies. They begin to run westward, not east, and they're carrying not buckets but shovels, hammers, planks of wood.

I grab a woman's arm. "What now?" I yell into her ear.

"They're mining the west wall, near the Porte de Poitiers—English mercenaries," she shouts back, balancing a hoe on her knee. "Send your husband and your brothers."

I hold her a little longer. "Did—was it Englishmen who started the fire?"

"Who else? Only the devil works on Easter!" She breaks away.

This has happened in Villeneuve before. There's been a lull in the king's ongoing war with the English, and some unemployed mercenaries have decided to plunder our market center to make up for lost wages and booty. They use an old method, setting fire to one quartier and then attacking another, digging under the city walls until the masonry collapses. If they succeed they will swarm into the streets like rats, grabbing at money, treasure, women—more than can be brought back to England. The wealth stolen here will likely get lost or spent on the road back to the Channel, and the English will revel in the waste of it, while we lose everything.

Or such is the Englishmen's plan. But the mood in our streets is strong—people are exhilarated with urgent purpose. The townsfolk rush by with glowing faces, shining shovels. Their hope is great. We're defending ourselves, our families, our country and king, and we may do it bloodily, knowing we have God's blessing. Our greatest treasures, the relics, are already safely away, and Villeneuve has always felt itself to be particularly fortunate.

And in the end it is always hard for outsiders to capture a walled town, especially a market center with such ample stores of food as sit even now in warehouses like Radegonde's. Our townsmen are already raining arrows down from the city walls, and a countermine is being built, a wooden wall inside the stone one—strong enough to stop an army of dogs already exhausting themselves with digging. By morning the looters may well be gone.

I feel a stitch in my side. I slow down, walk for a while. I begin to wonder where I got that terrible sense of urgency. Would it have been so bad for me to wait with Radegonde until the fire was out, the wall doubled, the town victorious?

THE BAKERWOMAN

Evil's long of foot, always afoot. Creeping through the forest, sneaking into town—what brings it home?

Home, the ovens by the north wall. From the ramparts they look tiny, but they'll burn with the rest in a fire. Be robbed with the rest if the devils dig that far.

Husband, boil the oil. Deliver us from evil— Hit 'em with a rock! Hit 'em with a plank! Hit 'em with a loaf! Scald them, bake them, kill them.

Cleanse us of this evil. Cut it off at the root.

I arrive at the bakery cold and smelling of smoke, bruised by blows from careless arms and tools. Still with the scent of *her* in my lungs, the feel of her in my eyes.

I find Hercule scrunched by our own little brazier fire. A shapeless brown mass writhes in his fingers; he is knitting fiercely and doesn't look up, even when I slam the door.

"Back so soon?" he says into the knotty wool, jabbing with his needles.

As if he really is my little boy (sulky, petulant), I rush to hug him. I feel quite affectionate. "I'm so glad you're still here," I say. "I'm so glad you're all right. There's a fire and the west walls are under attack—I was afraid you'd gone to watch."

"To watch, you say, but not to help," he mutters in my arms. His uselessness always a point of resentment.

"No, you might have helped, but—I'm glad you're here. The others, the burghers, will protect us," I say. My sense of anticlimax is keen; Hercule is all right, didn't even miss me. I stand up and shake out my skirts, which were clean just a little while ago today. "Every property man in town is running with a shovel or bucket to add his feeble little strokes."

"You speak sarcastically."

"You speak childishly." I give his head a tap and move toward the cupboard; I'm hungry.

"A boy came looking for you today," Hercule says as he resumes his knitting.

"Oh?" I'm well advanced in the rent, and the bakers haven't bothered me in weeks; maybe there's another chance at a job, something to tide me over until Radegonde delivers. I wonder if she will want me to decline it.

"From the new church."

"Did Pierre send him?" Perhaps I should be anxious. "Don't be coy—tell me. Did he want information about Mistress Putemonnoie?" This seems like a tiny matter now; of course I can't inform, have nothing to say about her to anyone. I think dimly of my clumsy attempts at kissing Godfridus, and I smile to myself.

"A *little* boy," Hercule says, ignoring the smile, "a real one. A stone-cutting apprentice. He came about—"

"Godfridus?" I bite into an apple's wrinkled flesh.

"Yes," Hercule says with satisfaction. "He cut his hand today, showing off. He wanted you to sew it up but you weren't here."

"Was it a bad cut?" I ask—concerned now, and sorry I wasn't here to help him. "It must have been, if it meant he wanted me after all these weeks. Did he call a surgeon?"

Hercule shrugs, his threads knotting rhymthically. "I don't know. I sent the boy away. Maybe the stoneman will lose his thumb."

More of Hercule's exaggerations and tricks, I think. I sit by the fire with my apple and take small bites, pleasuring myself with the slow satisfaction of this hunger. Hercule is annoying me. I think I should have stayed with Radegonde.

"We'll visit Godfridus tomorrow," I say out loud. "We'll both go. We can bring him some bread and the last of these apples."

Hercule's face knots together and his fingers fly. He doesn't speak.

All night I dream by our little fire. What's going on outside seems merely a detail in the background, business conducted between powers in which we play no part. Instead I think of Godfridus, and the dwarf, and of course Radegonde. My mind recites the words she spoke today and how she looked at me, and even the lines I read from her husband's book while she slept.

After some hours my breasts are full; I unfasten my dress, and Hercule drains them.

From Henri Putemonnoie's livre de raison
THE LORE OF THE TOAD
Despite their reputation, toads most often can be made to bring good fortune rather than bad.

If you hold a live one in your hand until it dies, that makes a cure for fever.

If you put a dead one under your bed, it protects you from the peste.

The crapal stone, which forms in the brow of a certain type, will sweat when it senses poison nearby. You or your mage must dig it out after death and cure it in manure for forty days before using it.

If you take the heart and left feet of this or any other toad and place them on a sleeping person's mouth, that person will answer truthfully to any question you ask.

There is a recipe that some midwives know: If you mix the fat of a strangled child with the venom from a toad, then apply the unguent you get to one of your enemies, your enemy will writhe in agony until dead.

Toads are also the signs of adultery.

GODFRIDUS
So this is the inferno. Yes, where heat beats with heavy sticks, and damned souls career through my own. Where I close my eyes and see a flower in russet down. On fire.

My heart is like wax, melting . . . I am a voice crying out in the wilderness.

You are simply sleeping—*I throw back the blanket and tell this to myself. It's only the fever from your hand. And that will go away. This is not the moment for death or damnation; you are not that fortunate.* You have not finished.

I feel a beating in my hand, as if something wants to get out. Beyond the windows, the screaming grows. My feet stumble from the bed, my good hand tears the door open—

Give me peace!

HE LONG NIGHT BRIMS OVER WITH SOUNDS
of fire and war. We sleep fitfully, and Hercule
groans in his dreams; but I can barely spare a
thought for him or the struggles without.

I am thinking of other bodies, other lips.
I lie awake burning; even my breath is a
flame. It's as if the fire has left the walls and
leapt inside me.

By matins, word below is that the fire is
out and the mining has been stopped. Men
flock by in proud, satisfied droves, rubbing
their backs and belaboring, with little smiles,
the feats and pains of last night's battle. I am
starving.

The bakery downstairs opens late. After a
night on the ramparts, the wife has baked the
bread by herself, without help from her husband. Today he is gathering news instead of
flour, and she's queen of gossip and loaves.
When I go down for our allotment, I have to
wait in a long line.

"Are the attackers gone, then?" I ask when
it's finally my turn.

"Not yet," the woman says darkly. She's
counting some coins in one palm, adding them
up before dropping them one by one into the

pocket at her girdle. She seems reluctant to surrender my bread; business is good this morning.

"But the fighting has stopped," I say, reaching for a loaf.

"Those English." She blocks my hand with hers, sweeping some crumbs into a little pile on the counter. "They're treating us to a siege."

When I don't respond right away, the woman behind me cuts in, "They think Villeneuve is the richest city in all France, and they want us to pay a tribute. They're trying to make us ransom ourselves off! My husband says they want twelve thousand livres, but old Richard next door says twenty-five. Whatever the price, the town fathers won't pay it—they think we can last out a year, even more, and the mercenaries will go long before that."

I ponder this news, wondering what it will mean to my own life. Radegonde's agents won't be able to get through, and there'll be no hunting—no summer venison coming from her big house to my little domus, unless the siege lifts. This was something I'd been looking forward to.

"They're camped by the west gate?" I ask.

"They're all around the city," says the bakerwoman. "More of them came during the night, it seems. *My* husband thinks there's no escaping now—not, that is, until they get tired of sieging." She sighs, rubbing her thin hands together as if to warm them. "That's what they're all counting on, the men. But who knows? Maybe the English will like it here. Maybe they'll last longer than any of us think—they're a sluggish people, and they don't get bored easily."

"Let's hope you're wrong."

"Let us pray," she corrects me.

"Of course." I pick up a loaf from the counter, my fair share. "Well, thank you for this." I stop, weigh the bread in my hand. "*Pardon*. It feels lighter than usual."

Her lips press together. "I'm making some adjustments," she tells me. "I have to—we have no telling when grain will pass through the town gates again. The town fathers may even stop fixing prices and weights."

I tuck the airy bread beneath my arm. "This siege appears to be a lucky thing for you," I observe to the bakerwoman. "You can charge whatever you like."

Behind the counter, she draws her loaves together protectively. "We have to conserve food," she insists. "And people are asking for more than ever . . ."

I go upstairs.

IT OCCURS TO ME that Marie must be frightened about what happened last night. She has no way of knowing exactly what took place, and the noise and smoke must have wound even into her tiny cell. So although this is not my usual day to see her, I pack up a basket with food for her as well as Godfridus, throw on my mantle, and take the dwarf by the hand.

It is exciting, walking through the besieged streets. Hercule dances at my side. People are everywhere and they are filthy, but full of energy and a kind of light. They tell their stories to one another and almost forget to frown as Bonne Tardieu passes. We are having a holiday. A priest I don't know tries to herd people into a church, to pray for fortitude and eventual deliverance, but there is no interest.

I am approached by a man I don't know. He says my name and asks if I'll join a committee to stand on the city walls and fling rocks at the English.

I have learned from Radegonde how to dismiss unwelcome petitioners. "Blessed earlobes," I say. "You may save your strength."

He scowls and turns to Hercule, bends down. "How about you, my boy?"

The dwarf shrinks farther back into his hood.

"This boy is in my charge," I say. "He won't be wasting his time, either."

The committee man straightens slowly up again, settling his belt. "You'll sing a different song when you see his legs bow for lack of food."

"Tossing down a few pebbles is a waste of time and won't feed anybody," I say. "You'll only expose yourselves to English arrows." And I drag Hercule away with me.

The dwarf laughs, skipping gleefully. The siege, mild adventure as it is, has got him excited. "They really think there's something to be afraid of!" he scoffs. "Why, when Sieur Robert's castle was under siege, we dispatched the attackers in three days. We blinded them with quicklime, and when they got the runs from eating a rotten hart we left outside the walls—we pretended they'd arrived in the middle of a hunt—we mixed soft soap with bits of iron and dropped the lot from the walls, so they slipped about and couldn't go anywhere. We picked them off like flies. It was great fun."

"Two townsmen were wounded last night," I remind him. "One was brained when a neighbor swung back with his hammer—"

"—and the wife of another man poked his eye out when he came home to bed. She thought he was an English devil coming to rape her," Hercule concludes. "The fools. Fools!" He prances.

"Hercule Legrand," I say, jerking him out of a cartwheel. "If you are going to be a child, then you have to act like one, at least in public. Your playing is too practiced."

He chews his lip. He is for all the world a child . . . with a thin wisp of a mouth, not a plump red pillow of one. I think about lips until the silence of Marie's district closes around us.

Here ashes are still falling from the sky. They land against my mantle and dissolve like faint white kisses. Hercule swats them away from his face and complains. The mist curls up our legs, twining into my skirts. Meanwhile Marie's voice winds through the budding trees: "Fan the flames of April's fire, in June you'll find your heart's desire . . ."

ONCE WE'VE GIVEN Marie her food and news—greeted, as always, with silence and a hard grab at the offerings—Godfridus is our next errand. My basket still holds half the morning's bread, a little flask of Radegonde's wine, and a few expensive honey cakes wrapped up in a clean cloth. Hercule trots grudgingly at my heels, but he accepts his punishment with surprising grace. Perhaps I will give him a honey cake.

We find Godfridus's landlord, the bibulous cobbler, sprawled in front of his shop door, asleep and drooling. We step over him and climb the alley stairs. There's no need to knock on Godfridus's door; it's off the latch, swaying slightly on its leather hinges. I notice the keyhole has fallen out.

When we get inside, I don't see Godfridus at first, only the dust and broken bulk of a dozen clay heads. A damp sheet lies draped over his buckets of clay; I see no sheet on his bed, only a pair of patched brown blankets covering what could be more wet clay or rejected statuary. But this bulge, it turns out, is my friend; he has pulled the blankets over his head. When I ease them away, I find his forehead moist and sticky with a fevered sweat.

"He is sick, after all," Hercule says in a whisper, almost awed. He clasps his hands in front of himself.

A blue eye peers out between sandy lashes. "Bonne," Godfridus croaks. "You did come."

For a moment I can't do more than nod. "I didn't know you had it so badly . . . I should have been here last night."

"You came," he says again. His lips are cracked.

"Are you in pain, stoneman?" Hercule asks.

"Go play in a corner," I snap at him, glad to have someone besides myself to be angry with. I turn back to the wounded man and soften my voice. "Godfridus, show me your hand."

With effort he pulls his left hand out of the blankets and lays it in my lap. It's up to me to pick the thing up, unwrap the dirty bandage, and examine the wound.

One entire half of the hand itself is puffy and red, and Godfridus catches his breath when I touch it. His thumb is three times its usual size; six knotted black stitches at the base are holding back a seam that's ready to burst. Virgini gratias, it's covered in a healing crust.

Hercule pushes a chair around from window to window and climbs on it, throwing open the shutters. "A little fresh air will cure you, stoneman," he says. "You know what I was saying as we came over here, I was saying——"

"Be quiet, Hercule. And leave the windows alone—you should know how dangerous cool air is to a sweating man." I hop up on Godfridus's bed and lift his eyelids, stare into the orbs underneath. Large pupils, bright irises. "How long have you had this fever?"

"Since nightfall," says Godfridus. His eyes search my face, trying to find words. I know what he will say, and he says it: "I'm going to lose my hand," in a low voice, for my ears alone. "And probably I will die."

I think, now, I can sense death on him. It's leaking into the hole in his hand, creeping through the rest of him. I smell it.

139

But—"Don't be silly," I whisper back nonetheless. "You're going to be fine—you'll have a long, productive life."

Hercule hears the whispers, pushes his chair to the bedside, and climbs up, staring curiously at the swollen hand. He looks as if he'd like to prod it. "You know about the siege, don't you?" he asks. "Last night it was all hands to the rescue."

If he were really a child, I'd smack him. Since he's a grown man, I send him away. "Hercule, I have an errand for you. We need an ointment for this hand, and you will buy it."

"Where do you think I'll get it? The city gates are shut and all the shops are closed."

I give his hood a sharp tweak and pull it over his face. "You should know—the district of shadows. Go down the narrowest street in town and look for a door carved with a half-moon and two stars. The man's name is Macchabeus; he's a Jew."

Godfridus stirs and starts to protest—something about Jews.

"Macchabé is the best surgeon in town," I say, and turn from Godfridus to reach my most private purse out of my dress. I give Hercule a coin. "Use this. Tell him you've come for a sculptor whose hand is septic. He'll know what's best to give you."

Hercule takes the coin sulkily. "What if somebody sees I'm not a little boy?"

"They won't see, and if they do, they won't care. It's the district of shadows," I say, and push him off the stool.

HERCULE

You are the son of man, not of god, though you live like that Christ who begged pity of fallen women. Both so fond of your wounds.

But since I must, I trudge through the streets on your errand. A left at l'Eglise Saint-Porchaire, then down the narrowest street I can find in a place I have seldom been. The buildings close in overhead and cut off the sun.

I won't take any longer than I have to.

Jews, midwives, fillettes de joie—citizens of the shadows. They stare as I pass, round eyes following me through the stinking murk.

"Looking for Macchabeus," I say in my little-boy voice. Silently an old Jewess, her head in a shroud, points the way.

Now I stand in front of a wooden door that sags in its frame. Its pair of four-pointed stars and sliver of moon look tired, as if the shadows have sucked away their painted light. I knock, and around the edge of door a pair of dark eyes peer from a wrinkly nest, rimmed in a wisp of wimple gone gray. The eyes blink and the head nods at me.

"Ancient Macchabé," I cry, not without a glimmer of pleasure, "have you grown so old you're ending your life as a woman, though your name ends like a man's?"

In reply the creature drags the door open, letting it scrape on the floor planks, and motions me to come inside.

Maybe she doesn't understand. I will refine myself. "Has age unsexed you," I ask, "so your club has shrunk inside, leaving you man in name only?"

She has started up a set of dark and narrow stairs. She turns around and motions to me again.

"An old man's root loses hair," I call up to her. "An old woman's face takes root with it."

When she still doesn't answer, I trudge upward, pushing myself along the walls. Maybe I can think of another joke. Or maybe another try will show me to be nervous.

Bonne is right—I'm too foolish to make a good fool.

The old person leads me into a small chamber, its walls so crumbled that I can see the horsehair holding them together beneath the plaster. A few bunches of dried herbs hang from the ceiling, and in one corner sit a very few earthenware jars, their mouths smeary with grease.

A little man with blue eyes and black hair, balding, sits wrapped in a blanket by a window. His head nods to a tiny rhythm, as if he's agreeing with the silence of the street. The crone gestures at him and at me. He gives his head a deeper nod, and she goes to sit by an empty brazier.

I stand with my hands on my hips. "Are you Macchabeus?"

He answers with a question. "What do you want with a wizard?"

"I'm sure many men were hurt yesterday," Godfridus says humbly, as I pour wine over his brow to wash it.

"That doesn't make their pain any greater than yours." I dab carefully around his eyes. I had to tear my shift for the cloth to do this, as everything Godfridus owns is impregnated with earth and stone. When I rinse the cloth, the dust from his skin tinkles against the washbasin and collects at the bottom like a red clot.

Once I'm done soothing his brow, I put the basin down and settle back next to Godfridus. The fever has made him drowsy, but his eyes are still anxious, so I pull his head into my lap and start rubbing it with the long, careful strokes I learned as a nitpicker. At the first touch, I feel him sigh. I chase a louse through his hair and trap, pluck, and crush it between my nails.

"I'm not afraid to die, you know," says Godfridus. "But I am sorry."

"You won't die." I pretend quickly to dig after another louse. "You've only had the fever half a day. It will break."

"I'm sorry to die," he ruminates, looking over at his collection of broken heads. "I wanted to—to give something . . . to Villeneuve, to God. To you."

I hug his head to my chest, where he's suckled from me so often. "You've already given us so much. Your friendship to me. Your work to the new church."

I see another louse then; it slides off Godfridus's head and disappears into my bodice, tickling its way down.

"Acanthus leaves and flat blossoms," he says almost bitterly; then, on a wistful note, "My Virgin was to have been a masterpiece."

"And she will be," I promise, refusing to follow his eyes back to the broken heads. So he has been making a Virgin—perhaps I should have known. I turn his own, living head to face me, and again I start furrowing into the thin red locks with my fingers. His eyes are turned upward but they don't see me.

"The best work I've ever done," says Godfridus, "was that sarcophagus for Henri Putemonnoie." He sighs. "Perhaps I should have carved my own . . . Have you seen it?"

"Not yet."

"Ah."

I pick out a flea, but it wiggles through my fingers. "She's told me there's a special room for it near the house chapel," I say. "So she must think highly of your work. As will all of Villeneuve, once the sarcophagus is installed in the Putemonnoie chapel at the new church."

Godfridus does not seem convinced. Maybe he thinks the chapel will never be built—that Radegonde will not produce an heir. Or maybe the fever is simply pulling him away. I'm conscious that he might fall asleep at any moment, or Hercule might come back. So I speak perhaps unwisely, asking a question that has been much in my mind.

"Were you ever—did you fall in love with her?" I blurt out.

Godfridus takes a moment to respond. "With who?" He has already forgotten our last words.

"With *her*. Radegonde Putemonnoie." I bury all ten fingers in his hair at once. "She was your patronne, and she is—I imagine she would be fascinating. Irresistible."

"Fascination should be for God," he tells me, eyes half-closed. "And to seduce a pious woman is doubly a sin."

"But if *you* didn't seduce her—if she came to you?"

"She would never come to a poor sculptor."

I find I'm pressing hard on his skull; I ease my grip. The man is ill, after all. "Did you want to—" I begin softly, then can't finish.

He doesn't speak right away, but finally, as if from great distance, he asks, "You mean, exchange solaces with her?"

"Yes." My palms, sweaty now, stroke his brow. "And the rest of it."

Very faint: "A sin."

"But a sin of love," I say, resting my fingertips on his eyelids. I know there will be no further answer. I address the dusty room. "Doesn't that count for something?"

HERCULE

My heart's in my throat. "I've looked all over France for a wizard."

"Then rejoice." His hand creeps from the blanket and hovers expectantly; gladly I lay Bonne's silver coin in it, as if to seal a bargain whose terms we've yet to name.

Macchabeus, the mage, appears satisfied. "You have a question, my man?"

So he knows—I'm man, not child. This gives me faith, though as my eyes dance from greasy jar to dried-stick bundle, the room does not brim with promise.

I will start with something small, what I came for. "I need a poultice. For a wound."

"What sort of wound?"

"A—" I hesitate. The blue eyes stare at me shrewdly—is he really a Jew? Can he be as old as he looks? "What difference does it make?"

In any event, he seems the man I came for. His knowledge is extensive. He tells me, "The preparation has to suit the balance of humors in each part of the body. A puncture in the stomach is different from a bruise in the head, and a thorn in the foot is different from a boil on the groin. A gash to the—"

"Let me tell you what I need," I interrupt.

I tell him—a sculptor, a cut . . . I say what I want. And he takes charge, sitting there in his blanket, directing the woman to fill a small clay pot with a smear of ointment here, a dab of unguent there, a pinch or two of the hanging herbs. She stoppers the jar and gives it to me.

The man resumes his shivering nod. "First salve the wound with this unguent, then make a bandage with egg white and rosewater. Bind it tightly." His hand is once more outside the blanket, stretched toward me.

"That should work. If it doesn't, come back to me."

I dig in a pocket for more silver—a bit of my own, for luck—toss it onto the cracked palm, and go on my way rejoicing.

GODFRIDUS

How curious: We have no record of what it is to sleep.

Black. Heavy. Still. Hot.

This is all I know of my sleep.

But am I asleep? What questions can a sleeping man ask? And remembering a dream is not the same as remembering the sleep.

Or death. The longest sleep. When do we know we are dead? Only when experiencing it. Only as we feel the rotten flesh slip away from our bones. Only as we wait for the trumpet call of the Last Day, to go before the One who never sleeps and humble ourselves, beg for mercy.

At what moment did Christ's spirit leave His flesh? Did He think He had fallen asleep?

A hand on my hand—dry, gentle, scratchy-skinned. Cool. Half-

remembered sounds of words. The smells of wine and milk and blood. Communion.

> *In the blood of Adam death was maken,*
> *In the blood of Christ were all up-taken,*
> *And by that blood I do thee charge—*
> *Let thou run no more at large.*

Whose voice is this? An angel's? Or my own?
> *The sleep is pulling me downward.*
> *My hand, greasy and wet. The feel of corruption ... and sleep.*

The Jewish poultice brings an instant change in Godfridus. He quiets down, sinks with a sigh into what I believe will be a restful sleep.

A moment ago, he was agitated to hear Hercule chanting—a charm he says will soothe and save the blood. Though it's usually an ill omen when a patient protests his cure, in this case I choose to see a good sign: Godfridus is still well enough to hate the dwarf.

"How did you know about Macchabeus?" Hercule asks as I set about tidying Godfridus's studio.

I pull a few more threads from my chemise and use them to tie some rushes into a broom; Godfridus doesn't have one. "He was good to my mother in the old days. He was interested in her case, and when she needed medicines he gave them to her, sometimes free of charge. He also helped her teach me to read."

"Ah." Hercule says nothing more. He seems to be hugging some delightful secret to himself; even his breathing is a prance as he looks first at me, then at sleeping Godfridus, then at me again.

I go to work first on the floor around the broken heads, stacking the pieces tidily (like the bones in the atrium) as I sweep.

"Macchabé seems very skilled in his art," Hercule allows.

I almost drop the broom. The Jew has a certain reputation, largely unfounded but still dangerous to those who traffic with him—can Hercule have found out so soon? "Macchabeus is a wise man," I say, sweeping to hide the shaking in my hands. "But remember he is an infidel, and Christians are forbidden to consort with him. We must be very careful, even when only buying simple medicines."

Hercule hops up on the chair and crows. "I was raised in an abbey and found in a church," he says, "but what makes you think I'm Christian?"

As if to reinforce (or sound a counterpoint to) his words, the bells of the new church—old Anne, Aliénore, and Blanche—begin to ring. Noontime, dinnertime. My breasts feel the pulse of milk. I lay down my broom.

"I hope you're Christian enough to look after Godfridus while I'm gone," I say.

His face is a mix of glee and mischief. "Where are you going?"

"It's time for my visit to the Putemonnoie house," I say, straightening my dress and wishing I'd thought to bring the nice surcoat with me. Today of all days I'll have to go without it. "I'll see if Mistress Putemonnoie has any advice about this wound."

Hercule looks scornful. "What can she tell you? Her only magic is in her face."

"A good Christian doesn't need magic—a good Christian prays," I remind him, saying a little prayer inside my own mind. I nod at the basket. "You can get your dinner from there. And stay out of the district of shadows from now on."

THE BAKERWOMAN

How the heart beats with the first rush of blood! The blood that once marked weakness but in these days shows a woman's strength, what others might feed on. I am hot with this blood, my face is red and my breasts are hard with it. I hold it tight between my thighs, steeping cloths like bread in wine. For our blood is our salvation.

When the people rush my counter, I shove them loaves like stones. Take this and fight the devils!

Radegonde Putemonnoie does not wish to see me.

My dinner is waiting in the scullery, as always, but she has left instructions that she's not to be disturbed. Even by me; the kitchen girl confirms it when I ask. So I sit alone, too warm, and tear into the chicken with my fingers. At least one Villeneuvian is not hoarding food.

Eventually there comes a stir in the courtyard. It seems there is to be a special service at Saint-Grégoire, the parish church, and the mistress will attend. She also plans to make a special donation.

"Fetch the mistress's veil!" I hear Agnès shrill. She must enjoy commanding around the servants of lower rank. I imagine she is the one who orders the gate shut and locked behind them, as she bears the mistress away.

I gulp my last mouthfuls and then I, too, go to Saint-Grégoire, where the tympanum's Last Judgment is a sober reminder of sin's wages. If we do not die in the siege, we will die some other way, and then where will we be?

The nave is crowded with rich people in Sunday-style finery, as if the force of their gold and jewels will turn the English away. I hide in the shadows of the north transept. This is where I see her, without her seeing me: She stands in the nave with her head raised toward the roof, praying. A string of black beads is wound through her fingers and her lips move to holy formulae, kissing her prayers out.

In my whole body my heart is pounding, from my temples to the cleft between my legs.

Did she kiss me yesterday, or did I kiss her? I can't tell now, know only that it was anything but a kiss of peace. And yet the mistress herself appears tranquil, as if that burning, sighing kiss never happened.

Her lips continue to move as young Father Michel delivers his sermon; she is delivering her own words up to God, disdaining the priest's. None of the other merchants and servants can follow his Latin, and they do not try. Instead they gaze around themselves at their wealthy church's ornaments, Christs and Marys and demons serene behind wavering veils of incense, their colors clouded by faint bands from the windows. With her prayer over, I watch Radegonde's face settle into just such a stone mask: mouth a closed curve, nose a still line, eyes two lashed arcs turning toward her own hands, where the beads glisten like black tears.

HE WEEK THAT FOLLOWS IS OF CONSTANT worry. What is my future? Godfridus gets steadily sicker, though he is sometimes lucid through his fever. But Radegonde Putemonnoie still refuses me entry to her rooms, so I can't beg her for help . . . if indeed she has any to give. And if she doesn't want me to read to her, she won't want me to suckle her child. I worry about this as I tend my false uncle, as I hush Hercule in his playing, as I collect the dinners that are still cooked for me. I become more and more certain she is going to abandon me, and I wonder if I will find a new employer. Who would want me now that I've been so publicly picked up and then dropped by la Putemonnoie? It is five—six—seven days since the kiss, and I have all but given up hope.

Then at last there is word in the kitchen: She will see me. More than will—she commands it. And it is Saint Expeditus's day, good for settling protracted negotiations. I fly up the many-sided steeple to the tower room.

Radegonde has been watching the siege. Her face is turned toward the distant ramparts, her widow's veil fluttering in the breeze from the window. When she hears me come in, she holds out a hand behind her in absentminded greeting and says there is little to see, just the English drinking their wine and gorging on animals from our forest; but the quiet activity has suited her for today. Then she sniffs, wrinkles her nose, and looks at me sideways.

"You smell like death."

Death—I see the bones in the atrium sliding damp against one another.

"Mistress," I say then, humbly and as if my lips have never touched hers, "the sculptor—my uncle—has been wounded. A cut to the hand that has corrupted his flesh." I wonder if this news will pique la Putemonnoie's interest, if it will make her kind.

It does make her turn from the window. In the movement her veil is blown aside, revealing the jewels in her hair; they are all yellow and green today, like the eyes she turns on me. "Has a surgeon seen your uncle?"

I tear my eyes away from her. "He had one to sew him up, but I don't think the man did it well. I've treated the wound with an ointment from the district of shadows."

"A cut to the hand," she muses, looking out the window at distances I don't want to contemplate. "Corrupted, an ointment . . ." She appears to be lost in thought. I know she has heard my unspoken plea. I also know now that we will not speak of or repeat the kiss.

While she thinks, she lifts a wisp of hair from my neck and makes it squeak in her fingers. "Bonne," she says, "what if you were to have a proper bath?"

I'm confused. "But what about—"

She inclines her head, like a lady bestowing favor on her knight. "Oh, I'll help your uncle." Her veil finally detaches itself and floats to the floor. "He'll have everything he needs—but you have to give me time to prepare. Come, let's have a bath."

Within a few moments, I'm sitting in a tub of steaming water, wooden slats against my back, flower petals and drops of oil skimming along the surface and licking at my breasts. My belly sags in the water like a big white pudding.

Radegonde Putemonnoie sits across from me, in the same tub. We are sharing the bath. I've heard this is the custom among rich people, but I never thought it would apply to myself. Maybe she thinks, as some women do, that bathing with a wet nurse will help ensure the health of her unborn baby. I know only that I do not know where to look.

Her body is as different from mine as it can be. My mother, Blanche Mirabilis, was wrong about one thing—nudity does not show every class of person to be the same. I'm conscious of every little vein and bruise and scar on my body, and that viscous belly. La Putemonnoie's naked back is smooth and light brown; her breasts firm and dark-nippled, belly stretched taut and as yet not much bigger than mine; legs sleekly hairless (I've heard rich women sometimes remove the hair there with strips of hot pitch).

Suddenly Radegonde laughs. She has left the jewels in her hair, and they laugh at me also. "Bonne, how you stare! Have you never taken a bath before?" She splashes me with one hand, in play, and tosses her head. I think she is showing me the smooth roundness of her neck.

"I've bathed at the public house," I admit meekly. "Always in a crowd, swimming around—never like this."

Agnès coughs and speaks to Radegonde. "Mistress"—she waves the wad of my clothes under the lady's nose—"what should I do with these?" My dress and chemise, my apron and bandeau, all look too dirty to touch—stiff in the armpits and around the neck, where the seams have turned white with oil and sloughed skin. There is even a grease stain on the overdress, and I just gave it a scrubbing last week.

"Take them outside and beat them," Radegonde orders, without looking at me. "Let them air in the sun."

Agnès gives a superior smirk. She knows I've been a laundress. She goes out, leaving only the little maid called Héloïse in a corner, and I can't look up.

Radegonde's voice interrupts my self-castigation. "Bonne, I've been thinking," she says, handing a sponge to Héloïse, who starts to wash her back, "when we read from now on, I want you to skip the pages of accounts. Find a part that looks like a story, something from Henri's life, and read that to me. It's what I chiefly need from the book."

I notice a louse, dead, floating among the flower petals. "Whatever you like, mistress," I acquiesce. I scrub my hands under the water.

"You see, Bonne, there is knowledge, and there is *knowledge*. The kind that knows how to swaddle a baby or drain the fever out of a man's hand. I suspect we won't find this kind—the kind you and I have, in our different ways—in my husband's book of reason. No, he'll take up pages with society manners and meditations on God and how many angels may dance on a pin. He wanted to go on Crusade, you know."

"You are right," I say, "about practical knowledge. I'm sure you're very wise about medicine and housekeeping and—other matters."

Radegonde Putemonnoie sighs and stretches, easing herself down farther in the tub. Her long bony toes nibble at my hip. "Yes, medicine . . . I'll see your uncle tomorrow," she says. "Tonight I will gather some baby herbs and other curatives in my garden. They have to age in the moonlight."

I shiver. I think I don't want to know more about this—her occult secrets—I don't want to learn anything I'll have to report to the priests. But then she winks at me, and I wonder if perhaps she was making a joke.

From Henri Putemonnoie's livre de raison

In the year of the great cinnamon harvest, I arranged to wed a young girl not yet nineteen, of good family, in a town two leagues away from Bourdon, where I had some warehouses. I had had some dealing with the father, and he was well pleased to see me wed his daughter. Our betrothal lasted one year, during which time five of my ships arrived from the East with melons, rice, lemons, and artichokes, and the seeds for a herb called spinach, which has since been cultivated in France with great profit to myself. I put aside the best portions of these exotic fruits for the wedding feast.

We were married before the church of Saint-Hilaire, in that precinct of Bourdon where I presently lived. Unto her I promised, as thousands have promised in centuries past: "I take thee, Radegonde, to my wedded wife, to have and to hold, from this day forward, for better, for worse, for richer, for poorer, in sickness and in health, till death us depart, if holy Church it will ordain, and thereto I plight thee my troth." And she promised me likewise. Upon which the priest blessed our rings and we did give them to each other, vowing, "With this ring I thee wed, and with my body I thee honor." And so moved into the church for Mass, with wax tapers and finest-quality incense, which I paid for.

In dowry she brought me three hundred livres of silver, plus a trousseau worth one hundred livres, with some silver plate, two golden serving platters, and linens for a large bed. In return I dowered her two hundred livres, and one-fourth of my wealth to be set to her use during her lifetime, with one hundred livres to be paid as a gift on the birth of each son, and fifty livres at the birth of each daughter. Her father was so pleasured by this arrangement that he then promised me, additionally, a fine bowl, twenty-four inches across, of Italian glass in a color of my choosing, and his black mare for my stable.

I was pleased with her beauty, her docility, and her fulfillment of the marriage debt.

"WHERE IS BOURDON?" I have to ask.

She mumbles vaguely. "Bourdon?" But I hear her sigh and breathe deep, and I know she's already dreaming.

I sit on a hard chest beside the bed, listening to the spring insects and visioning: a golden day, a blue dress for constancy . . . Touch blue, your wish will come true—who could stand next to Radegonde Putemonnoie as husband and not feel every wish had been granted? The legal words of love. Then, above it all, the Christ of the church tympanum: feet on the heads of the sinners, one hand summoning the virtuous to heaven.

HERCULE

Change, fester, smart, burn! Your whole body's a boil now. My ointment is working, though another will come tomorrow and take its greasy place.

So time is precious for me, a torment for you. Die painful, stoneman— but hurry up and do it before morning.

I knit these prayers into clothes as others sleep. As others dream of others, not of me. I need no sleep now—I have trust and means and magic. This is my first task, but I have many desires.

N THE MORNING, GODFRIDUS'S STUDIO IS close and fetid, a hot box smelling of decay. La Putemonnoie and I arrive together. She insists on it, and wants no other servants—in fact no one knows she has left her great house; we slipped out through a door hidden beneath the honeysuckle, and she wore a plain dark cloak.

My soi-disant uncle is lying limp on his bed, nakedness barely covered, and he sleeps through our arrival. Radegonde goes straight to him, not noticing the crumbling broken heads or Hercule rolled into a ball at the bottom of the bed.

"So there you are!" Hercule shouts, uncurling himself. He glares as if I have done something wrong. He looks rumpled and worn out, as if he's been here long; and I feel a twinge that he should be more devoted to Godfridus's care than I.

"The sun's barely up," I say weakly.

Yet Radegonde, too, has told me she's been awake for hours. I imagine that sometime in the dark of night she got out of bed and dressed herself, without a maid; then she went outside. This is when she harvested her special herbs, and she spent the rest of the night boiling and crushing and mixing. Her unguent did cook in the moonlight, and the process of scraping it into a jar has delayed us. We also had to assemble—as a secret from the servants—a collection of bottles, jars, and basins.

"How is the patient?" she asks briskly now, leaning over and feeling the heat of his brow.

"Still sleeping," the dwarf states the obvious. "The Jew's medicine gives him peace."

But even I can see this isn't the case. Godfridus's color is ashy gray, and his breathing rasps as in the last stage of fever. I don't like to imagine what will be next.

Radegonde is unperturbed. She reaches into her sleeve and pulls out a linen square, which she holds to her nose while she considers the case. A faint wisp of perfume cuts through the sickroom air and is gone.

"Unwrap the hand for me," she says, her voice coming muffled through the cloth.

I take the hand delicately, though it's clear Godfridus is beyond feeling pain. Gingerly I unwrap it, length after length of sticky cloth. Hercule stares sedulously out the window.

The whole hand and much of the wrist is red and yellow and puffy now, though I still can't see any dangerous green . . . yet. I hold it up for Radegonde's inspection, turning hopeful eyes to her.

"Have you been washing the wound?" she asks.

"Of course not! Yesterday I washed around it, but I left the wound alone. See, it's made the healing crust," I say—though my stomach does turn when I see the stitches all but obscured by hard yellow blood.

Radegonde sighs and tucks the linen square back into her sleeve. "Every wound must be washed," she says; "you've learned it wrong, like most people. Pour this vinegar into the basin we brought, and bring me a knife."

She uses the knife blade to scrape away the scab; then with the point she plucks out the stitches one by one. The hand bursts open and oozes out its contents.

Hercule coughs.

But now Radegonde seems to notice neither the smell nor the ugliness. Her face is intent, her pillowy mouth drawn into a smooth line. She asks for mint leaves from her bag. When I hand them to her, she chews them—a pleasant aroma—then spits them out into an empty basin and puts her mouth to the wound.

She sucks.

La Putemonnoie, sucking out a festered sore! As I watch her my head swims, my knees tremble. I've heard only of saints doing this; it is not recommended for ordinary people. I never saw even Blanche do it, and I don't think I could. It could kill a person. But I tell myself that Radegonde knows what's best, for Godfridus and for herself. She will set everything right.

The sucking fills her cheeks and makes Godfridus's hand small. When finished she spits into the basin again and tucks another mint leaf into her mouth. Then she dips a wad of flax into a vinegar jar and blots it on the wound. Godfridus begins to bleed, scarlet blood mixing with bitter wine.

"You see this?" she says to me, discarding that flax and motioning me to get her a fresh wad. "A good sign. The hand is washing itself."

Through all of it, Godfridus has not moved. Hercule, however, now grabs the chamberpot from under the bed and climbs on the chair by the window; with a shout of "Garde-l'eau!" he empties it in the street below. There comes a cry of protest.

Radegonde chooses to ignore the dwarf's pointless antics. She continues to swab out Godfridus's hand until the bleeding all but stops again; then she applies the ointment that she herself made, takes up needle and thread, and sews a tidy seam around the base of the thumb. Lastly she applies a green herb poultice and wraps the hand in linen once again.

"There," she says in satisfaction, tying the linen in a bow. "Now all it needs is changing twice a day; each time, you have to apply more ointment and poultice it on top. He should wake up later today, and he'll be better within a week."

"Will he be able to keep his hand?" I ask, knowing full well that a surgeon would have cut it off today.

"Of course."

"And his life?" asks Hercule.

Radegonde laughs scornfully, not even looking at him. "Certes."

We all look down at Godfridus, silent in his fever dreams. It is too soon to look for much change, but we all know. He is saved. Radegonde poises to step away.

"Is there anything else we should do?" I ask, holding her there.

"Well," she says, "if you like, I'll send him a ruby."

"A ruby!" Hercule repeats. He sounds excited at last.

"Yes." She begins tidying up the bedside herself, stoppering the jars of unguent and poultice. "They're said to cure infection and feed the blood. You can put mine under his tongue and have him suck on it."

The dwarf growls. "I can think of better uses for a ruby."

Now Radegonde looks at me. "This ointment you got from the district of shadows," she says, "I'd like to see it."

I have to look to Hercule. "Well? Where is it?"

"In the street below," he says serenely. "When you put the new one on him, I threw the old one out with the chamberpot. To avoid confusion."

"Thank you," I say, uncertain. My gratitude is more sure when I turn to my mistress—"Thank you," I say again, and I kiss the hands that sewed a seam as lovely as an embroidered border. "You may have saved my uncle's life."

"I have saved it," she says, and she pulls the cord on her bag tight. "It was only a thumb, after all—not a palm or a wrist. And now you and I will go home."

FEAST OF SAINT OPPORTUNA

Y GRATITUDE, MY FAITH, HAVE BEEN WELL placed. Radegonde Putemonnoie! The fever turns, the hand shrinks, Godfridus is better in two days. Not perfect, of course; it will take a while for his body to knit itself together again, and he is very tired. He sits up in bed and sucks on the promised ruby, gazing emptily out the windows, waiting. In the mornings, I sit beside him and stitch at practical linens for Radegonde's baby, eager to repay her for all she has done.

A ruby . . . I don't think it's the stone that has worked this miracle, but I am glad to see it. A merchant doesn't give a ruby where she expects no further business.

In the afternoons, I become an intimate of the great house. I am with Radegonde Putemonnoie almost every moment from sext until vespers—this is how my life has changed, how her favor to me and my old friend has brought about a new closeness between us, a new interest from her in me. And I am so grateful. Grateful to have become one note in a song, one page in a book, one petal around a glowing, fragrant center . . . My head is full of the sound and smell of my mistress, roses and musk and unnamed exotic spices.

Hercule glowers. I think he wants a ruby for himself—or at least he wants my attention. But his stories have dried up, and I'm tired of his tricks. Why should I watch him juggle when I can watch her work?

If I ever thought Radegonde lived a life of idle luxury, I know now I was wrong. Luxury requires work, from her as from others. The furs must be brushed, the pillows fluffed, the gold and silver and copper polished into gloss. And several times in the day, out come little clay pots and glass bottles of unguent, syrup, and powder—all for her personal use, because the magic of beauty's a science, and she is almost forty. There's a special order to the application of these concoctions: Her face must be massaged with the fingertips, the cord of each muscle stroked just so. There's a different way of rubbing for each bottle, a different fragrance and a different healing property. Her body also has to be rubbed, naked, with a special oil, until it's sleek and gleaming; there must be no burst veins or bulges of fat on my mistress's limbs. Agnès takes care of this.

Then there's her hair. The brushing, the combing, the hunting for lice; this I do, before someone else begins the braiding and coiling and pinning. I'm getting used to catching glimpses of my hands and even my face in a mirror, as Radegonde sits in front of it observing my work.

There is something about these looking glasses that keeps surprising me: If I raise my right hand, in the glass it looks as if I'm raising my left. Of course this is the way I've always known a reflection to work, showing movement in reverse; but earlier, there was always a film of water or a ripple in the metal to explain this change. To me it is astonishing that the man (or woman) who ingeniously married silver to glass could not also find a way to make the machine show a face truly. It is strange and almost troubling that even la Putemonnoie doesn't have enough money to see herself straight on, as others see her.

When Radegonde is finished with her regimen, if the afternoon is fine, we might take a promenade through her burgeoning gardens. We stop often, to smell a delicately scented bud or appreciate the music of a fountain. Our lips are red, our heads are a-spin with sensation. Her black velvets drink the light. Afterward we might sit in the sun, and Radegonde will have the livre de raison fetched for me while she works her broderie: stitching flowers and birds into her Garden of Earthly Delights or, more often these days, onto a dainty linen strip (the dull work of hemming already done by her washwoman). These strips are trims for the bodice of a christening gown, or sheets to fit the tiny crib of a newborn, even napkins to swathe its bottom. It's a shame to think what will happen to her delicate work—all the myriad body fluids and excretions that will sink and crust into the delicate folds. She seems never quite to believe that this is indeed the fate of every one of those linen strips. Perhaps she thinks her work will somehow ennoble both the objects and the filth that will stain them, as she ennobled my uncle's wound by sucking it dry.

Throughout the afternoon the mistress, like any pregnant woman, has to answer the call of nature many times. Usually she visits one of the indoor latrines (where I myself have now enjoyed the privilege of sitting, not squatting, and simply letting my waste disappear); but if she's feeling languid she has me lower her to a chamberpot by the bed or arbor, and then raise her up again. Each day she becomes heavier, slower, and we take this as a good sign for the heir.

We always end the afternoon in bed. I read while the mistress drifts into sleep. At her insistence I read in the big bed itself, wearing only a thin linen chemise she has cast off. She says my voice is sweetest when it whispers, so I must lie close and read into her ear; but she doesn't want my coarse clothes between her sheets.

I undress to the chemise slowly, shy about disrobing before her. First the belt, then the cotte, then the underdress—slowly over my head. I've learned to drape the garments over a chest or a chair whose legs make the shape of a cross; she likes things tidy. The hem of the chemise comes down midleg, and I'm glad this garment is both light and concealing. I have bought better cloths for my bandeaux, too, though the mistress cannot see them unless she asks to taste the milk. And my hair is always clean, even if I have to barter half my dinner to a peddler for the wash water.

Propped on her soft pillows, Radegonde watches me. I wonder if she knows my movements are always a lie; I want nothing more than to fling myself down beside her in the great downy nest of the bed and begin the reading.

"Your needs will be seen to," she says without provocation.

I am so grateful.

From Henri Putemonnoie's livre de raison

It was in the spring of the year in which I lost 30 sheep to murrain and brought home my first cargo of Asian silk that I first laid eyes on my wife, at a feast in the house of her father, favorite jeweler of the Pope in Avignon. She was not yet nineteen and dowered with 200 livres and an emerald neck-lace (her father advising me that an emerald dangling on the breast of a childbearing woman would protect the health of her offspring). We met sev-eral times again before the wedding, and I was repeatedly pleased with her, and she with me. That summer two more ships came in from the East, de-livering rich brocade and spices not yet given a name. Unfortunately, some of these seemed to be simply grass, tasteless and useless. Our vows were exchanged on the steps of Saint-Omer, then we processed inside for a Mass under the window donated by the jewelers' guild. Its reds and blues are justly famous. In his palace, the Pope blessed us and wished us many chil-dren; before his eyes I dowered my wife with 150 livres and a good quarter of my wealth. In the morning I also gave her a golden ring enameled with a scene of the Virgin's Presentation at the Temple, and we feasted for three days.

Another version! Was the truth so hard for Henri to pin down?

Radegonde does not comment on this reading. And I know I cannot ask; one question, even now, might mean my dismissal. I must learn to plan, and spy as Pierre has told me to do—but for a different end.

"I would love to see your rings," I say mildly, some days later.

She opens for me a casket full of rings, gleaming gold and silver and ivory, most set with luminous glossy jewels—emeralds, rubies, sapphires, diamonds, topaz, tiger's-eyes, garnets . . .

"And what about the gold ring with the Presentation on it?"

She laughs. "That one? If you can find it, you can have it."

I gaze at her, puzzled. Her beautiful face inscrutable.

"I was going to give you a ring anyway," she says, "when the baby came. Go ahead—pick whatever you like."

I slip them all on, one by one, until my hands are too heavy to lift. But all the rings are too large for me; they slide off my fingers and back into their own pile.

"You are too generous, mistress." Humbly I close the casket, bare-handed. Her laughter rings out like a bell, and she gives me a playful tap on the shoulder.

FEAST OF
SAINTS ANTONINA
AND ALEXANDER
[MAY 3]

GODFRIDUS
So I live. To work and sweat, sin and regret.

I ask for open shutters, and alone at night I count the stars. From my bed I can see ten of them—two are nearly invisible, and one shines brighter than all the rest together. All night I lie caught between their steady burn and the throbbing pulse in my hand. Each night the pulse gets weaker, and my head gets stronger.

I am almost afraid to get well. For weeks the rent is paid for me, food brought to me. I owe a debt of gratitude I'll never be able to pay in full.

One thing I will not accept—mother's milk is not for me now. "My body has been over-indulged," I explain to Bonne's incredulous stare. "I have sinned in pride and luxury. To live like Christ, the body must be reminded of its approaching death, not shown the comforts of an easy life."

"When," she asks, "has life ever been easy?"

Of course there is no answer to that, though in the long, hot hours of siege and sickness, the bustling old life does sometimes seem better than the new. I've thrust la Putemonnoie's ruby deep in my mattress and will give it to the poor, if I find any deserving. I don't deserve it, lying idle but alive. "Tell me about the new church," I say. "Has the work continued?"

"The artists have nothing else to do—so yes. There are some new corbels and a capital or two, and the Chapel of the Dormition's nearly done. The burghers are turning out to watch the work like a Mystery play—they even bring food. It has become our only entertainment."

Every day she washes me, following la Putemonnoie's orders, in a mixture of water and vinegar. My body has wasted away, and the muscles I once had are turning now to gelatin; I feel them quiver as she washes my face and neck, armpits, chest, legs, feet, groin . . .

"Don't worry," she says as she lifts my floppy root and quickly swabs the testicles, "there's no temptation here for me. Is there any for you?"

I can't suppress a wince. "Christ never let Himself be tempted."

"Then why does he have so many brides?"

"Your jokes are about as witty as the dwarf's," I say, and roll over to look at my failed heads.

I insist that the smashed heads remain as they are, a heap of dust and clay shards in a corner. When she tidies the place, she has to work around them.

"Radegonde Putemonnoie says it isn't healthy for a room to have so much dust in it," she tells me, leaning on the handle of a ragged broom. "It clogs the air, it dries out your humors."

But I make her leave them. At night sometimes I light a candle and from my bed I imagine them whole again. All those heads. Once I have them all reassembled in my mind, I turn them around, studying them from every angle. This one's nose was too big, that one's eyes wouldn't focus, this one had a lovely mouth but her chin was a disaster.

Ten broken heads crumble in the corner. Even the clay in the buckets has dried out.

HAT REEDY VOICE IN THE BLUE-GRAY dawn: "Laugh before light, you'll cry before night . . ." But who's laughing here? Certainly not the cell's lonely occupant, nor her only visitor.

I come to Marie in the early hours, holding my nose. These days her cell reeks of spoiled meat and fruit, and the smell gets stronger with each visit I make. Radegonde's provisions are too juicy, too ripe, too well preserved for an ascetic; Marie must be denying them to herself, probably breaking them wastefully on the walls. Anything to get temptation out of her reach.

I am wickedly pleased at this evidence that she's prone to enticement. And I think she is close to giving in—it's either that or, as the days get warmer, find herself swallowed by a rotten compote.

"Maybe one of these days you'll even talk to me outright," I say as I slide her usual bread and cheese, and a few particularly juicy early strawberries, through the window slit. As always, I catch the merest wet gleam of an eye, then her footsteps retreat from me.

"There's a bit of beef in the bread," I call

into the darkness. "Be careful how you handle it—after a few hours, it'll draw flies."

Lucky Marie! Elsewhere, the deprivations of Lent are stretching far beyond their usual span; it seems Villencuve's giddy confidence in storerooms and butteries was misplaced. Suddenly, in the fifth week of the siege, there's no meat at the butchers'—none that any of us recognize—and the only greens most people can get are wispy dandelions and grasses plucked before they're fully rooted.

Worst of all, there's danger of a bread shortage. The bakers have been selling lightened loaves at increased prices. Soon, my landlady has told me, they'll have to close up shop; they won't have wood left for the oven, and there's barely enough flour now to keep her and her husband.

The bakerwoman's eyes gleamed while she told me this, and she planted her skinny hands on her bony hips, where the old apron is now doubled, and told me we're facing hard times indeed. She made the sign of the cross and thanked God for deeming her worthy of adversity, which fattens the soul. It has fattened her bosom too, I think; at least one of her breasts looks larger to me.

I am well fed. I'm well fed, and so is Marie, and Godfridus, and Hercule, and of course Radegonde. No one but Radegonde seems still to have much livestock and staples and gardens—for, naturally, *she* has had the foresight to keep her larders as full-stocked as her warehouses. And these are not her only source of nourishment. Both Radegonde and Hercule are drinking their fill from me every day—she because it's good for pregnant women, he because it eases the pain in his bones. And thanks (I believe) to my good eating—or to God's benevolence—the more I nurse, the more milk I seem to have; sometimes there is so much left that my breasts ache with it. *This* is why the people hate me now: round limbs, strong stride, an overabundance of everything.

The pain in Hercule's bones is so slight that every day now he's out of bed and into mischief, dressed in a child's cotehardie and the hose he knit himself. This morning I notice his knees sticking out beneath the hem.

"Hercule, you're not just getting fat—I believe you've grown!"

Uncomfortably he tugs at the hose; though they fit a month ago, now he can't pull them all the way over his thighs. "I can't be growing," he says nonetheless. "I haven't changed in twelve years."

"You're changing now."

He looks comically worried—at least, comical to me though probably not to him. "I'll eat less."

"Your bones—and your heart—won't get better if you starve yourself."

He looks wildly around the room, clutching his hair in both fists. "Someday I'll have to earn money again. But I don't know how to do anything but be small!"

I hide a smile—foolish dwarf who would prevent his own cure! I give him a quick kiss on the brow and walk out to meet our mutual benefactress.

It is a fine May day, the feast of a woman who avoided rape and got a beheading. Radegonde and I walk through the town, two ladies going to market, with Agnès, the maid, swinging a basket behind. Radegonde has promised this will be a good day to buy little luxuries at bargain prices, since every artisan must be eager for a few sous. We take a winding route, weaving in and out of the streets: saunter past churches, where thinning priests pray with the hungry; stroll past shops where food won't be sold today, or only at a great price. We find the streets as crowded as on any working day, but quieter, less bustling. Now, as the workers go short of supplies, there isn't so much being done; people sit or walk up and down, chatting with one another, bickering out of boredom. They stare glassy-eyed at Radegonde and me.

"Don't duck your head." My mistress manages to make her voice sharp while keeping her face smooth.

"They're watching us." I say it as if it's something for me to be ashamed of.

"They're watching the basket Agnès is carrying. They think there's food inside."

"They hate us. They're angry."

"They have enough to eat," Radegonde says, patting the mound of her belly. "They just don't know how to cook to tempt themselves." A few steps farther on, she wrinkles her nose and takes my arm. "But what is that smell?"

"The sewers," I tell her. "The English blocked the drains last week, and they're backing up here. You don't smell them, of course, sitting in your garden," I note wistfully, then call back to Agnès, "A linen square and some perfume! Foul smells are bad for the baby."

Wordless, Agnès takes a vial out of her pocket and douses a handkerchief. She ignores my outstretched hand and gives it directly to Radegonde.

Radegonde takes the square without looking at the maid, and she presses it to her nostrils. Her everycolor eyes turn on me, blinking in relief. "Don't you want one?" she asks through the fine mesh. "Have Agnès fix it for you."

I can't help smiling a little smugly as I look at the maid, who wipes the bottle's mouth on a second scrap of linen and hands it over to me. I may be unused to giving commands, but I find I like it.

We walk on to centre-ville, stepping in and out the shadows of the new church's flying buttresses. Here we find the marché, greatly reduced in size and scope. Everyone knows Radegonde's warehouses hold more riches and objects of fine craftsmanship than could ever be offered here—they've heard of her Oriental silks, her Italian brocades, her collection of chess sets from Paris. So why is the great lady shopping in Villeneuve's lowly town market, strolling from wine seller to flute maker to bead stringer? Because, more than anything else, she loves a bargain.

"Can you play the flute?" she asks me, holding a crude wooden example in her hands.

Of course I can't.

"A pity." With every evidence of regret, she lays the flute down in front of its disappointed maker and moves on.

We visit a box maker's stall and a linen worker's, where she buys two pillowcases. She insists on paying in coin and hands the woman a sou; we wait for three deniers' change. These days a whole sou is needed for a single loaf of bread. Radegonde puts the pillowcases in Agnès's basket and says, "They will do for my steward and his wife."

At a bead seller's stall we linger, lifting up strings of amber and enamel, poking through a bowl of bone buttons. The craftsman follows Radegonde with prayerful eyes: She represents his next dinner. She must know this, but she seems oblivious as she passes over string after string, setting them in disarray. The seller turns beseeching eyes upon me, and I drop mine in shame.

La Putemonnoie spends a long time sliding heavy glass beads through her fingers. She picks some red and some blue off their strings; they stain her skin like berries. "For a gift," she tells me, as the seller wraps them in a twist of cloth. "The best come from Venice, though these are of course local. Now, Bonne, which of all these do you think nicest?" She waves a hand over the entire stall.

I look admiringly at the amber, then finger a carved wooden flower; it would make a good anchor for a rosary.

"You prefer sculpture, I see," says Radegonde, her head still bent over the strings of glass. "Something you've always loved."

As if there were some reproach there, I turn from the flower and look at a string of large globes with enameled designs—none so large or fine as her lovers-and-Death, of course, but there's one with a woman's face, perhaps today's martyr herself. "These are pretty," I say.

She darts me a look from slanting eyes. Then in a soft voice, she cuts right to my heart. "Bonne, I have a question. I must know. Is Godfridus your lover?"

The enameled beads clack on the table. The bead seller and Agnès have pricked up their ears, and Radegonde motions them away. The moment gathers in importance—or does it? I wonder how much store she sets by my answer; the question seems to come from out of the sky, but then I remember those days of open gates and countryside strolls—a kiss forced on Godfridus before my lips ever touched hers. And who's to say she'll care if and whom I kiss?

In the end I say merely, "He's my uncle." I say it loudly, so the others can hear.

Radegonde laughs a little; but I hear a trace of irritation. "Tell me," she whispers, "was he the father of your baby?"

I whisper back, "Godfridus came to Villeneuve two years ago. I became a wet nurse three years before that. And anyway, Godfridus has taken a vow of chastity. He doesn't want to father any children."

"Hm." Radegonde looks away, as if considering a handful of amber beads. "He isn't an unattractive man."

"Oh." I stare at the amber, whose string Radegonde has idly wound into a spiral. "Do *you* fancy Godfridus?"

Radegonde isn't taken off guard. Neither is she incensed by my impudence. She laughs again and tosses the beads carelessly. "If I were to marry again," she says, "I'd have to surrender my son and all his property to my husband's brother—especially if I married beneath me. And I find I enjoy certain freedoms as a widow."

These freedoms—they are the stuff of bawdy poems and plays. *You plan to take lovers?* It's on the tip of my tongue to ask it, and perhaps Father Pierre would want me to, but I don't. I can't. Instead I say, "No one would expect you to marry him, least of all Godfridus. But you did cure him and save his hand. He is very grateful. And perhaps you . . ." But I can't finish.

"Altogether," she says, "you and I have a great deal invested in that man."

I feel that I have trodden too close to la Putemonnoie's careful secrecy, that she is giving me a warning of some sort. I fall back on an old standby, "Godfridus tries to live like Christ."

Radegonde looks at me a long, level moment. And suddenly, "I've made a decision," she says. She picks up a whole string of amber beads and declares, "I'll buy these"—making the seller very happy—and plunks down a livre. He takes the coin without protest, though I'm sure it's much less than he usually charges (no one's buying amber these days).

Radegonde slips the string over my neck. "I don't know that I care for the color on you," she says, "but these are obviously the ones you should have. You like them. I'll give you a strong cord for restringing, or you can sew them onto the dress I'll give you when my baby is born."

I blush and thank her profusely.

Then she picks up a short strand of light blue glass and calls Agnès over. She feels no call to pay more for these, just hands them to Agnès and beams benevolently, confident she's pleased everyone, especially herself.

"We'll all get what we need," she promises, and she looks not at me but at the skinny, breathless maid. "Agnès, I have a special task for you."

GODFRIDUS

"Send her my thanks, but I already have everything."

The skinny maid—now plumper than most I see out my window—tries to pout with inadequate lips. "You can't send me away," she says. "You need me. Bonne, your niece, won't be able to come much now—my mistress needs her too much." *Deliberately she crosses to a corner (one without the dust of clay heads or crockery) and drops her bundle of belongings.* "I won't be in your way," *she says.* "No more than I have to be, watching you around the clock."

I struggle to sit up, but a weakness has come over me again. "I don't need you here," *I protest again, but too faintly.*

She is smiling with satisfaction. "Madame Putemonnoie has promised to send everything you need," *she says.* "*And* you need me."

I shudder for Bonne, alone now with the woman who saved my life, the woman who will give everything to us all.

"What lovely beads, my lady, and don't you look loverly counting them?"

I tell her Lady Anne once had just such a string, and crushed them all to fill a box with their powder. Our mage had told her the scent would ward off peste and guarantee love. She waved it about all summer, when peste loves to inhabit the air, and while she kept herself and all the castle safe, Lord Robert, her husband, bought a string of green glass for the virgin vavasour, who was virgin just a short while longer.

You might as well crush money itself. But—

"Don't you want to keep safe from the peste?" *I offer most humbly.* "And to shelter your loved ones as well? I know the charm to speak while grinding the stones. The aroma is like nothing you've ever smelled, rich and sweeter than incense. It's a sure protection, and summer is almost here."

She gathers the string in her hands. Her face is uncertain—one effect of her history, she'll never know who or what to believe. "Mistress Putemonnoie has all kinds of medicament and charm," *she says, clutching the amber to her.* "I'm quite certain we're all safe. Look what she did for Godfridus."

Yes, look . . .

I will visit the district soon.

FEAST OF
SAINT UMILIANA

[MAY 23]

TRUE HARD TIMES ARRIVE WITH SUMMERY heat. There is no food left, and the English show no signs of going. As I walk through the streets, I see Villeneuve turning against itself—people stealing food from one another, bribing the town council for extra rations, setting one dog on another for sport. In an alleyway, I see men butcher a donkey that's dropped dead with exhaustion. I see rats squabbling over the corpse of the Negro once displayed in the marketplace. I see the head of a captured Englishman, mounted on the city walls as a lesson to any who'd try to infiltrate us. I see gutters clogged with excrement and crawling with vermin. I see hatred in the faces of the townspeople.

At night the town criers shout their news: reports of promiscuity, blasphemy, wife beating. Two men have fought to the death over a pig's bladder, and a Jewess stands accused of murder. Children of both sexes have been raped.

Naturally, the people have stopped celebrating or even marking the saints' days; holiness is a luxury when children are eating the plaster off the walls. But within the walls of Radegonde's great house, we read daily of the saints' deeds, along with the doings of Henri Putemonnoie. Today, we see, is the feast of Umiliana, who was given the gift of shedding tears while at prayer. For a while the gift disappeared, and she tried to regain it by putting quicklime in her eyes; she was nearly blinded but became a saint nonetheless.

Radegonde receives this tale with a curl of the lips but without comment. She is embroidering a new corner in her Garden of Earthly Delights, a fountain flowing thick white balm.

Silently, thinking of weepy Umiliana, I turn the book's leaves, passing recipes and business accounts until I reach the blank pages at the end. They never fail to distract me with their yellowy smoothness. What would Henri have written here? The story of his child's conception and birth? The true tale of his love for Radegonde, and where he found her? I begin to understand the lure these cream-yellow pages must have had for him: the perfect confidant, the silent friend who receives everything, tells nothing.

"Bonne," Radegonde says impatiently, as if she has spoken before, "find something of interest to read."

Dutifully I turn the pages, stifle a yawn, and begin: " 'How to Cure Sickness of Wines . . .' "

This is the moment Father Pierre of the new church chooses to pay a visit to Radegonde Putemonnoie. When his name is announced, I scramble to put Henri's book away—who knows what he might think of it? Radegonde, however, keeps stitching tranquilly for a long moment before, hearing him enter, she rises in greeting.

It is shocking, and incongruous, and *wrong*, to see the priest's unwieldy body in Radegonde's solar. His dark serge looks pitiful against her deep black velvet, and his bumpy skin's an abomination by the smooth dusk of her cheeks.

I think he must feel it, too, this wrongness, but he gives no indication. He nods at me as he sits. "You are doing good work, daughter," he says, with a deep conspiratorial significance to his tone.

I blush and busy myself with untangling Radegonde's threads. "I am glad to contribute what I can," I reply, making myself think only of the nursing, not of the other promise he has extracted from me.

If Radegonde notices our exchange, she ignores it. She rings for wine and picks up her broderie, as naturally as if this visit were what she'd planned for the afternoon all along. "Well, Father," she says, "how kind of you to call on me when I am feeling too large to go much abroad."

"Blessings to you and the baby." He bobs his head benevolently, thinking no doubt with pleasure of the well-cured wine that is to come. "We at the new church wish you the best."

Deftly she licks a thread end and inserts it in her needle. "You are kind."

He watches with interest as she begins to surround her fountain with a cloud of beetles. "Your spiritual advisers know your heart is good," he tells Radegonde, "no matter what is said in the town."

I nearly drop the thread mass—Pierre has introduced his topic with such clumsiness, it makes me clumsy. It is far too clear what he wants, and thus it is equally clear he will never get it. Radegonde's hands move steadily.

"In the end," she says, "there is only one opinion that counts."

The wine arrives, and as I pour it out, Pierre refines his point: Villeneuve is dissatisfied with Radegonde's closed larder, and he has come to remonstrate.

"It is right that I should speak," he says, helping himself to a sesame cake from a tray. "A woman's heart may be good and willing, but sometimes it needs a gentle squeeze to see its duty."

He is here, naturally, to put the squeeze.

Radegonde's hand pauses for a split moment. "Are you suggesting, Father, that my sins, as you call them, are results of my womanliness?"

Gallantly he offers her an excuse. "Yours is the weaker sex."

She dips her needle again. "And yet woman is the vessel our Lord chose to bring his son to earth, and the being he has exalted above the angels."

Pierre chews with an expression of fixed thoughtfulness; obviously he doesn't expect much from Radegonde's powers of debate. Already he must be seeing himself with a fat capon in his pocket, perhaps a slab of salted dolphin won from a guilty heart. "Mother Mary," he says, ". . . ah, yes. How blessed that she was able to recover some of the sins of Eve."

"Eve," says Radegonde, "who was made from flesh, a material superior to the clay from which Adam was formed."

"Made from *man*," Pierre points out.

"And created in Paradise, whereas man was made outside and brought within, when it pleased the Lord."

Pierre sits up a little straighter, though his voice does not change. "Woman, as is universally known, brought the wrath of the Almighty down on man and was doubly cursed with a nature cold and moist. Why else would God see fit to purge her each month, from the head to the bowels?"

"Perhaps," Radegonde says serenely, "because she was fashioned from a crooked rib, and thus doomed by man to imperfection."

A sesame cake crumbles in Pierre's fist. I expect him to shout *Blasphemy!* but instead he says, keeping tight rein on his temper, "Woman was and is the nest of sin, as sure as Eve was Adam's temptress! Whatever the crime, it can be traced to her—greed, sloth, concupiscence—"

Radegonde quirks an eyebrow, knowing she has won a point. "Father, given the cold, moist nature of which you speak, is it truly possible for women to feel the fires of lust? A cold, moist woman's love can be mere affection, nothing stronger."

Abruptly Pierre gets to his feet. "Daughter," he says, "you must be careful. Certain persons, hearing you say such things, might suspect you are not a Christian."

Radegonde looks up at him, her eyes open wide in innocence. But perhaps this is a mistake: Those weirdly colored eyes, slanted rather than round, could well mark her not of our world. "I may be a Christian, or not one, and still know these things," she says, as guileless as a deer. "Are they not facts?"

Facts, I think: like the fact of my mother's elevation, or the fact of her death? The fact of her holiness or the fact of her sin? There are so many facts and factions in the church, and it seems Blanche (or Umiliana, or Solange) could have been the subject of this debate all along.

"In any event—" Pierre gathers himself together, brushing crumbs from his sleeves and sitting back down. "In any event, daughter, I have come on a mission. From my own heart, I have decided to let you know that your soul is in doubt—in the town if not in the church. Although the town naturally looks to the church for guidance."

Now he gets to the meat of his matter, what I have been expecting: "Perhaps if you were to make a small gift—a token of goodwill—"

"I've promised the new church a chapel once I'm safely delivered."

"But perhaps something before then," he presses. "A smaller donation, but a sign all the people can appreciate—some tiles for the floor, perhaps, or a golden aquifer . . ."

Radegonde smiles politely, playing the gracious lady—and wily merchant. "I will think what might be best," she says, tucking her needle into the cloth and standing up. "Meanwhile, please have the rest of these cakes, for you and your holy brothers."

"Thank you." Standing, too, he wastes no time sweeping the contents of the tray into his pocket. No doubt he's disappointed to be bagging only cakes instead of meatier game, and it's equally sure that he'll enjoy them alone, on his walk back to church. "And do think on what I said. Some sort of gift, no matter what the size, might enable the people to see your soul more charitably."

"I have promised to think," she says a little sharply, and he knows he is dismissed.

I am proud of my mistress for besting a priest, especially one I find so odious; but as I leave this day, I feel a dull ache around my heart. If the most a woman's humors enable her to feel is gentle affection, there must be an imbalance in me—for I feel much more strongly than that.

WHERE DOES CHARITY BEGIN? I ask myself as I walk home through the hungry city. For example, how many lives have given themselves to create the wealth Radegonde Putemonnoie now possesses, and the beauty that wealth has nourished and preserved? Aside from the animals whose skins now line her cloaks, and the trees that are now her jewelry boxes and combs, how many men and women have died from the hard work of prying gems out of rock, or starved themselves to feed a civet cat, or gone blind fashioning gold into a love-knot ring? In a world where the poor are parents of the rich, how many men, and how many women, have given their lives to shape her perfection?

I know that I—and Godfridus, who carved Henri Putemonnoie's sarcophagus—are two bodies in the pillar raising that house to heaven. And it keeps climbing upward, as Villeneuve devours cats and dogs and horses, even its own walls, its own earth.

I think of rich people making love. Their bodies are smooth and they smell good as they glide against each other. They stick out their delicate pink tongues and lick, lick, dainty, consuming each other.

I think this love must taste of gold.

THE BAKERWOMAN

The Lord finds work for busy hands—the merchants and ladies, knights and lawyers of this town may lie languid, but the peasants are pushed. For those who know how to work, the toil increases as we move day to day, sunup to sunset. New walls to build against the English, old houses destroyed to build them—new ways found to nourish spirit if not body. New rituals for the church, new paths to salvation. Above all, new work, new ways to earn bread.

In these black ovens, guarded, I make it. Before you wake, while you prowl through the streets, while you haggle for greens or a stringy squirrel, I bake it.

While other women sell their bodies, while other women beg, while my husband shouts on the ramparts, I make it—the bread which is so useful for so many things. Raw, it's a glue. Baking, a promise of heaven. Baked, a miracle! Sop a sauce, wipe a knife. A slice in each hand to protect when carrying something hot. A thin wedge to pack a wound, to dry the blood and seal the edges.

I bake it. My sweat shapes it. This is my body.

Buy my bread! Yes, buy my bread! It will keep you alive. It will give you life.

How sweet, the warmth of a loaf spreading against the body's budding hardness.

SAINT PETRONILLA'S DAY

[MAY 31]

FTER PIERRE'S VISIT COMES ONE LAST, FIT-ful rainstorm, and then the season of light. The sun comes early and stays late; our shutters are open all day long. Building stones bake in the heat and the light, and the ground mist in the district of shadows burns down to a wisp. Beyond the town walls, our fields grow, die back, stay empty. Traders come down the road, sell to or are robbed by the English, and disappear.

The roses in Radegonde's garden begin to bloom unseasonably soon. Their scent rises from the ground, creeping in at windows, pouring over the garden wall until people in the street swoon with longing. These may be the only roses that Villeneuve will see this year—the other bushes have been picked bare for salads, even the thorns, which come up again in shiny puddles of vomit.

In that garden of earthly wonders, my mistress and I tread pathways of crushed mussel shell, between banks of roses, pansies, carnations, and forget-me-nots that have been manured and pruned for the best blossom and scent. She gathers bouquets for her bedroom, carefully selecting the finest and most fragrant blossoms, breaking the juicy stems off in her own fingers. I receive them in my arms till I tremble with their weight.

I am so happy.

And I am miserable. Because I want to tell my mistress about my happiness but am afraid to.

In the late afternoon, we lie curled in her bed, on the mountains of pillows she's heaped there. The flowers beat out a heady scent; the book rests closed at my side. Her back is turned to me, her hair a burning tickle on my lips, my nose, my head, my chest. Her breath comes evenly, her ribs rise and fall. She sleeps like the babe in her belly.

Upon her smooth, dark back, with one finger, I write: *Dans le jardin de son aimée...*

She moves, tickled in turn; but her breath doesn't change. I write again: *Vous et nulle autre.*

Her breathing stops.

I write, recklessly: *Tout ce que je suis, tout ce que je ne suis pas...*

And then she coughs, and her ribs start to rise and fall again. A fine sweat clings to her back like dew, and in her sleep she kicks off the last of the covers.

I remind myself that she can't read.

From Henri Putemonnoie's livre de raison
On my 1st voyage south and east, I was blessed to fall into company with a number of musulman traders, who welcomed me, after their fashion, with meat and drink, and supplied my first cargo of paprika, which they called filfillah; ginger (jibera), and cinnamon (karfa), as well as a seasoning for which we have no name and they call juljulan, for which I never found a market. Many of these spices they use to make a poultry dish called treed, a dish so tasty that their Prophet Mohammed once said he loved it better than everything save his wife.

The women of the East are very beautiful in their way, many with light skins and strangely colored eyes. The wealthier among them are cloistered like nuns and they make good wives and needlewomen, but they are often fat, fond of a confection they call snake—a paste of crushed almonds, sugar, cinnamon, and orange water greased and wrapped in pastry leaves. Their lips invariably taste sweet.

That very year my travels took me unto Persia, where the men inhale the smoke of a fiber called hemp, that induces a heavy torpor in which every movement seems to take place in a dream.

With my first shipment of spices I could have profited over 200 livres immediately on landing in Marseilles, but carried the goods myself to Toulouse, where they gained me 35 additional livres. The hemp would be bought nowhere, so after storing it a year I piled it in a field and set it and the juljulan afire, sickening myself wretchedly on the smoke.

Take one whole chicken, cleaned, and boil it with a small spoonful each of salt, ginger, pepper (filfil), chervil, a green called parsley, 3 pieces bark from the outer layer of the cinnamon plant, a pinch saffron, and 2 cups olive oil. Make a pastry with almost 2 livres flour and some water, shaping into 45 balls the size of a small hen's egg. Each ball should be flattened until very thin and a hand's length across. Yet this dough should not be much handled. Oil a domed tray and place directly over the fire, and fry each side of the dough sheets. Then on a large plate lap 30 circles of dough, flatly, and cover with the chicken (from which you have removed the cinnamon bark) and 3 fat onions cut large. Then cover this with the rest of the pastry, and moisten with some of the pot liquor.

This is treed, a dish of the infidels. The flavor is not for every palate.

BELIEVE MY MISTRESS IS JEALOUS. WHEN I go to Godfridus I have to sneak, as she has laid traps for me: Agnès lies in wait, and a lackey lurks at every corner. I don't know the consequences if I am caught, but no more do I want to know them.

Godfridus and I have an arrangement: When I whistle below the window, he declares he simply cannot rest another moment without a sip of wine, and he begs Agnès to go out for it. She's eager to serve, and I hide in a neighbor's doorway until she's gone. This usually wins us a quarter hour or so together.

Today I'm glad to see he's sitting up, and his pale eyes follow as I plump his pillows and bring him a drink of the clean water he really prefers to wine. Radegonde plucked out her stitches in his hand weeks ago, and the skin has knit together nicely; only a little redness and swelling remain.

"You'll be back at work in no time," I tell him, sitting down on the lone stool. "In fact there seems no reason not to begin now." I am eager to talk, to tell of my days at the great house and what I have read in Henri's book, but courtesy demands I address the invalid first.

He makes a gesture of distaste. "To chip out more acanthus and trumpetvine on corbels and capitals? . . ." His voice goes dark, sober. "No, I won't do that again. More than ever, now I need to complete my great work—to honor the God who saw fit to spare my life. Because that *must* be why He saved me."

"But you also need to earn a living," I point out. Perhaps his weeks of enforced idleness have made him slothful. Radegonde may have given him too much, including the ruby he seems to have swallowed, for it is nowhere.

"This," says my friend, "is a higher duty." Absently he frays the edge of his sheet. "If only I had clay again—then I could get started."

I get up and inspect the buckets in the corner, still under their protective white sheeting. I touch the clay inside. "It's all dry now."

"Of course it is." He sounds impatient. "Solid brick. Even the buckets are ruined."

"Can't we soak it in water?" I ask hopefully.

"The oils are gone. I'll get no figure out of there." He sits farther up, crouches in bed, and fusses with the shutters. "If only there were *something*," he frets, and slats us into darkness, as if the light of day is too much for a man who cannot watch his own work grow under his hands.

"Godfridus," I say; then jokingly, "Uncle . . ." He ignores me. To distract him I say, "I've been reading about the women of the East. Did you know they live apart from men, like nuns, and never step outside? Some of them have light eyes and all of them wear jewels. And the things they eat—"

Gazing toward his shutters, he points out that Agnès will return soon.

As I slink down his alley stairs, I miss our easy way of being together, of offering companionship and trust while keeping our own counsel. Godfridus has changed since his injury—become more remote, as if in touching death he has forgotten his friends. He is a closed book to me, thick with writing I can't read.

SAINT

CLOTILDE'S DAY

HERCULE

A man shouts "Steaks!" and he's mobbed—folk starved for flesh fly to buy. To buy, to eat, to think of better meat.

I know the seller. He's the man who trained the dancing bear, the lady chained and offered to dogs for sport, the one that Bonne saved along with me by feeding mouths more hungry than ours. Now the townsmen are bearing my bear away. Her blood makes a trail starring out from the meatman. It's better food than locusts, sure, but wet dirt sticks to the shoes and the smell makes my head spin. It's a common man who runs to blood, and still people follow the star.

There was a star danced, and beneath it I was born. In a dream of meat, in a sea of blood, to a girl who dubbed me Miscarriage and sold me into smallness. I have told this story a thousand times—the only tale that remains is the only one I cannot tell. Anne's, the one that brought me here. I'm looking for a story that will light my way out. Maybe it lurks in the shadows, in the Jew's place, along with my only hope. So I head there with hope for a cure.

"But not too much," I mutter as I pass the ranks of fillettes de joie, lined up in this city

that hungers for joy as for flesh. I fondle the balls in my pocket. My trade, too, is joy, and my body's my trade. I can lose my pain but not my size—and then there are other things I want.

Can I be enchanted? It's not the food—I ate more at Coussin—and it's not my age—I'm past thirty-three. But the pain in my heart is different these days, and I have grown bigger. So big that a skinny fillette in yellow sleeves tracks my bloody footprints, as if I'm not a child but a client.

"Get thee behind me!" I scream.

The fillette jumps back. "Don't be afraid," she says like a girl in a dream. "It's only love."

La Putemonnoie and I sit in her garden, beside what would be the shade of a pear tree if the thing weren't espaliered so severely. The roses are a dizzying mass of color and scent. Bees buzz and fountains trill; a fat green frog hops by, following the honeycomb of shell-graveled paths.

I fan my mistress against the heat and relay the town's news. The wife of a wealthy burgher has died. A basket maker found a purseful of gold coins buried in his back garden and was jailed for his fortune, as the purse looked new and he couldn't say why he'd been digging.

Finally I tell la Putemonnoie that according to the bakerwoman, the new church is to have a labyrinth. "It will be one of the finest in France, if not the very finest," I say. Labyrinths are rare and expensive church ornaments, rich in prestige and reputation; people travel miles to visit them, as with the one in Saint-Porchaire. "The maze will be black and white marble from Italy, laid out in the pattern of the Search for the Wonderful and the Good, just as at Chartres. The rosa mundi at the center will be of pink marble, representing Christ's blood. The course's length will be—"

"Three miles," Radegonde says, "just as I ordered it."

My jaw drops. "Mistress?"

"Where in Villeneuve will you find Italian marble, outside my warehouses?" Her feet crunch restless on the mussel shells; a stand of lilies quivers. "I thought the nave floor needed something to complement the transepts' rose windows. I proposed it to your Father Pierre. He was pleased to accept, and the masons were glad to get the work. As you yourself have seen, the town is delighted." She sways backward, satisfied; of the little gesture Pierre asked, she has made a grand flourish. She must think it a good investment—or a slap in the face to Pierre—else she wouldn't have made it.

Few churches can boast such a marvel of planning and precision. This labyrinth will require vast stores of stone and skill, as one mislaid square or curve will ruin the complicated design. There can be only one pathway to the center, which represents heaven; the penitent pursue it on their knees. The priests say that anyone who reaches it will find himself changed for the better and that much closer to salvation.

But I think of the gaunt faces I see every day in the street. Hatred lurks in each hunger wrinkle, and violence. "Have you thought of also giving our townsfolk something to eat?" I say.

Radegonde's nose twitches. "Bonne Tardieu, you should know better than anyone else that whatever you give a person in this life, he wishes it were somehow better. But give him a promise for the life to come . . . The labyrinth will be Villeneuve's stock in salvation, with the added advantage that when the people find out what salvation is like, they won't be able to complain about it. Your Father Pierre approves. You see—I've seen to everything."

It makes me uneasy that she calls him *my* Father Pierre, as if she knows of the promise he exacted from me. Should I say that my first thought is of protecting her? I think of the amber beads she bought me at the marketplace, and of the flecks of dust inside each one.

"I'm grateful for all you've done," I say. "And I'm sure the labyrinth will be magnificent."

"Yes," she says, "it will be."

Then Radegonde closes her eyes, shutting me out. Along with the sunlight, which loses itself in the deep folds of her black velvet. She is tired.

As we sit without speaking, without moving, I watch a rose bloom. It uncurls from its bud like a hand, finger by pink finger, coming out of a fist. Driving Pierre and his promise from my mind, I wonder how far heaven really resembles a rose.

WE, BLANCHE AND I, once knelt in the white rose of Saint-Porchaire's labyrinth. The peste had been raging for weeks and the atrium was full of dying and dead; their moans permeated the stone walls, penetrated my flesh and bones. It was a steamy Sunday, and as others breathed their last, we prayed with every knee step for a miracle, for the town to be saved in this life. It was as if we knew that in their salvation lay ours. Though Marie, from her cell, prophesied only doom for all of us.

In the end, in the rosa mundi, all I noticed was soreness in my knees, and red and blue light on my arms and Blanche's . . . Blanche, first raised toward heaven then dashed to the very center of Saint-Porchaire's flower.

FINALLY MY BONES are aware of a deep silence. I realize Radegonde has made no sound for some time.

I look up and see she has stopped breathing. Her eyes are still closed.

"Mistress!" I jump up, give her a shake, start fanning again. "Are you sick?"

Then she opens her amazing eyes, in which all the colors of the world are found, and takes my hand and puts it on her belly.

"He's moving," she says.

The heir of the Putemonnoies is kicking his mother.

HOW CAN THE KICK OF AN INFANT not even born drive a grown woman from her place? But drive me it does—sweeps me right out of this version of paradise, away from the garden, the great house, to . . . where? Not home, where Hercule will be practicing his tricks; not Godfridus's studio, where Agnès will watch me with her sharp little eyes and my friend will ignore me.

Of course. Down the narrowest streets I can find, to the church that houses the bodies and souls of my progenitors. Yes, to the center of my world—I am pushed by a rich family's upstart back to the bosom of mine.

But I must ask myself again, *Why?* What has set my heart to pounding so, my feet to running? (My arms to aching, as if from an embrace . . .) Surely I can't be afraid of a fetus—and just as surely, I must be glad for the kick, since it's high time the thing showed some sign of life.

. . . The same life I felt trying to kick its way out between my legs— life struggling against the moon and stars and fate, vying with my own flesh, until all sensation suddenly stopped . . .

So often the childbed is a place of death. More babies, and more women, have died there than of peste or, truth be known, old age. I'm fearful of my mistress's fate, about what could happen in the hour she gives birth, and I decide that fear, made manifest in a tiny flutter, is what made me flee her side.

I resolve to find some way to protect her. To save her from death and from more men, other husbands or lovers, who would demand such sacrifices of her. And meanwhile I will pray.

So I am here, in a gray district made of gray houses, hemmed by perpetual mist. I cut across the atrium. Black walls, white bones, fragile wisps of grass; the stolid danse of death rimming the windows. There's comfort here already, in solitude and sameness; it's as good as an embrace, and I am heading for my mother.

Faintly I hear Marie's voice, and it's a strange comfort: "A bloom on the tree when the apples are ripe means a sure termination of somebody's life . . ."

This place is ever the same to me. In many ways I am grateful for that; in continuity there is comfort. So I say the first prayer I think of, one for the Nativity of the Blessed Virgin: "Nativitas tua, dei genitrix Virgo, gaudium annuntiavit . . . solvens maledictionem, dedit benedictionem: et confundens mortem, donavit nobis vitam sempiternam . . ." I like the way the words sound in the churchyard silence, so I say some of them again: "destroyed death and gave us eternal life . . ."

They are beautiful words, and give me peace. In peace I cross the atrium where men and women have died and decayed and their bones have been stacked, by me, in a monument that now means eternal rest. "Their voice is gone out through all the earth, and their words to the end of the world . . ."

My feet are soft against the ground. I reach the far end, the beginning of the crumbling, blackened church, and prepare to go up into the tower.

Then, from out the tower door, a man steps into the sunlight.

A soldier, an Englishman, I think immediately. The English have broken through our walls! For only a foreigner would come here, knowing the history of the place. I plant my feet on the ground and get ready to scream, to sound the alarm.

And yet I stop myself. He may be a stranger to me, but he's no foreigner: tall, dark, and dressed like a good French artisan, in brown cotte and hose. A respectable citizen; more so than I. Now he leans against a scabby wall, his arms folded.

"I've been watching you," he says.

I start to walk again. Like a cat, the man jumps straight into my path.

"Excuse me." I adopt Radegonde's haughty tone. "You're in my way."

"And you, mistress, are in my thoughts." Staring into my face, he licks his lips.

"This is holy ground," I say, and try to brush past him.

He won't let me go, stands there holding my arm. His eyes devour me darkly.

"Sir, I have no idea who you are."

"But I know you. You're Bonne Tardieu, single woman, wet nurse, and sometime laundress."

"Then you must know I am engaged by Radegonde Putemonnoie."

But even her name won't help me now. There's a light in the stranger's eyes, and he breathes heavily on me.

"Of course I know that," he says. "You're living off the richest woman in Villeneuve. You've sold her your milk."

"But I have no money with me now." I try to wrench away but can't. "I have nothing—no money, nothing of value. Please let me go." I feel myself near tears, in a terror that seems new although I think I am no stranger to it.

He says, almost regretfully, "I can't."

"But I have nothing!"

And then suddenly he rips my dress open, tears the bandeau away from my breasts. I find my back against the chalky cool wall, my wrists in one of his hands, his other hand pressing my pelvis into the wall to hold me still.

His head is at my breasts. He's feeding.

While my mind reels, my body betrays me, giving against my will. I can't stop it. Milk throbs out of with every pulse, as my heart pounds and he sucks life's blood away.

His lips smack wet against me, obscenely loud.

So, I think with a curious detachment, he wanted only the sweetness of my milk. Not my sex, not money, but a sweetness that I can't keep sacred even for Radegonde. And I feel in my traitorous breasts an ache subsiding. This man, my rapist, brings relief I did not know I needed.

I hate him for it.

His throat makes a great gulping sound. He switches nipples clumsily, ready to drain them both.

And at that moment I push. I draw on the wall for strength and I push. I push against this clumsy man and he falls sprawling in the dirt. And then I'm running, hands clutching my torn dress to my chest, running away with the sound of his mouth in my ears and the liquor of his mouth on my breasts.

GODFRIDUS

Today the morning sun hit me, popped open my eyes. I knew what I have to do.

I feel it in the prickle of my veins, in the itch of healed flesh. God has answered a decade's worth of prayers. My work is beginning again— beginning for the first time.

Now I have no need of sketches. Only of materials. I jump from my bed and soak last week's loaf in last night's wine—a gooey mess—and I knead it into claylike consistency. Eyes closed, I stroke and shape, and when I open them I see, for one heartbeat only, the absolute vision of what I want. And yet not what I expected—the nose so sharp, the brow so lined, the eyes—I know they must be closed—and mouth so tired.

But this is what I've sought for all these months. Perfection. Inspiration.

And then it's gone. Melted away, dissolved back into pliant mush. I must find something harder.

My pounding on the dried-clay bucket wakes the slender maid from a nap. She sits up on her pallet, blinking sleepily. "What are you doing?" She wears a coarse chemise to sleep, as I have done since she's lived here.

"Help me," I pant, and obligingly she rises and helps me pry the wooden bucket planks loose. Soon we have a brown cylinder of flaky stuff. It sits in a cloud of its own powder. Humble material; until fired it will be subject to crumbling and bumping. But it will do.

I take up my chisel, long unused; curl stiff fingers around it. "Be care-

ful," warns *Agnès, but I hardly hear her. Before I can lose that image—before it corrupts itself in the fragile medium of my mind—I start to carve.*

The filthiest shadow in this district of dirt and dark. That is Bonne Tardieu, defiled.

But where to go? Where to purify both soul and body? There are no bathhouses anymore, and I can't go to Radegonde's like this. I head for the street. And when I emerge—burst, rather, with prickling nipples and flaming face, still holding my garments closed—I see a girl.

The day's second chance meeting. Her body is gaunt, her pale hair lank. She wears a red dress and dirty yellow sleeves. She stares at me, takes a short step forward.

Instantly I know what to do. "You!" I cry, and wave my free arm. "Come here!"

The habits and command of a chatelaine must have rubbed off on me; the girl comes. Her eyes are wide, obliging, her face familiar.

I realize I've seen her before. I've seen her lurking about the alleyways, or walking circles around the church block. She always wears this dress and these sleeves, and her hair hangs in ropes down her back. For some time now there's been room to spare in the dress, and where her bosom should swell there's only a hungry flatness, like a boy's. When she comes close her breath has the sour smell of one who hasn't eaten in days.

"Mistress?" Her voice is timid, and I see her feet are bare.

"Are you hungry?"

She ducks her head.

I look around, clutching the rip over my bosom, at the buildings that shut out the sky. "Do you have a room here?"

"No . . ." she says slowly, as if with dawning joy, "but I know where we can go."

Apparently she's had women hire her before, or at least she's willing to accommodate one now. She asks no questions but leads me to the darkest pocket of the shadow district, under an eave in an alley barely wide enough for a dog. There she offers herself to me, turning with an open expression, her laces already undone.

"Open your mouth," I say.

She tells me she's a stranger in Villeneuve, driven out of her home city. I tell her to suckle first, then she can give me her story.

The gentle tugs of a woman's lips, the cleansing of a childlike tongue . . . Thank the Virgin.

You can sneeze your brains out, as Hercule says; you can sneeze your limbs off. Sneezing is the first sign of leprosy. But this time the sneezes lied, though the girl's parents—relieved to be rid of an extra mouth— had already sent her to a leprosarium. There she kept sneezing, but only in springtime, and spent the other months helping the monks sweep up the fingers and toes that fell off her campmates. She wept until her tears turned to blood. Meanwhile she kept waiting to come apart at the seams, but she only grew taller and prettier—though not plump, for it's impossible to thrive on a monastery diet.

She takes the last drops from my dugs, the last spit from the tips. She would lick me all over, like a cat.

"When the monks gave up and sent me back, my family didn't want me," she says as we rest. Her nimble hands have unfastened my braids, and she's giving my scalp a special, soothing rub. "They said I smelled of the leper camp, and no one in the village would touch me."

So she came to Villeneuve, to sell the body that remained so miraculously whole. She lives in the street of the fillettes de joie, in the gutter before a brothel run by a onetime nun who sold the girl's body over and over as *virgo intacta* and then discarded her.

As she scratches the dead skin from my scalp, she tells me I could make a fortune off my milk.

I miscounted: This is the day's third chance meeting, and far luckier than those with fetus or man.

GODFRIDUS

Blessed marble hardness yielding, the shape in-side so eager to emerge. What gifts! The vision, the stone—everything I need. Now I must give myself.

So, soon, I will see. A body released from my mind, released from this stone which so recently was released from a warehouse. The dress taut over the knees, folded between the legs, draped to reveal one hard, shining breast. And the answering globe of the skull that will drink from it.

I chip, I polish, I stroke. This is holy work for a Sunday, for any day, even the feast of a saint who ate poisonous spiders and lived. His blessing protects me, his life inspires me, as every life inspires and blesses me now. Even my own.

I thank you, Lord, for the gift of the marble. Porphyry, the queen of minerals; its crystals catch the light. I thank Christ—thank even Agnès, who secured it for me.

"Can I look yet?" she begs, her back to me, her stitchery work proceeding slowly.

"Not yet." I don't want her to see she isn't the model—I'll hurt no good woman's feelings. "And don't speak. The Lord's work is done in silence."

While the world without darkens, the light inside grows. No candle is needed, no fire, no flame of any kind. For even shrouded in sheets, even under a blanket, the column gives off unearthly light—the light of spirit making itself manifest, of life emerging from stone. The maid sleeps with her arm over her eyes, so as not to be blinded while dreaming. Myself, I need no sleep anymore; all night I chip away at one smooth foot, or at the leg above it. My chisel knows how to find each curve and follow it lovingly. And the face is carving itself.

Secrets. Contradictions. I've added to my little store of these, and despite what I expected, they've made me stronger. The rape of my breasts was not my downfall after all; it won me a new friend, an ally quite apart from Radegonde and the priests, or Hercule and Godfridus. A comforter, and a plan for my own and others' salvation. It gave me something to keep from my mistress—I'll never tell her about the man in the atrium or the fillette outside—and this makes me stronger in face of *her* secrets, and her questions.

Both our minds, inevitably, are turning to one moment these days. The one to which her swelling, struggling belly is tending; the moment at which death will cross birth, and the future be written.

This afternoon, in the midst of my reading, Radegonde unlooses her hair. It ripples across the pillows and down the sheets, covering her husband's book and disappearing over the edge of the bed. She props herself up and looks at me, searching my face but never finding what she wants.

"Mistress?" I inquire, brushing the hair from the page. We've been reading of ways to keep garlic from sprouting.

She pounces, like a spider. "Tell me," she says, "about your confinement."

I am able to close the book calmly. Suddenly I'm glad for that brown man, and glad for the baby-kick that thrust me toward him; because they've given me strength to face the last question I'd ever want to answer. The first I knew would come one day.

Twilight gathers in the room, though the sun outside is yellow and full.

"What do you want to know?" I ask.

Radegonde's fingers run through her hair, tugging feverishly at tiny snarls. "Was labor hard or quick? How long did the pains last? And how much did you bleed?" I think I hear a rustle of bedclothes displaced by the baby, kicking again; it's as if the heir himself is asking questions. "Did you have a boy or a girl?"

I close my eyes and remember that long time, the cold dark corner of the butcher's house. The pains, the eyes, the screams—the interminable silence. What good will it do my mistress to hear of this?

"I don't know what to tell you," I say at last, and honestly. When I open my eyes I see my fingers have been making tiny, tight pleats in the bedsheet. "Except that I don't think you can read your future in my past."

"Just tell me what it was like," she says, and flops back into her pillows. *"What is it like to have a child?"*

"I don't know." This is the most honest answer I can give her. "Everything from that afternoon feels hazy."

"Like a dream?" she asks. "Perhaps it was like being asleep and dreaming."

"Not exactly a dream, but a different life."

She mulls that over. I almost count the moments. "But it took only one afternoon?"

"It was winter, the light only lasted a few hours. I think the pains started in the darkness . . ."

"And blood?"

"Yes. There is always some blood." I seem to remember the butcheress cursing because when she tried to give her cattle the straw I'd lain on, they wouldn't eat it. I imagine the scarlet splash in the manger; I hear, above the smacking of her child's lips on my teat, the two cows whickering and clomping their hoofs on the other side of the wall.

Radegonde sighs sharply. "Well, what about your baby?" she asks. "Do you remember *that?*—Did it come out healthy, did it live?" Maliciously, she asks the questions I've always dreaded. "And where is it now?"

I have to close my eyes once more. There's nothing for me to say except, again, "Your fate will be very different from mine."

Far beyond our window the church bells ring, echoed by a peacock's cry in the garden. The room has grown cool.

Suddenly Radegonde pinches me. "Oh, why won't you help me?" She turns on her side and feigns sleep.

SHE IS A WITCH, I think as I leave her lair of fur and feather and scent, my head aching and my heart sore. She is a witch who has bewitched me.

I am glad I have secrets from her—many secrets, for this evening as she slept I began another. I took out a pen and inkpot I'd found in the solar, turned to the blank pages at the end of Henri's book, and started to write.

It was another birth.

I will write what I know about her. I will write what questions I have. I will write the truth about myself, the entire ugly truth about my life and my baby, and the beautiful secret of what I am doing now to protect her, my mistress.

Scratch, scratch, my hand unsteady against the creamy pages of stiffened skin. This will be my magic, and I start from the beginning.

If there is a sound or a smell to holiness . . .

HERCULE

Tonight the dark is everywhere, in every pocket of my skin. No stars, no moon. The house so dark I can see my breath, see something streaming off me anyway. I think it is my soul.

I follow la Bonne downstairs.

"Are you certain?" asks the man, and I hear her voice answer, "Please. It can't do any harm."

In a murky bedroom the bakerwoman lies, perhaps dying. Her man's tried to warm her by piling every blanket he owns on top of her, but typically she's kicked them all off again and lies there naked now with one thin sheet twined round her leg. A winding sheet. There's hardly anything left of her now but wrinkles.

"She started fasting before the siege," says the husband, so involved with getting Bonne out of her clothes as fast as he can.

The woman's broken out in gooseflesh; I feel it pimpling under my hand when, sly in the dark, I stroke her. One breast is like a wineskin with no wine in it, flat and flappy. The other's hard as stone, and bulges like it holds a

body. What could anyone, even the most learned of Jewish mages, do to re-
verse a case like this? For it is not life that breast is hiding.

"Hercule!" Bonne hisses. She must be able to see in the dark—I draw
my hand away.

The bakerwoman mutters. "You will be made slaves," she says, "and no
one will buy you."

Jehovah's curse on the Israelites. But who is she to repeat it? No one
wants her, and everyone wants Goodness. Pure milk—life's blood—to fash-
ion a speedy cure.

Bonne crouches and she feeds.

The bakerwoman is but thirty-eight, the same age as la Putemonnoie, but she has all the signs of being unwomaned—the fast-beating heart, sleeplessness, flashing fevers; her husband tells me her passage within has become thin and dry and short as well. He thinks she may have cut herself there, to urge the blood out—she bled heavy a few days in April, he says, and since then, nothing.

This puts me in mind of a tale Blanche told me when I was ripe for my first bleeding. My mother had few stories; she seemed to have driven fantasy from her mind. (Her reasons for doing so must be obvious.) With this one exception, the only story she ever repeated to me was her own:

It was a hot day by the riverside, the current frothing and scumming with soap; we were scrubbing out some rich woman's clothes, including a chemise with a spreading stain where the wearer might sit. Blanche, sleeveless and muscled, fearlessly breathing the summer's pestilential air, asked if I knew what made that mark.

Indigestion? I suggested. Tiny rocks?

No, she said. *It's the blood of unborn babies. Each time it comes, it means a woman has wished for and been denied a child.*

Then she told me a story about a young girl who started this bleeding and was so ashamed she told her priest, who then kissed her unchastely and stopped the blood. In the course of time the girl's mother found out what had happened, and she tied a stone around her daughter's neck, pushed her into the river, and watched her sink, to wait under the water until it was safe to come out and be married. One winter's day a prince was riding along the bank and saw a beautiful girl trapped in the ice; he walked across the river and stamped hard where she was lying, and he broke through the ice and pulled her up into the air. With a torrent of blood she warmed them both; she handed the prince a son, and soon they were married.

My mother, arms slippery and steaming, paused to look around. I know now she was checking for the priests who would throw her in prison for telling a fairy story to a child. I know this because she concluded the story, *And the man who did this thing, who heard the girl's confession and in so doing became her spiritual father, and who then kissed her unchastely— he had to do penance for twelve long years.*

(I was twelve years old.)

THE FEAST OF
SAINT VITUS
AND HIS NURSE,
CRESCENTIA

[JUNE 15]

O HENRI PUTEMONNOIE'S PAGES, I CONFIDE this, my best secret:

I am Villeneuve's wet nurse. I am nursing the town. I am a fountain gushing milk; I am a tree weeping life from my branches. Not just for the starving babies whose mamans' breasts have dried up, not just for the sick and the old, but for everyone.

It began on the day of the man in the atrium. That day I knew—I'd seen it in the false Englishman's eyes—that some part of me, at least, was wanted. And the thought of this wanting gave me courage, so I could approach first the fillette's acquaintances and then the baker, with an offer of nourishment for his sick wife, later the other shopkeepers of my neighborhood. If they hesitated, if they looked askance at the ugliness of the offered breasts, if they remembered I was still Bonne Tardieu, bastard child of a failed miracle, I did not mind; I merely waited till the lure of a full belly worked its magic.

It is mankind's oldest instinct: to suck. To save oneself. No one can resist.

Now I don't have to ask any longer; hearing of the bakerwoman's improvement, the people wait for me. I walk the streets unharmed, taking the most direct route to where I'd like to go, stopping perhaps to feed a needy face, walking in the sunshine. Men make way for me; little girls lower their eyes to let me pass.

I know they do this from obligation, not love. But perhaps that will come.

Some days Radegonde walks with me; she, too, sees the difference. "Behold the good a simple labyrinth will do," she says, serene as always. "Aren't you glad I made that donation?"

MY FIRST PROTÉGÉE, the false and prostituted virgin, tells me she's been flooded with work. This is due perhaps to her rapidly plumpening body—she's even growing breasts, I see, of a size that would show her nearly sixteen—or to the fortification of bodies and lust that's arrived with the offering of my milk.

I describe the man from the atrium, and she says she's never met or serviced him. He's never found me again, either—though it seems I've been visited by every soul in Villeneuve. Sometimes I ask myself if he ever existed, or if he could have been some sort of divine emissary sent to put me on the path of Christian duty. But would Christ's (or the Virgin's) messenger use bodily force? Even the Holy Spirit was content with mere words.

There's another question always in my mind, one I'd like to pose to the fillette. It's constantly on the tip of my tongue—as she puts her own tongue to my flesh, as she combs out my hair, even as I sit alone at night, awake while Hercule sleeps. It was so easy to persuade her to go with me that first day, even not knowing what I wanted; it seemed the most natural thing in the world for her to cranny up with me and observe my undressing. How many other women have summoned her? And if they used her body for the purpose to which it is usually hired, *what did they do?* I cannot imagine what of that nature could go on between women.

It's natural curiosity. But I can't bring myself to ask. Instead I ask for stories of the leprosarium, and she gives me tales of missing fingers and men who have to pick their virility off the floor, men who thereafter change into dresses and call themselves girls.

Hercule, to my surprise, finds the stories unequivocally unamusing. He doesn't care for the fillette one whit. "Can she dance?" he asks me. "Can she turn a somersault or pull an egg out of her elbow?" He stands ready to demonstrate his ability in all three areas.

"I believe she can put her heels behind her ears," I tell him airily, "and that's all that matters to the people she treats with."

The dwarf squats down by his pallet, his face turned ugly and sour. "Then you should send her to the sculptor," he says grumpily. "Perhaps if he saw that he'd finally finish his masterwork."

It's a surprisingly good idea. After all the talk I've had with Godfridus about whoredom and sin, flesh and doom, the notion of sending him a prostitute as a helper attracts me. Plus it offers a way to get the fillette off the street—she could step into Agnès's place, nurse him into complete health.

Yes, she would fill the maid's place admirably. And therein lies the plan's great flaw: With the fillette, Godfridus would send Agnès back to Radegonde, and my moment of primacy would end.

Hercule, noting my long silence, comes out of his grump. "Would you like to cross your heels behind your head?" he asks me. "Or can't you picture it? Here, I can do it and I'm happy to show you." He does it—but barely—rocking back on his spine, face red with effort.

"Doesn't that hurt?" I can hear strain in his bones and tendons.

"Yes," he grunts, "but no more than it would hurt you. My body's well now, you know."

I smile. I am grateful for my milk, as others must surely be.

Hercule continues to rock, trying now to unlock his joints. "Perhaps . . ." He is trying to stay confident, to pretend his position isn't awkward. ". . . Perhaps you should take me to your patronne. She is used to entertainments and might be interested in this."

First I laugh out loud at the thought of Hercule in la Putemonnoie's house—his glittering eyes and clumsy tricks. "Aren't you a funny monkey," I say. Then I remember that she once expressed an interest in this, too, and I kneel down quickly to help him uncurl.

THE FEAST OF
SAINT CYR AND
HIS MOTHER,
JULITTA
[JUNE 16]

From Henri Putemonnoie's livre de raison

A SUCCESSFUL TRADE

*Four days' negotiation were required before I
could bring home that stone and its mount. This
was entirely the largest piece of solid rock crystal I had seen before or have seen since: twice as
long as my hand, twice as broad as my foot, and
completely clear as glass, though much heavier.
It had been cunningly slit at the back so as to
admit insertion of a blessed wafer. The mounting was no less admirable than the crystal itself,
gold of a fearful delicacy such as I have seen
only in Eastern and Byzantine work, adding
greatly to the weight of the object. It encircled
the crystal cunningly, in a shape like the rising
sun, though without rays. When the whole was
raised high (as for benediction before Holy
Communion), it caught and seemed to concen-
trate the light of every window and even of the
sun itself—all of which appeared to emanate
from the host.*

*For this monstrance I paid five bales of
cloth-of-silver, one of cloth-of-gold, and two
matched horses. This price was far greater than
the value of the stone and metal; but worth-*

while, as I donated the object to the new church of the town and received countless priestly blessings. It replaced another monstrance, reportedly even finer and in the shape of a Virgin, which was buried in fire and rubble for its part in a false miracle that moved the town some years before my wife and I arrived here. The priests were glad of this simpler shape (and the quality of the crystal) because they felt it tempted people less to imagine themselves miraculous.

HENRI'S BOOK is much on my mind as, standing by my mistress in the new church, I watch Father Pierre raise the host in its serviceable circle. An icy finger tickles my spine when I think that if it were not for the wonderful monstrance I've never seen, the seductive golden Virgin, I would not *be*. Blanche might have met a kind young man and married him, and any children they had would have been half his instead of wholly hers.

Under Pierre's muddy eyes, I pray.

WHEN, LATER IN THE DAY, Father Pierre turns up to ask if I've any news for him, I resolve to put a certain plan into action.

Women are given but few advantages in this life. My breasts have won me respect—and wanting. I can put that wanting to use now. So I describe my situation: The town comes to me singly or in pairs, their cheeks hollow and their eyes pleading . . . or greedy. For two weeks now I have fed any who asked, but that will change. I'll continue with a mere few.

"Daughter," says Pierre. The bumps on his face look ready to burst with pleasure. "You are right to limit your pensioners. And of course you are right to seek the church's advice—"

"No advice," I say. "*I* will choose who gets my milk."

He gapes.

I explain. It won't be money that dictates my selection; even though my clients might promise the world for a suckle, I am not greedy. I will instead model my choices on those of a great judge—even Christ, who distinguishes among sinners and saints. I will use criteria similar (but not identical) to those of his Last Judgment: The receivers of milk must show a certain virtue—though this does not exclude prostitutes and a few liars. The excluded ones are food stealers, misers, and drunkards who brawl publicly; witch hunters, wife beaters, and women who've stoned their sisters.

I explain to Pierre that those I reject, I will nonetheless help: As much as they want the milk, they will aspire to be the person—the kind of person—to whom it is given. They will become better people by their wanting; they will model themselves on those who get it. And thus I will further not only my salvation but theirs as well. "This can't help but please the church," I conclude.

I don't bother to tell Pierre that there is an unexpected benefit in this system for me. To make such a choice, I must ask for a life story, and that is what I hunger for most. So, starting with this afternoon's visits, as the people wait for their turns at my breast, I ask the next in line to tell me something I don't know. And I find that they are all as desperate to get those stories out as I am to take them in. So as they are sustained by my milk, I will grow fat on the lives of Villeneuve.

I CONTINUE TO NURSE the baker's wife and the baker himself, who after all have let me keep a roof over my head some years now. Then a wife whose husband, taking license in these desperate times, made her leave the house and took a concubine; two city guards orphaned at birth; a hungry mother of twins who whimper at the trickle from her flattened breasts; a virgin whose bones began mysteriously to ache after the hair vanished from between her legs. In a matter of days I restore them all to apparent health, and my reputation blossoms. I feed travelers trapped far from their home villages, where their families might be prosperous or dead. Laundresses out of work, and girls who pick lice from men's scalps for money.

Others come and I turn them away. The brothel keeper whose girls are striped from the whip. The sergeant-at-arms who set a pickpocket on fire. The wool merchant who once kicked Hercule.

If I know nothing against them, how can I say no? It becomes hard to decide; my client list continues to grow. But my milk keeps flowing—a few sips here, a bellyful there.

When I take a tired head in my arms and fit its mouth to my nipple, I know there's one less sinner among us. We fill with grace. And I have stories to fill the hours when I'm alone.

GODFRIDUS

I'm up to the breasts now. Heavy, glowing, teardrop-shaped—one draped, one exposed, both nearly equal in size to the holy Baby's head, which is pressed facelessly into the billow on the right. I see how her nose must be— fine and long, with the slightest bit of uptilting point at the tip. Her eyes will be closed, the faintest of blue veins painted on the lids. The hand on the child's skull will be delicate in shape, fragile in appearance, but sinewy and strong. The hand of an artist.

I am tired. I am thin. These are my physical sacrifices, and I make them freely. I've scarcely eaten since this work began. My hands—hardly mine anymore—are now just skin and sinew, and in this they resemble more and more the tools they wield. La Putemonnoie's skinny maid tries to tempt me with meat and cake, but how can I stop for mortal nourishment when the spirit of the marble is whispering through my head, telling me to cut a fold here, a line there?

I haven't worked like this since I was a boy in my father's tiling work- shop, when my regular duties were to sweep away dust and check that the stacks of tile were orderly and appealing to prospective clients.

It was among the tiles' squared rows, in fact, that the divine spirit first entered me. My father and brothers were away, peddling their wares at a trade market; I was cleaning around a heap of tumbled-down merchandise, creating tidy piles and removing cobwebs heavy with shards of granite and clay. I'd just pulled the veil from one heap and was trying to peel the stuff off my fingers when I happened to look down.

A scorpion stared back at me.

I froze, my fingers trailing gossamered dust. The thing was immense, with a body as big as my hand, plated like a warhorse. How could it have hidden behind one of these fragile webs? Now the snapping pincers beat the air, and the fat purple bulb at the tip of its tail quivered, summoning up the poison to sting me. I waited, with a strange sort of calm, for my fate.

In a way I admired the animal. It contained such power and strength, yet it could so easily fit underneath one of my father's pitiful clay squares. A booted foot could crush it—but a slippered foot would shrivel at its sting, and the owner of that foot would die in agony, gasping for breath. At the very least, the pincers could clamp down and sever a toe or a vein.

A phrase ran through my mind: Deliver us from evil... *But I don't think I identified this creature with evil. I gazed in fascination.*

I don't know how long I sat there, waiting to be killed, as dreamy as if the poison were already in my veins, before my mother crept to the workshop door to check on me. She had been in bed with another miscarriage— in those days she scarcely left it—but was keeping one ear out for me, and my silence had caused her no small alarm.

"Godfri—?" was all she had time to whisper before she collapsed from lack of strength.

But it was enough for me. I shook myself out of my daze and went to her. The scorpion perched another moment in the sun, but as I helped my mother to her feet, it whisked away into the rubbled stacks. I heard a rustling at the workshop fence and I knew it had gone.

The rest of that afternoon, while my mother rested, I sat beside her bed with a bit of sopping clay from my father's slip bucket. Working carefully (for this was my first work), I fashioned the clay into a crucifix—smooth on the very top, but with arms that split at the ends, and a swollen bulb at the bottom. Almost as an afterthought I added a Christ—crude, my stubby child's fingers unequal to the challenges of the human form—His head bent in agony, His limbs twisted, as if His body were full of venom.

I gave it to my mother, and she took it without a word. It dried to powdery adamant by her bedside, cracking and crumbling from not being cured. When she lay dying some weeks later, she asked that it be buried with her.

Today my fingers tingle against the shimmering stone. It puts the spirit into me again. This statue, this work, I will never bury—the world will see it and wonder at the grace of the Lord, who art in heaven.

FEAST OF SAINT RAYNER THE TROUBADOUR

[JUNE 17]

OU MUST," PIERRE SAYS THIS DAY, "PERSUADE la Putemonnoie to lodge you. Once installed in her house, you'll be in an excellent position."

I hear the clang of a proverb about vipers in the bosom. But I remind myself that this discussion is for Radegonde's own good, as well as mine. The visit to the priests' house is part of my newly scheduled rounds; it is my way of keeping Pierre's favor, since my scheme for general nursing has only increased his hints about feeding at the orphanage, along with his queries about my employer. Now we sit in the priests' solar with green-veined Paul and trembling Thomas, surrounded by dying wooden saints, eating almond cake I brought from the great house.

I tell the priests, "Mistress Putemonnoie has said she won't let her son be raised out of her sight. I believe she does expect me to live at her house ..." For a moment I think of it—will some spare pallet or bed be found for me and my charge, perhaps a corner of the very room where the future mother sleeps ...

"And you are often there now." Pierre leans toward me, stroking the bumps on his nose, while Paul brushes the crumbs from his chest into his hand and eats them. "Tell me, daughter, have you noticed anything?"

"I—I don't understand you, Father."

His knobby face is full of tension. "Any strange chants, perhaps in tongues you don't know? Any unguents, salves, potions she drinks or stores in hidden places?"

I figure now he's testing me; everyone in town knows of my mistress's secret beauty aids. "Only those she uses on her own body," I say truthfully. "You know, to preserve her youth, to keep her fresh. They'd have the same effect on anyone."

Elderly Father Thomas speaks up: "Have you used these preparations, my child?"

Instantly I'm on my guard; icy-veined, I say, "No."

"Has she offered them to you?"

"There has never been a question of my using those creams and things," I say slowly, "although Mistress Putemonnoie gives me everything I need. I don't *need* to preserve my looks."

Both Pierre and Paul nod at me, approvingly. "Very good, my child," says Pierre. "Come close and receive my blessing."

I crawl toward him on my knees, head bent, and feel the weight of his dry hand on my skull. I think my neck might break.

Thomas asks if there is any more almond cake.

HERCULE

With a strange crow at the door, the answer is swift—"I have nothing new."

Lady Bonne, ever taxed by black men who'd know her secrets. She says she saw two of them today already and satisfied them. I can see her fingers itch to close the door—though then she'll be alone with me and my demands, which she knows grow stronger with each mouth she feeds.

This new priest looks puzzled, frowns, checks her bosom as if to make sure he has the right place. Then he says simply, "I am hungry, mistress," and guarantees his welcome. My lady wides the door.

Though scarce older than myself, he's thin and grizzled. When he holds his hand up, the light shines through it. "My name is Etienne. I have no parish, but I've heard that you sometimes—" He looks helplessly at Bonne, at me, letting the light in his hand plead his case.

Magicians' hands are said to glow—*I gaze at my own plump paws, hunting for an answering glimmer. Then I notice the stranger's black robe is shabby, and it's tangled round his body like the guts of a butchered stag.*

Lady Bonne, temporarily without a mouth, takes pity on that luminous hand and invites its owner in.

But I in my corner am cautious. "Tell us your story," *I say, though it is not my place to do this*—*as Lady Bonne reminds with a needling look. But I pretend not to see, piping,* "How can God's men go hungry? When they aren't fasting from choice, they're lardering from the parish. When each confession means an egg or a loaf—"

Everyone knows that priests eat sin, I am about to say, but this one interrupts me.

"Then that is my story—how a priest came to starve."

La Bonté gives him the good chair and sits herself on the edge of the bed. I see her breasts perk up like falcons. They are ready for this story, eager to give its teller his reward.

As if he knows this, the priest begins to speak rapidly. "I was first ordained at Lors, to the north. I remember lying with my arms outstretched on the floor of the cathedral, with cold dust pressing into my forehead ..."

"A nice detail," *I offer sotto voce, creeping toward Bonne's hem. I am past master of pretty tales.*

He continues, oblivious, "I was twenty years old. And my first assignment was to visit the sick. I liked the work, going in to people in their homes, comforting them as they lay there ..."

"Going into ladies as they lay."

Etienne looks surprised, then sorrowful. He does not like this clever child clacking his balls at Lady Bonne's knee, but he'll endure, and bless, me if he has to.

"In Lors," *he says,* "we were plagued with devils"—*and now I am all ears.*

"Devils?" *repeats la Bonne. She is afraid, with a fascinated fear. The falcons huddle to her ribs.*

The stranger nods. "For some months," *he says,* "our young people were falling ill and taking to their beds. Good boys and girls, diligent workers and pious churchgoers in the first years of maturity. I was assigned to confess and comfort them. What is wrong? I would ask. What is ailing you? One

by one, they said that devils were pinching and burning their flesh with pokers, and I saw no reason to disbelieve them. In those days, to walk down the
street was to be deafened by howls from behind closed doors and windows."

"Were you a handsome man?" I must ask. La Bonne tweaks my ear
until I yelp.

"Mistress," says the priest, "I became an exorcist." He spreads his
bright fingers wide. "Myself, I could not believe it. But many said there was
some magic in the laying on of my hands. Both boys and girls claimed that
by touching their bellies I could pull the devils out."

I seem to hear, dimly, the cries of "Miracle! Miracle!" from the marketplace. I notice the falcons are weeping.

Modest to a very fault, the exorcist explains, "It did appear that I had
been singled out from the men of God. None of the other priests or friars
seemed to win such a result. So in time, the devils left Lors. The town re-
joiced. And I must confess I myself felt there was something to my reputation, that I was doing good work."

"So what do you need from me, Father Etienne?" asks la Bonne. "You've
led a blessed life."

It takes him a moment to answer, while I count the ticks of raindrops
against shutters. His head is bowed, showing the shiny pate within its fringe
of gray-streaked black. "I was sent away," he says at last. "The devils were
in a nearby village, and my superiors felt I was needed there. They gave me
a mule and sent me off. They sent me to a place called Matours."

"Oh!" I clap my hands.

Bonne looks down at me. "You've heard of it?"

Gladly I recite, "Have you been to Matours? Town of virgins and
whores? Dirty priests there conduct their amours—"

"Hercule!" She stops me just as I reach the end of my memory. Her eyes
threaten me with enclosure in the clothes chest. Then she invites the other,
"Please continue."

"Matours is a small place," he says, not looking at me. "But its fame has
spread, obviously . . . I lived with the aging parish priest. It was winter, and
in the cold I felt the floor of my ordaining church. I was homesick. I imagined the dust still on my forehead, a gray circle my patients could see.

"It did not go well for me in Matours. I exorcised two demons but they
reentered their victims the very next day. The devils seemed to be taking

older persons there, mostly around nineteen years of age . . . and one un-
lucky Friday I was called to the bed of a twenty-year-old woman. Bad for-
tune caught up with me there, with the girl's mother and aunt watching.

"The first part of an exorcism, as you may know, is always the inter-
view of the victim. How long has the devil been occupying the body? By
what signs does he, or she, make presence known? This girl's answer to the
first question was, 'From time to time over the past three months,' ever since
a demon had invaded her next-door neighbor. It was not there every day,
but often enough. Her demon was a male, an incubus, she was sure. He an-
nounced his arrival by setting afire and violently agitating her most secret
parts. As is often the case."

Lady Bonne and I nod. The story's getting better.

"Mistress, her private place would swell and burn and provoke her
dreadfully. In the course of my duty I asked—I had to ask—to see the part
afflicted. Remember that her mother and aunt were there. They pulled up
the sheet and showed me the part, and the girl swore the fever there was
scorching. I saw nothing, and when I put my hand there, as is common prac-
tice for an exorcist, I felt no particular heat.

"I suggested she get to her knees and pray with me for deliverance. She
was reluctant to leave her bed. The demon, she said, had threatened to in-
crease the agitation if she moved upright. When I tried to insist, she began
moaning and thrashing her limbs, which made the bedclothes fall away and
exposed her afflicted part again. This time it did indeed look inflamed."

He stops, overcome.

"Then what did you do?" I ask.

He sighs and responds to me for the first time, but looks at the light in
his lap. "I tried the laying on of hands for which I was known. I laid them
on her belly, as in previous cases, and massaged her gently. After some time
she quieted down, and though I felt nothing, she swore the devil had left her.
Her mother covered her again, and I, too, left.

"For some weeks afterward I was able to live in Matours more or less
peacefully, visiting the afflicted there and in nearby villages. The demons
seemed to be abandoning the young people, though I no longer felt I could
take credit for any exorcism. More often I was summoned to deliver last
rites or to pray with citizens suffering more usual physical ailments. Tu-
mors, boils, catarrh—

"I have to tell you," he interrupts himself, "I was happy in Matours. I hoped my superiors would let me settle there, that the demand for exorcism had ended. I was eager to take over the church when my gentle host retired, and give the holy sacrament to the people I'd come to know so well. But it didn't happen.

"That twenty-year-old woman had . . . well, she had responded too well to my treatment."

I realize he's making a feeble joke. Or is it?

Bonne murmurs, "She'd fallen in love with you."

"Not even that. But she announced she was pregnant. And though her mother and aunt had been in the room while I exorcised her, they insisted that I must be somehow to blame."

I look at the man again, with interest. That light seems to come from his whole body now, like the lumens that are said to emanate from a ghost. A man whose hands alone can stir life in a virgin belly . . . His eyes, though, are dark, two pinpricks fastening him to this world. He is no saint.

"So you see, mistress," he continues, "I was immediately condemned. Though I was not dismissed from holy orders, I was demoted. Even after all the exorcisms I had performed, I found myself without powerful friends, and even though eight months, nine, ten passed and the girl was not brought to bed—"

"You don't have to continue," says Lady Bonne. Her hands are at the fastenings of her dress. "You are hungry now."

As she frees the falcons, I say, "The problem is that the girl was never brought to bed. You should have bedded her, to keep her quiet."

"Perhaps"—the priest can't help licking his lips, watching the birds stretch their wings—"I'm being punished for my early fame, for the pride I may have taken in it."

Mouth fastens at last to beak, and I let the stranger take the first edge off his hunger. When he comes up for breath I ask, "What finally happened to the girl?"

He looks at me with sweet milk dripping from his lips. "I don't know." He says it not to me but to our mistress, who is still leaking. "Now I only scrub the church floors."

The falcons reach out to draw him close.

 GIRL WHO, ABANDONED BY HER LOVER, RID her body of his child; the sage-femme who helped her: These women I feed, as they were doing their best with what they had. The gossips who condemned those two, the man who promised marriage and summarily wed elsewhere: These I turn away. I feed a gentle exorcist, wrongly accused of venery, and, always, my fillette, who calls herself Marguerite and is becoming a friend of sorts. I still hope to find the courage to frame the questions I feel I need to ask her.

So much of men's and women's lives have been hidden from me. So much unfolds for me now. I hear of love, anger, sorrow, revenge. Of fathers and mothers, lingering bedridden deaths and urgent, moonlit courtships. Of childish pranks and regretful hurts. Of life.

Meanwhile, Hercule keeps begging to visit the Putemonnoie house. Like the rest of Villeneuve, he has a natural curiosity about my mistress; but I also suspect him of some darker purpose. Though I have no idea what he wants within Radegonde's walls, it is my sworn goal to keep him out. I drug him with milk until, near ecstatic, he can't budge to chase me down the street. Then I walk my rounds, nursing those too weak to leave their beds, visiting Marie, before I finally make my way to the great black gate.

Today Marie prophesies about midsummer, which is fast approaching: "With the swallow comes midsummer, Saint Jean's fire and sometimes water . . . If there's thunder in June, we'll have fruit soon, for c'est le mois de juin qui fait le foin . . . If a fire does light on midsummer's night . . ."

I wonder how much time my grandmother spends composing her rhymes, or if they come to her during her hours of prayer and meditation. Can they be sent directly from God? In any event she finishes the last one quickly, as if she's heard my footsteps but can't bear to leave a prophecy half-voiced: ". . . the-sun-will-shine-with-greater-might."

Today I have a poem of my own, and I pass it through her slit along with the usual bread and cheese. "Whether it's cold, Marie, or whether it's hot, there's going to be weather—whether or not."

The gray hand takes its rations and retreats. Silence. I notice the window's wild rose is in full bloom and heavily laden. It drowns out even the smell of the rotten fruit Marie's rejected.

"Better hold your nose," I say. "The air might flavor your bread with too much sweetness today."

Feeling uncommonly cheerful, I sink against the wall—I don't mind a prick or two from the rose's soft thorns—and enjoy the sight of so much greenery, and the little smacking sounds of Marie's feeding. I wonder how she would sound at my breast; probably louder than even the littlest, hungriest boy. And then I think it's funny that she insists on bread and cheese when all this time she could have had the richest food in the world, a food people will rape and bribe for.

Blanche, I seem to remember, nursed me very late. Maybe there was no other food she could give me. There in the sunshine, I get a clear picture of myself: out of swaddling clothes and standing on my own two legs at Blanche's knee, drinking my dinner. I seem to recall looking up and seeing her face, not tired and lined as it is in other memories, but clear and serene, smiling down at me. Perhaps, I think, this is how I managed to survive that tenuous childhood. Perhaps . . .

As I ponder it, Blanche's posture grows into a resemblance of the images in churches I have visited—the countless Virgins and minor female saints—and her face seems to melt into the face I see in Radegonde's mirrors.

Holy Virgin! For a moment I panic, try desperately to recapture my mother's looks. What color were her eyes? Were her cheeks round or gaunt? Forgetting Marie, forgetting the sunshine, I start to stumble blindly for the bell tower, thinking that if I enter Saint-Porchaire I will be able to remember. Or what if la Putemonnoie's looking-glasses have made me forget the one thing I've spent my life recalling?

Can it be she planned it this way? Could she really be a witch?

Below the June sun, the ruined roof bakes and pops. I stare dizzily down from the tower's edge at the rippling lead and recall a few lines of poetry. They feel in my head like a prayer, and when I say them aloud, they echo off the rubble in a voice that is both Blanche's and Radegonde's but belongs to neither, rather to a parish friar from my childhood: *My dove, my undefiled is but one; she is the only one of her mother, she is the choice one of her that bare her.*

ON MY WAY to the Putemonnoie house, I pass face after languishing face; bodies, slumped in doorways, that straighten as they see me. Though I draw the linen veil around my face, my figure can't be mistaken, and soon my name resounds around me—*Bonne Bonne Bonne* . . . I pause to pass a drop to one or two in particular need, and I receive their thanks impatiently. I long for the green quiet within Radegonde's walls.

I am come into my garden, my sister, my spouse . . .

When at last I arrive, I'm told the mistress is in the solar. This surprises me a little, as we have long been intimate enough for the comfort of the bedroom. But today, clearly, she intends to hold court. She's sitting in an x-chair and has had the rest of the seats removed; the broderie frame is in her hands, and a row of neatly rolled silks sits on a table beside her, next to the usual tangle of her threads. A huge bowl of roses blooms at her other side.

As I enter, I seem to hear a whisper of fabric, as if of a dress in flight; then Radegonde delicately pulls a thread taut, and I see she's working on a thorny border to her Garden of Earthly Delights.

"Good afternoon," I say, feeling as if I should bow or kneel at her feet. She is that cool and collected, in spite of the black velvet belly and heat-flushed face. "Where is your husband's book? Should I fetch it?"

She waits a moment before she replies. She focuses on the linen, holding the frame between herself and me. "We won't be reading today."

"No?" Despite a growing dread, I try to make my voice as colorless as hers.

Radegonde Putemonnoie weaves her needle through the stitches on the back of the linen, fastening off the thread; then she selects a strand the color of a peacock's tail and fits it through the needle's eye. I sense I've displeased her very seriously, and even the comical detail of a green thread stuck wormlike to her belly doesn't soothe me. I'm quaking in shoes still black with holy soot.

"Are you sure?" I ask in a faint voice. "I think I know a page with a story on it."

Carefully she anchors the bright new silk. "Why should I be interested in my husband's secrets today?" she asks. "Assuming that he had any worth hearing about. He's dead, and as we have seen, his secrets come to nothing. I'm much more interested in yours."

"*My* secrets?" I ask, fainter still.

She takes a stitch and picks it out. "Yes." Stitch, pick. Stitch, pick.

This is torture! I'm ready to throw myself at her feet, tell her about the day I gave birth, describe my life with Blanche, pretend I know my father's name. Which of these—or is it all of them—does she want? "Mistress, I assure you . . ." Of what?

She startles me by throwing her tapestry hoop aside, tumbling the silks down with it. She folds her arms, looking square at me. "You think I don't hear about what you do?" she asks. "You think no one tells me what goes on in the streets? *You think I can't see with my own eyes when I mount my tower?*"

"What—what have you seen?"

"You"—she points a long, accusing finger at me—"have been giving your milk away. *My* milk. My son's. For days now."

"You shouldn't go up in the tower, you know," I tell her. "At this stage it could be very dangerous—heights and stairs . . ." But it's not her clean view of Villeneuve that fills my mind, it's the black ruin of Saint-Porchaire, where I myself nearly fell just now.

She ignores my warning. The needle, still between her fingers, snaps. "What do you have to say for yourself, Bonne? Why have you been giving away what is mine by contract? And to strangers in the street—"

"I speak to them first," I defend myself. "They tell me their lives' stories. It's a sort of payment."

She vents an inelegant snort. "What do you want stories for? You give them milk—blood—life—for what? Stale wind!" She tugs at the heavy pendant on her bosom. "Stories aren't good business."

"I'll tell them to your baby as he grows up."

"My heir—why should he hear the lives of defrocked priests and prostitutes, or drink in the bad humors these people pass on to you?"

"They take my body in their mouths," I say. "Not the other way around. And I give each of them only a mouthful, so there's always more—"

"That milk is mine," she insists. "We have an agreement. Who gives you the food that produces the milk, so good and in such abundance?" It's unclear whether she's describing the food or the milk with that phrase, but I don't question her. "You have no business running around town offering your body like a—"

"I know what you're going to call me," I interrupt, quite calm now. "Others have said it before—but if you'd gathered your news well, you'd know that nobody is saying it now. The town is grateful to me. They've accepted me. And through me, I hope, they will accept you; they know I'm fed from your larders."

"They don't *have* to accept *me*." She tosses her head so the jewels flash. "I'm the one they should be begging for favors. And anyway, I took care of all that—I bought them that nice labyrinth, didn't I? Even now it's being fitted into the floor of the new church."

"They don't want a labyrinth," I say gently. "They want food. Everyone is hungry."

Her foot taps for the space of a heartbeat. "Why are you feeding people who've shunned you all your life?" she demands. "Your first patronne wouldn't even give you a bed to sleep in—yes, I know she made you lie in a pile of straw. Why should you waste yourself on them, when you know I'll take care of you?"

I think. The first picture that comes to my mind is the fillette, her dirty red dress and yellow hair. "Christian charity?" I offer. "Ensuring my place in heaven, cleansing my soul of past sins?"

"'It feels good to do good,'" she mocks. "You're simply afraid, Bonne Tardieu. And you know you have no call to be—I can give you everything. I will even give you a home."

I don't know how to tell her that what I really fear is exactly that, living in her house, sleeping by her bed, utterly losing my life in hers. I haven't realized until this moment just how much I need to have my separate life—my friends Godfridus and Hercule, the little domus hung with old linen, even my visits to Marie and Saint-Porchaire. The life I've made myself. If I lived here, I would have nothing but Radegonde. And Father Pierre's questions.

Suddenly Radegonde holds both hands out. The everycolor eyes focus entirely on me: commanding, pleading? "Come here, Bonne. Live here. Now," she says. Palms up, arms open, eyes melting. Pulling me close.

Despite myself, for a brief space I fantasize. I would bathe. I would read, I'd breathe and perhaps even wear her scents . . . But just as I long to throw myself into those arms and vow my everlasting loyalty, just as I step toward her, I see the kick under the black velvet.

The baby, whose fate will determine Radegonde's. The baby, who will be my charge to swaddle, burp, and wash. The baby, whose body will share my bed and whose smell will fill my nose and whose demands will put an end to our reading together. The baby.

"I can't." I say it baldly, and I offer no explanation.

Stung, quick, Radegonde folds her arms again. Her body rolls into a ball of fury around the stomach. "Then go!" she shouts. "Leave here and don't come back! There are plenty of wet nurses in this town!"

I don't point out that virtually every breast in Villeneuve has dried up except my own. That doesn't matter. She knows full well, as I know, that mine will wither too, once I'm banned from her kitchens. And there are no other pregnant women to make wet nurses these days; hard times make for miscarriages and infertile wombs. But even though we both know we're each other's only hope, we say nothing more. I leave, and she doesn't stop me.

HERCULE

When she comes home, she washes herself, scrub scrub scrub beneath the breasts, in the armpits, over the face, even between the legs. She's fixing herself up as clean as a virgin.

"All those mouths," she says, but she doesn't meet my eyes. Her hands shake.

"There's some smells that don't come off," I tell her from my squat by the cold hearth.

She rinses the cloth in red wine—these days, it's cheaper than water—and starts sliding it between her toes.

"They didn't suckle there, did they?" I tease her, and I grab the cloth and whirl it over our heads, anointing us both with red rain.

"Give me that!" She grabs for it, but then she starts to laugh, so hard she falls to the rushes. Her laughter's too fast and too hard for my trick, but I think it must be better than tears.

"Give that to me," she gasps, "or I'll—I'll have your balls on my girdle string!"

"Very nice!" I say, and snap the cloth smartly on her rump, leaving a big wet stain like a handprint. Then I tumble down beside her.

Suddenly the laughing stops. I'm staring into a pair of pale gray eyes, in the middle of which—tiny black circles—I see myself reflected.

It is the best moment of my life.

What an awkward pause in time, staring into the dwarf's eyes. My face looms large and white in his pupils. It is upside down and framed in yellow-green, set off like an artwork, like the face of someone crucified headfirst. It is my face, swollen and nearly transparent, but a different face than I'm used to.

The farmers say that if you see yourself reflected in another person's eyes, that one is your destiny. Can it be I'm supposed to end up with Hercule? Here, in this mean little room? Instead of—instead of where my mind has taken me these last weeks and months, instead of the fate I hoped I'd sealed with what I see now was a misguided, misplaced kiss. Instead of what was just offered and refused.

"Vanity," I murmur, as the eye image wavers before me. *Empty, foolish* . . . My own eyes well with tears, and I can't see Hercule or myself or anything else.

Hercule notices this. As a tear drops down my cheek, he wipes it away with his hand.

I can't help it. I flinch. I have come to like Hercule in these months, and I no longer fear the dwarf in him—but his is not the hand I want to touch me. His is not the body I want next to mine.

Immediately I whisper, "I'm sorry." But in this moment of our gaze, he has understood me—how deeply I am not sure, but at the very least he knows how I feel about *him.*

Hercule does not speak. He gets to his feet, pulls on his hood, and is quickly out the door. It slams and I am left alone.

HERCULE

The sun might shine with all its height, driving the shadows away, but I couldn't see to save my life. I see water—water for washing, water pouring in sheets from the sky. Water becoming wine. Cold stone, warm arms. An ugly breast, a tiny picture of myself.

I see love. And hatred. And there is only one place for me to go.

My feet take the narrowest streets they can find, well buried in curves and corners. We trip over mist, my big clumsy feet and I, and our stomach growls. Irreverent now as at every important moment of my life.

I speak to my stomach—"If you're hollow, think of the barren heart that's fed you."

No, that's not funny either. And what's more, it isn't true. What of that skin-and-bones whore, that disproved demon teaser, that bitch of a baker's wife—all lost souls that somehow touched hers, filled her heart till its blood burst from her chest, transformed into life-giving liquor that she shared freely. And that she enjoyed sharing.

It has always been easy to hate the ones she has loved, just as I can love those she does not. Chief among them myself—the dwarf she damned in saving.

I swoop down the narrowest street imaginable, my dwarf arms spread and grazing the walls on both sides. I am small, but this place is smaller...

I don't know if the Jew will help me. I don't even know what to ask for—something, a potion, a chant to bring about a revolution in Fortune's wheel, the lowest brought high and the highest, dashed. But I open the crescent-moon door and climb the rickety stairs anyway, greet the old woman and cross the mage's palm with silver.

There is no light in his hand. Only streaks of black dirt, traces of the too many generations he's lived. But still I ask for my spell.

It is the simplest of requests, yet he looks at me with jowly eyes.

"Surely you know this one in your sleep," I wheedle. "You could do it while sneezing or"—I look at the crone—"making a baby..."

"The best charm I can sell you," he tells me, "is one for giving up hope. Think of it—emptied out of foolish expectations, of desire itself."

But I don't want to give up my hope. It's what keeps a man alive, as the Christian fathers knew. To lose hope is to stop praying, and that's perhaps our ultimate sin. But I don't tell Macchabé this, because how do I know? Maybe the Jews cut away hope with their foreskins.

"Just sell me the charm I asked for." I make myself grim to please him. 219

Macchabeus sighs. "I can see there's no dissuading you."

My heart leaps. "None."

"Well, then..."

Now a cackle in the corner—the old woman, delighting in some private memory or joke. The wizard stares at her a moment, braiding his paws together, then sighs again and addresses me. "For a charm of this sort to work," he says, "there is something you must do first. Certes I could sell you some cheap trick that would win momentary happiness, but for real power you must do as I say."

"Anything, Father." Or have I spoken too soon?

"You will have to empty yourself out. Not of hope, yet"—raising one dark, crooked hand—"but of ill will. Just as a dove won't roost in a storm-tossed branch, so love won't nestle in an angry breast. Make peace with your enemies, learn not to envy or feel wrathful."

"I have to become good...?" When I think it over, this seems a seemly, though undesirable, demand.

He explains. "You have to become free, if you are to tie yourself to another heart. If the spell is to work, you must become like a still pool, giving back the reflection of the other. There is a rite with glass and silver that may come later, but you must prepare yourself in this way first."

If anything, his words increase my hopes tenfold. Reflections—an easy job, I think. There are just a few obstacles to clear away, and then I'll be seeing myself in a loved one's eyes every day.

For to become empty of anger and envy, what better than to remove their objects? I'm sure he or some apothecary can provide a suitable instrument. My path is clear, and I'm soon on my way—rejoicing. I even ignore that cackle, repeated as I plunge down the stairs and out into the street, where between peaked roof and oversailing I manage to see—yes—a real moon and two stars.

FEAST OF
JULIANA
FALCONIERI

[JUNE 19]

 SUPPOSE I SHOULD NOT BE SURPRISED TO find Agnès with Godfridus, but I am. I rather expected that when she heard about yesterday's quarrel with Radegonde—and she must have heard by now, since today has already passed nones—she would pack her bundle and go. Perhaps she is more loyal to Godfridus than I thought. And in a way he is loyal to her; today he won't play the trick we developed, won't send her out at my whistle.

I'd like her to go, and I don't care where. I slump on Godfridus's only chair and rest my head against his bed; in times of trouble, I think, the old friends are best. But as yet I haven't said the first word to him. I haven't had the chance.

Godfridus has no eyes for me; he is pacing up and down, hands in his armpits, wispy hair on end. His agitation, I think, has something to do with the tall shape he's draped with a sheet. The thing catches all the light in the room, and he keeps stepping up to it and twitching at the cloth, furtively caressing the shape beneath. Agnès herself is watching him; there's some mending from the great house in her hand, but her attention is all for the sculptor, her patient.

"You must sit down," she tells him, anxiously soothing. "It is good to interrupt your work once in a while, no matter how inconvenient you find it."

He perches then on the side of his bed but is up again immediately, smoothing the drape of the sheet. He reminds me of an ungainly stork about to lay an egg, fussing over her nest as if a twig out of place will break the shell.

"I'm ready for paints," he says, abstractedly. "I need colors—the finest lapis, ground stone and eggwhite . . . a good deal of brown, and coral pink. I can grind them myself."

So he's managed to finish something. Perhaps he re-clayed the dried earth, soaked it in water or wine to make something he could work with, found some baker's oven to fire it in.

My head sags heavier against the hard mattress. "You won't be getting materials from me," I say. "I've been dismissed."

Now the other two really do look at me. "You shouldn't have told him that," Agnès hisses. "The last thing he needs is to know that." Out loud she says, "The paints are on their way, Godfridus. I've already asked. The eggs, too. They should come tomorrow—peacocks' and swans', and I'll help you break them."

"Dismissed?" Godfridus asks me. "You won't be working for la Pute-monnoie?"

I nod my head, then shake it, uncertain which reply would mean my destiny is sealed. "No more nursing. No more meals." No more anything. I ready myself for a hand on my brow, a soothing touch on my shoulder. But Godfridus just stands before his long sheeted wand of an opus, on the brink of despair for its fate.

Agnès says again, "The paints *will* come tomorrow. Don't worry. You'll still have everything you need." She gives me a sidelong glance, as if she's satisfied now, knowing she has a power I do not, and she goes to lay a hand on Godfridus's forehead (the gesture, I think, that should be comforting me). "Don't upset him," she whispers. "He hasn't slept in weeks."

At this I get up. But before I leave, I have a few words for the maid. "If I'm banished, you know, you'll be wanted back there. Mistress Putemonnoie will send for you again, and you'll be waiting on her night and day."

I can't tell how Agnès feels about that. Of course she longs to resume her intimate association with a great lady—who wouldn't?—but it seems she's found something of almost equal satisfaction here, at the home of a great artist. Of course, such terms are always particular to the mouth of the one who utters them; I think especially of the broken clay heads. And then I notice the heads aren't there anymore. Godfridus must really have done something he's proud of.

AYS PASS, EACH TWICE AS EMPTY AS THE ONE before, but only half so as the day that is to come. I feed less, knowing the day will soon come when I have nothing left to give. But I do keep feeding—for if I don't, what good has my resistance done?

I am reminded, as I nurse, of the blessed Juliana Falconieri, who fasted until she could eat no more. Her wasted body refused all food, even the holy host, and in the end she took the last sacrament through her breast; it marked her nipple with a cross. I, too, am fasting now; but if I wait for signs of divine grace, I wait in vain. I have only belief in myself to fall back on, and my sense of what is right.

"I lost my husband," a petitioner might say, or, "I lost my children."

These days I follow up my expression of sympathy with a question: "How did the loss occur?"

Today's bereft mother wrings bony hands, watching me wetly. "I had two daughters, mistress, two little girls, and the Jews stole them both."

I have a bad feeling. "The Jews?"

"We were gathering plants in the siege's

early days, the three of us. Grass and herbs for a soup. When suddenly, from an alleyway, came a party of the heathen beasts . . . five," she says, wringing some more, "there were five of them—three held me down while two carried my girls away."

Hercule says, "This sounds less like a story than a problem in mathematics."

"What made you think they were Jews?" I ask. "Can you be certain?"

"Their caps, mistress—tall and yellow, the caps all Jews must wear out-of-doors. And the yellow circle badges on their breasts. They carried my girls away kicking and screaming, and my three attackers gave me such a blow to my head that I fainted away, and when I woke up they were gone."

I close my eyes and try to picture it: five men fleeing through tangled streets, their yellow hats bobbing at the peaks, two wriggly little girls caught in their arms.

"Mistress, clearly they planned to eat my girls in one of their dark rites," my applicant says with an air of desperation.

I think of my own little lump, buried some unknown place beyond the walls. "How big were your daughters?"

"Four years old and three, mistress."

Hercule makes some signs in the air. "Five men and two girls, combined age of seven, divided by one grown woman and an apronful of herbs—"

"Boy"—she turns to him with sudden sharpness—"how dare you make light of a mother's bereavement?"

"The boy is right," I say. "There is much fact in your story, no feeling."

"But I do feel!" She spreads her hands wide; I see the dirt settled into the lines of her palms. "I am—was—a mother! I grew those babies in my womb, I fed and swaddled them—"

"And then abandoned them in an alleyway."

She stares at me, eyes wide in horror. "Jews took them!"

"Would Jews bent on evildoing wear badges that would identify them later?" I point to the door. "There were no Jews. Perhaps there were no daughters."

She flings herself at my feet and wets my hem with her tears. "Mistress—mistress, I am hungry!"

Gently I detach myself, then Hercule and I drag her to the door. "These are hard times," I say, feeling almost sympathetic. "Perhaps I wouldn't blame you for abandoning your children. But I can't let you lie to me about such a loss."

She goes out weeping. Hercule and I look long at each other, and I see myself reflected once again.

FEAST OF SAINT PAULINUS OF NOLA

I LINGER ON IN MY DOMUS, WHICH ONCE seemed such a palace, and I think of the one that truly is palatial. The garden! The windows! The tapestries, the carpets, the down pillows and velvet hangings! And food—meat and fish and fowl, breads lighter and more delicious than from any baker's oven, sauces like nothing of the known world.

I believe Godfridus is still getting these, courtesy of Agnès. When I stood beneath his window last night, I saw her outline against the shutters. And the shadow of Godfridus's arms, whirling about his column of light.

They are dark times indeed when one friend can't rely on another. Or on the town's goodwill, or on her own resources. I can no longer count even on my bakers' loaves; the woman is on her feet again and doing well, but the man spends his days cursing on the ramparts, and anyway there is no flour. It would seem that I, Bonne sometimes-known-as-Tardieu, am all we have left.

Reports reach me that thieves have broken into Radegonde's garden. They came at night, over the walls, and grabbed at the green stuff inside. Grass, flower buds, rose petals. They urinated in the spring, fouling it at its source; the next day the water burned the soil instead of quenching it. But in their haste and greed, they overlooked the unfamiliar kitchen garden and left the lettuce and carrots and spices in their orderly rows. They also overlooked one of their own number, who broke his leg when falling from the wall. He is now in the town prison, awaiting execution; Radegonde's own guards dragged him there.

This is the news that circulates, as people scrounge for similar treats. Sweet things. Savory things. Melt-in-your-mouth morsels . . .

Today I am content (or *will* make myself so) to nibble at what Hercule buys in the streets with our last coins. I won't take rat or dog, but there are some strange leaves and a piece of hard, flat bread, mostly ground plaster. Hercule and I lie on our bed and gaze at the rafters, each thinking our own private thoughts. We agree not to answer the door; we turn the key together, shutting out our hungry neighbors. All afternoon the people come and go, knocking long and losing hope. I feel nothing now, and fear my flow is ceasing.

Toward evening, one visitor does not bother to knock. A hand tries the door latch straight away. It is the priest, I think; it is Father Pierre (I missed my visit to him yesterday). He will leave.

But then there are the sounds of iron clinking and of a key being fit into the lock. I sit up on my bed, letting the straw crackle loudly under me. The baker? I wonder.

That key does not work. But before I can feel relief, there's another in the lock, and then another. The visitor must have twenty keys or more, perhaps a hundred; one by one, they're fit in, until I lose count. And then—just as I'm almost ready to scream and open the door myself so I can push this person down the stairs, break his bones and bloody his nose—a key works. The latch lifts, and the visitor walks in.

She is wearing a mantle, long and brown; it is the garb of a peasant woman, but there's no mistaking the body inside. It has her bearing and her gait, her enormous belly. It has a maid behind it, with a basket of keys, iron rods gleaming in the half-light. *Her* eyes shine out from the hood. And then she's thrown the mantle off, and there is the black dress, the heavy pendant, the long sleeves belling around the big hands. A smile—

beseeching, I think, or can it be merely commanding—quivers around her sharp nose and pillowy lips.

"I will give you a banquet," she says. She sounds almost timid.

"A BANQUET?" I am faint with hunger. I keep my eyes down, so she won't read that in them.

Radegonde steps restlessly around the room. She tugs on a piece of the wall linen, and it comes off in her hand. "For the sealing of a contract, we will have a feast," she says, dropping the rag. "Yes, once and for all I have decided you *will* be my wet nurse, and the world may know it. In payment I'll serve you anything you've ever heard or read of. Anything you want."

Now I see the two of us in the bath, feasting on a great pie as our skins pucker. Feathery bones crunch between our teeth, and the water's scent embraces us . . .

Hercule picks up his wooden balls and begins to juggle. By this I know he's anxious—of course he wants to keep me out of the great house and devoted to him, but we both have to eat. He must want me to say yes and to find him a position as a fool.

Radegonde catches her breath and emphasizes, "Whatever you like. Whatever you want." She's walking toward me now. "Birds, beef, fish, pastries—I'll fill your mouth with things you've never even dreamed of eating."

Over by the bed, there is a loud *crack!* as one of Hercule's balls smashes into the shutter.

"Anything," says Radegonde. "Everything."

I feel weak, afraid. I must not let myself be commanded so easily; I think of all she's had me do these last months, all she has wanted from me. At this moment, I must convince myself I have some power—after all, *she* came back to *me*. And came herself, instead of sending a servant.

"It seems like so much for just two people," I say at last.

With a grand sweep of the hand, Radegonde replies, "Invite your friends."

I think of my friends—who are they? Godfridus, Hercule, the fillette and the exorcist? The bakers? Or perhaps all my clients, all who've told a tale and suckled from me?

Before I can answer, Hercule begins to jump around the room. "We accept!" He's cartwheeling, juggling, acting as much the fool as he can. "Name the time!"

But I say stubbornly, "I don't know."

Radegonde bites her lips. "Don't know?" We both recognize that tone in her voice; she's trying to hold her temper.

But I have to ask one question: "Why do you want me?"

HERCULE

I forget how to caper. The maid drops the keys. For everything in here has changed.

The women's eyes are flashing like black stars. Their pupils portray each other. My heart pops out my ears—can all hear it? I'm juggling it now with the keys. The air cools but annoys it, and my grip is slippery. The walls close in on us all.

At the end, as we're all about to choke, la Putemonnoie speaks out loud: "Your milk is the best, Bonne, and I must have the best. That is why."

It's all she needs to say. For with this, we understand.

Their eyes can close now.

From the other side of the room, I feel Bonne's spirit swell. It seems to press against the bed, the chest, the chair, to ooze out the window and into the street. I am important, she is thinking. I am loved.

I slip a few keys in my pocket.

Radegonde Putemonnoie wants me. She will do what I ask; she will honor my friends; she will feed and fete and court me. She is looking at me now.

Still I have an objection. I tear my eyes away and say, "If you do give this banquet—*if*—shouldn't we share with the town? People are hungry—"

"I thought you were taking care of that, Bonne." Radegonde tosses her head but then bows it, determined to be humble or at least forgiving. She understands what I'm intimating, and after all she wouldn't want the town to resent the feast either. "All right. Now please listen, because I'm prepared for this, too. If—when—you come back to me, I will build you a booth. A wooden hutment with a soft bench inside, big enough for you and a—a guest. It will sit inside my courtyard, and my servants will stand at the gate and admit your visitors. They will protect you. Think of it as a chapel, if you like."

"A chapel." I blush—Radegonde is looking pointedly around, beneath her lashes, at the wall linens, the straw bursting from the mattresses, the unswept floor. "We shouldn't call it that. I don't think . . ." But I realize I must make some concessions, too. "I accept," I say, very humble. "May I deliver charity baskets from the feast?"

"You may not. I will share my food in the form of your milk, but I won't give what I myself might eat. That's no bargain. And the people you service must promise something material in return—work on the labyrinth, perhaps, or if that's finished, as it will be in a very short time, they'll help build the birth chapel my Henri endowed. No stories."

No stories. But now I'll have the great-house tales again, perhaps Radegonde's own story . . .

Hercule jumps between us. "When is the feast?"

"Soon," she says with an everycolor eye on me. "Three or four days."

"Friday's unlucky for gatherings," says the dwarf. "But tomorrow is Midsummer's Eve—la nuit de Saint Jean. A most auspicious choice."

She throws up her big hands. "Tomorrow, then. I will have my servants start immediately. If Bonne agrees."

Why not agree? Let the feast be soon, if there is to be a feast—let the hut be built, if there is to be a hut.

I allow myself to smile. "I accept."

We seal our bargain with a kiss—the kind any woman might give a sister.

As I lie in bed by Radegonde, watching her have her hair brushed, I count up my blessings. Radegonde came back to me (or told me to go back to her); my friendship, like my service, must mean something. I'm even—shamefully—pleased about the stall she's planning to build. My feet get tired on their rounds; soon they'll have a pleasant place to rest, out of the day's heat, and I'll be almost like a lady taking callers. Virgini gratias.

Perhaps best of all (though I'm ashamed to say so), I'm to be the guest of honor at a real banquet. Even Godfridus will have to speak to me there; I am inviting him and Hercule. I get to request specific foods— everything I've wondered about, heard or read about, even foods forbidden by law to people of my station. I want roast peacock, fried flowers, everything spicy and honeyed. I want the Eastern food called treed.

Even as the hammers and saws go to work by the gateway, Radegonde throws open her pantries and larders and butteries, pries open barrels of salt fish, and unstrings ropes of onions and garlic. She runs around the house, carrying the great burden of her stomach too lightly, it seems, and supervising all the work. She is to approve every crust rolled, watch every chicken slaughtered. She seems to have gone a little mad.

"You'll see," she says. "After tomorrow night, you won't have anything to reproach me with ever again." Then she laughs wildly and pulls me down on the bed with her, where her hair swathes my face, and my body crumples a page of Henri's book.

"Are you sure you want to do this?" I ask, unpicking the fine black web of her hair. "There's no telling when the siege will lift and new food will come into town . . ."

"You have no idea how much this house holds. Other merchants may have run out, but I could host a feast every night for a year." Playful, she pulls her hair over my face again. I feel the spine of Henri's book straining under my rump. "And besides," she continues, lying back, "I'm bored— aren't you bored? There's nothing to do in town anymore. It's time we had a treat."

I duck out from under the hair and rescue the book—intact, I note with relief; the very definition of durable. "Shall I read, mistress?" My question sounds uneasy even in my own ears; I hope the reading will have a calming influence on her spirits, which I decide have become overheated by the ovens.

"By all means," she says, lying back with a sigh. "Read away." She closes her eyes and soon gives the impression of sleep.

GODFRIDUS

It whispers from my brush, each stroke a beat of blood through stone: crystals of blue, of brown, of red, and of white, fluid for now, dissolving and sink-

ing, marrying marble. What quiet work this is. What delicate work. Sometimes only one hair is needed in the brush; it paints one hair on a holy head, one wrinkle in a sacred garment. One pore in saintly skin. Finer and finer the detail, till I can see inside the very body itself, the heart and bones and viscera; I am painting them, too, in a way.

So it is a shock when the door swings open, when Agnès throws down her mending and rushes to intercept—unsuccessfully—the body of a speeding dwarf.

He plants himself before the statue, legs wide apart. I can't sheet it now, or the layer of color would smear. I try to make a shield with my body, to limited success—but he doesn't even seem to notice.

"A good evening to you, sculptor. And I mean that sincerely." He makes an elaborate bow.

"Is that why you're here?" Agnès grabs the dwarf by the chin and leads him toward the door. Her eyes stay averted, as I've made her promise not to look on the Madonna till done. "Save your greetings till tomorrow, when we'll all be forced to see each other again."

Yes, I remember, a manservant from the great house came some hours ago with an invitation that I wanted to refuse—but, for the duty owed to gratitude, could not.

The dwarf—who is scarcely a dwarf these days—breaks away from the maid and plops down cross-legged on the floor. His arms cross, too. "I'm here for a visit," he says stubbornly. "I have important words to say."

I stop Agnès as she starts to drag him away by the hair. "It's all right." In these few moments, with the dry air from the door, the paints have turned past their prime; I'll have to mix others, and so I may as well sit and rest my hands, and uncramp them from the brushes.

I take the chair. Agnès kneels down beside me—she likes to rub my fingers with wine and oil. My eyes stay on the work, which is glowing now with multicolored light. I love the knees, the feet, the shoulders and head, but there's a tricky problem with the nose. "What is it, Legrand?"

"I want you to forgive me," the dwarf says.

HERCULE

"Forgive you?" says the stoneman, his face a mask of hardened dust. "What is there to forgive?"

I remind myself to stay civil, to open myself to the magic. "We have dis-agreed in the past."

"But I," he says, as the maid fetches two bowls and a cloth for his hands, "bless them that curse me."

I slap my legs rather than his face. "Do you have to make this so hard? I need forgiveness. I have to make peace. I'm emptying out my heart."

"A new miracle?" asks the maid tartly, rubbing his fingers with wine. She could do with a slapping, too.

But I continue to address the sculptor, with whom my business is today. "You know I gave you the wrong medicine. You know I've never wished you well."

"Oh . . ." He smiles—there's nothing stronger than hate, he means to say, except what keeps it in control. He stinks of oil. "I pray for them who persecute me. There is nothing to forgive."

"Of course there is."

With an air of obliging me: "Then I forgive you." He waits for me to go.

"I won't leave till you really *forgive me," I say. "Till you admit that I wronged you and give me your blessing. That's my task. Call it penance, if you like, but I'll stay here all night if I have to."*

The maid drops his hand in the oily red basin. It makes an irritated splash.

"I forgive you," the sculptor says again, though I can tell his mind's not on me. "But I'm not qualified to give blessings . . ."

Aha. Jealousy, resentment perhaps? Something I can work with.

"Maybe you're thinking of Bonne," I say. "—Oh, excuse me, your niece. Well, I can give you a full account. She's living that same dissolute life you've always warned her away from. You do know what she's doing, don't you?"

"I do," says the maid, but who cares?

I tell the stoneman, "Oh, I've tried to make her stop—I've begged her! I've warned about the wages of the flesh trade and the sin of uxoriousness. But the only answer was the smack of lips—a stranger's—on her tit."

I see his eyeballs swivel, turning to that dark shape in the corner, the one that seems to be making all the shadows in the room. "I had heard rumors," he murmurs disinterestedly.

"Maybe we could save her soul together?" I suggest.

The maid interrupts, "You want to know how to stop her milk?" She's cleaning under his fingernails now. "If the wet nurse somehow got her monthly curse, or if she got pregnant"—a weighty pause—"that'd stop it."

I don't need to hide my disgust and disappointment. "There's no trick to that," I say, "and we'll be waiting a long time if we want this man to do the job. He won't even take her milk anymore."

But the milk is still in him; we can both tell. Even now we smell it on him, see it in the whites of his eyes and the strength of his bones and those yellow teeth that squeeze out false friendship to me.

Late, I think maybe the maid wants me for the work. To stop Bonne's milk! The one way possible—no, I won't think that; I can't. I am to empty myself.

The maid dries the sculptor's right hand. "We must leave Bonne to the life she has chosen," he says.

I think I hear a noise from the corner, a stone joint creaking into life.

"Forgive me?" I try one last time, and I get the same answer.

"There's nothing—"

"Damn you." I mutter it as I'm leaving, removed bodily by those holy two above. "Damn you. Damn forgiveness. Damn thwarting me." Will I never have my heart's desire? "Damn you damn you damn you."

How will he bless me now?

GODFRIDUS

At last she is perfected. Every fold in her robe, every bend in her curls, every line around her eyes and ears and mouth as she smiles down at her Son, blessing Him with life, feeding Him from her body.

Agnès sleeps, and for this I am glad. We have had visitors today, but I can't recall who.

Life! The room is full of light and life. A slow golden pulse from the faceless Babe, from the beaming mother, a yellow perfect light that stretches out my window and rolls through the streets, lighting the town all the way to the house where tomorrow I am to celebrate.

DAY OF SAINT ETHELREDA, ON THE EVE OF SAINT JOHN

[JUNE 23]

N THIS, THE MORNING OF OUR BANQUET, THE cesspits round the bakery overflow. When I poke my head out the window, I see the stuff oozing up wet and black through the soil; it's as if the bakery's sailing on a lake of merde. The stench is enough to make a person deaf, dumb, and blind, to lay a healthy man out and strike a sick one dead. I'm glad to have one of Radegonde's linen squares to clap over my face; it's beyond me how Hercule can sleep.

A crew of neighbor men are shoveling the stuff away, trying to get at what's blocking the drain into the gutter. "Good morning, mistress," they greet me, in deference to my clean dress and full breasts.

"Good morning," I choke out. "Have you seen the bakers who own this place?"

One man gestures around him. "He's somewhere back here. She's inside, I think, hiding from the smell."

"And who can blame her?" Another man laughs, gazing nonetheless hungrily at me.

I go in search of the bakerwoman, my patient. I don't find her in the domus; she has been feeling better lately and is sometimes to be found behind the counter in the shop below. She says she likes to see people, likes to sell bread when there is some; she spends long hours doing neither when the shop is empty—she just scrapes the counters and the walls down to the iron they're nailed together with. So I leave by the alley door and go around to the shop front.

One of the workingmen, a fuller called Joseph, lays down a plank for me, a bridge over the swamp of excrement. "I hope the morning finds you well," he says.

I smile behind my linen square. To Joseph, I used to be invisible at best; his eyes would look right through and past me as I went down the street. Until this siege, that is. "Well enough." I look down and see white maggots writhing in the sludge, as if the horror is making them sick, too.

There are no customers in the bakery, and no bread; the window's shut tight against the smell in the street, but the door's unlocked. I find the proprietress keeping busy inside, collecting imaginary crumbs and whispers of flour, sweeping them into her palm and then into the all-but-empty bins for reuse. She is so thin now she barely makes a bump in her clothes.

"So it's you." She watches me warily; she hasn't quite made up her mind what to think of my amazing supply of milk, though she's not going to disallow it entirely. It might be good for business, and it may even have saved her own life. Though today she seems eager to avoid thinking of that, to avoid even the sight of me.

"You're feeling better, then?" I ask, wincing at a slight pain. At the sound of her voice my bosom started to flow—but then there are plenty who'll take what I have if she won't. "Thank the Virgin."

She crosses herself. "Deo gratias." She starts to scrub at the counter-top, picking at a minuscule fleck of flour. "I've got a baking of flatbread in the oven. Come back after terce, and you'll get your share."

"I won't be needing it today," I say, mindful of the dunged-up fug that will be baked into the dough. Blanche once told me that's what smell is—a tiny humor from something delicious or foul that's found its way inside your nose.

"That's right." Scrape, scrape. "I hear you're going to a feast."

"It's a celebration and a dedication," I tell her, aware that I'm more than half lying. "Mistress Putemonnoie is building a shelter from which

I can nurse, a little stall dedicated to helping the people of Villeneuve."
For the first time it strikes me that in some ways this stall may resemble
the dreaded orphanage, inasmuch as it will be an institution of charity for
the desperate. The poor, the diseased . . . I put that thought out of my
mind. "It's going to be finished this evening, and tomorrow I'll be sitting
there."

"Hm." I'm sure she's scraping sawdust now, but most of the bread in
town must be half that. So I don't interfere when she dusts the next handful into the bin.

"It's a good idea, I think," she says suddenly. "We should do something to protect those who stand between ourselves and death. In this
town, however it happened, that's you."

I bow my head. "I'm not making any such claim."

But now she's watching me with suspicion in her eyes, dusty hands in
her armpits. "Those priests have been around here," she says. "Pierre and
Paul, from the new church."

"They have?" A shiver on my spine.

"They were asking about you—small things, like what you eat and
whether you sleep at night."

"I eat your delicious bread," I say. But she isn't fooled.

"They wanted to know about your mother, too. They know I knew
her."

I lean across the counter on my palms. "And what did you say?"

She's silent a moment and begins sweeping the tabletop again and
again, sweeping under my elbows, around my hands. "I told them how it
was back then—reminded them—with the elevation in the church. Dust
from Blanche's feet sprinkled down on my head. I believed in her."

"And now you don't."

She shrugs. "Hard to say what's a miracle and what isn't. The church
doesn't give us any rules. Or if there are rules, they're in Latin and no ordinary person understands them."

I wait. When it seems clear she won't add to this last speech, I say,
"These priests—while they were asking about me, did you tell them
you'd tasted my milk?"

"Oh, they knew. Why do you think they asked at all? They have the
name of everybody you've fed in this town."

I close my eyes as if against a sudden slap. "But it's good milk," I whisper. "It helped you get stronger, didn't it?"

I feel a long, weighty pause, in which the bangs and scrapes from outside echo, in which the stench slowly swells.

"Here." The bakerwoman reaches for my hand, pulls me across the table—eyes still closed—until my fingers are pressed hard against her ribs. Under her hand my own travels upward, tracing the outline of a long, hard lump.

"Now you feel it," she says needlessly, then lets my hand drop. "And you must have seen the kind of thing. I've seen it."

My hand is strangely cold where it touched her. "How long has it been there?" But it seems to me to have been there always—as if I did notice it, long ago.

"What does that matter? A month, two months. There's no point in trying to get stronger now—I'd be better off just wasting away."

I whisper, "I'm sorry." Tears smart at my eyes. I've never liked the woman, but still.

"Don't tell my husband." She takes a deep breath, filling her lungs. "He thinks I'm cured . . . But now, if I'm not mistaken, the baking's done."

Moments later, with a piping-hot splinter of dust and ash pressing into me—what is now called food—I stumble out into the stink where my name is called on all sides.

ONLY AN HOUR LATER, I hold Marie's basin in hand and see smoke coming off Saint-Porchaire. Billows of pale gray lofting toward the sun, streaking, glittering . . .

That's just the night fog, I tell myself, burning off in the heat. Midsummer is no time for ghosts or mists; even the mist on the ground is just a faint shimmer now, the summer's grown so hot. The air is dry and still, begging for flames; it's danger weather—peste weather, weather for war or despair.

I wonder if Marie even remembers the town is besieged.

She takes the basin from me silently, as always, and the hand vanishes into its cool darkness. I wait around to see if she'll have something to say.

There's nothing from within the cell. Yet. But I notice that the wild rose outside the slit is in bud again. I have to resist the desire to pinch a green knot between my fingers—it's so tempting when a bud is that young and juicy.

When I think about it—as perhaps when the priests do—there's not much difference between the English mercenaries and me. Or the man who raped my breasts (can it be only weeks ago?) and set me on my new course, the one who I have hoped will guarantee my safe passage through this life and the next. We all take advantage of our advantages.

"What do you think about hell, Marie?" I pinch the bud then and toss it recklessly—*prong!*—against the wall. "You must have come to some conclusions as you lived your holy life."

No answer, and of course I didn't think I'd get one. I ask myself what Blanche would say now. What might she have told her mother when the two of them fought over the swelling beneath her apron?

"Some people say, Marie, that hell is just as pleasant a place as heaven. They say Lucifer was the first son of God, and everything in his world mirrors the realm of the second son, Jesus Christ. Though hell was an ugly pit of flame when Satan fell into it, he's planted grass, flowers, and cozy tunnels of fruit trees. There's plenty to eat, and it's never too cold or too hot, and you're with all the people you've loved most in the world. Or so I have been told."

Naturally I didn't get these words from Blanche. I learned them in an afternoon of awful, hopeful speculation, from the lips of my first lover, Laurent. But what is the harm in blaspheming to a woman nobody visits?

I continue, somewhat wickedly, "I sometimes think that a sinner would make a better ruler—a better parent—than a saint. Don't you think a sinner would be more forgiving, more nurturing, than one who'd never sinned at all?"

Marie does not answer. I think that if I asked her for a kiss, she'd stick her bum out the window.

And how *do* we know hell isn't like this? When so often the line between sin and charity won't come clear.

"I'm leaving now," I say, unnecessarily loud. "And do you know what I'm going to do, Marie? I'm going to let strangers undress me. I'm going to sit half-naked in front of them, and I'll be proud of it. They'll put their mouths on me and tell me stories of their misbegotten sinful lives. And then I'm going to a rich woman's house to wallow in luxury and stuff my belly until I burst like the toad who looked at the bull."

I hear the sound of water flowing into a basin.

Hercule

They've cleared the trench but not the stench; there's merde in the air thick as love.

Love. She spins around in front of me, wearing an old wool dress, a clean linen wimple, a string of uncrushed amber. "Is it good enough?" she asks of her best.

And I, in tight velvet motley—my own best—and home-knit hose, offer my hitherto dearest possession: two gloves, finest silk, just as finely stitched and embroidered.

"Gold thread," she marvels, pulling them happily on. She ignores the patterns that don't match, the hands of differing sizes. "A peacock and— what's this one?"

"A lute." And I think of the gesture that drew this sheath from its hand, enabling its owner to play—my master's wife, the foolish woman, lighting her lamp to music. This glove was hers.

But no matter. As Goodness admires her hand within the dead woman's shape, I tie a pocket below my jaquette. It bulges and clanks, heavy with tricks. Tonight will be my one chance, and I will use it.

So we set out, dressed in velvet, bedecked in beads. We wear the cast-off finery of noble court and bourgeois warehouse. We look ridiculous.

Tonight the streets are full, brimming, close. Everywhere people are pulling a shingle from a roof, a plank from an oversail; though everything's in short supply, Saint John will have his bonfire. The people will dance and sing and drink what wine there is. They will hold the greatest debauch they can.

John is the saint who pointed humankind's way to Christ. Christ's cousin, he dipped the faithful in a holy river and made us all what we are today—in some ways, I admire him more than the carpenter who got all the attention. Each year, we celebrate his water with fire.

Hercule and I, en route to our own feast, step carefully, mindful of our finery. I washed and beat my dress myself, and I've got Radegonde's beads around my neck; he's in velvet and lace. We're both wearing mantles to protect our clothes from the dust. Under them we sweat, and I'm worried about the stench of the cesspit still clinging. I hope we'll be offered perfume at the great house; I've heard this is the custom at parties.

There's noise all over town—people destroying their homes for fun. I see Godfridus's landlord dragging a window frame. A sort of desperate joy billows from street to street.

"Help me pull this door free!"

"What'll we do with the plaster?"

"There's a wagon—jump on!"

I'm doubly glad for the mantles now, since they give Hercule and me some anonymity; this merriment frightens me, and I'd rather not be stopped now. My friend the fillette will have business tonight, and there'll be bastards conceived in the dancing. Or would be, if the mothers' bodies were strong enough to nourish them.

In the marketplace and in front of the church itself, the wood is being piled. Over by the Palais de Justice we stumble into a crowd—an angry crowd kicking at a bundle on the ground. A man. He's curled up into himself, protecting his genitals, one arm over his skull. His nose bleeds and his clothes are torn.

"What are you doing?" I cry involuntarily, then push Hercule behind me for safety.

"We caught him selling bad wine," a woman says. There's a stone in her hand, ready to throw. "Can you imagine—in these times, and today of all days! When wine is all we have . . ."

"What shall we do to the villain?" a man's voice booms out.

"Draw and quarter him, and feed the pieces to the pigs!" another roars. "They're used to eating shit."

Amid some cruel laughter, a woman says, "There are no pigs anymore; we've eaten them all."

I clap my hand over Hercule's mouth lest he say, *La Putemonnoie still has pigs.*

"Good people," I beg, "be merciful."

But no one listens. They're all bent to their work, punching and spitting, gloating over their victim. I'm afraid suddenly, and I bolt away, dragging Hercule after me through the dirty streets.

A HUNGRY THRONG FOLLOWS US—Bonne, la Tardieu, and her young charge. But I have seen the limit of their enthusiasm; if they were to suspect a bad business, they would turn on us in a heartbeat.

I stain my dress from the inside out, as our followers' famine echoes in my gut. If it weren't for Hercule I would stop; I'd never make it to Radegonde's. But now he's pulling me, his hand an iron vise around my wrist, and I must follow. All I can offer the masses is a promise: Tomorrow the booth will be finished; I will be in it; Radegonde's men will apportion time with me to those in need. I emphasize this name: *Radegonde Putemonnoie*. They have only to wait until morning.

The people follow us through the quartier of the great houses, where the homeowners have bought wood for the people rather than sacrificing their own domi; they follow right up to the gate, where the same men who will guard me tomorrow, perhaps, are putting the final touches into the building of my stall. What might have been a crude wooden hut has become a miniature palace—well, perhaps a castle, a little fortress with three walls, a roof lined for shade, shingles, even two slender columns and a tiny cross on top to bless it. Two men are just now hammering the rood in place; two others stand waiting with buckets of paint.

One of these comes to open the big gates, allowing Hercule and me to slip inside. A manservant strides from the house with a torch, needless in this golden evening.

As the lock clangs shut, there's a moan from the crowd.

"Tomorrow," I promise, "tomorrow! Come back at dawn, and Mistress Putemonnoie will have the stall ready just here . . ."

Then the manservant's bearing me away, and Hercule, and there's Radegonde herself in the doorway—smiling and holding her hands out, with eyes only for me.

HERCULE

Outside, the people smolder. Their souls are filling their minds with smoke. Inside there's scent and sound, a carpet of flower petals and a gallery of musicians. Oils to dab behind ear and elbow, bowls for the dipping of fingers and wrists. A fresh frock for Lady Good—blue-green brocade—and a rib-

bon tie for her waist. She is instructed to forget the wimple and wear her hair down like a cloud. Like a virgin.

And for us both . . . Linen towels, ivory combs, golden plates, enameled salt cellars. Jeweled goblets, silver knives. Wax tapers, shining eyes; flushed cheeks and a gust of feeling that reeks like incense . . . Thank god for the bottle in my pocket, my apothecary vial of sweet, sweet release—sweet for me, release for someone else.

From Henri Putemonnoie's livre de raison
At meals it is polite to provide a bowl of scented water for each two diners to dip their hands in as needed. Boil rosemary with orange peel one hour, then strain the water through a cheesecloth and let it cool to just above room temperature. You may also use chamomile or sage. Avoid cinnamon for this use, as it may lose its strength of scent.

The table salt must be white. Boil it in 3 parts water, then strain and dry it on a tablecloth in the sun.

We are—*it* is—about to begin.

Our mistress sits at the head of the table; I am at her right. Across from me, Hercule, who stares at the space between himself and Radegonde as if he'll gobble it up before it's even laden. There's an empty place at the table's foot; Godfridus is late, and Radegonde declares we can't wait without spoiling the food. Truth to tell, I'm too hungry myself to wait—too filled with greed and lust for the delicious smells that fill the hall. (How different from what I feel still clings from the bakery!). Radegonde has lent me a shift and overdress, just slightly too tight and too short; the skirt shimmers over my knees in its complicated brocade. Green-blue, the shade of courtly romance.

Hercule tried to turn a cartwheel when he saw the table, but he fell over and cracked his elbow instead. The long stretches of plank have been blanketed in Persian tapestries, then set with chased plates and studded goblets, tall candles, piles of fruit. It is a riot of color. Manservants make the circuit of the table, filling our goblets with wine, while in the gallery at the far end of the room, musicians playing flutes and lutes and trumpets spin out tunes for our pleasure.

Radegonde raises her goblet to me. "A toast to Bonne Tardieu! To your good health!"

Hercule echoes it—"To your good, to your health"—and I blush.

I have to answer. I raise my glass to Radegonde in thanks; but what is there to say? "How much sweeter than wine is . . . thy, um, love."

She looks at me curiously; Hercule crows and claps his hands. "The Song of Solomon!" he says. "And you've thrown wisdom out the window."

He is right. For once I accept this feast, I accept that I am hers; Radegonde will truly be my mistress, and I'll be her contracted minion.

Radegonde whispers to a manservant, who comes around the table to box Hercule on the ears. "No more of that," she says. "You're here only by Bonne's good graces." She says right out loud, looking at me, "Everything tonight is for your pleasure, Bonne. I've ordered it all the way you've heard and read about it. Just name what you'd like first."

Hercule sits sour in his chair, ears flaming.

"I want—" I hesitate; I almost can't bear to start eating, the anticipation's so painfully delicious. "Oh, I wish . . . where's Godfridus?"

And just then, in he walks through the door, trailing Agnès behind him. The trumpets blow a kingly blast, and a manservant shows my artful uncle to his bench. Hercule squirms, almost as if he's glad to see Godfridus; I try to greet my friend, but his face is turned in on itself, the skin sagging exhaustedly, unseeing. He must not have eaten in a while; perhaps he hasn't slept. He needs food. He needs this night, which is for him as much as it is for me.

Once Godfridus is settled, Radegonde gets slowly to her feet, eyes reflecting and outglowing the candles that light a yellow trail down the boards. We all stare—she looks so fine and so strange. Her soft breath blows around the hall, wavering the flames.

"Well," she says simply, "let us begin."

She claps her hands. And the servants circulate again, this time bearing trays and tureens, and a great mountain of a pie. Agnès is serving now, bustling about with huge knives and spoons. Her blade flashes as she approaches the enormous pastry.

"Let me do that." Radegonde fairly grabs for the knife. Agnès bows quiescently, simply holds the pie steady. Radegonde cuts a deep, ragged slice. There's the crackling of bones. "Doves," she explains as she sends a piece down to me. Her smile is satisfied.

This is the first offering I sample. I've never eaten dove before—people of my class are forbidden to. It's delicious, delicate and fatty and flavorful. It makes me drunk ("O blessed Virgin!" under my breath). I eat of it until the edge is gone from my hunger—but somewhat distracted by Héloïse, who stands behind my bench to wait on me, refilling my trencher and goblet without my asking.

And when I'm done with the pie, there's much more: slabs of meat, vats of soup, boats of sauce. We could feed an army, or at least the throng of nobles that would normally attend a feast such as this. I am almost too busy to notice how my mistress eats, tearing dainty morsels from the food on her plate, fitting them delicately between her pillowed lips.

By contrast, Hercule dives in, greasing his face and dirtying his arms to the elbow, like a midwife. Godfridus just toys with his food, as if he isn't interested; he only nibbles at an end of the bread trencher, and the one thing he seems to enjoy is his wine. Even the choice tidbits Agnès slips him do no good: He simply isn't tempted.

Radegonde calls down the table to me, "Bonne, why won't you take some pork? The pepper sauce is delicious."

"I don't care for pork." Of course I'm thinking of the disgraced wine seller. "The meat is said to be similar to that of human flesh."

Hercule looks up from his trencher. "Cannibalism is a great tradition," he quips. "Or are you against Holy Communion now, too?"

Quietly Agnès refills Godfridus's wine goblet. I think I see her blow a kiss into the cup, but I am besotted with food. The rest of us are eating as if our appetites will only grow, as if there's no tomorrow. An illusion of fairy-tale fantasy fuels our hunger: Here we are eating the foods of the wealthy, the foods that appear when a dragon is slain or a magic ring worn, only to disappear in the blink of a witch's eye. They are the foods of ballad and legend—

The fried squash flowers are a poem.

The Parmesan pies are a song.

The salted dolphin (boiled twice in wine) is a treatise on the art of love.

The peacock is a fan-tailed roman courtois; it is stuffed with chickens, which have been stuffed with smaller birds, telling of noble deeds and daring amours.

The treed is a phrase of infidel prayer, oily and wet with a flavor of smoke.

Our last pie is a fabliau; when the steward cuts into it, live frogs and turtles pour out. We all jump away from the table, shrieking and laughing, falling against the servants and ourselves. An enormous toad lands *plop* in a hot bowl of mace-and-ginger broth, and drowns.

Calmly the servants collect the frogs and turtles and carry them off for a new soup.

Hercule holds up a goblet. "A toast," he cries, "to jokes and jokers!"

Radegonde looks pleased.

HERCULE

But I must remind myself: Make peace. Empty my heart of greed and wrath, gluttony, lust . . . empty my belly, maybe, if someone'll hand me a pot. So that, soon, I may empty my vial into a cup.

But how to get close?

Should I try flattery? Since bribes will not do. O mistress, your eyes are like herrings, asleep in the brine of your tears . . . Pray let me touch your lips that are like two ripe fruits, savor the seed of your tongue . . . *Oh, balls.*

Hercule dazzles us with his juggling, tossing apples and pears to the rafters and catching them again, defining circles and arabesques, making them sketch portraits of each one of us in the air. We sit and watch in silent awe, jaws still, as he step-hops lightly down the table, over the candles, toward the mistress.

Can it be we have reached the end of insatiable hunger? Our stomachs have distended and they hurt, butting against the table planks. I split my borrowed dress long ago. Radegonde leans exhausted against Agnès, who stands steadfast behind her, like a wall. Even Godfridus's saintly face is flushed.

Growing before our eyes, there's an air picture of the mistress. Her sharp nose, her long lashes, sketched in flying fruits—can Hercule have learned this at court?

Then suddenly Hercule's toys drop. In fact, we all startle. The flautists have piped a shrill trill. Hercule lands on a candle and snuffs it with his bottom; his jaquette rips. The trumpets round off with a blare.

Radegonde stands again with slow majesty, mystery. We hardly see Agnès help her. "We haven't finished yet," says the lady.

Hercule mutters, "Of course not." He stands on his head on a quince and belches.

The musicians play with renewed gust, and six small boys dressed as cherubs stagger in, carrying an enormous sculpture. I have never seen the like before. It is a subtility, a model of a grand house and gardens, with the trees in full golden-green leaf, the fountain plashing silver wire, and under an arcade a tiny model of a widow in black, head veiled in a long wimple, holding a swaddled baby. A figure in a blue-green dress stands behind her holding a basket.

The house is pastry, I realize in a moment; it's food. Pastry molded and tinted and gilded—with real gold—and baked.

"It is my house, you see," says Radegonde, getting up and opening the front gate, then the front door, then an upstairs window. I notice my little stall has been shaped in dough, too, and sits there waiting for me.

Godfridus is gazing with interest. "A wonder . . ."

The cherubs' legs wobble, then fold suddenly at the knees. They set the creation down on one end of the great table; the whole oaken slab gives a shudder.

I find myself, curiously, blinking back tears. Radegonde holds out a hand and gestures for me to come and inspect the subtility. We all follow, carrying our wine goblets, dazed and enchanted by the monumental, edible work, so lifelike except for its size and the inevitable bubbles in the pastry.

"Well, Godfridus," asks Radegonde, "what do you think of my cooks' talent for sculpture?"

HERCULE

What is a man to think, when he's spent his days and ways on some higher purpose?

I sidle to the side of the lady. At last, all eyes are diverted. As the stone-man reaches for the bread house, I reach for what lies in my pocket, and I

pour it into her goblet. Madness, cracking bones, misfortune of all sorts—
who cares, as long as one of them results?

But I hope it's madness. The sort of disorder that drives a person from
home, from loved ones, that renders her repugnant.

Slowly, the scarred hand reaches out. Godfridus plucks up a tree and inspects it. Each leaf has been molded separately, dipped into green dye and
bound to the trunk with gold wire. His hand trembles in awe.

Suddenly the tree vanishes and crumbs pour out of my uncle's fist.
Like sand through an hourglass. What remains, he brushes off on the seat
of his cotte. Hercule breaks into hand-clapping laughter.

"Flour and water," murmurs Godfridus. "See how it crumbles? When
those with any gift from God, any talent for shaping, should devote themselves to returning their gift to the great Maker. Not for the glory of any
one person, but for anonymous absorption into the One——"

Radegonde's face is flaming with anger. "Are you some kind of market preacher?" She grabs her goblet and hurls it at him. It misses, lands on
the floor with a clang, stains the rushes and tile bloody red.

Hercule gasps. Tracing the path of the goblet, he sinks to the floor as
if to lap up its contents. A servant brings him more wine of his own, but
he sets it down untasted; the spilled wine drips from his fingers like tears.

Godfridus doesn't see any of this. "We have forgotten why we are
here," he whispers. "On the eve of Saint John the Baptist, who pointed
the way to——"

"Shh, Godfridus." I grab his arm and give it a shake, startled for a
moment at how skinny it's become. "We're here for a party. For Midsummer."

Agnès explains to her mistress in a loud whisper, "He's just tired. He
finished the thing today, his great work. It's standing by the window in
his——"

This is interesting news indeed, but Godfridus will have none of it. In
a near shout, he continues, "Saint John, who wore a tunic of camel's hair
and lived on locusts and honey, who beseeched us, 'I am the voice of one
crying in the wilderness. Straighten in the way of the Lord . . .'"

I shake him again, violently now, and find Hercule on his other side,
slapping him toward sense. The little hands leave wet prints on God-

fridus's ear and cheek and mouth. Do I imagine it, or does Hercule kiss his brow? Only when Agnès comes with a brimful goblet and fits it to his lips does my friend calm down and lose some of the prophetic light in his pale eye.

GODFRIDUS
Let this be the last supper, my last time among these people. I will drink no more wine on this earth.

I spit, but I taste the dwarf's hands on my lips. His flesh is bitter.
My head, a fish that swims in a pot about to boil.

"Well," Radegonde says, with a forced laugh that tries to say she doesn't care about the sculpture's fate. "Your uncle did have one right idea, anyway. Choose a wall, my guests, and make it yours. This house is for eating—so let's eat it!" She tears off a chunk and stuffs it in my hand.

I look down at it. The tower room. Shingled in gold, with tiny almond-paste doves on the rood. I touch my tongue to it, tentative. It melts against my muscle.

"Delicious," I say out loud.

It seems wrong, even sinful, to dismantle such a work of art—to dishonor the hours that went into the making of it—but I can't stop myself. I eat the tower room, then a gold tree, a gold turret, a gold chicken. I nibble around windows, punch a hole in a roof, pull down the walls with my hands. I grow queasy—but I keep going. Under Godfridus's blue glare, Hercule and Radegonde and I are stuffing ourselves now, grabbing the shiniest parts of the building, our mouths melting with the buttery flaky tenderness of fine pastry, teeth grinding against the gold. We are eating wealth itself.

It has no taste.

From Henri Putemonnoie's livre de raison
Balance must be achieved in diet, as in all other things. This is especially important when planning a feast or other large meal, as the quantity of food consumed will proportionally increase any imbalance in humors and result in bursts of cholera, or bouts of lethargy, melancholia, or bile in your guests.

Have your surgeon or another reliable man of science draw up the menu. He must allow equal measures of hot and cold, dry and wet: For the combination of foods eaten by a man should echo his own nature, which the scientists say is warm and moist.

Spices will dry food out and most make a dish hotter, too.

Beef is a dry meat and should be boiled. A cold, wet meat like pork must be roasted, which makes it drier and hotter; spice it according to your desires. Herring is a dry fish, dolphin a wet one; if that your dolphin has been salted, then you may have it boiled.

Most vegetables are wet and cool in nature, with the exception of the onion, which is wet and warm.

Bread alone is neutral, and can be used as the canvas on which to lay your strips of hot, cold, dry, wet.

We've finally sickened ourselves. The subtility now resembles no building so much as Saint-Porchaire, roofless, with walls half-eaten. But what do you do with such a work when you've gotten what you can from it?

We all look as if by agreement to Godfridus. He's oblivious, taking a privy apart flake by flake with his fingernails.

"So, sculptor?" queries Radegonde.

He looks up, eyes distant. "She came arrayed in scarlet and pourpre, drunken with the blood of saints . . ."

"Ah," Radegonde says. "The whore of Babylon." She picks up one of the pastry figures—the widow in black—and holds it in her arms as if to protect it. At some point, she must have collected the human dolls for safekeeping; the others lie on a chest at her elbow. "You're as drunk as she was. But what should we do with this sculpture now? It's too pathetic as it is . . ."

Godfridus comes a bit to himself but hesitates, looks helplessly over the wasted house. "We should—" He pulls a shutter off a window and drops it. "We must—"

"I know!" Before we can anticipate him, Hercule jumps bodily into the subtility and smashes it—every wall, corridor, window, room. He rolls on the thing like a pig in dung, destroying, if not God's work, then the pastry chef's. Crumbs and gold leaf coat his body, and when he stands, his whole shape seems haloed with them.

In their gallery, the musicians scarcely miss a note. They must be used to such debauchery.

Now Hercule stands with his hands on his hips. I think we are all relieved; a pile of crumbs is easier to look at than something half-finished.

"And how about you, lady?" Hercule says to Radegonde. "You must offer us some entertainment. Can you dance or sing?"

Radegonde stares him up and down. "My voice is too low for singing," she says, "and to dance in my condition would be unseemly."

"Then—oh-ho!" He hops down from the table. "I have an idea. A real entertainment, as fantastic as anything that trips off a minstrel's tongue. You must now show us your house—your *real* house. Let us see it top to bottom, with all its treasures intact." Above the fooling smile, his eyes glitter. It's almost as if he is angry—but how can he be? We've been given everything tonight.

Radegonde looks uncertain. She lays the widow down on the chest, watching Hercule. "Why do you want that, dwarf? You can't think there's something in it for you."

"How can there be nothing for me? When your husband's religious prizes, relics and medals and paintings, are renowned all over Christendom. When it is said that just the sight of your altar, fashioned from a plank of the True Cross, will send a man's soul soaring to heaven!" He laughs, and it's like the crackling of thorns. "I've heard—listen well, stoneman—that the plank is so long a man can lie down on it full length, and many have done so, to their souls' everlasting delight . . ."

"All right, all right!" Radegonde holds up a hand. "I'll show you the relics. If the others want to see them. Bonne?"

I nod.

"Godfridus?"

He nods, too, dazed—or dazzled, maybe. A True Cross fragment that long . . .

"Fine." She says it as if for just this one evening she'd wanted to escape her merchantdom, the bales of cloth and trunks of spice in the bowels of the house, the holy relics stockpiled like so much bacon. She gathers up her skirts with a gesture that shows me, at least, that she is vexed. "Follow me."

G*ODFRIDUS*

Turning. Packed. Writhing, wriggling in the dark, and tight and hot. Face stinging. Wearing a camel's-hair tunic . . . Climbing downward. All panting now. Then we squeeze out one by one, falling from the darkness into— deeper darkness.

My head, my heart. I am sick and I taste—
But I want to see.

"Where is that maid?" Radegonde's voice. "She should have brought a light."

"I've brought several, mistress." Agnès steps from the stairwell calmly, a dish of burning oil in her hand, a stock of tapers in her pocket. "I thought your guests would each like one."

We take the tapers—the night's last extravagance, perhaps—one in each of our fists, and light them from her dish, then step back. Our eyes are caught by first this color, then that gleam; we wander away until corner by corner the room flickers into sight. This is the first of the fabric storerooms, where piles of brocade and cloth-of-gold lie slipping against each other, splashed with a length of green velvet.

"What lovely things," Hercule says, his voice not one bit impressed, "but how carelessly you care for them."

Radegonde holds her taper high, lighting the way to the next door. "This room isn't much used," she says. "Follow me and you'll see what you came for."

She leads them through, as she first led me: from gold room to scent room to cloth again, and again and again. Their eyes glow, their fingers twitch; even Agnès, who must have been down here so many times, gazes in wonder. The jeweled sticks and prickets; the metal dishes; the crystal boxes of myrrh and sweet-smelling musk . . . Once again I, too, am lost, lost in the splendors beneath the house of Putemonnoie.

Hercule has a quip for each room, a caper for each chest of treasures.

253

Treasures—that's his word: "For where your treasure is, there will your heart be also," he says again and again, until I'm sick of it.

"How can you presume to know our mistress's heart?" I ask, and in answer he gives me that old idiotic grin.

"You'll see, you'll see!" he trumpets.

I tell myself I'll check his pocket before we go; there's no telling what bit of her "heart" he's already tucked in there.

"Bonne, where are you?" Radegonde's voice echoes down a dark hallway; she sounds weary, and of course a long walk with many stairs is no good for anybody after a big meal.

"Coming!" I hurry after.

"Bring the dwarf—I'm about to open the reliquary. Agnès, the key . . ."

Behind me I hear a great gulp, as of excitement or somebody choking. "Hercule," I say, "stop playing. Hurry up!"

THE RELIQUARY VAULT looms over our heads, a thick iron door over the very heart of the house. There's a sound of blood beating—perhaps an echo of drums or footsteps overhead, the servants having a party of their own—or maybe the noise of our own excited organs as we wait for new mysteries to be revealed.

I can't remember where I've been anymore, whether I've seen this room before or not. Somehow tonight on this tour everything has been new again, even that puddle of green velvet. A fog lies over my vision.

And there—the key is in, the bolt scraping, the door swinging free. I feel Godfridus tremble at my side; I'm sure it's his heartbeat I'm hearing. But then Hercule's the one who darts in first, so fast he blows out his light; and the rest of us shuffle slowly after, waiting for awe to strike us.

What strikes first is a blast of cold air, cold and sour. Then the light comes up like the dawn, as we bring in our candles: Radegonde, Godfridus, me, Agnès. And we see, all at once, Henri. Lying on a box of death.

Yes, this is the bent man I saw last year. But he has become horrible.

A crooked body reclines on a flat lid, arms crossed piously over chest; this is topped by Henri Putemonnoie's face, slack in death. And death is not peaceful for him, not the least bit serene. Worms crawl out of his arms, his fingerbones crumble, his flesh swells around the embalmer's stitches. Stone frogs suck at his eyes and lips, and the creatures seem to pulse as they feed. This is a real man, a man who might rise from the lid and join us—if his flesh weren't too rotten to move.

Henri has been waiting all this time, through all this merrymaking and wealth-squandering, for us. The room reeks of him.

"My husband's relics," says Radegonde. Do I only imagine the wink she gives me?

GODFRIDUS
this is the face
and this is not the face I saw—
"I am corruption," she said,
and the light died.

Shivering, barely able to see, I put out a hand and touch—not soft, yielding rotten flesh, but cold, hard stone. Painted.

So this is not Henri's body, just his portrait—a sarcophagus carved and painted to a kind of perfection, complete likeness. It is far more terrifying than Saint-Porchaire's danse macabre, which at least has nothing but death about it.

Radegonde turns to Godfridus. "I thought you'd like to see the box's resting place. And we really must congratulate you on your work. It is spectacular—the craft, the detail . . ."

Godfridus gives a choked cry. It sounds as if he says, "Christus clarus." A blasphemy. Or just "Clara."

Hercule meanwhile falls back into the shadows at the edges of the room, and sounds as if he, too, is choking—though perhaps with thorny laughter.

This is not a very nice trick you've played, Radegonde, I think. Even though Godfridus mocked your subtilty.

I reach for Godfridus's big, dry hand. "It is—a very moving depiction," I say to my friend, the poor man who labored over this nightmare for weeks. His fingers refuse to clasp mine, and I realize the wounded hand may still be sore. His eyes are fixed on the box, his lips moving in silent prayer. So this work disturbs even its maker. And rightfully so—I think that if this is Godfridus's true art, he must be prevented from carving more, or we'll all descend into madness.

"Yes, everything is as my husband wanted it," Radegonde says. "His expression in the moment of death. His body as it would appear some months afterward, at the birth of his heir. Or of his daughter—you see he lies equally ready to share my nun's cell for eternity . . . I really must congratulate you, my man; this will be your legacy to the generations."

Godfridus cries out again, as if in great pain. His scarred hand presses on his heart; he drops his candle and the wax spatters on the floor and my skirt. "Clara," he says again, and runs out into darkness.

"Uncle—" I call and start to chase him; but my candle blows out, too, and Radegonde holds hers away from me. She keeps me in place with her blazing eyes. In any case, Godfridus doesn't hear me.

"Agnès," says Radegonde, "follow him. He won't find his way out alone." Her breath is coming in short gasps; clearly she's overtired, though still elated from the wine. She needs rest, and perhaps a soothing dose of Henri's innocuous book.

So Agnès goes, and there are just three of us alive here. I anchor my candle on the stone box, take Radegonde's hands, and stroke her wrists, as my mother used to do when I was upset.

Just as I think this, Hercule speaks up. "The stoneman has looked on the face of corruption," he says in that stentorian prophet's voice. "The emptiness within. Turn around and see."

HERCULE

*The stage is set. My bag of tricks has changed this room from grim to . . .
eternal.*

Just a few dozen shards of glass, coated in silver. Each one small in itself, but taken together—infinite. La Pute's house is full of them, and I have the keys to find them. And the occult angles from a secret book.

The room is a mirror box that shows life lasting ever into death. The glasses reflect each other and what's at their center. Whatever it might be, coffin, dwarf, or woman, the glass will reflect it over and over, smaller and smaller, until the image is too tiny for human eyes. Which is when it becomes not just what we see but what we are.

I jump from the box and leave the center empty. So, for the others, time opens into itself, into nothing—images repeated a thousand times, countless times, in reflected light, dwindling down to the least of all, a pinprick, a mere nothing.

This is how to void a heart. And a head. Vanity of vanities! And I am waiting to fill them . . .

My face flits through the glass eyes. Hercule claps and says a string of odd sounds: *Pix plus pax plus matrix vide plus . . .*

But Radegonde is laughing, too, or smiling anyway, smiling serenely, strongly, as she lifts her taper high and steps into the very center of the mirrored galaxy. She stands there at the hub, turning slowly, smiling into her own eyes. She inspects her face, her body, from every angle; sees into every fissure of herself. She smiles. She admires the infinite portraits of herself.

The words die on Hercule's lips.

HERCULE

Vanity, vanity, all magic, religion, love . . . And my heart is like wax, enlarged in my misfortune, shrunk in my prosperity. But not empty—no, not empty, or I would not be looking at this.

The Jew swore I could have what I want. Revenge, love, everything, all for a simple trick and a few foreign words. I would be exalted in the eyes of my beloved, my enemies cast down. And instead—

The bitch is pleased. She stands there glowing in the maze of my illusions, where she should have seen herself and quailed. Where any Christian would have fallen down to her knees and cried out to be forgiven the void inside.

Bonne hasn't even stepped into the center, and I stand on the edge like vanity, caught in a snare of my own weaving. So all my tricks have failed.

Lady Bonne is at peace, not reflected but reflecting, because in this labyrinth of mirrors and horrors she sees only one face, not hers, and it soothes her.

She looks at me with eyes of puzzle. "Hercule," she says, "what was it that you wanted?"

I cut and run.

Hercule's footsteps fade into the crowded storerooms. He, at least, will find his way out safely; he has a knack. No doubt he'll help himself to gold as he goes.

But I don't have much mind left to think about him.

Because now we are alone. Around me still I see my mistress's nose, her eyes, the dark tendrils of her hair, all repeated to infinity. Dazzling. Confused by this multiplication as by wine, I begin to speak: "I must apologize—the dwarf . . ."

I'm silenced as Radegonde turns to me on her toes, her exhaustion gone. She asks, "Would you like to share a secret?"

"I . . ." Which are her eyes, and which are reflections? "I'm not sure . . . I think we should find the others. We are all too drunk . . ."

Radegonde puts her hands to her head and shakes out her hair. She sinks to the ground as if its weight has overcome her. Or as if taken ill.

"Mistress?" I find myself on my knees.

Her right hand reaches to me.

WHEN I SAY IT ALOUD—impulsive, still drunk, head reeling—her eyes shift away. She can't look at me. She sprawls on the floor in her puff of black velvet, leaning against her husband's box with her hair spread around her and that smile still dying on her mouth, not looking . . .

At once my lips open again: "Don't answer." I'm afraid she is the kind of person who, when told she is loved, will ask, *How much.* (I would say, *Thank you.*)

So I roll my gaze to the left, to see what she might see. There's nothing—toads and worms, the flame's yellow flicker in her hand. I attach her candle, too, to the sarcophagus. Hers at Henri's head, where his lids push at the stitches holding them shut; mine at his feet, where his stone toenails grow in creaky, cracking spurts.

I try to like the idea of myself as one who loves without asking anything in return. "Are you ill, mistress?" In this light her face is pure gold. I put a hand on the immense curve of her black-velvet belly. Beneath my palm I feel a feeble kick, and now I know I want to feel it; I want this baby to live.

"Bonne," she says, "kiss me."

THE BAKERWOMAN

Bring on the axes—bring the doors, counters, clothes, and stock! Let it all burn! We are martyrs, so let us dance.

In the smoke I see my spirit. Blotting out the sky.

There is a time to break down and a time to build up—a time to cast away, a time to dance . . . To waste, to save—your soul!

Kiss me, my husband. Kiss me here.

How sore the mouth uncustomed to use. A feast of food, a feast of kisses— So many kisses! The slow lick learned in the straw stack, the forked dart of green velvet. Our mouths, our hands, our bodies twisting upside down and backward; a thousand tendresses to each other. So careful. So soft. With cold stone at our backs and hot sweat in our clothes.

She lifts mine for me, my borrowed skirts. She purses her lips and blows to cool me—but I don't cool . . .

And now a mouth is nibbling where no mouth has sucked or nibbled before. But then again, how natural: another course in the night's endless feast, this bite a kiss, too, as the tapers burn steady and the sweat rolls down my neck . . . And as I stretch my neck, I feel a pulling down below, where the other mouth is, as if the folds were sewn up and are now ripping free.

How will she know when to stop? When I come unwound completely?

GODFRIDUS

Turn, turn, turn . . . upward through the darkness. I know where she waits.

She waits wet with the blood of saints. She waits with body full of light . . . Filling my bed and my mind with light.

Good, good! *She is. My best.*

They that wait upon the Lord shall renew their strength. By gazing upon His works.

She's the one who judges when I've had enough. All of me is on fire, in flower, and my sad paradise aches. But instead of visiting further she sits up, wipes her lips, and says, "Now show me what you've learned."

How my legs burn—a frustrated ebb, slowly sinking—while I kneel obediently before her. She lifts the softness of her own skirt, and between my lips I hold my breath. I am willing but unsure. I bend and begin in turn to feed.

At first I don't like this. The drunkenness is gone, the good feeling's going, and doing this is like sucking an oyster stuck in a bird's nest. I hear a thousand rushing noises—can la Putemonnoie's house have rats? Radegonde's fingers bury in the hair at my nape. When I breathe I smell her sweat, and the odor of roses and musk, soured.

It is both sweet and salty, hot and liquid. It is like fire. It is like blood. It occurs to me that *this* is the taste of wealth.

And then a thump, and a thump, and a thump. Radegonde cries out. She has grown a second heart, and it is beating in my mouth.

HERCULE

"Ahh, Bonne, Bonne!" The devil's own sound. It seeps through walls and around corners—Good, Good, Good . . . How can I escape?

I fling my empty vial; it shatters on the stone. I dash the bitch's treasures to the ground—gold and crystal, silver and glass. I smash her mirrors, making more mirrors. But there is no end to the sound, the moan, their solace.

This whole place must be built like the curl of an ear, whorling in upon itself, trapping noise. Because there's no escaping that name, no matter how I try. And no finding the source again—no plugging it up . . . Good, Good, Good. God.

I may escape. But I will always hear her, everywhere.

Now we both rock back, side by side, back by back against the stone box, faces glistening. Radegonde's chest heaves; her eyes swoon half down. The pendant's gotten twisted to the back, and its chain lies tight against her throat. I can see the pulse hammer against it madly—or is that only an effect of the light? Above our heads Henri lies in peaceful repose, rotting.

I feel crushed. To a pulp. My lips, my nose, my heart, each part of me that has touched her. I'm a pulp that tingles and vibrates all over, like the skin of a drum that's been given a good thump. Like the heart of a chicken that keeps beating after the bird's been beheaded and plucked.

Radegonde's hand finds mine. It covers, squeezes just a little too hard for comfort. After a moment, I squeeze back.

"Bonne," she says, her pillowy lips, red and swollen, smiling faintly. "What a feast."

Unaccountably, I blush. I remember haystacks and the nunnery that Radegonde will die into if her baby is not born a boy. I remember the bread Blanche painted with her blood.

"I . . . pleased you?" I ask.

Silently, Radegonde nods, and swoops down to nestle a kiss in the nape of my neck.

I think at this moment that I have held Radegonde Putemonnoie's heart in my lips and lived. I pleased her; I made her cry. This has been my power over her. Then why am I so afraid?

"WHAT WILL WE TELL THE PRIESTS?"

"The priests?" Radegonde laughs. At that word she is her old self again; if she had a needle, she would thrust it into me. "What *will* we tell them? What is there to tell?"

I stir against the coldness at my back. "We have to confess."

"To what?"

"To—to—" My lips form the words with difficulty, swollen, and she isn't making it easier. "I'm sure"—though, momentarily, also confused—"that this . . . that we've just committed a sin."

"Oh, Bonne. What's the sin in a kiss?" she asks, as I asked myself some months ago. "And that's all that we've done: exchanged the solace of a kiss."

"Very many kisses, where people—do not kiss."

"Perhaps they do." She laughs again, slyly. "You haven't had the advantage of two decades' wedlock, Bonne."

Henri's box feels suddenly hot against my back. "I don't think what we just did would pass as the marriage debt."

Radegonde is quiet a moment, then, with breath under control, asks me softly, "And what about what you said? What you said when we fell to the floor, before the kiss?"

I'm on fire with the shame. What a child I am. What a—servant. "I owe you everything," I say.

This is enough for her. She touches my cheek and finds it still taut. "Then relax. Remember," she adds, "you weren't forced into anything. You weren't chased."

"That's right," I say miserably. "I was the one who said the words."

"If you didn't like what just happened, it doesn't have to happen again. But if you did like it . . . There is no sin in—liking."

I will not answer her implicit question: will not say I liked some parts, found other parts strange. Well, all of it strange, but only some of it in bad ways . . . Perhaps it is best to keep a secret.

Radegonde shivers, and I realize she's still waiting. Waiting for me to answer, as the sweat dries and chills her flesh.

"We'd better go upstairs," I say, though reluctant. I dread facing God-fridus, Hercule, the servants—they'll all know, I think, somehow. My very face will be a confession. But the longer we spend down here, the more they must wonder.

Then tomorrow—the booth, the line of hungry townsfolk asking to be fed . . . How will I dare to put my breasts to their lips, when every gift from my body must damn them to some torment? —And then another thought, even more horrifying: *What if I have no more milk?* If God or the Virgin takes it away . . .

And Radegonde still will not say that she loves me.

She is stirring at my side, pulling herself up by the edge of the box, wrenching a taper free of the wax trap. Her skirts whisper against my face, but she ignores me.

"Very well," she says at last, looking down. "Let's go. Upstairs. The feast is over."

Still I hesitate, knitting my fingers together, anguished—there's so much I want to say to her, more solace (of the spiritual kind) I want to get and give . . . but the words won't come. I am mute.

"Fine," she says. "So then, adieu." For a moment she leans down close to me again, and her hand dives to the place her mouth was earlier. She touches me quickly, makes me twitch. Then she turns on her heel and leaves me.

IT TAKES A MOMENT to realize she's truly gone, that she would abandon me down here in this strange, dark place with none but Henri for company. I keep expecting her to come back, to ask for another kiss—of peace—and take my hand again and tell me everything will be all right.

My heart is still pounding, but my breasts feel empty. I can't remember if Radegonde drained them just now or not. Instead I remember, again, the look on Blanche's face as I gazed up at her, nursing. I remember it as rapture—the way I imagine she looked at her elevation.

This is when it happens to me. Suddenly, all the feeling that has been building in me, in my heart, in my stomach, my breasts, comes crashing to a single point of flame. Between my legs. Right where Radegonde touched me, in the center of the haystack where she gave me her licking kisses.

Rapture.

Now it is my own heart that splits in two, and the second one beats a mad drumsong. I put my hand there, feel the second heart dancing. It spreads warmth through my whole body, through all my bones, dizzying my head the same way heights do. I throb, and throb, and throb, and the heat of it blankets me in dew.

I love Radegonde, I think. In spite of everything we have done, I love her. Without shame or even gratitude, purely . . . This is the feeling of love.

Yes, this is how Blanche must have felt when she was miracled, when she made her slow journey round the nave, borne up by invisible hands. When God himself beat inside her.

He beats in me now.

GODFRIDUS
. . . drunken on the blood of pearls—liqueurs, les cœurs—I hear in my heart now
Bonne . . . Dieu . . . !

The throbbing resides, pulse by pulse, slow.

When it is over, I feel both elated and ashamed. Elated because the sense of the second heart has been indescribably good, perhaps the best feeling I have known. Ashamed because I know this feeling rose in me out of an illicit embrace, out of sin. Maybe even out of magic.

I check the candle and find it has burned to a thumb's length.

One more thing I know: If I don't go now, I'll be spending the night with Henri. Alone and in the dark; because Radegonde, no matter how she has made me feel, is not coming back. So I rise. I am inexplicably weak, and my knees pop; my skirt (lent just a few hours before) swishes down, wrinkled and stained. I take my taper and shut the door. And start to ravel my way out of a labyrinth from which the penitent cannot emerge unchanged.

BOOK III

DANSE
MACABRE

HEN BLANCHE MIRABILIS, FIFTEEN AND A
virgin, set foot once more on God's earth, she
found her legs would hardly hold her. Her
feet had lost the ability to sense a difference
between air and stone; she wasn't sure if she'd
stopped flying yet. Maybe she'd melt right
into the ground, dead center of the flower in
the labyrinth. And she seemed to have grown
taller—but no, that was only because the
people around her were on their knees, everyone staring upward, waiting to see if she'd
produce another miracle.

She waited, too. Until the stone beneath
her feet firmed up and resumed its customary
chill, and the pigeons in the rafters took up
their usual flutter and coo, and the yellow-
eyed priest finally set down the monstrance,
his hands shaking, and collapsed against the
altar for support.

They wanted her to say something. They
were watching her mouth, expecting some
message, words of guidance straight from God.

Blanche cleared her throat, tentative,
waiting to feel it come. She coughed again.
Then at last she parted her blood-drained lips
and said,

"I think that's all there is."

OF ALL THOSE WHO KNOW Radegonde, know her secrets and the twists and turns of her mind, I am perhaps the one who's come closest, who knows best. So why can't I find my way out of her warehousing? I should be able to anticipate the sequence of the rooms, the layout of barrel and chest, the stocking of each shelf. But I am lost. I wander from room to room, into dead ends and around in circles, confronting again and again that splash of green velvet.

The candle, pinched between my thumb and forefinger, burns so low I feel the flame. My lashes curl in the smoke. Will I ever see daylight again?

And then—a door. A stair. A way up, a way out. But even as my heart lurches in relief, it registers also a twinge of regret. I almost want to be trapped down here—because it seems I am much more afraid of facing Radegonde again.

HERCULE

I didn't get here on my knees. But holy lobes! I've found liberation. A spiral stair and a willing door, and I sniff the sweet, smoky air, catch the servants' glassy glare, hear the bang and clang of door and gates as I burst forth.

The crowds of the town roll like waves. They are drunk and dancing, writhing and thrashing. Among them tonight I am invisible, I move free.

Liberation: from liber, *meaning free—this much the monks taught me in their locked cells. But their freedom may be another version of the Jew's emptiness—no place to go, no one to see. Will I even be welcome at home, if Good—Good—Good ever gets there?*

I follow the crowd. Why not? And so I see a gray cloud billowing up from the new-church square. The Christian walls and buttresses bask in reflected light, turned to a uniform orange. I have found the town bonfire, the burning of—what else?—empty vanities. Houses, carts, and trees.

This is the source of all the pleasure—the brilliance of burning, the wonder of waste. No more do the dancers tout Saint John's eve—in fact midnight passed belowground. It's full Midsummer now, and the church's lessons go unread, the facade's virgins and kings, judges and virtues stand-

ing stone-cold beneath the flickering light. The people dance and worship their own bodies for tonight.

How could I have thought of changing? How could I ever become an empty soul?

But I'm getting an idea.

Liberation!

Vanity.

They seem interminable, these stairs. I've forgotten how far down we were. My taper gives out at the eighty-first step, and I lose track after that, feeling my way in the dark, leaning into the curve of the spiral and measuring progress by the ache in my calves. I feel as if I'm climbing to heaven, shinnying up a cord that connects earth to sky, a snailshell big enough to house the human race.

How many hours, I ask myself, have I spent negotiating the staircases of Radegonde Putemonnoie? And what will I say to her when I emerge from this one, to find her among the crumbs and spills of our great feast?

As I ask myself these questions (and get no answers), I seem to sense a thinning of the darkness. Soon each step is bringing new details: In dim brownness I make out square blocks under my hands, triangles under my feet. And then I emerge—into the sky.

This is a sky thick and umber, padded in clouds that retain the orange light of torches and English campfires and the bonfire I know is burning at centre-ville, far below. I'm in Radegonde's needle tower, under the eaves with the doves and the desk. I seem to have lost my sense of time— it could be anywhere from vespers to compline, Saint John's being the longest day of the year and, I begin to think, of my life.

With my hands on the center of the spiral, I must have missed a door—maybe several—somewhere on my upward climb.

The orange light swirls at the windows, but I have no interest in following it. Soon I will go back down, groping for such a door; but for now I'll sit in Henri's chair and rest. Listen to the doves, watch as the sky changes colors. Think what might happen now between myself and my mistress. And what I can tell the church. And what I have felt in my body . . .

There comes a tapping on the roof. A light rain has begun to fall.

He hath made everything beautiful in his time and you, my Lady, are beautiful beside me. Your flesh cool. Hard. Luminous, in the peace of a sheetless bed, beneath a roofless heaven. My love.

Outside, the city burns, as it has burned before. Inside, I feel your clarity. Opening to me.

When the rain begins outside, the doves fly in. They light first on the windowsills, then on the shutter tops, then on Henri's desk. They flutter their wings and scatter their feathers. Only too soon will the inevitable happen— filth—and with a sigh I get to my feet to chase them out, wondering how the servants can have been so careless as to leave the shutters open.

I get rid of the birds and fasten the shutters, first those facing the back of the house and the west part of town, then those that overlook the courtyard. I try not to look out and down, too sick already to take the vertigo. But my eye catches a movement in the yard and suddenly I freeze, lean out the window, stare down.

The courtyard is full of men. Men in dark, bulky clothes, holding smoky torches, standing eerily still. They are waiting for something. I recognize Maître Civis, the prominent wool merchant; there are other town fathers as well. And Fathers Pierre and Paul, lurking discreetly at the back, hands tucked into sleeves.

The torches streak the drizzle orange, long orange arms reaching up to me. Why has Radegonde assembled these men? What does she have to tell them, or to make them do? The paint is melting off the hutment built today.

Soon the front door opens, and Radegonde comes out. There is a man on either side of her, supporting her arms. She says nothing. I stare down and see, at first, nothing but the top of her head. Her hair is still loose, and it looks like her only clothing. She walks away from the house, and gradually I see more—her black dress, her hands behind her back. Shackled.

My head spins—noticing at last the great height from which I'm watching.

HERCULE

Holy heels and anklebones! The woman's heavy.

How comic it must be, how freakishly funny, to see a spindly man-child drag a gleaming girl through the night streets! His forearm under her chin, his sweat dripping on her brow. Her bare virgin feet scraping, complaining with a loud grr-ouch *as she goes—a rape in progress, the spectator must think, or at the very least a love game. For now, let us ignore that baby— smug fat and bald, a chaperon nonetheless.*

Love! The funniest freak of all. The mysterious monster, the ridiculous rape—of all that makes man or beast.

". . . returning it to the great Maker. Not for the glory of any one person . . ." So the stoneman said, and here I am. One with a stone.

My next steps are clear. To put out a fire, to open a door: These are the tricks of a minute, what any street mage could do—given a thundercloud and a skeleton key (merci, la Putemonnoie). The bonfire fizzles, the crowds run away, the door swings on humid hinges. So onward, inward! Planting the body, wiping the brow, guessing the angle of morning light. A thousand fine adjustments. And that gives me time to wonder where the maker is. Having abandoned revelry, why did he leave his rock alone? And why lay her in his bed, with mattress rumpled and a wet stain spreading . . . In love with his work, so why leave it?

I wanted only peace. But in that tangled domus—open now to wind and rain—I made use of some things. Under his own chisel, and upon the flesh he had carved, I shaped three words: GODFRIDUS ME FECIT. *Godfridus made me. So will his name be made tomorrow, fingered in the first rays of the sun. He who claimed to labor for God will be known a vainglorious villein. And the work of his hands not so holy—just a common version of an ordinary woman. He'll be disgraced, a blasphemer.*

And this I do for love. Vanity!

Blasphemy.

If you believe in that sort of thing.

Radegonde doesn't glance back. She follows her captors in proud docility, as if she knew they would come for her, as if she was expecting them to cap off our revels—hers and mine—in this manner. Perhaps she watched them approach from this very window.

The men close around her, making a silent procession, and I watch, numb and afraid, as they disappear into the golden darkness of the street.

The courtyard becomes an empty cradle. Where are the Putemonnoie guards? Why am I not with her, when we both have sinned? *What has just happened?*

It is beyond a church matter now. Our town fathers do not tolerate women who share with women; in my youth the judges cut the hands off a pair so they could not touch each other, and last year a nun was burned for corrupting the novices, and the novices were flogged.

They will come for me.

THE RAIN GROWS STRONGER, fatter, while below me in the house I feel energy gathering like a thunderclap. I wait for my doom. And the house erupts.

First there's noise—raucous shouting. Of joy, triumph, maybe rage . . . Then the doors open, flooding the yard with light and with servants. Aprons over their heads against the hammering rain, Radegonde's staff run with arms full of treasure—linens and ewers, dresses, the odd necklace from an unlocked coffer. The sight of this looting frightens me almost more than seeing Radegonde led away, for if servants feel induced to steal, they are pretty sure their mistress won't come back to punish them.

Now Agnès comes out, a brown whirlwind whisking between the gates and the booth I was to occupy tomorrow, bravely blocking the way. As her fellow servants squeeze past, she tries to pluck the goods from their arms. She seizes a white box, a blue mantle, a bit of yellow linen from the baby's layette.

One man runs with a peacock, flapping and squawking; Agnès grabs it, tries to save it—and accidentally breaks its neck. The bird lies shining dead in the gutter until someone else scoops it up.

After a long time the storm slows, and brown clouds yield to black sky and stars, crowds to silence. The looters are finished. Agnès vanishes, melting into the street—probably afraid to be in the house now, heading instead for the shelter of Godfridus's studio. She was here tonight as a mere guest.

One last boy dashes out of the kitchen, a string of sausages trailing from his pocket. He climbs up my booth and snaps the cross off the rood; then he, too, is gone.

There's nothing more to see, though the bony moon shines white.

I curl up under Henri's desk, knees to chin, and try to think. What shall I do next—where can I go? I think it might help me to reason out the situation if I were to write it down. There is in fact much about this night I could confide to the blank pages of Henri's book—and this may be my last chance to write there. So I crawl cramp-limbed to get the book from its shelf, and I spit into the old ink bottle to make the stuff move. But before I can lift the quill to write, the book falls open and my hands fall to my sides. What I read is both ridiculous and terrifying, and it dams my words up. The doves come back and roost as I sink onto the floor in a deep, jelly-boned stupor.

From Henri Putemonnoie's livre de raison
THE LORE OF VIRGINS

It is said there is a special scent to virgins, a mingling of florals, incense, and divinity. We are supposed able to recognize them by this, as by their colorless urine. Yet all that is certain is that virgins inevitably produce a passionate reaction in those who are near them.

Poets urge virgins to gather rosebuds while young.

Mages use their monthly cloths in charms.

The Virgin's rose-crown anticipates the crown of thorns worn by her Son, whose blood stained roses red.

It is widely known that virginity is the period of a woman's greatest powers, which are destroyed, like Eve's, by fleshly knowledge. And doubly so if, like Eve, she takes joy in that knowing.

273

DAY OF JOHN
THE BAPTIST

RIME'S BELLS BRING A FRESH BREEZE AND
dew on the building stones—our town kissed
by the morning star, birthing a lovely day for
the denuded city. And the English are gone.
Overnight.

As gray-blue dawn seeps over the rooftops, I see the camp's just a wasteland, all mud
and garbage, animal bones and black blisters
where the cookfires used to burn. So while the
bonfire raged, while the town danced, while
Radegonde was arrested, the soldiers at our
gates packed up and moved on. Maybe they
saw the flames and thought the prize they'd
waited for these long months was being destroyed from the inside. Maybe they just got
tired.

This is the feast of Saint John the Baptist,
the one saint feted on the day of his birth
rather than his death.

Shutter by shutter, Villeneuve comes
awake. To discover there's a door missing
here, part of a wall gone there: The townspeople look around in perplexment, as if not
remembering that they themselves pulled out
the nails, chopped at the boards. They cross
themselves and pray.

It takes a while for the town to learn of and then believe in its liberation. But once this happens, I hear shouts of joy and ringing bells. The city gates are thrown open and the people swarm into the countryside, crawling over it like ants in their dirty garments. Some jump into the river. Some root in the campsite debris. But most rush on unsteady legs for the meadows and farm fields, to rub their skins against green growing things and cram their mouths with wild berries and peas in the pod. Leaves crinkle in hair, flowers erupt from bosoms. Tiny figures dance in the wavering distance. Who knows how many babies will be made *now*? And what I would give to be out there among them . . .

The town is deserted. The town is silent. This great house has become nothing more than a tomb. Still I stand at the tower window, looking out, waiting, knowing Villeneuve has no more need of me.

GODFRIDUS

> *In too much goodness there is danger*
> *In too much pleasure Christ's a stranger*
> > *It was my first time.*
> Humble, poor, and—
> *I will find myself   outside*
> > *green*
> > *Sleep for a hundred years be wakened by a—*
> > *flood, and a pillar of salt, and sin.*
> > *My love's a stone and yet not a stone, dead and yet not dead. De-*
> *filed. Unchaste.*
> > *I am wild, wild, and I rave.*

275

As the sun climbs high, it makes my tower room an oven; the birds, my companions, now shun it. Below us all, the rejoicing continues, and no one comes. Can it be they don't guess where I am?

After hours of revelry, the priests start to herd everyone back into town. A flock of black robes scatters across the green fields, flapping their arms like beetles too heavy to fly. The church bells begin to ring again, hard and quick. Somewhere Anne, Aliénore, and Blanche are swinging dizzily, singing out the joyful call to prayer; only the broken tower at

Saint-Porchaire stays mute. I imagine the midday sun—brighter than ever today, I think—shining down upon the lead-lined nave.

Then I imagine Radegonde in a prison cell. The Villeneuve prison lies beneath the earth; down there she won't hear a single bell or shout of joy, won't see a solitary sunbeam. She won't know what's happened to anybody but hers.

I tremble, afraid of where my thoughts are leading. Straight to Radegonde's side, the dark heart of the town.

AT LAST.

I see them down at the great house's gates, four town fathers—Pierre and Paul, and the merchants Civis and Froisson—surrounded by guardsmen, followed by a small number of townspeople. The guards lead the way inside and rap on the big door with their halberds. I hear my name. *Bonne.* They are calling; it is my time, and there is nothing I can do. So I gather up my skirts and, without a word, wind down the long staircase and into the hall, to open the door with my own hands and let all the fathers in.

I bow. The merchants bow, too, and fall to their knees, perhaps in apology; Father Paul signs the cross.

Wordless, Pierre reaches for my hands.

"Wait—" For the moment, the worst I can imagine is the feel of his skin on mine. "I will come, but you don't need to bind me."

The mud-colored eyes widen. Pierre—and Paul—and the merchants—all feign astonishment.

"Sister," says Paul, with veins pulsing in his tonsure, "we're here to take you to centre-ville."

My knees shake, but I think of Blanche and the way she met her own fate, walking steady to Saint-Porchaire. "I will come," I say again. "Only do not touch me . . ."

The guards shift, sore of bone or confused of purpose—I don't know. It's sure I suckled some of them.

The wool merchant, Maître Civis, says, "You know what has happened?" His breath smells of sheep, as Froisson's does of the wax he molds into candles.

"Of course," I say. "I know."

"And you are still here?"

"Where else would I go?" I spread my arms. "You would find me anywhere."

"That is true," Pierre speaks up again, "for God's eyes are everywhere. And He is summoning you."

And so we go.

I FIND THE STREETS surprisingly dead. Only a few souls stand about to gossip, and most of them fall in line behind my arrest party. Now that their bellies are full, my doves take me to prison with flowers in their hair.

So I walk, as ten years ago my mother walked and as ten hours ago my mistress walked as well, toward my destiny. I walk between Pierre and Civis, with Froisson and Paul behind, dragging a train of guards. But my hands are free and my head is high.

Bonne Bonne Bonne . . .

Voices are raised all around, but this is the only word I hear. For one last time the air shimmers with my name, while the inevitable bells rain drops of joy to drown the sound of me.

Bonne Bonne Bonne Bonne . . . I think I see a plume of smoke above Saint-Porchaire. But no one will waste a building for just one sinner, or even two; nor, I am sure, would they reunite me with Radegonde, even for death.

We enter the new-church square, where the rain has washed the signs of bonfire into the gutter. The voices fade to a gentle thrum beneath Anne, Aliénore, and Blanche; I am strangely glad my grandfather's bells will toll me into prison.

Here our steps are forced to slow, because the square is packed with every soul now in Villeneuve—men, women, children, peasants from outside the walls. Priests and friars and minor brethren are organizing them into a complicated pattern, a folded lobe that makes the most of this limited space and will eventually guide them like fish into the nave, where they will register their gratitude for freedom, their condemnation of me.

I hear a monk: "Bless you, daughter, God be with you, son, no shoving please . . ." His hood is off, and his eyes are burning. He looks at the bakerwoman.

To mark the time, she and the others pray. "Benedicta," they say in unison, "tu in mulieribus . . ." Some have even gotten to their knees and shuffle as the others walk.

From a sea of dirty scalps and grass-stained garments, the steps of the Palais de Justice rise. The great doors gape like a maw, ready to swallow. I think I hear the word "Virgin."

We cut directly to the very center of the coil. The town fathers, Pierre and Paul, Civis and Froisson, take me there, and I have the sense that the people are holding their breath—but they will not stop the procession.

From the grande place's center point, the trip inside is straight. A path opens before us. This is how it is to be: I will be taken inside—to be excommunicated, I think, perhaps beaten, in Villeneuve's largest gathering place.

Bonne Bonne Bonne Bonne . . .

My feet slip on the blood laid down by faithful knees. Pierre's hand catches my elbow, and I ease down. I go forward on my own knees, knee by knee among the bodies I have nourished. The people murmur.

Closer, the shadows inside the door form colors, pools of sunshine that shower the faithful with stained light. Then there is the butterfly feel of a hand on my head. I look up into the eyes of our chief confessor, Thomas.

This is my worst moment. He gazes down at me, his eyes as kind as a real father's.

"Sister," he breathes, and those eyes fill with tears. As, now, do mine.

And somehow I am on my feet, and the faithful are on their bellies, and Thomas—suddenly strong—and I are walking across their backs up to the very altar.

It is the moment I've dreaded, the one I knew would come. We stagger together.

Someone is standing there, on the holiest spot in Villeneuve.

The Bakerwoman

Husband, you may pull me down, but you've no right to make me look. I pray to Our Lady, to the real Good—I'll worship no false idols anymore.

The knot in my gut's no child of yours or mine.
Husband, her foot crushes my very neck!

Now I can see it clearly. On the altar stands a woman, in a blue robe and half-fallen veil; she is dead still and nursing a child. There is something vaguely familiar about her. In a moment I realize that of course she is not a woman but a statue, a representation of the Virgin Mary; it is only that she is remarkably made so as to look like a real person.

"She appeared overnight," Thomas explains in his voice of an ancient confessor, privy to the sins and mysteries of the universe. "She gathered Villeneuve to her bosom and blessed us all. The siege lifted."

My head buzzes. Is Thomas telling me to worship a statue? One about whom there's something I feel I should recognize . . . She looks to me like an ordinary woman, tall, slightly larger than life-size, with wide child-bearing hips and big capable hands clasping her baby's bottom. *His* face is obscured, his mouth fastened on her right breast and almost engulfed by it—for these are no dainty ladylike bosoms, but immense billowing sacs meant to nourish an entire race. Her drapery does nothing to disguise the fullness of her body, the strength of her belly and legs.

Mary bends slightly around her suckling infant, smiling with eyes and lips shut; a few strands of brown hair have escaped from her veil and straggle against her neck like vines on the tree of life. She glows, lost in a moment of rapture.

Then with a little lurch I realize this, too—why I know this Virgin without having seen her before, and why I could not at first recognize who she was: because she has my face, my body, my hands. And a baby.

". . . as you have blessed us, Bonne," Thomas continues softly, and dodders back into the arms of my guards.

I fall, too, and there are bodies to catch me. There are hands to set me up, to brush me off, to straighten my garments and turn my face once more toward my own image. They stop just short of raising me to the altar.

As I gaze at the Virgin—the Mother—who wears my face, I notice that I have lost a shoe, and it is not the one with the hole. Another hole has been torn in the skirt of my borrowed overdress. I am dizzied by this shingled chaos of human shapes where the church's ordered labyrinth should be, and I feel my clothes being eaten off me.

From the floor, a woman says, "We are grateful for miracles," and first one man and then the rest of them take it up. They press scraps of my garments to their lips.

I don't understand. I stand alone and frozen, not wanting to look at the statue any longer but even more loath to walk across these people to gain the door. A miracle. A mystery. It is almost with relief that I see Pierre and Paul tread the living carpet in a path to my side.

"Sister." Pierre waves his bumpy hands not quite in a cross over me.

Paul echoes, "Sister." He doesn't even try to guess what gesture should accompany my new status. He and Pierre stand still with pleasure for a moment, looking at the two of me.

I can't believe that *they* believe some sort of holy thing has taken place here; they must be planning a special punishment. There is nothing I can do to protect myself, not here in the very center of the citizenry. So I wait.

Pierre says, "We will surely name the new cathedral for her. Notre-Dame de Villeneuve."

Paul adds, "Once it *is* a cathedral," almost inaudibly, and Pierre ignores him.

He says, "See, Bonne Tardieu, how the souls above and below have blessed our good work. What a gift you—and we all—have been given."

The people on the floor beneath us shout, "We are grateful for miracles!"

I stifle a shudder. "Good fathers—"

I stop myself before I can go further. The people believe in this miracle, and whether the priests believe or not, they have decided to play along with it. Perhaps I am indeed the only one here who knows this statue must be Godfridus's work, not a divine reward for collective virtue or a commemoration of my body's output; my uncle's weeks of retirement have removed him from general memory. And of course my mind goes to the lowly cell where, I imagine, Radegonde sits awaiting her fate. My role in this miracle play might help her.

At last I say, "We are grateful for miracles." Though inside I am asking, Where is my uncle, and when will he come forward to destroy this latest wonder?

ON ALL SIDES, the murmur grows again: *We are grateful*... Heads poke up, dust on their lips, belief in their eyes. The air feels fragile as glass, and they, the faithful, glitter.

God slopes toward the west windows, glowing blue and red. In his light the Virgin *could* be alive. I am honored, and ashamed. Though—finally I think it—maybe it is wrong of me to doubt this miracle. Maybe the statue is truly divine. After all, even I did not know Godfridus had found the stone for it, and even if his hands did fashion her face and body, weren't they guided by some greater force? A holy spirit of inspiration . . .

I feel such a force directing my life now: if not God, then his minions. He, or they, have chosen me, have shown what I must do to save Radegonde and myself. He, or they, bow my head and move my feet, show me the way out through a transept. They guide me to the priests' house, where I am given a chair in the office chamber and a footstool and a glass of cool wine. I sit with five Christs, each one more gilded and bloody than the last; a large Saint Catherine, wheel at her feet, weeps by my shoulder, and at my elbow a Sebastian turns his eyes to heaven. I am but one of these, miraculously spared.

The laymen call me mother; the priests, sister. But I am not here to rest. Pierre, Paul, and Thomas gather round me to gloat over—to discuss—our town's latest wonder. They make me think of a war council planning, plotting, strategizing. Their words are a barrage through which I try to drift, not to think . . .

Paul spears me with a smile. "God has chosen your face, sister. For your good work in the town, God has chosen you."

I open my mouth, but Pierre rushes quickly into the breach.

"During our time of trouble," he says in a benevolent tone, "you helped many souls in this town. Now gazing at your image will help even more. The people say they feel consoled and joyful looking at this Virgin's face. Imagine what pilgrims—and princes—and the Pope himself will say and do when they come here and feel that same consolation, that same joy. Think of the benefits to our town. We will get our bishopric, and our cathedral."

Paul adds, "Merchants who stayed away for the siege will come for this; we will quickly resume our place as a center of commerce and pilgrimage."

"Resume?" says Pierre. "We will increase it!"

Weakly I ask to be allowed to talk. I must do it, this thing that is in my heart.

"Certes, sister." Thomas smiles, a trembling hand raising the cup to his lips. He drinks the wine as if it is mother's milk—as if it is—

"My milk," I say, "may have flowed abundantly during the siege . . ."

"More than abundantly," Pierre says.

"Well, if it did so, it was due to the generosity of one person. I am sure you know who I mean."

Paul says, "You were most generous."

"I mean"—I swallow, then say the name—"Radegonde Putemonnoie. She fed me the best from her larders during all those weeks, and it was her meat and drink that kept my milk flowing. *She* fed the town."

The two priests exchange speaking looks. "Mistress Putemonnoie," says Pierre, "refused several direct appeals to her charity. You yourself witnessed at least one."

"Because she was already feeding people through me," I say desperately. "And she did donate the labyrinth that the citizens are walking over—or lying on—even now. I'm sure you know her warehouses are the one place that such fine materials could be found during the siege."

The priests flutter, as if I've come too close to blaspheming. But quickly they marshal their forces again, and Pierre says, "That is true. Which is why, again, the gift of this Virgin is so astonishing and yet so fitting. She was sent as a sign of recognition that the town is finally dealing properly with la Putemonnoie; when we justly arrested her for a witch, the English tormenters fled and the Blessed Mother appeared."

I chew on my lip. I am beginning to feel that any further defense will be useless; even if Godfridus were to appear with chisel in hand and paint stains on clothes, bearing the imprint of his work, he would not convince the fathers of his authorship—they'd be much more likely to clap him into prison for sacrilege. And perhaps, I am beginning to think, this is for the best.

Only in a small corner of my mind does the charge against Radegonde register. For the moment I realize just that the priests will not help her, and that her arrest supposedly has nothing to do with the Putemonnoie wealth. Though they can't help discussing that now.

Meditatively, Paul asks what is to be done with the fortune. "Now that the city is open again, we don't need those larders—but there is the business to consider, and the house itself."

"It is a good question," says Pierre. "With the widow in prison, the entire domain is without supervision. Perhaps it is time to claim it for the church."

Thomas says, gentle as always, "The house and business are not hers. They were her husband's, and will be her son's if she bears a son."

"But what if she has a daughter?" Pierre asks hopefully. "Or a miscarriage?"

"There is a brother-in-law in Paris, I believe." As Thomas speaks, I look at him—I never thought him so sharp before. And he seems almost to be on Radegonde's side . . . He sees me looking and tucks a cake into his mouth, smiling with crumbly beatitude.

Pierre is even better informed, and his answers are ready. "If she's found guilty of witchcraft, her personal wealth will be forfeit to the church. And while she's in prison on such a charge, the income from her property belongs to us."

"Ah," says Thomas, almost in a whisper, "but can we be sure what is hers? Do we know what her dower was, or the value of the gifts her husband gave her?"

Now they all look to me again. I think I might see an opportunity. "I know something of her business," I say. "I've seen her desks and warehouses, I know a bit about how she behaved. I could look for some kind of accounting." Though not, of course, the contradicting reports in Henri's book.

Pierre nods approvingly. "That is an excellent idea, sister. No one would question *your* honesty."

I flinch. Under those words lies a clear invitation—a command, rather—to be highly dishonest. And for that expectation I am indebted to the statue. I am now an ally of the church . . . or perhaps I should say, its serf.

Now the priests return to the miracle, sweeping me with their plans to sponsor pilgrims, to invite princes and the Pope, to erect a chapel for the statue.

"For though we'll leave her where she is for now, she cannot stand on the main altar forever," says Pierre, and the others agree.

"We'll call it the Chapel of the Milk," says Paul.

"In my youth," adds Thomas, around a mouthful of nut cake, "the treasury at Chartres held a vial of the Virgin's milk. Perhaps the brothers there would lend it for display."

The others pronounce this an excellent suggestion. "Along, perhaps, with some of Bonne's," Paul says, turning to me.

Pierre frowns. "I don't think—"

For once we are in agreement: To put my milk next to Mary's would be truly to flirt with blasphemy. "My own milk is not ready for holy traffic," I say. "In fact, it still belongs to Mistress Putemonnoie, who bought my services some time ago. Will she stay in prison long?" I continue bravely, stubbornly. "I've promised to take care of her and her baby."

"She'll stay in her cell until the trial," says Paul, ever direct. "She can't be tested till the baby's born, but—"

Pierre takes a different tack. He makes his voice as soft as Thomas's. "Do not worry about what you've promised, sister. No one will dispute your right to a wage for what you've done for the Putemonnoie family. Indeed, for all you've done for the town—and will continue to do—"

"I don't want any special consideration," I interrupt him. "But I have given my word in contract—"

He smiles at me with indulgence, tinged with the slightest degree of impatience. "You have done good work, sister. Now you must forget those who have not worked for the greater good—cultivate your own soul, and set an example for all. Your investigation into her accounting is task enough for now."

Thomas brushes the crumbs from his poor hands and adds vaguely, "Miracles are good for the people."

I subside then, and hear them plot till the lay brothers arrive with dishes of burning oil.

GODFRIDUS

I am the voice of one who cries in joy— I may rave, but I understand. You have followed. In blue.

This is consummation—perfection—of my love for

      God   clarity   goodness

    The locks that frame you—are they red or brown? Your skin golden or white? And does it even matter? I sweat and you smile, and you are one with me, we are one with each other, and you have forgiven my sin. Your whole body's a kiss and your eyes closed in tenderness. So delicate, the fine blue veins . . .

    But look at me, look at me!

    The eyes open.

    "Godfridus," she whispers.

    Corruption.

After curfew, as a woman of the church, I am allowed inside alone. To commune and pray with the statue, as the priests believe; in truth, to go over every inch of her with a bright tallow candle. I examine the painted stone from head to heel, and it is here, below her long Achilles tendon, that I find my proof. Letters scratched as a sign of mortal authorship: D   I US ME FECIT. Their shape is rough, unseemly given the woman's perfection, and the spaces between are uneven. As I peer closer, I see the paint and some of the stone have been worn away on this heel. It is the work of a mere moment to fill in the gaps with what I know: GODFRIDUS ME FECIT. *Godfridus made me.*

    Alone in the vast, drafty blackness, I know I should tell the church and town fathers what I have found. My lips part as if to speak the words aloud—my uncle was proud of his work. But then, in the flicker of my flame, I see that the gaps could be inscribed differently: DOMINUS ME FECIT.

    This I do say out loud: "God made me." And my hand trembles so violently that, despite its steadfastness against drafts, the candle blows out and I am left in darkness. A darkness so complete that it almost seems my hands have not grabbed a smaller bit of stone, are not scraping at that heel, not rubbing, rubbing, rubbing stone on stone into the night until the marble is smooth and wordless and pink, painted with a drop of my blood.

    I hereby stake my life, and that of my mistress, on a miracle. On divine authorship. Since God alone can save us, I will let the people think he has done so.

Until I can think of something better . . .

HERCULE

Through alleys and shadows, between bricks and through walls. Who will house a freak who's failed? Miserably.

Oh, but the world is a purse of pockets and loose strings; there's a hiding spot for every coin or splinter worth keeping. There must be a place for a swollen dwarf. Holy mother of the mother of Good! The black place of my second birth, of heights and fears and prayers and death. The one nearly empty place within these city walls. The sinners' sanctuary.

It is quite dark outside, in this half-destroyed town. The people are sleeping the sleep of too much joy. Or at least, so I expect them to be, and therefore I make no special effort to hide my face.

It is as if they have been waiting and watching from every window. I cannot say where they come from, only that as soon as my feet hit the street they're upon me. The people who have seen the statue, the people I have fed. They are silent, don't even speak my name, only follow me with skirts beating like wings. They terrify me with this silence. I begin to run.

And where should I go? Where is my home now? A crowd waits at the bakery, a reeking splintered pile. When they see me they run, too, with swift feet and pumping heads, gray and menacing in the darkness. I head east. But instead of Godfridus's atelier, I find the drunken cobbler reeling inside his house's skeleton—the panels and the roof of the building, including most of Godfridus's room, sacrificed last night. What has become of my friend? I duck where I think the people will not follow, into the quartier des ombres, but like pigeons they do follow.

The fillette isn't at her usual corner, I never knew where the exorcist lives, and who knows what might be waiting in the atrium? I give the church a wide berth. But nonetheless I seem to hear a voice issuing from the black ruin—the local genius, the forgotten weather prophet. "Warm days in June," she wails, "harvest comes soon . . ."

How could bounty be a cause for moaning? But there are reasons we'll never understand. A miracle can mask evil.

Wings beat behind me—I must not think. I run in an arc, through the unholy square (dancing death laughing at me), into the bone-dead, all-but-deserted ruin. Even the hardiest souls won't follow me here. So I settle in.

The miracles have trapped me.

HERCULE

Your milk may be marble, but you cry real tears. Wet tears. How plainly the lashes sop, the eyes swell, the cheeks redden, how ugly it makes you.

But you have come—to me!

I think you may be a witch. Are you? Because now, after everything, it is my heart that is moved and my eyes that moisten, as I watch from an overhang of stone in this place where you found me. Are you one of these? One who anoints herself with honey, then rolls upon a bed of wheat? And do you take the sticky harvest and grind it in two stones and cause bread to be baked from it, to feed your man and waste him away for love? Shame on you!

But of course you are no baker. You are a sailor, awash in a sea of your own eyeing.

And you made me grow.

I could reach out my strong new hand and take yours, but I won't. Instead I'll let my heart—new also—swell, to pillow you in this hard place.

The hours are long and quiet. I weep, soaking my skirts, until I fall into lonely stupor, a half-sleep of exhaustion. And eventually I begin to hear a hum: *Bonne Bonne Bonne . . .* It is all around. And I think I know the voice.

There is no vertigo now. I clutch the ruined walls, I close my eyes and lean over the nave—and it is as if I can see my mother floating there, bright-haired and virgin-limbed. Blanche the Astonishing. *Bonne,* she says. She smiles, and from her smile, I know she feels two hearts inside her—the best feeling she has ever known, better even than nursing her child.

I open my eyes and there she is still, shimmering, white.

A breeze blows from Blanche onto me; the fine hairs tickle my cheeks. She continues to smile. Slowly, I let go of the walls—but do not fall. I stay there, floating at an impossible angle, looking at my mother. She parts her lips, as if to speak, but there is no sound.

I whisper her name. "Blanche . . ."

Then suddenly a wall of flame whooshes up, and the room is an inferno. Blanche's eyes fly wide in terror. She plummets to the floor, where her screams mingle with the screams of others. My hair singes, my eyebrows disappear. I fall—backward, always backward.

I DON'T KNOW HOW LONG I lie there before I realize my breasts are on fire. Hot and hard, they've been full for hours, and they burn with each breath. So I squeeze them like wincing udders, drip-drip-drip against the floor: milk joining ash, blood to blood. I lie back again and do not sleep.

Witches are meant to dance in the wilds of the forest, never in tunnels underground. They smear themselves with menstrual blood and the blood of virgins, not creams and unguents imported from the East. They eat insects and children; they do not cure wounds or give birth, unless it is to Satan's spawn. Radegonde is no witch. But how am I to tell this to the fathers? For witches also feast between each other's legs.

I look down into the nave from which my mother rose. Every bump in the lead blanket is someone's face, elbow, hipbone, breast; large swells are bodies lying together, arms and legs entwined by chance or love as the last hope died. I will never know which of those ripples engendered me.

Some of the bodies are of course gone, burned into air. What will become of them on Judgment Day, when flesh is meant to rise again? Those whom animals have eaten will be regurgitated and reassembled, but what of those who have become ash in whole or in part?

FINALLY, as dawn streaks the sky with clay, I sneak back toward the center of town. I am going to the great house; it is the one place I can think of where I can not only feed myself but also be alone. So in the early-morning twilight I unlock the iron gate, crack it open, and slide inside. I lock it again immediately, then do the same with the big house door.

The silence of this place has its own echo.

The servants took what they could carry from the main pantry and buttery, but the stores belowstairs are still full. I find everything I need; I know where the mistress kept the keys. Not even Radegonde's guardsmen could break down the doors to the wine cellars and cheeseries.

I never have to leave here again.

DAY OF
SAINTS LUCEJA
AND AUCEJAS

 OURS PASS, A DAY. I DON'T EAT. INSTEAD I wander through the denuded house, noting the absence of portable furniture and bibelots, listening to floor and table boards creaking in protest at their burdenless state. Watching the banquet's crumbs decay while luffs of dust float by like ghosts.

When darkness falls, I go to Radegonde's bedchamber. I fill the room with light from candles and climb onto the smooth counterpane, put my heels by my buttocks, and spread my legs wide. This is the way rich women wait for childbirth, propped open and slowly dilating—women who don't have to make do with a heap of straw in a corner of someone else's house. I set Henri's book on my thighs and turn to the blank pages at the end. I have cut a new quill. I write.

When I'm done there, I read about the symbolism of snakes and the proper keeping of a tame wolf.

It is said that men's stories are full of tension, that they lead to an upsurge of activity and emotion, and that after such a moment they reverse direction and wind quietly to a definite close. These stories are told in taverns and by fireplaces, eased along by wine and mead; if women are there to listen, they only listen—never speak. Our stories get told while we slap laundry against a river rock or wait for a stew to boil so we can stir it again; our stories are criticized for not fitting the pattern.

If I have to find such a turning point in Henri Putemonnoie's history of his life, it must be his marriage to Radegonde. But there are so many versions of the wedding itself that I can't make sense of his life before or since, and anyway it doesn't seem to be *his* life that changed when he married her. He was the one who already had money.

And yet, if my mistress's life altered so dramatically, why doesn't more of that show in the book? In the long, empty night, I turn the leaves, shuffle and reorder them, unbend some and fold others together, put recipes in one section and trade accounts in another. Still I don't find a clear, visible Radegonde anywhere. She's like a tiny drawing that a monk has carefully removed from his manuscript, paring away at the parchment until the image is just dust and a faint outline under his knife. Why has he taken her out?

I look for a page, in Henri's cramped writing, that might save the wife I am sure he loved. I find instead twelve ways to store onions and how to keep ants out of a garden.

HERCULE

I juggle when the pain's not too bad, I knit when it's not bad at all. I am getting bigger.

It was a good idea, coming here. I have a whole church to myself, a staircase and a tower of my own, ample room to grow in. Protection.

And I have the hounds of hell. No wall, however thick, can keep out those tales of rain and thunder, wind and stars. I toss my balls of rock and listen, for "Sound that travels far and wide, a stormy day does oft betide." I watch the hair sprout from my arms, my legs, my fork, and ponder, "Curls that kink and cords that bind: signs of rain and heavy wind." I eat rotten fruit and dried meat as the gray hand passes them to me, and know "A bloom on the tree when the apples are ripe is sure termination of somebody's life."

But when, but when? "They are green now," I say, and drop the rock balls thunk, thunk, thunk.

I remember that cross against the white mist . . . Bonne.

Days pass, a week. All alone, I rattle through the house, furnished now with great piles of the hairy dust. Four, five times a day, I squeeze my milk into a basin. The nipples' former pallor has darkened from many mouths, and the red and blue veins stand out like stained glass. At night I pour the milk onto Radegonde's rosebushes; they creep upward and grow thick with leaves. Still I do not sleep.

During the day, I remain inside. I take a back route to the kitchen, keep the shutters closed, and avoid the courtyard at all costs. For there's a mob without—people peering through the gate, calling out my name. They know I am in here. They think I'm praying.

They, themselves, actually are at prayer. They're praying to me. From the shutters in the great hall, I see them tie ribbons and other tokens to the gate's iron bars. I sneak out after curfew and pull those scraps from the gate, filling a basket with the gaudy offerings. The people, those who can, have written out their names and sometimes the requests they want me to make of God. They believe my milk will protect them from evil, will keep them strong, will bring money into town, cure impotence, and make them pretty. And they all ask, very humbly, that when I feel ready to rejoin the world, I come to them.

One by one, every priest in town rings the house bell. The sound booms through the hollow rooms. When I hear it, I climb up to the needle tower and watch until the black crow goes, or I run to the bedchamber and bury my head under the pillows. Always, the sight of a priest's robe stirs the fear in my heart.

I never thought that once assured of a place in society, I'd be so scared. I never realized how terrifying it is to have something to lose. If I misstep now, Villeneuve will take revenge. Radegonde and I might both be burned for witches: The line between miracle and magic is so fine.

One afternoon I take all of my mistress's clothes out of their chests and spread them around her boudoir. No matter how I move the heavy sleeves and skirts, I can't create the sense of anyone inside. And I can't bear to think of the body they used to cover.

There is an emptiness in me. I'm hungry. Not so much for food—I have all that I need. No, I crave something to occupy me. Something to fill the thick, blank pages at the end of the book.

NCE MORE I SIT WITH MY BACK AGAINST THE
pillows, knees up and legs open. A looking
glass lies beside me, reflecting rays of unshut-
tered sun. Its ivory handle points toward my
hand as it waits to tell me of myself.

Am I a witch? What do I fear? What
should I confess? What is holding me here?

I must track the river to its source: find
the second heartbeat. If I am brave enough.
Thus, slowly, my left hand raises the mirror as
my right divides the forest of curls and pushes
them back, glueing them down with saliva.
And I look.

The glass of this mirror—the one in
which Radegonde first showed me to myself—
is of such quality that I see an almost unwa-
vering picture: the slicked-back hairs, startling
dark; the snaillike wetness in between. I know
the priests would say it is wrong to look, that
this is the worst kind of vanity—but I can't
help myself. Not since my breasts began to
grow have I been able to see myself down
here.

The glass shows me a little cave. Below it,
a jagged scar runs back between my legs.
Fleetingly I remember the tug of the mid-

wife's stitches there, an echo of the greater ones upon my belly, as I stood and walked into my new life.

But I will not think of that day. I aim the glass higher and my hand peels back the outside lobes to reveal a tide of rippling flesh. Complicated petals, my flower. The inside is completely pink, except for two blue veins that run in the deepest channels. And there's the bump at the top, swelling (I can feel it), a tiny sepal, a red recluse's head poking out of a pink cowl. In the glass, my hand pushes the cowl back, then lays a fingertip upon the face of the recluse.

Lightning!

My finger jumps away, then—curious, rebellious, a novice caught playing when she should be in chapel—slides down one of the inner ripples, pressing on the central ridge. There's a deeper feeling here, as if somehow I'm pressing into my spine, my backbone. I feel it even in my brain.

Suddenly I find two fingers are rubbing and nibbling—rubbling—at the recluse, worrying and washing her face, divesting her of her cowl, turning her fiery red. For a moment I forget myself and moan out loud.

I stop the hand, disciplining it. The sentiments recede.

But the hand persuades me to let it start again. And it resumes differently, more urgently, with a flurry of small tugs and peelings. *Radegonde taught me,* it says. *Now just lie back.* It rubbles and worries the anchoress, making me weak, until finally she gathers her strength and heaves.

The mirror drops. Both hands falls away. The nun is full of fury, writhing and twitching, spitting in anger. I feel her heart beat. I scream so loud the glass in the moving panes rattles. The recluse shudders, and shudders again. Then lies still, exhausted.

What am I? Covered in sweat, I swoon.

SAINT
pHOCAS'S DAY
[JULY 3]

HEN I WAKE IN THE MORNING, THE SUN shows blood on the oversheet, and a big grayish yellow lump.

It is a tooth. My own, the first I've lost since bleeding made me a woman. It slipped out overnight.

I check between my legs. Nothing. The blood is from my mouth, too.

Though I didn't feel myself lose this tooth, my tongue goes directly to the hole it left. It was the right upper eyetooth, the one Radegonde's mirrors showed me had rotted. I remember that the last time I looked at my face, on the night of the feast, the tooth had taken on a bluish sheen. Now its former seat in my gum is soft and swampy, like a slug, and it tastes like base metal.

I pick the thing up carefully and push myself sitting to examine it. It's gray from the outside in, the only shading being the pinprick of a black root at the center. I feel curiously tender toward this tiny part of myself, so small, yet so well formed for its space; when I fit it back into its hole (my fingers smelling like the sea), it sits there snug for a moment.

I'm used to seeing matter leave my body—blood, milk, tears, the usual—but nothing so substantial, so *hard*, as this. When it falls against my tongue, it makes me feel its loss. I spit it into my palm and know what I must do.

I have some idea where Radegonde keeps her things. I climb down from the bed—soft carpet for my feet—and go key by key through the basket till I find one that unlocks the chest I want.

This is where Radegonde stores her private luxuries. And in an ivory box inside, I find just what I'm looking for: a pouch of red satin with a mouth that draws shut on a golden thread. I pull it open, and a green stone drops out; this I lay aside. I replace it with my tooth and slip the cord around my neck. The double line of it runs between my breasts, and the pouch with my tooth inside slaps lightly over my ribs.

Then I look at the emerald. The surface is cloudy and dull, but inside it's more green than anything I've ever seen before, and its green is deep as if the stone—no bigger than my thumb pad—holds more space within than its edges take up.

This must be the stone la Putemonnoie is said to suck on all night, the one that guards her youth and luck. I blow on it and rub the sides against the counterpane; the outside gets a little brighter, but not much. Then I put it in my regular pocket, for my own luck, dress quickly, and am soon out in the street, having locked every door behind me.

"MOTHER!"

"Bonne!"

"There she is!"

"Mother Bonne, over here!"

My doves swarm around me, pecking at my clothes, begging me for a suckle, a blessing, a word.

I run away.

They follow. They catch me. I'm frail from fasting and slow with in-activity—easy prey for those with faith.

"Please, Bonne—"

"My baby!" A woman shoves a spavined creature in my face. "Scro-fula, since birth . . ."

I shudder, holding my skirts tight against my body. "Good people . . ."

"She spoke!"

They fall silent, listening, waiting for me to deliver the word of God. I realize I must frame my own words with care; this will perhaps be what distinguishes my fate from my mother's.

"Good people," I say, "God wants you . . . to go home. Go home and pray. Or pray in church"—that will please the priests. "He has delivered you—delivered us—from the Englishmen; now we must give thanks where it is due."

"The new church—"

"The Virgin—"

"We are grateful for miracles!"

But no one departs. They watch me with eyes no less hungry for their bellies' fullness.

"Please, Mother, show us your breasts." The man who says this is highly respectful, not lewd; even though he has removed his shirt, it is only to flog himself with a tree branch, raising thin red welts. He flogs even as he speaks.

"Good people," I say, averting my eyes and with the resignation of desperation, "you may escort me to the new church." I will let Pierre and Paul take care of them. I touch my tooth in its pouch, and the people think I am touching my breasts. They cheer.

We make a little parade as we head through the streets, collecting more of a crowd along the way. People are eager to leave their shops, their tools, their children in order to follow my bosom. Somebody pulls out a flute and begins to play, and then it's impossible for the rest of us (yes, even Mother Bonne) to keep from marking time with our footsteps. The respectful man and his fellow flagellants also keep time, lashing themselves with every step; the sound of tearing flesh makes the drumbeat of our music.

In a quarter hour, we're at the narthex of the new church. The chisels inside cease as the workmen learn who's without. Soon the door swings open, and a young priest beckons. I lift my hand. I have a speech ready.

"Good people, let us in and pray. Let us be grateful. Let us remember"—the words come from an old page of Scripture—"we all go unto one place." I offer my personal benediction to each man, woman, and child who has followed me here. I clasp their hands as singly, dutifully, they file inside. I do not think it irreligious of me; it makes them so happy.

And when they're all in, I turn my heels, cover my head with my apron, and flee. Up one street and down another, past the big well, across a square, and to the house of one Maître Civis, citizen and prominent member of the town council. The priests have a stake in this miracle, and in Radegonde's confinement; perhaps a wool merchant will be more amenable to reason.

As I pull the bell cord, I wonder again: Why hasn't Godfridus turned up to dismiss the misbelief? Doesn't he, somewhere, resent the use I'm making of his work—he who was proud enough to sign and display it?

Footsteps approach the door, and I pull myself straight.

When the elderly manservant sees me, his jaw drops, and as he ushers me in, he bends deep at the knee. "I—I will tell the maître you're here," he says without asking my name.

This from a man who, in younger days, once emptied a piss pot on my head as I slept in a doorway. I run my tongue into the tooth's groove and remind myself to keep strong.

In a very few moments, Civis himself stands before me—then kneels, carrying my hand to his lips. "You do me such honor, mistress." He is burly now and bearded, his barrel chest heaving; that smell of the sheep still clings. Beaming, he orders the servant to bring up some wine and offers me his arm. "If you come to the solar, my wife will be much honored to receive you."

This man's of an age to have torched Saint-Porchaire—but I won't think of that. I've chosen him because he's prosperous and therefore must be practical.

Upstairs we pass through rooms crammed with bales of raw wool. There's wool all about: cloth, thread, fluffy fairy lumps that, like the dust in the Putemonnoie home, are clogging the passageways. In her solar, Civis's wife has been spinning—wool of the finest grade, of course—and the air's full of fiber, the smell sour and oily and stale. Her windows are small, and I'll bet they haven't any glass for the winter. And yet Maître Civis is one of the wealthiest men in town.

When she stands, Civis's wife looks me in the eye and searches my face intently, though her lips keep smiling. Blanche once told me that women who aren't absolutely consumed with religious ardor are reserved around female mystics; it's as if they can't believe in a miracle worked with a womanly body. Or perhaps they envy the nod of divine approval—they'd like to claim God's heart, too. But we can't all marry Christ.

Paradoxically, I am somewhat relieved to find in all the town one soul who questions the Miracle of the Milk. Though she makes my work here harder.

The wool merchant doesn't notice our exchange of glances. He is rubbing his beard, scratching excitedly as if after a louse. "Are you well, Mother?" he asks me. "Is there something I—or the town—can do for you?"

"Please, sit," urges his wife, more conscious of manners though more doubtful of me.

A puff of sheepy dust billows up when I land on my bench; the cushion is flat and lumpy. I decide to take a bold tack. "I've come about Radegonde Putemonnoie," I announce, then wonder if I've said it too loudly. The name weights the air like a bad odor.

The wife snips it free. "Does she owe you money?"

"No." I resist the sudden impulse to laugh, as if my womb has wandered into my head and made me hysterical. Once more my tongue goes where the tooth used to be. "But I am concerned about her. You realize Mistress Putemonnoie is very far along in pregnancy and has now been imprisoned"—I hesitate, but add—"unjustly."

Maître Civis looks uneasy. "I'm sure she's taken care of as well as any other prisoner of her rank, and in her condition."

"Prisoners of rank aren't usually kept in prison. They stay at home."

"Do you understand the crime?" asks Civis's wife. Her dress is stained where neck and wrists emerge. "People are calling her la Pute. She is accused of—"

Before the word can be spoken, I say, "I understand the prison stretches for miles underneath the city, and the air down there is very foul. Extremely dangerous for a woman in her situation."

Maître Civis is scowling, perhaps at his wife, perhaps at me, perhaps (I hope) at being a decent man in an indecent situation. "Her kind of prisoners," he says, "are usually kept until they confess."

This word strikes a chill in me. "She has nothing to confess," I croak. "And in her condition, I fear the prison keepers' methods of persuasion." When Civis doesn't reply, I press on: "Thumbscrews, pokers, the pear . . ."

The wife winces at that—the large, toothy bulb that masters of torture insert in a womb and screw open, letting it bloom bloody until the subject tells them all they wish to hear.

Maître Civis says weakly, "I assure you, there is nothing to fear on that score. She has a belly, after all, and she won't be tried until the baby comes. You have my word of honor—as a master."

I press my palms together and dig the nails into my wrists. A pregnancy is usually good enough only to postpone an execution; if the fathers are putting off her trial, it means they do intend to precede it with torture—torture that may result in death.

At this moment, the man arrives with wine (always wine, now), and in the bustle of pouring it out, I come to myself again. When we are alone, the Civis couple raise their cups, gazing as if to toast me.

I look at them over the rim of my cup. "I would feel much better," I say, "if I could assure myself about Mistress Putemonnoie with my own eyes. I am her servant, you know, and responsible."

"*You*—visit la Putemonnoie?" Now Civis looks deeply distressed. "Mistress—Mother—I can't encourage that. Imagine the dangers to you down there! And no one thinks of you as her servant now. Rather, it is she who—"

His wife puts in, "If you go down, your milk might sour."

But, stubbornly, I restate my case: "You see, I'm still under contract to her. I feel a certain duty . . . for the baby, if for none else."

Civis gulps his wine. "*Do* you realize what the mother stands accused of?"

I set my cup down untasted; we all seem to be merely reminding one another of what we already know. My chief aim for the moment is to keep Civis from saying the words out loud, as they'll only strengthen his own resolve to keep me away. "Yes, maître, I do. But shouldn't you also realize that in the end she may be proven—"

"Witchcraft!" the wife trumpets suddenly. Her russet dress now bears a red wine stain. "Witchcraft and heresy! The richest woman in town, and nobody knows where she came from, or her wealth, or her people. And just look at her! She's lived here almost twenty years and not aged a day—"

Now Civis, afraid to give me offense, claps his hand over his wife's mouth. "These are serious charges," he says to me. "La Putemonnoie may be found guilty."

"But the baby she's carrying is entirely innocent."

The wife yanks the hand away from her face. "How do we know? That could be the child of—"

"Certes he is the child of his mother's middle age," I interrupt smoothly, "and thus at some risk, especially if his mother isn't receiving the attention she's used to. I'm worried about that baby. Do you realize"— I focus particularly on the maître—"that if the baby dies, the entire Putemonnoie fortune goes to Henri's brother, in Paris?"

In the ensuing silence, I think I hear the wool bales bleat.

Civis asks at last, "The money leaves Villeneuve?"

I feel a tremendous, perhaps premature, rush of relief. Finally I have said one right thing. I think perhaps the priests have been keeping this a secret from the laymen, who might not want the money to be churched. "And all the business, maître. The warehouses, the traveling agents . . . You know a woman can't inherit all that property, and there's no one else but the brother."

"Ah." He beard-scrabbles.

"So you share my concern."

The wife's eyes have gone bright and indignant, like a rat's. "You plan to suckle the witch," she accuses me. Clearly she's made up her mind about my soul as well. "A viper at the—"

"Naturally," Civis says, "we should not let the innocent suffer for the crimes of those who have harbored them."

I nearly fall out of my seat. "Then I may visit her?"

But I've pressed my point too soon. Civis's face has a worried, furtive look, and he gets to his feet. "I will visit her myself," he says.

"I'd really prefer—"

He cuts me off. "We must protect the innocent," he reminds me, almost using my own words. "And you, *good* mistress, are the person most to be protected. You and your milk. The town fathers would never forgive me if . . . Well, I will investigate the case and see that she has what she needs."

I have to bite back certain words—bite and chew and swallow. How quickly my darker past has been forgotten; how quickly I have become a civic treasure, when once the prison was too good for me. But I try to accept this outcome calmly, and as if grateful.

"Will you broach the subject at the next council meeting?" I ask, and he agrees, gracious in his relief. In return I offer my hand to kiss and take a sip of wine that stings my mouth.

The sheep weaver and I part cordially, like persons of business.

GODFRIDUS

I am on fire.

His circuit is unto the ends of heaven, and there is nothing hid from the heat thereof. He bakes the clay of His shaping, making it adamant, making it stone.

I burn, I bake. My skin turns red and falls away. I bathe and the river steams. I have sinned.

He—not I—hath made every thing beautiful in His time. And He hath left it pure. It is my time to cast away stones, my time to refrain from embracing, His time to gather stones together. Also He hath set the world in our heart.

> *in our heart*
> > *we have Stones*

I am cast away.

Again I drape the apron over my head, but I attract attention. The streets are busy, and I must step slowly; people see my face. They gather. I ignore them and they trail along in silence, glad simply to be near me.

As I walk along, my hand touches the tooth beneath my dress, the tiny hardness in the red silk bag. My breasts know it is nestled there; they are warming it, perhaps turning it . . . *blanche.*

I remember my vision that night at Saint-Porchaire: my mother smiling, beckoning to me. I know now that she was choosing me for greatness, asking me to do some great thing. Which is why she blew me backward to safety instead of pulling me down, with her. And so, instead of returning to the Putemonnoie house, I lead my flock once more to the new church.

Again I shoo the doves into the church itself. They leave the living me and flutter in to contemplate my image. But *I* am going to the priests' house behind. I plan to strike a bargain, a pact, with Father Pierre.

And I am most welcome. The two men, Pierre and Paul, make the sign of the cross on themselves as they see me—Pierre's bumps and wrinkles expressing transcendent joy, Paul's powdery pink baldness gleaming with the god within him. *Entheosiasm.*

"Bless you, bless you, sister," the men say. They seat me on a velveted bench, themselves in x-chairs, and the glossy saints ignore us. Thomas comes in on two lay brothers' arms, and he sits, too.

"What happened to your brows?" he asks abruptly. The near-blind old eyes are keen after all.

"I—" I put up a finger to touch. The hairs are bristly and short, as if newly grown. *Blanche,* I think.

"It is the milk, perhaps," Paul suggests. "It draws inside what's not needed without."

"You're getting thin, sister," is Pierre's comment. "You must take advantage of the larders at your disposal. Keep up your strength, and your flow. Don't you have a cook?" He seems to regard Radegonde's house as mine now; but surely he knows the servants left on Saint John's Eve.

Three sets of eyes, three mouths, sit before me dissecting. "Thank you, my fathers, for your kind concern. All is well with me, if not with every soul in Villeneuve. I've come to— I hope you will bless my mission in coming here."

"What is that, sister?" Thomas asks, blinking. "Would you like a Mass said in your name? Perhaps we can—"

"Every church in town has been praying for you these past ten days," Paul puts in. The skin works over his bare skull. "The people are saying—"

I blurt it out: "I want you to free Radegonde Putemonnoie. I demand it."

Silence lengthens, stretches, takes on body and consistency.

I turn to Pierre. "I know what you accuse her of. But you wanted me to watch her . . . I watched, and nothing I saw convinces me she belongs in prison now. You must let her out."

Pierre frowns for a moment, but then his brow clears. He really is trying to think the best of me. "You watched her, yes. And now you want to watch in prison?"

"I want her out of prison," I murmur, or maybe I only think I murmur it. For now, before these men and these painted saints, I realize just what it is I'm asking them to do for me.

"Regular visits," Pierre continues thoughtfully, "readings from the Bible, a few questions about her unguents and her doings in the full moon—that sort of thing?"

"I'm afraid we could never let her out," says Paul. "She'll stand trial as soon as the baby comes." Pierre glares at him for saying too much too plainly.

Thomas only quivers, but that is his way. I realize he will help neither me nor his brothers. And then he smiles at me, gently, and I see he's missing his left eyetooth. I believe this is a sign—this is the one chance God will give me. I must make of it what I need.

"Yes, Fathers," I say, mustering Radegondian serenity. *This* is how to bargain. "I could . . . interview her for you. I could watch her. I'm as concerned in—for—her soul as you are. She trusts me."

The three priests speak to one another with their eyes. Trust, confidence, confession—they will make me their thumbscrew, their pear. And I will assume my power slowly.

"We will have to confer," says Pierre.

"There are dangers to weigh," adds Paul.

Thomas merely quivers.

How well I know the dangers. "Shall I wait outside?"

"Thank you."

In the passage, I think of all the conferences that have been held in the priests' house over the century since founding the new church: conferences to save immortal souls, to save marble; to promote piety, to promote contributions to the building fund. Even to decide how the church, and thus the town, should treat my mother and me. I'm borne down under the weight of all this conferring.

So I close my eyes and imagine the priests. They whisper behind raised hands, fingertip to fingertip, lips almost touching. The skin stretches and contracts, veins knobbling, over three tonsured skulls as they weigh dangers. Then, willfully, I imagine the bare heads smoothed over, the coarse stubble on them softened into downy fuzz, the parched aging mouths wet and supple. And I feel an answering trickle over my ribs.

When the priests call me in again, they say I can't see Radegonde.

"We can't take that risk with your person," Pierre explains.

"You are this town's greatest treasure," says Paul. They both sign the cross.

"But you may pray for her," offers Thomas, gently smiling.

It is what I expected. Almost before I know it, my fingers are at my clothing, loosening the laces in back and tugging the dress down over my shoulders. The bandeau is stiff; it unwinds with a brisk crackle, and my nipples pucker and harden as they're exposed to the air.

The old men stare at me. Their hands have dropped; their mouths are open. Two spheres of milk hang from me like cloudy pearls, the red bag of tooth in between.

"Fathers"—I cup a breast in each hand, squeezing them to keep up the flow, as I did with the dogs in the bear ring; my eyes are closed—"I beg you, humbly, please taste my milk. I have so much of it, and I know I would please God by offering it up to the church."

I feel the clothes heavy around my hips, my flesh heavy in my hands. A Christ regards me sternly. But the priests don't seem shocked; I hear their footsteps clack-clack approaching and feel the air move to hold them as they take up the half-stooped position before me. By the time their bellies are full, I know I'll be granted this small request. Not even a priest can resist me . . .

Now they are trapped. Licking, being licked. Tongues of flame making love to the walls as they climb higher and higher—tongues loving limbs, arms, necks, legs; consuming hair in one blossoming burst . . . The roof supports catch fire, the whole body of lead collapses . . .

It is the judgment of the Lord. Their ashes melt together.

Soon it is over. The black crows stand, wiping their mouths on their sleeves, and I start to wrap my bandeau. Tucking the tooth between. I am embarrassed before these men in a way that I haven't been with my clients, yet the holy fathers do not watch me, do not speak of or look at my breasts.

Pierre turns his eyes to the ceiling and says, "I've been inspired. I have an idea."

"You've thought of a way I may see my mistress?" I try to phrase it as if this is Pierre's own fondest hope. I wonder, incidentally, what good it is to be known as a miracle woman if I can't get the church to satisfy my wishes.

In his corner, Thomas snores.

Pierre produces his scheme like a busker pulls a sword from his throat: "Your milk is still abundant, sister——"

"And Mistress Putemonnoie has paid for it, to nurse her baby."

"Sister, the great famine of Villeneuve has ended, but there are still mouths that must be fed, bodies that need nourishment."

I swallow bile. "Fathers, I would be——happy to share my milk with the priesthood any time it can be useful."

"Thank you, sister," Paul says, watching the breasts disappear into my chemise. "Perhaps we——"

Pierre lifts a hand. "I have another notion. As priests we must think of our parishioners. In this time of prosperity, when most souls are well nourished by their own means, we must remember those without enough to eat. The sick children, the indigent babies . . ."

"You mean the orphanage."

"Sister, you anticipate me!" He beams and scratches a wart. "Perhaps you yourself were going to propose this very thing. If you could nurse the abandoned babies—you must have enough for *them*, when you've been feeding so many grown folks—it would be another work of wonder."

I pull the dress over my shoulders and lace it. "I'm not sure how much good I could do at the orphanage."

Pierre's next words are for Paul. "Think how pleased the cardinal would be if we lowered the mortality rate. If *all* the babies lived——!"

It's common knowledge that nine out of ten children at the Hôtel-Dieu die within their first year. The rest grow into spavined, weak-lunged adolescence, capable of only the most minor menial labor and doomed to early deaths. Most of my life has been aimed at keeping myself out of the place.

"Yes," I say dully. "The cardinal would likely increase his contribution to the new church. It would be the richest in the province." And if I can't keep the babies alive—well, I will be just one more failed holy woman in Blanche's family. Perhaps another church will sustain a fire.

Pierre looks quickly back at me. His nose is positively twitching. "The souls you'd save, sister—think of the souls."

"Yes, the souls . . ." Paul nods. "And the cardinal *has* promised to make us a visit soon. For the statue—and then to see its living likeness in such an act of charity . . ."

"One more thing." Pierre coughs to signal delicacy, and I dart him a look from my singed brows. "Sister, we are aware that milk cannot flow unless a woman be in a certain state. Namely, that she abstain from congress with men."

Once again that hysterical laughter bubbles within me, and this time I can't prevent a little gulp from escaping. How do the priests think I have been living all these years? I nearly do not think of that night with Radegonde, or of the one time that got me pregnant.

Pierre seems to mistake my chuckle for a cry of pain, as if giving up men will be a sacrifice. "The Lord has chosen you for this work," he says on a note of reproof. "You must honor His choice. Your . . . uncle . . . will understand."

"Pierre." For the first time I use his name without honorific. "I don't even know where Godfridus is. But as to your condition, I completely agree. I will honor the Lord's request"—it will be easy—"if you honor mine. Let me at least visit Mistress Putemonnoie. She has a soul, and so does her unborn baby."

Pierre and Paul exchange a look of victory. "If you agree, sister, I think that might be arranged," Pierre concedes at last.

It must be what he intended all along.

As I take my leave, Thomas awakes. "Daughter," he says, fixing his kind blue eyes on mine, "you must allow me to give you a gift. In these hot days, with their risk of peste, you must be safe. I will give you a pomander of my own making."

I sink down beside him and say thanks, if not for the charm then for the goodwill. I will carry his token into the very Hôtel of God.

fEAST OF SAINT BERTHA THE ANCHORESS

[J U L Y   4]

HERCULE

She's a lady now, but she couldn't pay anyone to come here. She comes herself, and climbs the wall, and empties the basin, and slides in new food. I watch.

She wears the dress of blue-green brocade, too short and tattery, and her ankles show like sticks. It is also too tight across the bosom, though she's made it to lace up in front. But she looks beautiful, with her basket and an orange stuck with cloves.

So easy it is to slip along and between walls where the sun never shines, following her glow of silk traced with gold, the fruity rope of smell, the jingle of keys at her belt. The fool foldeth his hands together. But she doesn't see.

"Marie, I have a new duty," she calls into the stone slit, as she passes meat and loaf. "I'm going to the orphanage—at last. Even though I managed to keep out when my mother died and her mother turned her back."

There is no sound. The voice speaks to me now.

La Bonne spends some moments gazing at the black slit framed in roses. Not even a flicker of flesh, not a whisper of weathery doom. Bonne sniffs her orange and says, "First, the prison."

When she's gone, I scurry to the hole like a rat. The gray hand passes me meat and bread, the old voice whispers—"When Venus is full, Mars rides the bull. On such a night the moon will be bright . . ."

I chew and prickle my ears. I have my teacher at last.

I've been granted half my wish. I can see Radegonde.

I take such care in dressing for her that I am late to feeding Marie. I tell Marie of the new arrangement, my pending visits to orphanage and prison. She knows of the dangers; she knows she might never see me again, if the air is diseased and Thomas's pomander doesn't do its work. She knows she might starve, as no one else cares about feeding her. Still she says nothing. So I shake out my skirts and proceed belowground—to another cell, whose prisoner has been most intimate with me.

I don't go alone. Once I leave the shadow district, my doves trail me to the main prison door, a hatch between the tiny chapel of Saint-Médard and the looming Palais de Justice. Studded with iron, streaked with rust, it is framed by a pair of guards and a fringe of homeless prison widows, hands out for alms. There Pierre is waiting.

"Ah, sister," he says, pretending to bless me and my believers. The widows wail that he has given them nothing; some venture to say their husbands are wrongly imprisoned. Pierre does not notice. "Are you ready?" He lifts a spotted hand to show a book of Bernard de Clairvaux's writing in the vulgar tongue. "For you to read," he explains, "aloud." I complete his thought: to improve Radegonde's mind, save her soul, see if perhaps she falls down writhing and foaming at the mouth when she hears the word of God.

I am glad I've not described all my former activities in the Putemonnoie house. There is no telling how a priest would interpret Henri's book and its various accounts of Radegonde's past; *that* tome now sits tucked beneath the mattress on which his wife used to sleep, embalmed each night with milk.

When the guards throw open the doors, a billow of cold, sour air knocks me backward. Feeling faint, I squeeze the pomander and grope for

Radegonde's linen square—I've tucked one in my pocket, where my fingers also brush the reassuring hard weight of the emerald.

This is no worse than the Hôtel-Dieu, I tell myself as I straighten up. No worse than anywhere.

Pierre and I enter. Immediately we must step down a set of stairs into the earth itself, where tiny tiles web the walls and floor. Light travels weakly from above. At the bottom there is a second door, which Pierre unlocks himself. The air gets darker and damper.

"Breath of God." I clap the linen square tighter over my face.

"The air here never changes," Pierre confides as if this is a thing of wonder, a gift from Christ. He does not reprove me for blaspheming. "Winter, spring, or summer, it is always the same in temperature and quality."

A man emerges from the murk. He carries a pine torch, bright smoking shadows all over us and the tiles. "Afternoon, Father."

Pierre coughs and, nodding to this new guard, gives his nose a swipe. "We are here for la Putemonnoie. Bonne LaMère and I."

Stocky, gray-complected, breathing easy, the guard peers at me. With the linen square over my face, I'm no more distinctive than a swaddled baby, and he must be wondering at my reputation. I feel my milk shrinking deep inside, breasts wrinkling; I look around and see more of these tiny tiles—fragments of tile, really—winking whitely in the light.

"I see you're studying the mosaics, mistress." The guard raises his torch. "This is a very old place. When we was digging the town hall foundations, we discovered the first tunnel, and they seemed so useful it would have been a sin to fill them in. Nobody's ever escaped from this prison."

"Then," I say, "Villeneuve isn't really new after all."

"In a sense," Pierre says piously, "there is nothing new under the sun."

The guard gestures with his torch. "The women are kept over this way."

He takes us through a brief corridor and down a short staircase. At the bottom, four or five dark tunnels branch away. We take the second from the right and head (as far as I can tell) east, probably under the wide street known as the Grand' Rue. The farther we go, the less tile there is; finally there's just a mixture of stone, brick, and sometimes wood holding back the walls of earth. Dirt falls like a light but constant rain.

When we're some ells up the Grand' Rue, we find the first of the cells. It appears to be empty, an iron grate that holds nothing but two squabbling rats. They don't bother to run when they see us; in fact they sniff so boldly that the pomander drops from my hand.

The guard's torch sends up a puff of smoke. "Watch your step, Father."

Pierre has nearly fallen into a puddle of gray muck. Clucking fretfully, he gathers up his skirts. I wonder if he's been down here before; specifically, if he's come to visit Radegonde. Somehow, seeing him so clumsy, I doubt it.

A little farther on there's a scratching sound, but no rat. Behind this rusty grate, a gnarled woman is scraping the wall with a piece of broken pottery; she's already made a dent a few hands' breadths deep and doesn't stop when we walk by.

"That's Nicolette de Jardinier," the guard volunteers. "Seems to think she can dig her way out."

"She can't?" But even I know the answer.

"These walls are thick, mistress, and passing hard. She's been working that hole for three years, so you see how safe the place is." He sounds proud of it.

I shiver, but I'm not going to look at that poor wretch again. I can think of only one woman now. We pass more cells, the figures in them still, hopeless, lying on their heaps of straw and rags, their heads turned any which way . . . They don't seem to care if their eyes are open or closed.

"Why are they here?" I whisper, around the burn in my throat. "Are they all accused witches?"

"Or debtors, or illegal prostitutes. One is a murderess." Pierre answers shortly, as if to speak down here is mortal danger.

At least, I think, Radegonde is not completely alone. But then we pass a string of cells that appear to be empty, populated only by piles of dust. We are so deep in that the rats won't follow, and the earth's evil smells seem to have accumulated here.

Pierre stops in a cul-de-sac, a thumbprint of earth and stone. "Here."

I have to look. I see a woman sitting on a heap of straw, her back to us, in a dark dress creased and clotted with dirt. Long black hair hangs tangled around her shoulders—matted, or perhaps woven, into a blanket. It looks to be of a piece with her dress.

The air closes in. This can't be—but it is. I sway. "Radegonde!"

Father Pierre starts fanning me, hands flapping at the black-robed wrists. "Mistress Bonne, please!" And the guard gives me a good shake. Still the woman in the cell doesn't move.

"Is she alive?"

"Was last night," the guard assures me. "I checked her myself."

We all stare, as at a dismal panther in a traveling menagerie.

"Madame Putemonnoie?" I call tentatively. "Can you hear me?"

Then something in her snaps; the blanket of hair heaves for a breath. "Oh, go away, Bonne." Her voice is cross, as if I've interrupted her at dinner.

I am relieved, and ashamed. "I came as soon as I could—as soon as they let me . . ." This sounds lame even to my ears. "Will you turn around, please? To look at me?"

I'm afraid there's something wrong (the alternative is unthinkable, that she simply doesn't want to see me). I imagine her cheeks scored, her eyes gouged out, her nose split open like a peach. Has she been tortured in prison? Has she been raped?

"I have to see you," I say low, as if in apology. She doesn't answer. So I look up. "Father Pierre, please—"

The burly guard unlocks the gate, and (with me holding the smoking torch) together he and Pierre seize Radegonde by the shoulders. They have a struggle to turn her around: She's sitting heavy, not fighting, just increasing her weight the way children do when they don't want to go to bed. My sense of shame increases—but so does my fear.

I let them hoist and prod and pull until I'm looking at her front side. Her head has dropped, sunk into her breast. I see only the matted top of once-beautiful hair.

"Lift her face. Please."

Pierre starts to do it, cupping her chin in his hand. But then she comes alive, shakes him off, and looks square at me.

"Satisfied?" she says.

I bend, holding the torch closer. And I breathe again: It is the same face.

The same, only different. Her pillowy lips are withered, dry and cracked. Her cheeks are cracked, too—but no, those are shadows, frown wrinkles magnified by shadowy light. There's dirt all over her face, and perhaps a dried wisp of blood on her chin (the candles turn everything brown). But her nose is still needle-sharp, and her eyes are still bright—glowering at me from the savage hair.

"How—how can I be satisfied?" But I do wonder if perhaps my face has revealed what my treacherous heart felt for a moment—pleasure. Of course I'm sorry she is here, and that she's dirty, and disheveled, and tired. More sorry than I can say. But seeing her like this, I love her more than ever.

Pierre gazes at the prisoner with a sort of workmanlike pride. "She has not been tortured," he comments to me. The guard takes the torch away.

Radegonde won't raise her eyes from the straw. "So you're here, Bonne. Did you come to gloat?"

"Mistress Putemonnoie, I hope you don't think I had anything to do with your arrest."

She shakes her head impatiently and does not bother to reply. "How long have I been here?"

"Eleven days." I know I'm blushing, but it's too dark for her to see. Again I explain, "I came as soon as I could—as soon as the council and church would let me."

"We have to look after Mistress Tardieu," Pierre puts in. "She is our treasure." Does he emphasize the possessive? "We all must protect her—"

"From me?" Radegonde's downturned face is stone. "I'm the one who saved her from the gutter. You're the ones who tossed her there."

"—from herself," Pierre continues smoothly. "From her own good heart. She might unknowingly expose herself to danger, whether to body or soul, and all of us in Villeneuve have an interest in her survival."

Radegonde looks at him. Just looks.

As if he feels the weight of her former power, Pierre seems compelled to rush on— "The milk, you know, the blessed miracle of life in the famine. God gave it to us through our sister's body . . . And the statue that appeared in the new church, exactly her likeness—a sure sign from God."

"Statue?" Radegonde repeats, lips twisted. "Of finest white marble?"

"Painted," Pierre corrects. "Exquisitely. And precisely the image and coloring of Mistress Tardieu here, nursing an infant. A Virgin, of course, and the *Holy* Child." He weights that word as if to remove the statue, as he would remove me, from this grimy little cell and the child that might land in its pile of straw.

"The dauphin's coming to see it," the guard says, competing with Pierre for importance. "And the cardinal. People walk in every day from the country all around. A miracle—why, our Virgin's famous all over France."

I break in: "I said that if they let me visit you, I'd nurse at the orphanage." She knows how I feel about that.

"Saint Bonne," says Radegonde, unimpressed. "And all God's bastards." She flicks a glance at me and adds, "So you finally lost that tooth."

My tongue flies protectively to the space. For the first time I think I was wrong to come. Radegonde is so cold, so brittle—she'd rather snap in two than show me any kindness. She blames me. Maybe she's jealous. And maybe all this is natural.

"Mistress Bonne is doing holy work," Pierre says with more than his usual force.

"How is your baby?" I ask—one last try. "How do you feel? Are you all right here?"

Radegonde lets a silence develop. I think she might be hoping we'll hear a rat scratching somewhere, or a deathwatch beetle in the walls. But no—that's more like one of Hercule's tricks, cultivating pity. Anyway, what can she (used to velvet and silk and servants) say about this place?

Radegonde, I want to whisper, *I am sorry.* Sorry for many things I cannot voice before the priest.

The silence snaps when, in the dust and smoke, Radegonde sneezes.

"A vos souhaits." Without thinking, I give the traditional salute: To your wishes. And rush heedlessly on, "Radegonde—Mistress Putemonnoie—I am doing the best for you I can."

She looks at me with her everycolor eyes, the weird eyes that hold a world inside and might in themselves have damned her. The priest and guard seem to disappear, and I think again of the night of the feast, the night she arranged in my honor and for my pleasure. I think of holding her in my mouth. I know this is in her mind, too.

Finally she speaks. "Are you waiting to hear that I love you?"

I flinch, as if she's slapped me. The words may seem sweet but her voice is cold, too cold even to be hateful. I remember that with her, honey always comes with a sting.

The guard laughs nervously.

"God loves you, Bonne. And blesses you." She sounds colder still—such that the guard stops laughing and Pierre turns to me, hasty and urgent.

"Are you ready to leave?"

I look at the book still clutched in his horny hand and find my tongue is tied. The church is protecting me.

"You see," Pierre whispers (scratching the back of his neck with Bernard), "she has no complaints. And if you are satisfied, sister, we may return . . ."

Radegonde just wipes her nose on her sleeve in a gesture that reminds me of feeding the priests. Yes, it is time to go. She wants me to, and the men are edging around each other in the cul-de-sac. I have only a moment to linger—to fish the emerald out of my pocket, throw it through the bars, then dash after the light before it's gone.

"You need not come again," Pierre says, and I know it won't be allowed.

DAY OF SAINT APOLLONIUS

HERCULE

So it's the cell for me, the voice and the tricks. "Two moons in May, rain every day. Two moons in June quicken the womb. Two in July, someone will die. Two moons in August..."

"And if the sun's ray singles you out at a funeral," I answer, "you are next to die. Yet the sun strikes you as soon as you step up to moan about it, and you're still with us. Yes, everything's evil under the sun, and more evil in the shadows—like you and me, old walnut. Come, now. Teach me a trick."

In answer, a missile flies from the slit and lands, plop, at my feet. White cheese fuzzed with mold. I brush it off and bite, then juggle as I chew.

Quickly the taste becomes bitter—for we are not alone. And it's not Bonne who comes but one of those black beetles, stepping around bone heaps, swiveling at the skeletons who dance, dance, and dig upon the walls. The walls that once housed his brother beetles and later boxed their dying flock.

He doesn't see me. I dive for a bone heap.

And soon he's up to the very slit itself. He waves at a wisp of mist and parts the thorns like one seeking maidenhead.

"Marie?" he calls. "Are you in there?"

I stifle an impulse to laugh. Who else would he find? The bones around me rattle. But I must quieten if I want to learn his purpose, so I hug a skull and make myself still. A mouse. A rat. A spy.

Silence from the cell.

The beetle gropes his pocket, pulls out a stylus and a tablet smooth with wax. A sharp white stick pressing sticky gray syrup, taking notes—now he's a pupil, too, and kneels at his prophet's wall. His knee squashes my cheese. He should be a stylite.

"Marie, my child, the church has a question for you."

What could he expect the witch to say, when she's been locked away two decades and has seen no one? Or only one. And that, of course, is why the beetle's buzzed here.

"The wet nurse," he says, "Bonne Tardieu. What do you know of her soul? You must tell me everything—for the good of the town, and in the name of God, whom you swore to serve when you were walled in here."

There is a long, long quiet. Does the witch own Bonne's secrets, and will she give them up? Or will she offer the weather to a man of God? Flies hum into her slit and out again. A frog hops by and eats one.

When at last the words come, they are both of weather and of God. "What profit shall you ever find," she says, "when you have labored for the wind?"

I stare at my face in the glass. This is the face of a false saint, and Radegonde will have none of me, even in prison. All I can do is watch over her house and business.

With this, at least, I have an army to help me. Now that I'm out in the world again, Radegonde's household is reassembling. One by one the manservants and grooms and maids and gardeners turn up at the door, or else (admitted by a friend on the staff) slip quietly into their old positions overnight. The one difference is that now they come to me for orders, as if I've formally taken over the office of chatelaine—which becomes, by usage, essentially the case. There seem to be far too many of them, and I am at a loss; I assign various tasks as they occur to me, cleaning and folding and scrubbing.

Agnès is among the last to return. She does not say where she went or ask to be taken back, simply greets me one morning in the hall. We are not friends, but I feel I must let her stay. She watches me with the shrewd eyes of a herring dealer's daughter, and I suspect she may have been enlisted by Pierre.

Agnès says nothing when I tell the maids to collect any ivory objects that have yellowed and to spread them in the sun to bleach. She hides her grin in her sleeve when, that night, the maids bring the boxes and combs and chess sets inside, all cracked and the color of dark morning urine. After that she takes a sort of promotion, supervising the other maids, instructing them how to mend and turn the sheets sides to middle.

Even as she watches me, I watch Agnès. She knows things about running a big house. And from years of observation, she also knows something about how to deal with the agents who come in, and the orders that must be placed or filled from the warehouses. She's a good bargainer—I know because I've seen men leave the house cursing. So I study her.

Agnès puzzles me. She seems different now—more substantial, somehow—and I wonder again where she's been. She no longer owns that blue mantle—did she sell it to buy herself lodging and live for a while in leisure? I wonder, also, why she—who watched the statue take shape under Godfridus's chisel—doesn't say something about it to the church. She must have a plan. I wonder what she thinks when she sees that Villeneuve's best trade these days is in miracles—samples of marble dust from the new church, tiny vials of milk pretending to be mine. (Bottles of the real stuff sit in the church treasury, awaiting their moment.)

She has mounted Radegonde's unfinished Garden of Earthly Delights and framed it on the solar walls, a constant reminder of the house's true mistress. She stands in front of the Garden broderie, stroking the satiny stitches. "I hope the mistress is well," she says, again and again. And again I wonder what she knows.

"We should have the mirrors polished," I say.

SAINT SARA'S DAY

ITH SHORTER DAYS, OUR AIR BECOMES HEAVY and thick, foul everywhere—to breathe at all is danger. In the streets, fires burn to keep the peste away; even the men who are rebuilding ruined houses have braziers close at hand. Their sweat falls in the streets like rain, and makes people look to the windless sky.

Every day, with linen square and pierced pomander, I walk to the Hôtel-Dieu by the south wall. Fat, gray, rubbled, the Mansion of God: home to cripples, mendicants, and children unwanted. Monday to Sunday I go, and the stench of the place—unwashed bodies, madness, and death—never leaves me. Every mouth there howls for me; the weak ones lie three to a bed, waiting. It is too gray inside to recognize faces, and I wonder how many might be brother and sister, parent and child to each other, and not know it. I wonder how many will end up where Radegonde is now. I suckle the little ones blindly.

"No nurse can save every child," I tell the nuns who work there and the priests who oversee them.

"You are no ordinary nurse," says Thomas. "You are our Bonne." He keeps me supplied with oranges from Spain.

I stop wearing the tooth. I am afraid it could look witchly—the Putemonnoie servants might talk.

The people continue to delight in my work and the glory it might bring our town. Believers escort me to the Hôtel-Dieu and wait outside. When I come out they give me flowers and ask for suck—until Pierre preaches a sermon about the virtue of conserving miracles, and then I am reserved for only the scabbiest, hungriest mouths.

I am exhausted, drained, sick at heart. I've lost my pleasure in feeding; who could rejoice at the orphanage? For days I haven't seen Radegonde. Or Hercule, or Godfridus—my three friends, together at the feast and all behaving badly, disappeared at once as well. How strange that I know where only one, the mistress, has ended; the cobbler hasn't seen his tenant, and the bakerwoman asks what's become of my young charge. She is doing a brisk business, though I'm told her bread has made people sick. The smell of sewage has never entirely left the bakery, but people still buy its wares because of who used to live above.

Today the bakerwoman leans toward me. "Our bodies are ovens," she confides.

In the crowds that surround and beseech me, I have only myself for companion. And the constant reflection of myself. Day after day I am taken to the statue whose heel I pinked with blood, and I'm held up for admiration. People say the Virgin glows with an unworldly light. To me she is the darkest spot in the church.

One good evening my two special nurselings happen by for a visit. They are curious about the great house—how different, I wonder, would Saint John's Eve have been if I'd invited them, too? They bring the countryside with them—the exorcist, a jar of honey he collected himself (and he has the bee welts to prove it); the fillette, a bouquet of late-blooming iris. A priest and a prostitute together in Radegonde's solar, helping me organize the baby's layette: He makes a cap while she sees to the blankets.

Marguerite has also brought news. She tells an interesting tale of a wild man living in the forest: "A tall man all naked, mistress, and red as a copper kettle." She delivers this news calmly, even dreamily, cutting the fluff from a blanket. "A fellow I know found him sleeping in a hollow log, and he was up and off like a rabbit. They say he hunts at night, and throws stones at travelers, and ravishes girls who stay out past curfew."

Etienne pricks his finger on a needle. "Many a man's been falsely accused," he says, "simply for losing his luck. Maybe this poor soul lost work in the siege and became penniless. Maybe he was robbed and beaten on the road. Perhaps he's been too long in the sun . . . He may have lost his senses, even, but we shouldn't condemn a man for losing his clothes."

Myself, I gaze down at my shoes—new ones, soft leather against a floor left bare for coolness. I think of my own adventures beyond the city walls: the day of the haystack, with Laurent, and the day of the clay, with Godfridus. I feel lonely.

"You could come here," I say impulsively, forgetting the wild red man. "Both of you. To live and work, I mean—for room and board and wages."

The two of them blink.

Marguerite's nose wrinkles. "You mean to be some kind of servant? A maid?" She cuts deep into the blanket. "I don't know how to sew or to wait on fine ladies."

"That doesn't matter. I could teach you," though I wonder how I myself might learn. I may be wearing Radegonde's clothes now, but I don't have her graces.

"Father Etienne?" I ask.

He gives me a sad smile, holding my eyes a long time. "You are generous, as ever, and you've earned my gratitude for life. But of all people, you can't take a dishonored priest into your home. No, I'd better stay as I am." Tearing his eyes from me, he puts a few more clumsy stitches into the cap and speaks more kindly to the fillette. "But you, daughter, should accept this offer. What a wonderful chance for you."

Yet her mind, too, is made up. "In all gratitude," she says to me, "I thank you. Though I don't think I will accept. Now that the city gates are open, business is back—I make a much better living now than I ever could as a maid."

"You are how old, daughter?" says Etienne to Marguerite. "You should think of your future. It's a hard life, and youth fades fast. A woman who lives off her body is left without a sou before she's thirty—not to mention the cost to your eternal soul."

She laughs indulgently. "My soul? If you only knew how many of your kind have come to me—and isn't it much more wicked when a priest sins than when a harlot does it? Even the priests of the new church—"

"Stop." The tiny cap crumples in his fist. "The church may house corrupt men, but it tells us the truth about God."

"You sound like a man who's on fire. Do you know how to quench it?" Marguerite dreams, slicing away at the blanket, ". . . Someday I might get a house of my own, and girls."

"Then you might become rich, but you'll still be damned." Etienne pleads with her like a lover, and I am amazed—he could have been her father. "Meanwhile you could be pregnant, beaten, abandoned . . . We both know what men are."

"When I have my house," she says, "you can live there and clean my floors. Since you, too, want to continue in the life you've got."

I cover my ears with my hands. "Stop! Stop bickering! —I'm sorry. It's nearly curfew. You'd both better go to these homes you're so determined to keep."

As I LOCK THE DOOR behind those two, I wonder if I'll ever squeeze my milk into their dying mouths, or if I'll nurse one of Marguerite's babies at the Hôtel-Dieu. Tender lips scaly from hunger . . . I wonder, also, how long I'll have to keep going to God's Mansion. How long my reputation for wonders will last.

I am taking more stock in that these days, for I have realized that if people believe in the miracle of the breasts, they'll believe in the miracle of the elevation, and Blanche will live on. Perhaps this is the great thing she was asking me to do that night at Saint-Porchaire.

When I am alone, I stand before one of Radegonde's mirrors (still bright under its dust) and look at myself. I touch my face; I study my body. I undress. I watch my bosoms swell and leak, watch the play of candlelight on my hair above and below. I stay there for hours while the church bells ring and fade, ring and fade.

I ask myself what I have become. I ask if I Believe.

FEAST OF SAINT BONAVENTURA

[JULY 14]

HERCULE

"The Lord maketh his sun to rise; it riseth on good and bad. On just and unjust he doth the rain shed. I see men as trees, walking."

These words unroll below my tower, and by them I know the black beetle approaches. The old witch—Bonne's ancestor—mouths nothing but Scripture these days—it's her own special language, which I can decode, and it's told many a tale already. Of her family and Bonne's, of naughty Blanche and the priests who courted her. Of bodies that swelled . . .

I go down, to dig myself into that pile of bones and listen. "Ram thou thy fruitful tidings in my ear," I say—"it's been barren too long. And don't be a log, lying." But I don't say this last out loud.

Because here he is, Pierre, the rock on which the church was built, his black bulk framed in the human rubble round my eyes. He blinks at the stench of the cell, the urine and fruit festering in the summer heat. But he kneels, takes out his tablet, and rubs the rod on his skirt.

"Marie, I have brought you something," says our holy father, as if to a child. "Something to eat."

The witch hasn't eaten in weeks—she doesn't want to. But above a cross of femurs, I see the beetle pull out a round bit of white. He places it at the lip of the slit and pushes it inside.

"How long has it been since you've taken Communion?" he asks the tense silence. "Here I am giving you the Lord's body. And to accept it, you know you must first confess . . ."

Seventh day, confess and be shriven. Wrapped in a dark cloak of Radegonde's, slinking from shadow to shadow, I go far from her house, far from anyone who knows me, to the tiniest church on the outskirts of Villeneuve. I can't bring myself to tell my sins to Thomas; I think a young priest might hear them best. Kind Father Antoine welcomes me, as he would any wimpled and veiled parishioner.

I take a deep breath. "I've been angry, Father, and jealous once, and I may have taken the Lord's name in vain. And this is only a beginning . . ."

There's a silence at my side—welcoming, I think, receptive. What a relief. Someone besides the book to confide in.

"I may be falling prey to vanity, too. Sometimes I look at myself . . . Father?"

The young priest speaks; his voice is strained. "I did not hear you clearly, good sister. Could you repeat?"

Sister. I hear it with a sinking heart—not *daughter*. "You know who I am." So now I have to think about what I'm doing here. Don't I want to be a good sister? Don't I want to be *bonne*? "My life has changed since the siege."

"Deo gratias. So many blessings."

"I've been nursing at the hospital. And so far no babies have died." In the folds of my skirts, I cross my fingers.

"A blessing."

"But I'm afraid . . ."

"God will comfort you."

"I don't think I can do much good there. You see, I'm really not—"

"Modesty is a virtue. But to give up hope is a sin."

"I won't give up. In fact, I can't give up. I struggle with my feelings . . ."

"Bless you, sister."

And then I do, in a sense, surrender. "Thank you, Father." I'm shriven.

HERCULE

Holy menses! as Mary said when she heard she was pregnant. I am lost . . .

I scurry after the black-brown smudge of the beetle, out of the shadows and into the town. It's getting dark all over, and moths with the flies dive at his shoulders.

This time the witch said nothing. Not of Bonne, not of Blanche, not even of the weather. Her mouth was full with the flesh of Christ—maybe she's holding out for his blood, too—and when she gets it, who knows what she'll say?

In a shady arcade, Pierre steps in a horse heap. He streaks a butcher's stoop with his sandal and the housewife shouts. He blesses her dungily, and here I catch up. If someone is going to speak, it had best be me—best for me—and the shadows will hide how I've grown. I remember to speak like an orphan. "Father!" I pant. "Listen to me! I'll give you what you want."

It takes him a moment to figure where the voice is coming from—there are so many souls now about. But only one stands still for him. He peers under my hood and thinks he knows me. "Young Legrand, is it? Who used to live with our sister Bonne. You wish to help the church, my little man?" He sounds full of doubt.

"Yes, I lived there. I know everything about her." I hear the echo: Bonne . . . Bonne . . . Bonne . . . "I can help better than anyone!"

He tousles my head in its hood, and I almost kick him. "No wonder you're infirm," he says. "Knowledge endangers the young." He looks up at a passing side of beef, thinks, and then turns back to me. "Very well, little man," he says. "I have to give a service now, but we can talk tomorrow. Where will we find each other? Will you come to the priests' house?"

Too many people there. But where else do I have? "Saint-Porchaire," I say, shrinking deeper into the shadows. "Where you were today. Come at sunset."

Bemused, amused, and not expecting much, he agrees and beetles off. When he's gone I jump up and down in the bloody dirt, stamping the memory of his lumpy face away. Then I fling myself into that very dust, to hunt for bits of flesh that haven't rotted yet.

Forbidden confession, thwarted in apology—what can I do to prove loyalty to my mistress and remorse for our sin? I would fast on bread and water, as the penance books dictate, if I weren't afraid I'd dry up my milk just when I seem to need it most. More practically, I would hire an advocate for Radegonde's defense. But no lawyer in town will take la Putemonnoie on, no matter what I offer—gold, jewels, a miracle—for she's considered irredeemable. I ask among my believers for a name, any man in any town who might look kindly on her cause. Only Marguerite can give me one, and even she is not sure. She met a lawyer once, but was he called Louis or Clovis? Martin or Martial? It was so long ago, and sometimes their names are just borrowed . . .

I give Etienne a horse and send him to Poitiers to look for anyone who might help. "I will do everything," he vows, gazing down from the saddle. "Everything in my power."

"That's all I can ask," I say sadly, and off he rides.

 AINT SWITHIN'S COMES WITH A THREAT OF thunder. Air clogs the lungs, insects cake the nostrils, and church bells try to ring away a storm. I imagine what Marie would say: *As weather is on Swithin's day, so six weeks thence, the farmers say.*

Underground, the air is always the same.

At the council's request, Maître Civis has brought me again to the prison. The town fathers say Radegonde is behaving strangely— fasting, refusing to answer the fathers' remarks—and they are worried. Until they figure out about the money, they need her alive.

I follow the man's ovine-smelling bulk, a linen square on my nose to filter out what smells worse. In the past weeks, more of the cells have found occupants. The very tiles and dirt of the prison seem to live, and there is a stir in the tunnel along the Grand' Rue. Radegonde's doings are big news here, and word of them has radiated from her cul-de-sac.

"Mistress Putemonnoie!" Civis calls as we approach. I think he may be a good man. Even when he stops, he shifts his weight from foot to foot, worrying his hat in his hands. "Your nurse is here."

"The nurse is here," echoes a voice in the next cell, and the prisoners up and down make it a chant: *Nurse—nurse—nurse* . . . I can't tell if they're mocking or not.

Radegonde sits on her cell floor, her back to us. Her dress is torn, and her hair is gone. Cut. Shorn off in ragged lengths, the rest sprouting unevenly from her skull. Her beautiful hair . . . Her head is thrown back; her neck, creased in the middle by her spine, looks pale and very skinny. I hear her voice murmuring, but I can't tell the words.

I croak, "Radegonde . . ."

This time she is complaisant with me—even docile. Slowly she unfolds and comes to the grate, an ethereal smile lighting her face. Her hands are clasped in front of her (where I kissed and feasted); she stares straight at me but cannot be said to see me.

She's close enough to kiss. Instead I feel her breath across my lips—a wisp of warm air, which I inhale deeply through my mouth.

She speaks in a voice more musical than ever. "I have seen," she says softly.

"Seen?" I try to speak without breathing out. Seen what? This is the Radegonde of the bear ring, I think—this is Lady Kindness. She's forgiven me.

"I have seen *him*," she says, flooding my lips again. "He's coming back for me . . . Perhaps tonight!" Then, like a page who's just delivered an urgent message and can now die free, she staggers backward and falls with a kind of eerie grace to her knees, then to her nates. Her lips move, but no sound comes out.

"You see?" Civis whispers to me. "Most strange behavior. Though this is the first time she's spoken . . ."

I can't answer him right away. I'm staring into a whitish bald spot in the middle of my mistress's head. I don't know where to start.

"Why did you cut her hair?"

"We didn't," says Civis. He grabs his hat and twists it. "She cut it herself. First she gnawed it with her teeth, then she broke it strand by strand with her fingernails, then she pulled what was left out by the roots."

"Did it herself, she did," says the voice in the next cell. I can't see her, but she will be heard. "They say she's bald as a nun."

Civis weaves his fingers together uncomfortably, shouldering away from the common wall. "See if you can get her to eat," he urges me.

I fish a honey cake out of my pocket and wave it before the bars. "Mistress . . . I have something nice here for you." My voice wheedles already, as if she's a child I'm trying to wean onto oatmeal.

Her hands, still clasped, travel from her lap to her breast. "I have everything I need." She goes back to her silent speech—a kind of prayer, I'm certain now.

Nonetheless I feel encouraged to press on. After all, she's still speaking to me; that means she's still interested in being catered to, in the gifts I might bring.

"Honey cake," I almost sing. "I'm sure you don't have honey cake here."

"We do our best," says Civis.

The next-door woman cackles, "Our best!"

Radegonde's lips keep moving. But I, who know her body so well, think I detect a listening tenseness in her. So I go on, sterner now, "You must eat! They tell me—the fathers do—that you've been starving yourself. You know no good will come of that. Come, eat this honey cake. I brought it for you."

She waits a few heartbeats, then she says, "He's coming back for me."

Involuntarily, my hand convulses. My thumb goes through the cake, crumbing it. "Who's coming?"

Now her features fall into an expression of rapture, such as I've seen her wear only once before. But she doesn't speak now—just as she didn't speak at that earlier time.

"Who's coming? Why won't you eat? Radegonde, you have to talk to me!"

While the wretched woman nearby laughs, Maître Civis plucks at my sleeve. "We may as well go . . ."

I, of course, ignore him. I'm imagining an old lover coming to Radegonde, swearing to help her escape, kissing her hands with feverish passion—or, more probably, a guard who's plaguing her with sexual demands, threatening to return again and again. Even her belly and the dirt don't make her undesirable . . . but I must think only of how to help her.

"Remember the baby!" I whisper. "Eat!"

Radegonde gets to her feet. She moves, swaying, to the bars again. "He says he'll give me his heart, and he'll carry mine in his breast." She leans closer, confidingly: "Maybe I'll bear his wounds."

My basket drops. It's clear now what Radegonde means—what she's claiming for herself, subtly, very subtly. She won't come out and say the name. Or is she so lost in her ecstasy, so convinced, that she doesn't feel a need to say it? I, who know her better than anyone else, peer into her eyes, trying to see whether she truly believes herself or is having us on. If she thinks this is the way to save herself and her child, or if she's gone completely mad. But it's impossible—I see either too much in those eyes or too little.

I choose my words with care. "Madame Putemonnoie . . . you've been arrested for witchcraft."

She smiles, radiantly indulgent. "Yes, He sent me this trial as a sign of His love. And I thank Him most humbly for it. Praise Him! Gratias!" I notice a fine line of sweat on her upper lip.

Civis, too, understands by now. He appears truly agitated. "We have to go"—taking my arm in his fist. "I can't let you stay—a meeting must be called, the council has to—"

"Praise Jesus!" Radegonde says, in a pleasant conversational tone, "and pray that I receive the Heart soon."

Before Civis can drag me away, I thrust the honey cake into Radegonde's cell. "Take care of the baby," I urge, wondering if my words mean anything to her. "He'd want you to." Just in case she isn't playacting, in case she believes.

In the neighboring cell, the woman laughs under her breath, then says, "Jesus loves the children. Bless Jesus." She's taking no chances, either.

Radegonde gives a hushed sigh. When she parts her lips, I think I see the emerald. And I think I hear her say, "I love . . . you."

My heart stops. But she isn't looking at me, not even at the honey cake, and I don't know if I've only imagined the words. Because her neighbor is saying, over and over, "Love . . . love . . . love . . ."

"Mistress. Mother." Civis gives my arm a hard pull. "I will investigate this case, I swear. But you must come away—"

"Radegonde, we're going," I call as I give in. "But I'll be back. Be

"Remember the baby!" I whisper. "Eat!"

Radegonde gets to her feet. She moves, swaying, to the bars again. "He says he'll give me his heart, and he'll carry mine in his breast." She leans closer, confidingly: "Maybe I'll bear his wounds."

My basket drops. It's clear now what Radegonde means—what she's claiming for herself, subtly, very subtly. She won't come out and say the name. Or is she so lost in her ecstasy, so convinced, that she doesn't feel a need to say it? I, who know her better than anyone else, peer into her eyes, trying to see whether she truly believes herself or is having us on. If she thinks this is the way to save herself and her child, or if she's gone completely mad. But it's impossible—I see either too much in those eyes or too little.

I choose my words with care. "Madame Putemonnoie . . . you've been arrested for witchcraft."

She smiles, radiantly indulgent. "Yes, He sent me this trial as a sign of His love. And I thank Him most humbly for it. Praise Him! Gratias!" I notice a fine line of sweat on her upper lip.

careful," I add for no explicable reason. "Bless you." If she's in her right mind, she knows what I'm trying to say.

Radegonde beams at the ceiling. "I'm not alone."

H*ERCULE*

He reeks like bad soap—too much lard and insufficient ash. I smell him above the whirl of my balls, above the clack of my needles, above the roar of my thoughts. The beetle is coming, and I have prepared a web.

I've laid out the bones where the priests used to live and swept off the mist so they're seen. A mortal reminder is always in time. As I assembled each of my pestilential dead—using one's ribs, another's skull, the legs and feet of a third—I made them ask, What will you leave behind?

And here he is, studying the bones as the sun sets. May his answer to their question suit my needs . . . Magic has hurt me, but not miracles. Yet.

"Father Pierre," I say from my hood, "you and I will both be glad you've come. Please sit."

I've centered a stone in this great bone dance, and he lowers himself, each skin bump dripping sweat. "Who arranged these bones? Was it you? Should you not be learning some trade instead?" He has no notion of my true age, my true work.

"Father"—I crouch at his feet, where only the top of my head can be seen—"I have a question for you. Why is LaMère's soul your study? Do you have some complaint?"

Pierre says, "Not yet." And by this I know I was right—he's just casting about for a weapon, a miracle prophylaxis. He will shake what he finds in her face, make her quail.

I am aware we're alone, he and I, with the bones all around us. They ask their question of me. They're bones of the folk that the church killed—and I recall I've killed, too, a soul much finer than this priest's. But I am no murderer! I'll just use my knowing for strength. So I make my voice cracked and feeble, like a cheap cooking pot, the voice of the last child who'd trick. "What do you have to know?" I ask.

The questions come fast. Have I seen demons dance over Bonne's head? Have I heard her make charms against pregnant women, to secure herself employment? Has she fashioned implements in the shape of male members? Have I seen her kiss unchastely?

I remind myself of death and I answer. These answers do not please. So I offer more: "But I have seen demons dancing. I have heard charms being spoken. I've seen evil statues carved and I've seen kisses—"

Pierre is not interested in who might have done these things, if they were not done by la Bonne. He stops me from naming other names. "By God!" He snaps his stylus in two. "Have you ever even heard her wish for rain?"

And then the voice of the weather speaks. That wailing witch cries, "Where it listeth, the wind blows, and thou hearest the sound thereof. But ye know not where it goes, no more than fatherly love."

"Be quiet, old woman!" I shout, forgetting myself. What if she interferes with my plans now?

The priest makes me shush. "She is speaking!" He runs flap-skirted to her hole. "What can you tell me, Marie? Have you seen and heard Bonne do these things?"

It is clear, now, that my craving for mastery has produced twin desire in her. As I follow, slowly, she whines, "A wise child makes a father glad, and he is a wise man who fathers good from bad."

More Scripture, modified. My ears are pricked.

"Why do you talk so much of fathers?" asks the father with anger. "Tell me something about that woman. Tell me something I can use, or I'll have your cell pulled apart brick by brick."

She says, "He is Antichrist who denieth he is father and son."

She doesn't bother with a rhyme, but I can finish for myself— And you should know that you're the one.

The beetle's legs click. "You are wrong," he says. "You are lying. And no one will believe you."

But in this he is wrong. His town will believe anything, and he knows it.

We wait for the witch to reply. There is a tiny scraping sound, and the host appears once more on the lip of her slit. The beetle stares at it, his white wafer now gray and ready to crumble. By this he knows he's failed. His skin bumps bulge; his face goes yellow to match his suddenly amber eyes—he's not a beetle, he's a toad.

The host goes in his toad pocket, the tablet as well. Then he looks at me sharply and croaks, "Never speak of this."

By folly perishes a fool—or else thrives. I have an idea . . .

DAY OF SAINTS
JUSTA AND RUfINA,
WORKERS IN CLAY

[JULY 19]

HE COUNCIL MEETS, DISCUSSES, DEBATES. They can't decide what to do, except to swear the guards and me and one another to secrecy. There's no telling what the townspeople might do if word gets out that la Putemonnoie has been seeing Christ.

But word inevitably gets out. Word jumps from tavern keeper to nightman to baker, makes its way through priest and midwife and married lady. Radegonde Putemonnoie, locked away in a cell beneath the streets, is having visions—heavenly visions of Christ, who gives her His heart; who promises her the favor of stigmata; who kisses her brow and speaks to her of love. One night, it is said, He parted the edges of His side wound like a curtain, and she walked in and discovered Eden.

Now Radegonde, too, has her believers. Vigils are held in her honor; sometimes the street outside the jail is filled three deep. But the vigil holders have a way of disappearing; the prison cells have a way of filling up. Belief is a dangerous thing in a climate where a fortune is still to be accounted for. Lucky the woman whose miracles suit the church—or better yet, who is not holy at all.

Agnès is often queasy, and she eats too much.

Someone must be held responsible for Radegonde's reputation. So, discreetly, further arrests are made. Quietly the guards become the guarded ones, and new prison workers are imported from the countryside. A minor priest, whose duty once was to visit the tunnels and take confessions, is now consigned to a cell. There's only one person outside the high clergy who can be trusted with complete knowledge, who can be trusted to speak to and of la Pute, and that one is . . .

I know I have to do something. I visit some of my former, well-placed clients, display again my breasts; I assemble a list of names and addresses. They ask for favors, and I grant them. I must do something.

Then, one sultry day midmonth, dust rises on the Poitiers road. A traveler. He rides a bay horse from our stables, and a black hat sprouts like a mushroom from his graying hair; he comes straight to the Pute-monnoie house, shaking the dust of the road onto the courtyard cobblestones.

He is the advocate I've ordered. Reputed to be the best that Poitiers has to offer, sent posthaste by Etienne, who will return on foot. Day after day, I've watched for this man, but I'm not watching when he comes. Agnès and I have been treating the furniture with a special oil whose recipe I discovered in Henri's book. We're doing the work ourselves, rubbing down the wood until the veins bulge in our arms and sweat mats down our hair. Agnès looks green around the mouth and puffy in the face, but she insists on continuing the work.

When I hear the advocate has come, I drop my rag and go running. Here is our savior, I hope and I pray, as water rolls down my face. Radegonde's steward has led him to Henri's public office, on the first floor. There he sits with his hat in one hand, keeping his upper lip pinched in the other, looking thirsty.

"Bring us wine," I order the servant. By now I'm forgetting to say "please" almost as often as I remember.

The advocate bows and sweeps his hat before me. "Didier de la Clyte. Avocat de Poitiers." I notice he has a slight harelip, a crease that runs from his left nostril to the center of his lip, where it tugs the skin up in a permanent teeth-baring smile. Or sneer. For all that, he is a well-looking man, one with a presence likely to convince and persuade.

"You'll have to tell me everything," he says.

At his request, I fetch writing materials; when I come back, there is a ledger open before him, and his hand lies on a blank page, curled expectantly. He wastes no time.

"How pregnant is the woman?" Didier taps the quill on his scar.

"She'll deliver within the month."

"Ah." He writes, what looks like a meaningless scribble to me. "I ask because I must know this: Did her strange behavior—her witchlike proceedings—commence with the time of conception? Can you date their beginning precisely? Can you surmise a cause?"

I think of the face creams, the lotions, the powders. Of myself. "I don't know. I only met her in February. But you should know—she's been having visions . . ."

As he writes, the man's face is a mystery. He seems unimpressed by miracles, Radegonde's or my own. With the dust of the road still upon him, he's of a larger world than ours.

At the end of my story, I propose some stewed walnuts and go myself to fetch them. While the kitchen maid scoops up a bowlful, I belatedly wrap myself in wimple and barbette and veil and remind myself that I must breathe, that I must stay calm, must tell him the best truth I can. He is *our* advocate, after all. He will do his best for us.

"Holy Mother," I pray, "please let this work. Free Radegonde, and I promise I will be good."

Then I shiver, because—without realizing it—when I imagined the Virgin's face, I saw my own.

GODFRIDUS

I believe

> *in God the Father Almighty, Creator of*
>> *Heaven and earth;*

and in Jesus Christ, His only Son, our Lord; Who was conceived by the Holy Spirit; born of the Virgin Mary; suffered under Pontius Pilate; was crucified, died, and was buried

> *While the whore wrapped her legs round His cross and rubbed, and His mother threw her hands toward heaven, in grief though not despair; and she touched heaven, and He rose*

and He descended into Hell . . .
and burned
and cast out what offended Him.
   what He loved
         He destroyed
I understand

OW THAT I AM ABLE TO SLEEP, I FIND MORE and more that I've slid down from the pillows, to wake up curled on bare sheets. And that I, too, am bare, having kicked off the covers, my white behind pointing shameless at the window.

Sometimes I find my fingers curled into my body, nestling in the salty folds. I don't always take them out again. Sometimes I push them deeper in, or flirt them around the edges, or use them like a little mouth. Each time the nun's heart beats, she gets less angry, and I become less inclined to confess what I have done.

IN THE DAYTIME, Didier de la Clyte accompanies me on my visits to the rich and powerful. He seems to sneer when he sees how I persuade them to speak, yet I am sure these people will prove his best witnesses.

He gathers information elsewhere, too, from Putemonnoie servants, clients, and debtors. I continue to search Henri's office and papers.

And news continues to leak from the jail,

taking to the air, rooting in the earth, spreading like fire. Once again, everyone is speaking of Radegonde.

—She's a saint, say some.

—An impostor, say others; and,

—Women shouldn't be actors. Or saints.

—A woman shouldn't have to be a martyr either.

—God would never choose her.

Now the priests decide to make prison visits part of my schedule. I suspect they use me as a proving stone, a certified worker of miracles against whom Radegonde's visions can be measured. Agnès packs food for her, and faithful followers slip tributes into the basket (some for me, some for her) as I walk toward the jail. I think, once again, that Radegonde is the cleverest woman living. Or else the most mad.

I have to be as clever. With each step, I know that if I say or do the wrong thing, I might not be allowed to leave. For Pierre is always waiting, hands inside his dark sleeves, hoping I'll preserve my own holiness by debunking hers.

Who can know the truth? Even I can only guess, and my guess changes from day to day, with the direction of the wind. I don't know whether she tastes the food I slip through her grate. I don't know about her baby. Will it survive? Does she even care anymore?

All I really know is that on these visits, even then, she barely looks anywhere but the ceiling, barely halts the flow of whispered prayers. Each time, I hear the words *I love you;* but they are meaningless, merely prayer.

HERCULE

Above the town, a steeple snags the moon. The clouds are feeding famishedly, and everything is dark.

"What does this mean? Where's your God now?" I call out, and receive—and expect—no reply. Since the day she returned the host, the witch has stopped her wailing. Even the beetle has vanished. He does not visit, and it's been days since I knew what the skies were trying to say. The moon waxes, and I wait for the second sighting that foretells death.

"Marie!" I shout. "Marie!" And try to peer in her slit, but the sky will not shine for me.

FEAST OF SAINT
ANNE, MOTHER
OF THE VIRGIN
[JULY 26]

HESE DAYS OF HEAT AND RAIN ARE NATURE'S
finest. Plants and bushes once denuded are
now releafed and retwigged; they grow by
leaps and bounds. There may even be some
flowers out before the first frost. At home,
every rose in the garden burdens the air,
and there are cornflowers, carnations, mar-
guerites, poppies, peonies—a riot of color,
texture, and fragrance. Even inside, we're
dizzied with scent. Breathing it, we know that
here, at least, we are safe from the peste.

Before going to the orphanage each day, I
spend an hour in the gardens, feeding bread
crumbs to the peacocks and sitting on a bench
of turves, where I unsnarl the knots in Radegonde's embroidery threads. A neat little
pyramid of silken spools is growing in her
workbasket; when she is free, I think, she can
resume her Earthly Delights with ease. This
task is soothing to me. Maids come and go
with messages that have nothing to do with
God's work; the Putemonnoie fortune grows
abroad. Peacocks cry my name.

It is out here, in the clear morning air, that
I realize I haven't been to see Marie in some
time. Not since the day of my first prison visit.

Radegonde's threads spill on the grass. "Mother of God!" The servants come running.

"MARIE!"

The only sound is of insects, buzzing, chirping, flying with loud wings. And of the toads that eat them. On the walls the wood skeletons caper and laugh in silence—and below, the bone ones have left their piles to make a maze. How? Who could have come here?

I step carefully over these new shapes, respecting their rest. They have banished the blanket of ground mist, and for perhaps the first time I see the earth here—not white or black but green, growing vines that reach up to fondle a leg here, to part two ribs there. I have a basket with fresh strawberries, new bread, and our best cheese, plus a flask with springwater. But surrounded by skeletons, such things seem useless.

At Marie's slit, I part wild rose leaves and flowers. The slip that Blanche and I planted so long ago has flourished such that its tendrils now reach inside, and I have to pull them out to look. Of course, when I put my face up to the slit, I block out the only light, and I see nothing.

"Marie?"

Buzz, whir, gulp—I think I hear the vines grow, too. I try to step closer and trip on a skull that's rolled its way here. "Are you alive? Make a noise—anything—to let me know you're all right."

Somewhere, a bird twitters. A mockingbird, I think; it has caught an insect or a toad. Otherwise, the air is still.

The cheese I've brought is a particularly fragrant sort, temptingly pungent, well veined with deep blue mold. I take it from the basket, peel away its cloth, hold it up to the slit. A smell like the odor of swaddling leaks out.

No one grabs the cheese; no one speaks. Not so much as a mouse squeaks.

So I wrap the cheese again and drop it inside the cell. I don't like the thought of dirtying food, but I drop the bread in, too—I don't know what else to do. I can't drop the glass flask; it is too fragile. And the strawberries would bruise.

"Marie." I try to sing the words, coaxing, "I'll take your chamber-pot—it must be full by now . . ."

. . . My soft child hand in Blanche's, walking over and beneath the skeletons, with my mother's voice explaining: *When Marie no longer fills the basin, she will be cleansed of sin; then God will take her to paradise, and she won't need a basin again . . .*

I start to panic. What have I done by my neglect? I speak fast, too loudly. "Come, give me a prophecy. I'll hold my breath and pretend I've left, and you can tell my fortune as if you're reading it in the sky. It's Saint Anne's day."

I realize tears are streaming down my face. My teeth chatter, as if I've caught a chill, but the sun still looms like a hot eye above me. ". . . Anne, the mother of Mary. The namesake of that bell your husband made for this very church—I wonder if you minded that he didn't name one after you? Anyway, Marie, I know your air is always the same, but out here it's hot and moist. There was a beautiful sunrise. And I know what you'd say—'If red the sun begin his race, by night the rain will fall apace.'"

The cell remains silent, but I babble on: "'If Saint Anne's night is rainy yet, the yearly harvest will be wet.' 'If it rain near Magdalene's day'—that was Sunday, Marie—'she's washing her hair to dance away.' 'Burn fern, bring rain . . .'"

But of course there's no answer.

HERCULE

La Bonne sinks to the green, crying as if to wake the dead. The vines rise up to hold her.

"Marie!" There tumble basket and flask. The glass bounces, then falls to bits that ping-ping in the leaves. The vines run fingers over Bonne, damping her clothes and curling her hair, entering her. It is Anne's day, and the sky, like Bonne's eyes, rumbles with rain.

Anne . . . How you wept for the vavasour's daughter, wept for her death and her life. When I took a glove from you that day it was wet, and it has never dried.

Today Bonne waters the bones with her tears. Perhaps she loved this old woman as she, too, has been loved. Completely. Unquestioningly. Inexplicably.

Now the clouds lower, and a black figure joins the danse. It walks bravely, crunching bones, fluttering like the angel of death. It draws close to Bonne. Then kneels down, gropes among the vines and bones—pulls her up, head then shoulders, tugs her free of the clinging suckers. "Mistress!"

"Ah—" She barely struggles. Her shining face, the darkening sky. "Oh, Etienne."

Fervently he kisses her, a kiss most unfathered. "I've just returned—I knew you'd be here. Mistress, I am so grateful. I did what you said, and I've had such a blessing! And there is much more I would do—" He kisses her hands, face, breasts—if they were truly falcons, they'd pluck his eyes out.

She scarcely seems to feel him. "Then grant me a favor," she says. "An exorcism."

The rain breaks over their heads.

When darkness falls, I dig Radegonde's biggest, most draping cloak out of the winter chests and wrap myself head to ankle. I'm already wimpled, with starchy linen binding my chin; I've hidden as much of myself as I can.

In a near bedroom, the advocate snores.

Bundled like this, faceless, as anonymous as can be a tall woman in wool at the height of July, I slip through the streets, shielding a candle flame, avoiding the night guards and the nightmen who empty clogged gutters. My shoes splash in puddles, my skirts become muddy. But over my head the sky is clear, and a moon nearly full (for the second time this month) is shining.

In the shadow of the new church, my dark man waits for me. He goes down on one knee as if to be blessed, and the moonlight pours over him.

I whisper, "Etienne, get up."

He found me today at Saint-Porchaire, mourning Marie. He wanted to tell me he has been given a parish on the road to Poitiers; he wanted to credit me for it and thank me. He did not think he'd be asked to do *this*. For I am going to make some peace with Marie at last.

When he stands, he wipes my brow with his wrist. "You're overheated."

"After we get there, I'll take the cloak off."

"But for now . . ." Solicitously, he pulls the hood down farther over my face. "If we are seen, you must not be recognized."

He picks up a bag and we start. A breeze winds its way under my hood, reeking of manure.

"Etienne," I say suddenly, "do you believe in the Miracle of the Statue?"

The bag's contents clank. "What do you mean?"

"You believe in God's teachings," I explain, "and you believe in the church, if not all the people in it. Do you believe in—in me?"

His eyes are very white. *He* is very white. "I believe we must be grateful for what God has given us." He waits a few moments and adds, "I believe in hope."

We round a corner, and there's a guard. Etienne is brave and calls out, "A visit to the dying."

The man crosses himself. "Walk on, Fathers."

Sometimes it is a lucky thing to be with a priest. A priest who regrets seeing you as a woman while exalting you as a savior. A priest like many men.

"Hope," I whisper.

343

"We must not give it up. Hope will save us . . . and forgiveness."

I smell the vines growing, smell the stones decaying. It is the new smell of Saint-Porchaire, what has replaced the sound and smell that used to reign here.

I shed my cloak as I walk up to the cell and put my lips to the slit. "Marie?" One last time. If she's there and conscious, she'll answer. If not, the sanctity of a twenty-three-year seclusion is about to be violated.

We listen to insectuous silence.

"All right"—I feel a thrill of excitement to be *doing something*— "We are going in."

First the roses must be cleared. They lie in a green-and-pink heap while we pluck the thorns from our palms and wipe the blood away. Then I order Etienne, "Hand me the chisel." The wooden grip feels warm, as if my uncle's (my friend's) hand just left it. Yes, these are Godfridus's tools we're using—the exorcist went by the studio today, to root in the rubble for what we need.

"And the hammer." Another warm grip, a heavy lump of iron at the head, pulling my arm down. Etienne lifts the candle and I choose a likely vein of mortar, slide the chisel along, feel for a crack. It lodges. I strike.

"Holy wishbone!" The hammer falls to the ground. I shake my hand and clamp it between my knees, trying to get dominion over the pain. Even in her death, Marie is fighting me.

Etienne examines the hand, kindly overlooking my blasphemy. He picks up the hammer. "Let me."

So he takes over, pounding diligently away. *Thonk. Thonk.* He hits much harder than I did.

As I listen, sheltering the candle, the pain in my hand subsides. I think about my vanished uncle. Now at last I understand why he pursued his trade—for the glory of God, and for the glorious pain he felt each time the hammer hit home: like a nail in the hand as he struck. I wonder if all sculptors feel this. And how many of them enjoy it.

Under Etienne's hand, first one block drops inward, then two. The hole they leave will barely admit a head. But soon the third and fourth blocks fall.

He steps back, dusting off his hands. "There. It looks big enough now."

I reach the candle inside, onto one of the fallen stones, and curl myself up to climb. I feel a little of the old vertigo, though not far off the ground. I grip the wall. And by exhaling and holding my breath, I find I can fit.

"What do you see?" asks Etienne.

"Nothing yet." But I smell something sweet. Shielding the flame, I sweep the light around the tiny space.

I can't believe it. Look again.

There's the earthenware basin that I bought in the marketplace, empty. There's a heap of moldy bread and cheese by a wall. There's an old blanket, ragged, torn, and threadbare, that Marie used as both bed and cover . . . But there's no Marie. Not a bone, not a trace.

Instead, in the middle of the cell, in the center of a paving stone, a plant has rooted. A lily, blooming, snow white.

HERCULE

It's a tight fit, said the man to his virgin bride, and there's nothing to come of it but more labor for you.

How kind, nonetheless, that they cut me a passage.

When they go, my turn comes. Pushing my way in, shutting my lungs against the reek of the place, scraping my elbows and my new-knobby knees.

What a stench! Call the nightmen! I dump the overfilled basin and pluck up that weed in the floor.

She is well and truly gone, my teacher.

Cobwebs string the new breeze, night sweats film the walls. Where is their owner? Has she left to find the priest, to fulfill the omen of July's double moon? Or has she simply . . . died . . . and if not to live out her own prophecy, then why?

DAY OF THE SEVEN SLEEPERS

TIENNE AND I WALK FAST WHILE DAWN creeps into the heavens, trying to shake the discovery off ourselves. My dove, my first and last pensioner, has disappeared. I imagine her spirit leaving the cell on white wings. Perhaps she roosts even now atop Henri Putemonnoie's tower.

Etienne still holds the hammer and chisel, as if letting go will set him loose in a maze he can't fight free of. Perhaps, seeing what's become of Marie, he is questioning his belief in me.

Our next job will be to haul new mortar, seal up the hole again, stanch the tide of miracles. But that will have to wait for dark to fall once more.

At home I ring for a maid and send her with a message: Bonne LaMère is at prayer and will not visit God's Mansion till after nones. In the long, hot morning, I take a cool bath and climb to the tower, wet hair tangling around me. I try to write and my hair drenches the pages. When the church bells ring, it seems that each peal lasts longer than usual.

In all last night's events, my one consolation has been that pile of cheese and bread. It tells me that Marie had food, she just chose not to eat it; she must have been fasting for weeks before I stopped coming. That midden-heap makes me less a murderess—but I find it makes me no less bereft. Where *has* she gone, leaving no clue but the lily behind?

And how can I miss someone who hated me?

I can't work; I can't hold a pen. I take out my rosary and pray. "Blessed are you among women," I start. "And blessed is . . ." I find I want more than the usual words. "Blessed is Marie, who has escaped this world. Blessed is Hercule, who is I know not where. Blessed is the wild man in the forest. Blessed is . . ."

Around nones, a knock comes on the door.

"Bonne, can you hear me?" It's Agnès.

"I'm praying." In a whisper I continue, as if to weave a web of safety with my words, "Blessed is Agnès, who feels no remorse."

She rattles the latch, then kicks at the door when she finds it locked. "Come fast," she says. "Madame Putemonnoie is in childbed, and it's going hard."

From Henri Putemonnoie's livre de raison
To make a man impotent, some women feed him forty ants boiled in one cup of daffodil juice.

To fill him with lust, some mix their monthly blood with his meat. Some others, up from childbed, drown a fish in the afterbirth, then boil and roast the fish and feed it to their husband.

All these women must do five and two years' penance.

When Agnès and I arrive at the prison door, we find Pierre, Paul, and Civis. They are waiting for me, for a miracle. They make my knees weak.

"Deo gratias!" Maître Civis flings himself to the ground and kisses the hem of my garment. The prison widows snicker until Agnès shoots them a daggered look.

"What is happening?" she demands to know.

Pierre pounds on the door. "Radegonde Putemonnoie is in labor, daughter. We thought your mistress, Bonne LaMère, would want to know."

I speak hurriedly, above the maid's response. "I do want to know. But we hear it's going badly. Where is the midwife?"

"There is no midwife," Paul blurts out.

The door swings open and Pierre lets it hit him.

Civis gets to his feet, wringing his hat. "Wet nurses know how to deliver, don't they? You gave birth yourself . . ."

I am Bonne LaMère. And now they believe me an expert in childbed.

"Why haven't you found a midwife?" I ask. But I think I can understand—no sage-femme wants to be responsible for a bad birth, especially if the mother might be Villeneuve's latest saint or greatest witch. The dangers here outweigh the possible glories by far. "Never mind—take me to her."

We leave the priests behind as first Civis, then I, then Agnès scurry down the splintery tunnels. All the prisoners are whispering; they know who I am by now, and they know what's happened to Radegonde. One churchwoman going to succor another.

"Virgini gratias!" the wretched women call, and, "We are grateful for miracles!"

I stumble past, my hair full of dirt.

Radegonde has a real bed now. She is sitting up on it, naked, using her own clothes for a pillow; it pleases me that she won't have to give birth into straw. Her arms are folded over her belly (the baby riding very low, in position for delivery), her bosom heaving, lips folded to stifle her cries. Sticky tears snake down her cheeks. She is clearly in agony.

Agnès stares in horror.

It's up to me to act. "How long has she been like this?" I ask Civis.

He can't bring himself to look. "The guard found her in labor this morning. She seems to be in some pain, but she won't speak. I brought her this bed." He twists his cap again, wringing its neck. "Mother, please save her."

I look on his broad face, and I see he's fallen in love. He believes, and he can't bear to see this body broken under torture.

Agnès has thrown the apron over her head. "Do something!"

As I approach the bed, I wonder which Radegonde I will be speaking to. Will it be the one of needles and relics, or the one of visions and blessings? "Mistress," I say in a low voice, "I need you now . . . Hear me."

I take her hand, not knowing what else to do. I've been present at only two births, and both were my own. I know just that I should comfort this suffering soul. So I take her hand.

"Radegonde," I say softly, for her ears alone, "I will do for you what you need."

Then I straighten, tightening all my muscles, trying to remember what the midwife did to me in the early stages, when I was still awake.

"Mistress, I am going to investigate your case. Agnès will hold your legs apart."

The maid does as I say, her face averted.

"And you, maître, hold that torch close." He, too, obeys; he, too, turns his head.

Gently I push Radegonde's knees up. "Try not to move."

So I crouch before that sad paradise where a month ago I was a visitor. Her lips are swollen and purple, and I see a small tear on one side, leaking blood. This I take as a sign the baby will come soon.

Holding my breath for strength, I plunge my hand inside.

Civis groans.

Inside, Radegonde is slick, wet, and tight, hotter than anything I've felt before. I push her legs farther apart, worm my hand up to the very top. "I'm sorry if this hurts." Here I feel for her womb's expansion, the opening of that inner mouth that will spit out an infant. I feel ridges, concentric circles, a long smoothness.

349

"Has the water sac burst?" I ask, hand still inside, trying to seem authoritative.

"I don't know." Civis, the man, appears to feel every movement of my hand. His body twitches as I probe.

I push on the center of the circle. A sudden gush, scalding fluid pink with blood, drenches my arm and the bed.

"*You* broke it." Agnès can't help staring now, fascinated, revolted. She swallows as if she'd like to vomit.

I feel a little sick myself. "A woman once did the same for me."

In the deluge, my hand was washed away. I put it back inside, feel the top of the womb again. I still can't find much opening.

"She's too tense," I say, withdrawing the hand and looking around for a cloth.

Agnès produces a linen square from her own sleeve. "What can I do? Should I rub her temples?" Sometime in the last moments, she came to accept my command; her own knowledge belongs to the days of luxury and leisure.

I wipe my hand, rub it hard; then use the damp cloth to clean both arms up to the elbow. Too late, I remember that Radegonde said it is important to wash before treating a sick person.

"I need supplies," I say curtly, trying to recall what was brought to my own childbed. "Both of you, fetch water, basins, fresh cloths. Vinegar. And pillows—she should be sitting up. Hurry!"

When both are gone, I lean in close to Radegonde. Half one wall is metal bars, there's a neighbor on each side now, and wall torches are smoking all around, but this is as much privacy as we're going to get. "You must relax," I say softly. "My love, you have to let him come."

I gaze down at the lips, the body I have kissed. They are wrinkled, straining, popping with veins. The very picture of silent struggle. "Radegonde," I whisper, "you have been very brave. But you may speak now. Even saints feel pain."

I push open her eyelids. The everycolor irises, bright with agony, stare ahead unseeing. They do not swivel even when I pass my hand before them.

Either she is in complete control of her body or she has left it. And in either case, she's waiting for me to save her.

THE BAKERWOMAN

Come to me, my husband! See me, feel me! While I still have flesh . . .

Displeased with her husband, Saint Liberata prayed to become unmarriageable. In the morning she woke with a beard.

Do not be a saint who fasts with a banquet before him! Not when it may be your last . . . My body will burst.

Alone with Radegonde, I sing. Comforting songs my mother sang when I was sick, bawdy songs of the street, slow songs from convents. I make up my own words. "You must relax," I hum. "You must give in. You must let this baby come . . ."

Finally Agnès is back, carrying two basins in one hand, a bucket of water in the other, and a flask of vinegar in her pocket; she has wrapped linen towels around her head. The essentials.

"Civis is bringing pillows," she says. "I also told him to find a midwife, even if he has to arrest her."

"Good for you." I mix vinegar and water, soak a towel, and dab at Radegonde's brow.

Agnès folds and refolds the linens. "Will that do it? Will rubbing her head bring the baby?"

I keep my voice soft, for Radegonde's sake. "We have to get her body to open up. To relax. Can you sing?"

So Agnès sings, and when her voice gives out, I sing again. We repeat ourselves. Guards visit the other cells, rattling the grates and offering food; the prisoners fast to sing with us. And I keep bathing Radegonde's forehead and arms, and Agnès keeps fluttering around, rinsing and cooling cloths.

"Relax" . . . a tinkling as Agnès wrings a cloth; she sings *Amours mi font souffrir* . . . "Radegonde, think of something pleasant. Think of . . ."

My mistress's stomach ripples.

Late in what must be afternoon, Agnès goes out. I don't notice at first, but she stays gone a long while. I myself haven't been to the privy all day; that part of me has gone to sleep. Likewise—I notice now, and grope them to be sure—my breasts haven't swollen or leaked. My whole body is shut down, to strain only for this baby's delivery.

I climb into bed beside Radegonde. "We are alone," I sing into the curling ear. "You must give in . . ." I give her belly long, smooth strokes, trying to straighten the baby's path. "You must . . . You must . . ."

A knocking comes on the bars. Maître Civis and Father Paul stand looking in. Their arms are full of linens from the great house, Henri Putemonnoie's initials on pillows and sheets. I get up.

"Is she all right?" Civis is crushing his pillows.

Paul stares.

"I'm doing my best." My hands itch to touch my breasts again, to check them. Instead I take the pillows and put them at Radegonde's back. "Did you find a midwife?"

Paul says, "Let us pray." He needn't say more.

But Civis explains, ripping his hat apart, "The midwives have fled to the forest. That's what people say. They heard they were to be arrested for witches . . ."

The men leave. I get into bed again.

Around vespers, Agnès returns. "I couldn't find anyone," she says wetly. "Not even a surgeon. They've all disappeared, like someone's taken them. I even went to that Jewish doctor's house."

Never mind. Macchabé wasn't able to cure Godfridus anyway.

"This baby will be born," I say.

"But what can we *do*?"

I hold out the basin. "Bring me some fresh water mixed with wine."

I sit in bed, holding Radegonde's hand and recounting to her, in a whisper, all the good moments I remember.

Around nine o'clock, the first scream comes.

From Henri Putemonnoie's livre de raison
A LIST OF EFFECTIVE TORTURES

- ✦ thumbscrews
- ✦ a tongue clamp
- ✦ an iron helmet with screws to tighten as a vise
- ✦ the rack
- ✦ the wheel
- ✦ chained down, feet smeared with lard that a goat will lick till the feet are raw and bleeding, even to the bone
- ✦ similarly, a hungry rat trapped under a bowl on the subject's belly, eating his way free
- ✦ removal of the fingernails
- ✦ various whippings, brandings, etc.

It's like this for all of us—this is when death comes closest. As we lie giving life, Death sucks our breath down his lungs; he peers into our throats, our hearts, our entrails, and takes what he likes. This isn't a business— there is no bargaining.

Not even for Radegonde. Her body slips away from her in scream after scream, one moan following another. Her legs begin to thrash, her arms to clutch her belly. She kicks at death; she clutches at life. Agnès and the chorus of prisoners sing louder.

When I check between Radegonde's legs, I see a trickle of blood. Inside, still, she is closed tight—nothing but smoothness, as if her womb has no opening at all.

"God!" she screams to the ceiling. "Oh, God!" And a stream of sounds that make no words I know.

I know now that she is going to die. And that, for my sins, I have been condemned to watch it.

DEATH HOLDS MY MISTRESS in his arms and plays. *In the fire there is music, a howling of timbers, a popping of knots. Every body dances to the plainsong of pain—elbows lash and shinbones churn; it is a release of sorts, a dance with Death. Only stone stands still till it bursts.* But Death won't take Radegonde yet. First he wants her to scream herself hoarse, then mute; wants her to pound on her stomach with both fists; to cry until the tears turn to blood.

. . . Bloody tears. A sudden light blinds me.

"Agnès," I say, "there is something for you to do. You must go to—"

"Not now! It's too close!" And even she knows that "it" is no longer joyful.

"It will be closer still, if you don't do as I say. And you may be able to save her . . . You are her only hope, Agnès. You."

So out goes Agnès. I think it must be morning; the prisoners are being given their bread and water. If this is a new day, it belongs to Saint Nazarius, who encouraged martyrs. I watch Radegonde in Death's dance grip and try to join her, but they two belong to a world apart. The guards avoid this cell.

Agnès returns quickly this time, with the fillette de joie floating behind.

The next best thing to a midwife is a whore.

"I'm so grateful you sent for me, mother," says the girl who once wept blood. She hardly seems to notice the writhing on the bed. "I am so glad."

I grab her red-and-yellow arm and drag her over, as Radegonde screams again. "Marguerite," I say urgently, "I believe that you have seen a lot of—this. *Do you know what to do?*"

Thoughtfully, the fillette passes a grubby hand over Radegonde's brow, watching the contortions of her face as she readies another scream. "Oh yes," she says. "I know. We need a rag."

"Here." Agnès gives her a towel.

Marguerite folds it, rolls it, and twists it; then she opens Radegonde's lips and teeth with her fingers and slides the bundle in, like putting a bit into a horse's mouth.

When Radegonde screams again, the sound's just a faint trill—a salvo from a flautist. She looks furious. Marguerite regards her with satisfaction.

"*Do something,*" Agnès hisses. I am as dumb as if the gag were filling my mouth, too.

"First I must investigate." The fillette bends down between the dark thighs; Agnès and I hold the legs apart. The thin hand disappears up inside for a moment, then Marguerite stands up, wiping it on her skirt. Too late I remember she didn't wash it.

"Yes," she says again, "I know what is wrong. This baby is being born in reverse."

Agnès shrieks and I gulp. "What do you mean?" But I know; I have heard these words before. My marrow turns to jelly.

"The womb is ready to deliver—wide open—but the baby's bottom is at the opening, and she can't push it out." Dreamily, Marguerite turns to me. "I saw it over and over with sheep at the leprosarium. And goats."

I must have been feeling the baby instead of the mother when I checked.

"Sheep and goats?" says Agnès. "Those are the babies you've delivered?"

"Yes." Marguerite does not bother to explain or excuse herself, if indeed she knows that is what Agnès expects. She pulls Radegonde's legs out straight, making her comfortable. "I know who this is," she says irrelevantly. "This is the prison saint. The martyr."

Agnès flings herself on her mistress's body, sobbing.

But I force myself to hope. At least now we know what is happening. "Does Radegonde have to die?"

For a moment a frown flits across the fillette's vague face. "No. Not if we do this right. We have to turn the baby in the womb . . . I've seen it done."

With sheep and goats, I could add—but this is our best hope. I've heard that with some women it does work. "What do you need?"

"Help me take off my sleeves."

So we tear the yellow sleeves from the red dress; bare the girl's arms. Her skin shines in the torchlight like marble—to my eyes.

"Now hold her legs down again," says the fillette. "I think this is going to hurt her."

Radegonde's flesh splits open as Marguerite works inside, trying to move the baby. We have to stop to tie Radegonde's hands to the bed. Then it's back in, twisting, turning, fighting with that stubborn scion of the Putemonnoies . . . The red stream between Radegonde's legs flows thicker.

"It's no use," Marguerite says at last, withdrawing and wiping her own face on her shoulder.

"No use?" Agnès wails. A look from me stops her from bursting into tears again. Instead she retreats into a corner and vomits into one of the towels she brought.

Radegonde jerks against the bedclothes. Her eyes are open now, looking from one of us to the other, accusing, damning. She seems to have come back to herself. She has something to tell us.

"Take the cloth out," I say.

Agnès does it.

Radegonde looks straight at me and says, "You have to cut me open."

Agnès swoons. "Mistress!"

"Cut me open," Radegonde continues stubbornly, "but don't cut the baby. Without him there's no point in saving my life."

I close my eyes, seeing the straw of my own childbed gather before my gaze. The last thing I saw when they cut me, the first when I opened my eyes. "Isn't there anything else we can do?" I ask Marguerite.

"If you'd summoned me earlier," she says gently, "we could have made her sneeze the baby out, or we could have picked her up to shake it loose. But it is too late now—he is stuck."

"Can *you* cut a baby out?"

"I've never done it. I wouldn't dare."

The three of us gaze down at the bed, emotion rippling over our faces. Regret, sorrow, fear, and certainty.

355

Radegonde—taut and bound, stomach heaving—stares back. "If you won't help me," she says, "I'll tear him out with my bare hands."

Agnès swoons again. Even with her hands tied, we know our mistress could do it.

And I know what I must do. "All right," I say. I put my hands on that belly. "I need a—" But I can't say the word.

Marguerite pulls me down so she can whisper in my ear. "Wait here for me. I will get what we need."

And while Agnès and I wait, bathing Radegonde and murmuring to her, Marguerite (far away now) gives a guard a kiss, many kisses, and plucks the knife from his belt. She floats back to lay it in my hand.

"Avoid the veins," she tells me.

At first cut, blood sprays us like a fine red fountain.

I SLICE THROUGH THE LAYERS OF FAT and flesh beneath Radegonde's omphalos; they peel away in shades of pink. Agnès and Marguerite wipe the blood as I plunge deeper, deeper, into the very core of Radegonde. I hold a finger on the blade, to feel the mother's tissues springing back. I hope not to slice the baby.

"Can you tell if I'm close?"

Radegonde grits her teeth, still crucified to the bedposts. She is fighting to stay with us, to help us. "It all feels the same," she squeezes out.

And then I know I'm there—the last layer of muscle pares away, and the blood stops flowing for a moment, long enough for me to see the curve of a little thigh beneath the sparkle of the blade. I throw the knife away.

"There he is!" My eyes meet hers. "I have him!"

And, amid the prisoners' joyful cheering, I reach into her stomach and pull her baby out.

Her daughter.

AGNÈS

The rest is easy, cutting the cord, wiping blood and yellow cheese off the baby. Any two women can do that, so I'm allowed to help. It takes a saint to return inside and grope, to fish out a big purple liver of a thing with a cord still attached and veins like rivers everywhere.

"Don't let air into her," says the whore, who jumps to hold the vulva shut and bandage it—though nothing much came through there. Tardieu gets a needle and thread to stitch the gash.

Being sewn, the mistress passes out.

That leaves me to hold the baby. It's still sticky and smells like blood—or can I tell anymore? Little eyes shut tight, black fuzz on squashed head. This bug that's eaten its mother, as all children do. I hold it tight and hard. It's only a girl. It's only our doom.

Bonne's never been much good at stitchery. She seals this seam with a kiss, and doesn't care if I see.

Mistress! *I want to scream it, though she sleeps.* I would give you everything . . .

In her sleep, she murmurs, "Bonne . . ."

This is the baby!

A warm, moist bundle of doughy limbs, a half-set head misted black; black lashes over blue eyes, pinpricks of dimples and nipples and nails; a masculine omphalos (it will fall off). Whimpering kittenish cry; smell of warmth and wool.

How soon is too soon to nurse? While the mother sleeps, I put the mite to my breast. She isn't interested.

I wash Radegonde and then myself, making us both clean for mothering. I wish for perfume, to scent her brow and my bosom.

Agnès insists on swaddling the baby right away, so her limbs grow in right; we all tear up some towels, and I do the binding myself—even Agnès agrees I'm the one who knows it best. Looping carefully, hand over hand, wrapping this little bud up safe as a second womb.

I check the cut. (Baby slumped in the crook of my arm, already feeling right.) We are all surprised at how quickly it has stopped flowing. Radegonde's breath is even, if shallow. And if her womb doesn't suppurate, we tell ourselves that she might live.

We are exhausted. Enchanted. And free to go—our work is done; we could call the guards, ask to be let out, but we'd all rather stay. Agnès and the fillette curl up together in a corner, sharing the extra blanket; I lay down a fresh sheet and get into bed with Radegonde, baby tucked between us. When the little girl wakes, I'll nurse her.

The placenta ("mother cake," the farmers call it) sits in a basin by the bed. Tomorrow we'll bury it in Radegonde's rose garden.

Radegonde sleeps next to me, limp and stinking despite her bath. I snuggle down in bed and—one last time—kiss her on the lips. The baby mews.

S A I N T
M A R T H A ' S   D A Y
[J U L Y   2 9]

HERCULE

*Inter faeces et urinam, nascimur. Between piss
and shit are we born, and the road to heaven itself lies between the two. This I remember as, in
the darkness, I run from window to window
and whisper through the slatted shutters:*

Pierre is the father of Bonne. Pierre se-
duced the saint, Blanche. It was Pierre!

*This may not be enough to imprison him,
but it's surely enough to make rumors. Rumors
that will seep through the town's dreams and
leap from one bed to another. Rumors that, in
the morning, will cause people to see him anew.
Their spiritual father, prey to the sins of the
flesh.*

*In the ruined church, under the full moon,
I cut a vein. My blood pours into Marie's basin,
I spit three times, and here is what shows in the
bowl: A woman who loves. A woman who dies.
A chance for myself either way . . . and this, too,
I do for love, my own.*

I cradle this miracle in my arms, half-asleep
and half-atrance, hardly aware of the mother
at all.

A daughter. A pink-white bloom of a girl.
But now Radegonde is tossing and moan-

ing beside me, her fingers fretting at the cut, coming away all aglisten. The sheets are wet. I have to put the baby down. I give her to Marguerite.

But the little thing can cry in earnest now; she's eager for the breast. And praise the Virgin! Milk springs to the ready. Torn, I nurse, with one eye on the patient.

Agnès hasn't a thought to spare. She's fussing around the mother, wiping the maternal brow and offering a pot to piss in. "She's sick," the maid announces, looking at me as if it's my fault.

The cut has begun to swell, puffing around the sutures I so carefully threaded and tied. It sends forth a liquid that looks like water but feels thick and sticky. I probe with my fingers and the cut seems to suck at me. "It isn't serious yet. The fluid is still clear—if it turns yellow, then we'll have to worry."

We all know it's just a matter of time.

"What can we *do*?" Agnès frets.

"Vinegar," I say, as my breasts leak. "Wash the wound with vinegar."

I reach out for the baby again—milk over soft gums and rosebud lips. It's such a good, quiet feeling, nursing her. Somehow she is not like any other person, infant or adult, I've had at my breast. O Virgin, I pray, let me succeed where before I have failed. Let me protect this baby.

Radegonde plucks at my elbow with her broad, soft hand. "Let me see."

So I pull the child away from the nipple and resettle her, facing outward for display. Radegonde looks a long minute while her daughter gathers herself up for a scream.

"A girl?" asks the mother.

I nod. Radegonde sinks deeper into the pillows, and I put the baby back where she wants to be.

"What saint's day is this?"

I think. Time has lost meaning, and I have only the guards' visits to other cells to judge by. "Martha's, I believe."

"Marthe Putemonnoie." Radegonde's lips crack in distaste. "A housewife."

I say timidly, "Rose is a nice name."

Radegonde sighs. She doesn't answer, and I think she's falling asleep.

Soon after, the baby drifts off, too, and I pull back the sheets to check the cut. Its water has turned white.

A GNÈS
There is more.

In the night, she moans and gives birth again—to a lump of hair and splintered bone, tangled and clotted together. It starts out between the legs and gets stuck. The bandage bursts.

"Goodness." Even Bonne LaMère is shocked awake. Our Bonne, who thinks I don't see. She pulls out the strange thing and lets it drip through her fingers a moment. Then she tucks it in the basin.

"Never seen this before." Pushes it under the bed. "And didn't see it this time, either."

Maybe it snaked down the cut in the mistress, collecting blood and hair and bone, to push all the disease out in one lump. Maybe it is what will save her. Or maybe it's what the priests have been looking for.

Inside me, though it's very soon, I feel the flip of fins.

And she says again, "Bonne."

N THE MORNING, FATHERS PIERRE AND PAUL
are the first visitors. They come to gather the
final news, to see the baby for themselves.

I leave Radegonde beneath her sheet.
"She's sleeping," I say, and hope for the best. I
unwrap Rose so the church can witness her
perfection. With my shoe, I kick the basin farther under the bed.

Virgini gratias, Pierre doesn't ask to see
the placenta. Agnès and Marguerite watch,
tense, while the old priests contemplate the
wiggling, protesting mass of new person.
Pierre enters the cell to take her in his hands
and turn her this way and that—looking for
marks of the devil, perhaps; but little Rose is
perfect, the very image of purity (if a little
dusky, like her mother).

Finally Pierre holds her up to the torch to
comment on her black brows and lashes.
When the light hits her eyes, she screams, and
he nearly drops her. I take her from his spotty
hands and hush her in the time-honored way.

"A healthy infant," Paul pronounces.

"So she seems," Pierre tempers.

"Yes, Fathers. A good strong *girl*." I emphasize the last word, perhaps challenging

them to comment, but they don't. Although they must be thinking of the brother-in-law from Paris.

Pierre wipes his palms on his robe. "We hear you had to cut the mother open."

Word travels fast, even underground.

I admit, "That is, unfortunately, what must be done in many cases—to save the child or give the mother a chance. I hope I have done both."

"Hm." Pierre studies sleeping, sweating Radegonde a moment, then offers me a benediction and departs with his shadow.

Tiptoeing, half-afraid, the guards come by soon after. They're relieved to see the prisoner still alive, glad to see her delivered of a living child. One of them has a ribbon he wants her to bless; his wife, he says, will soon be in labor.

Radegonde's wound weeps milk.

SOON AFTER, as the prisoners break fast, Etienne comes with special news.

"The town fathers are meeting this afternoon. They will decide Mistress Putemonnoie's case." He peers through the bars at the tiny creature in my arms, then at the woman in the bed; he has a detached interest in the baby, and none in her mother. But he asks, "Is there something I can do?"

"Exorcism won't help," I say, jiggling Rose in my arms. "Her problem isn't a devil, it's wound fever."

Her problem is also motherhood—of a daughter. The town fathers might have been inclined to keep the mother of Henri's heir alive, and his taxes and business in town, but the mother of a useless girl can be conveniently called a witch and shunted off to the stake.

I wonder when she will be *put to the question*—the magistrates' gentle term for torture. As if they could invent anything worse than she's already endured.

"What about the trial?" Agnès breaks in. She's deliberately not looking at me, as if I am to blame for the mistress's fever (am I? Would a chaste woman fall ill?). "Father Etienne, when will the trial be? Should we go to the Palais de Justice today?"

"I wonder why they're calling the judges now," Marguerite murmurs, combing her hair with her fingers. "When . . . anything . . . might happen by nightfall."

"That's it," I say over the baby's soft skull. "They don't want to let an innocent woman, a visionary, die in prison. That would make her a martyr. They have to find her guilty first."

Guilty by reason of a girl.

GODFRIDUS

I have said to corruption, Thou art my father. To the worm, Thou art my mother and my sister.

I eat my mothers and sisters. I loved spirit but it was made flesh, and it is corruption. I am corruption. I, I, I am such as the worms churn with their filthy lust. And I eat them with disgust.

We are born to die. I eat.

God moves the worker's hands, and the work is good, but when the breath of mortals blows upon it, the body turns to dust. To worms. To corruption. The Queen of Heaven cannot rise unless she is dead. Murder brings us close to God. I eat.

"I'm dying."

My body jolts. Have I been asleep? The baby, Rose, rests in my arms, and we are in bed.

I roll halfway to one side, facing Radegonde. We're alone; Etienne took Marguerite and Agnès away. "Of course—"

Before I can say *not*, she interrupts: "And I don't mind. What is there to live for now?" She is utterly lucid. She doesn't even look at her baby— perhaps it's too much to bear, the thought of this rose growing without its mother.

Tenderly I stroke Radegonde's face. The bones there seem softer, despite their prominence; in her fasting she lost flesh, and she lost strength, too. "Don't you know a cure?" I ask hopefully. "You if anyone should be able to—"

"Bonne." Even dying, she can command with a word. "There is no hope. But I want you to do something."

"Of course." I close my eyes against what she has said. "Anything."

"Bring me the sculptor, your uncle."

In my arms, Rose leaks a long wind.

"Godfridus?" I try to keep the hurt out of my voice—hurt that, at such a time, she wants him. And is willing to send me away to get him.

"Yes, that one . . . You see, I want a sarcophagus like Henri's, carved, decorated, inscribed with my name and dates. So we'll be laid side by side in the new church crypt."

"I promise you'll have the sarcophagus, when the time comes—many years from now, I'm sure." I don't mention that her body will probably never enter the new church again—Pierre will see to that. "But God-fridus disappeared weeks ago." I add with a flash of clarity, "I think he's somewhere in the forest."

Radegonde looks at me with eyes whose colors have ebbed away. "So go to the forest. Find him."

She's addressing me not as Bonne-the-miracle-worker but as Bonne-the-nurse, former whore, former laundress, former picker of nits—it's my job to find hidden things. And because of that, I know she's the old Radegonde, miracle-ignorant, publicly pious, occult of soul, and used to command.

Now she's marshaling her own death. And proud of it.

"Yes," she breathes what might be her last, "bring me the sculptor—*quickly*. Take the baby with you . . . And one more thing." She's smiling now, seems to have recovered her serenity (and thus I know her prison visions were real; she ordered Christ to come to her, and he did). "Come here and kiss me."

I lean over and we kiss. A kiss of peace, with the baby between us.

THE BAKERWOMAN

Just a plain brown mouse by my husband's side. They don't see the pain that lifts my soul up.

On earth, my legs feel uncommon strong. Or rather, they don't feel at all, and that is their strength. They stand before the only palace our town has ever known.

Gray and square, like a tomb, the Palais de Justice. My husband calls this our oldest building, because as soon as there was a town there was a need

*for punishment. It has three doors in front, as to a church. Latched wide
open. Empty. Something will happen here soon.*

*Why let the woman die in prison? Let her instead burn by the market
cross, let the world know what she's done!*

"To the Palais! To Justice!" Criers sweep through the town.

I am here, I am ready.

We make a sound like fire, Rose and I, walking through the forest. She is
tied to my chest with a sheet, and my steps fall heavy on twigs and leaves.
Branches feather over us; the river flows loud beside, while its gouts of
light prick our eyes.

We are in the wild, and our world has dwindled down to two. My
palm caresses the soft little skull, sheltering it, fingers tucking it into a
fold of the sheet; I gaze into the pink rosebud face. "The daughter of
Radegonde and Henri Putemonnoie," I say out loud. She returns my look
unblinking, her mouth puckered like a raspberry.

"I found a needle in a haystack once before," I tell her. It's half a joke,
and her lips work their way to a coo. Like a mourning dove. But then she
smiles.

A feeling wells up in me. I must do something.

"Godfridus!" I call. "It's Bonne! I've come for you . . ."

I step with the sound like fire. The forest gathers its branches, listening, watching. But surely it is more than the forest I feel. My very bones
are alert: They detect the brush of a distant step, the break of a far-off
twig, the weight of eyes on my back. I smell it, too; it's not an animal
smell, not the odor of bear or dog, but the smell of a man—a man like the
one in the atrium, a man like the one in the haystack, who knows? A man.

I stop, turn—see no one. There's plenty a bush and a bank to hide behind. "Godfridus? Is that you?" After a moment, "Hercule?" But our fol-
lower is neither of these. And he could be anywhere between me and
Villeneuve.

I speed up, trot—deep, deeper into the wilderness, into the tangle of
boughs and trunks, green vines and prickles. Short of breath and reeking
of fear. Glad at least that Rose is hidden, bound so tight to me and so silent.

I should not have traced her parentage aloud. Anyone would covet a
child of the Putemonnoies. Even a wild man. Even a friend.

Burn the witch! Ring, ring the bells, summon the judges! Maître Civis, a wool merchant; Maître Froisson, maker of candles; Maître d'Orage, the town's richest meat man. From the priesthood we have Paul, a ranking father; Père Christophe, who's young and handsome; Father Luc of the lepers, who has looked on evil and kept all his fingers. Their table has been placed in a square of light.

Father Pierre shares his light with the prosecutor. It is this priest who brought the suit and chose the lawyer. His choice is a plain man, stout and wrinkled to dignity but no further. Like all advocates, he wears a floppy black hat.

The accused's defender has a harelip.

The shouting begins. Burn the witch!

In the romances, a woman in my position (alone, afoot, in danger) almost always twists her ankle. Steps in a snake hole, a rabbit hole, a toad hole, and falls to her rescue—a dark handsome man who sweeps away her attacker with one blow of the sword, sweeps her into his arms, sweeps the hair off her brow.

367

Some part of this happens to me. Deep in the forest, I fall.

A twig trips me. The baby unbalances me. I pitch forward but manage to twist myself and land on my back, Rose atop. She wails; I pant; branches whirl overhead, scissoring the sky. We wait for our fate.

And there is the creature herself, last to enter. A baby was cut out of her last night, and it lived, and here she is anyway. Alive as well. Her body sags, her weight depends on two guards to drag it along, but she lives. There is a dark wet spot on the front of her dress.

"A miracle!" A man dares to shout it. Then he disappears.

The crowd surges forward.

When the whirling stops, silence sinks like a blanket. Whatever was behind us has gone.

"It is all right," I say to Rose. "I was imagining things." I pat her swaddled bottom, catching my breath. "Just imagining."

The judges find the defendant impudent in her refusal to stand. Even the subjects of torture—which they assure her believers she is not—must stand trial. The lids flutter over her eyes, and her breath comes faint. Her lawyer says she cannot stand.

"You are accused . . . You are accused . . ." It goes on.

Pierre approaches the judges' table. His robe opens a hole in the room and fills it with light. "Good friends, I have long suspected la Putemonnoie of witchcraft. But I would not come to court without complete proof, and now my proof is sure. The testimony I offer is sanctioned by Mother Bonne. It is her careful observation of the woman, and the reports she made to me, that confirmed my suspicions and enabled the town to bring this woman to justice."

I am a good woman. Burn the witch.

The harelip speaks. "Father, were you Mistress Putemonnoie's confessor?"

Is this the kind of question, the kind of justice, they teach in the big city? The so-called center of bread-making, tale-spinning, and law. My husband visited there once.

"As far as I know," says the father, "she chose not to make confession."

I had heard that the woman—the witch—took Communion every week, and to do that you must confess. But would a priest lie?

"So then," says the lip, "if she did not confess, you have no direct knowledge of any sins, misdeeds, or practices of the mistress?"

"I have reports."

"Reports are not confession." The man turns to the judges. "I propose this person be disqualified from giving witness. He can present only rumors."

Who then should give witness?

"They are not rumors, but reputation," says the priest. "Mistress Bonne told me herself."

I remember. There's another bundle I'm carrying. Wrapped in linen, bloody, rotting—the mother cake and . . . the other thing . . . I take it all from my pocket and bury it by a shrub. So deep the animals won't know what's there, I bury the wastes of motherhood.

I feel ashes drift over my lips, my hands . . . When I try to brush them away, I touch nothing.

THE BAKERWOMAN

"God may make a woman beautiful, but the Devil makes her enticing."

At last the prosecutor has found the meat of the matter. La Putemonnoie is exactly my age and far from my equal, and we all want to know why.

Her advocate, de la Clyte, taps his finger on a ledger. "Can you name me one man," he says, as if he has the testimony of every townsman with him, "whom Madame Putemonnoie can be accused of tempting and betraying with her body?"

The reply is ready. "Can you name me one she has not?"

Husband . . . my husband, what would you say? You who loved the White saint, who saw her fall and still loved her. Who inflicted her daughter on me, over my head, walking on my floors and hailing plaster into our bed.

Marriage is contract, not sacrament. Look at me.

Did that woman tempt you?

You look. You smile.

"Judges," says de la Clyte, "Fathers. This woman has been set aside by God."

A sudden squawk. I have been in a stupor, staring into the air and seeing nothing. But this cry, this wail—my body responds and drags my heart after it, through the ducts of my dugs into somebody else's mouth.

There is a baby in my arms. It wants its belly filled and its bottom wiped. I have a choice between this life and a long-ago death.

So I unwrap the baby, clean her, rewrap. I pull my clothes to my waist and let her latch again to my breast. We set off along the river and into the heart of the wood, the trackless evergreen thickness where sun never shines.

Rose is an excellent navigator. She doesn't need to speak or even keep her eyes open; it's the pressure of her tongue on my teat, the heat of her breath on my flesh that tells me to turn this way or that, to push through this thicket or step around that one. She has me leave the river that was my guide—and this is good, for just moments afterward I hear a splash and a day-waking wolf swims from the very spot on which we just stood.

Rose leads me so deep that there is no more day-waking or night-sleeping; the very air turns black around us. I can't see her or even my own hand in front of my face. It is the long dark time of the womb, or of death. But still we go forward.

THE BAKERWOMAN

He stands before the town with forked beard trembling, dust swirling from his robes. He whose face should not see light of day. Why he? We all know the woman would not trust her face creams and eye salves to other hands, not even the hands of a Jew. She makes them herself, at midnight, under the moon.

"Judges," says the defender of the wraith, "Fathers. This man knows nothing of the accused. Moreover, he is a Jew, and by law Jews can no more testify in court than women can."

"He is a witch," says Pierre, "and thus can indict another."

The lip twitches scornfully. "He is no witch. Jews poison wells, they do not work magic . . . You have a coop of confessed witches in your prison— why don't you call one of those? I will tell you why. Those women have been living side by side with the accused for weeks now. They know her spirit, they know her soul. You may put them to the whip, the poker, and the thumb-screw all you like—and I am sure you have done so—but God will not let even a witch blaspheme against His saints."

A stir in the courtroom. The defendant's head has swooned.

I stop, look around. My eyes have become accustomed to the blackness and can make out shapes and colors within it. An ebony tree, a dun flower, a leaden stump. They give me the truth I have always trusted. I use them to gaze down at my Rose. She looks up at me, still nursing, her eyes new-born cornflowers in the thicket of shadow. Mouth on the nipple, she smiles.

Ahead of us, in the darkness, there is a sudden stillness. Slowly I look up.

I think I am dreaming, or having a vision. A man does indeed stand there. Or something in the shape of a man. To my steeped eyes, he looks entirely red—hair, body, eyes.

Hastily I free a hand and cross myself, then sign the cross over Rose and shield her. "We are Christians," I say to him. "I stop you in the name of God, and of Christ and the Holy Virgin."

He parts his lips. I see a yellow gleam and I'm ready to dash.

But under my hand, Rose explodes. The entire tiny bundle of her puts itself into a scream, and she shakes my hand away. Then smiles. And puts the pink tongue between her lips and blows at the devil.

He steps forward.

I step back. "You can't have her!" But Rose is still beaming at him, and I look harder. And behold the face of my oldest friend.

THE BAKERWOMAN

"Remove the Jew!"

"Raise Radegonde!"

The crowd beats like a heart. They want to see her for themselves—someone has said blood's flowing from a ring around her skull, and her cropped hair is scarlet with it. Has Christ given her the ultimate honor, a crown that echoes His own?

At the judges' order, the guards surround her. Their broad backs make a fortress, and we can see nothing. But those in front still insist there is blood spurting from her brow, and the news travels backward.

A priest shoves his way to the front of the room. He wears a cowl, but his hands glow. "Fathers," he says, "judges. I am an exorcist, an expert in the subject of demons and witches. Let me investigate the case. I need only an hour—"

The men on the bench turn to Pierre. He runs his hands through his hair. But before he can speak, Maître Civis says, "Yes. Yes, you may have an hour."

The other judges look at him. He stares defiance.

She is taken away.

AN HOUR, my husband, my spouse. An hour of pain, of the hand squeezing my belly and breasts. We wait. Can you not feel it?

How I have loved you.

And in an hour she is back. Her eyes still closed, her head still wobbling. Yes, there is a little streak of blood, but it isn't dripping—it could have come from anywhere. The guards carry her now.

The investigator mounts the dais. In his own words, he tells the court what he has sought—breath foul from the Devil's anus, a womb cold from the Devil's prick, an outsize bud, swollen like a man's for orgies, and an extra teat, disguised as wart, birthmark, or scar, for nursing the Devil's spawn. Lastly, he says, he doused her with holy water, which will raise welts on a witch.

Aside from the smear of blood around her head and the gash already on her belly, he says he found nothing.

Handsome Father Christophe has a question. "What is your name, brother, and have you a parish?"

"My name is Etienne. My parish, the Little Church by the Side of the Road to Poitiers."

Judge Father Paul frowns. "That is not within our demesne. Your evidence must be considered inconclusive."

The crowd roars—but not for him.

Someone has said la Putemonnoie's hands are bleeding.

I scream, "Let us see for ourselves!" and my husband hoists me up.

Yes, this is my friend, my putative uncle. I recognize his bony nose, his sparse hair. He is red, but that is because he's naked and burnt by the sun, briar-scratched and mud-soaked. It looks as if he's flayed himself on purpose, removed his skin for martyrdom. The glow around him is the glow of pain.

"My friend," I say, "you must come back to Villeneuve."

He dashes off, to hide behind a tree. And he peeks around the trunk like a wood sprite. His lips form part of the word, but no sound at all: *Ville . . . vie.*

"I *think* you are Godfridus," I say. "Do you recognize me? I am Bonne, your—niece."

His lips mouth, *Bonne.* He approaches slowly, then flings himself down on his knees. He can't keep himself from me. He stares, rapt, as if all the light of the world is contained in me. Or isn't. When I follow his red eyes, I see they are trained not on me but on Rose.

She burbles and waves to him with her eyes.

I shrink. "This is not my baby. But you must know that. This is Radegonde's baby. And Radegonde needs you."

He smiles. At the baby. As at something he has created.

"I never saw the face," he says.

THE BAKERWOMAN

I see nothing. She's surrounded. And there's a rumor now that the exorcist cut her hands himself, to help her cause. Pierre has discredited him.

And so the final witness is called. A slender maid with swelling eyes, Radegonde's personal servant, Agnès of Paris, maid to the woman I could have been. It is said that she begged Pierre to let her speak. It is said that she promised him much. It is sure that the church has done something to get her here, as we all live by a rule that forbids women voice.

Each pair of lungs reserves its breath. What has occasioned this great bending of the law?

It is so quiet we hear pigeons outside.

The prosecutor begins, "You have known the accused how long?"

"I have always worked for the Putemonnoies," the maid says. "Ever since I was a child."

The judges nod approvingly—this woman deserves to speak. Satisfied, the prosecutor says, "And you have seen her with her husband, the late Henri Putemonnoie?"

"Of course. I worked for both of them."

"And you were there at his death." This is not a question.

"I was."

"And what do you know of this death?"

"That it happened in his sleep, after a long illness."

The prosecutor paces up and down through shafts of gray sunlight. He turns and asks suddenly, "Did the accused bring about the death in any way? By witchcraft, for example?"

The courtroom gasps. The maid stays calm. "No," she says. "His heart went bad."

There comes a cheer somewhere behind us—husband, do you hear it? The prosecutor goes white. He must have counted on hearing differently. It is a long time before he speaks again, then he asks, "Did you witness the birth of Radegonde Putemonnoie's child?"

Agnès looks level at him. "I did."

"Will you describe it?"

"I will." She does. The woman's water sac would not burst, and the woman's fetus would not come forth. The child's limbs were wedged against nature and could not be set to rights.

This we knew already.

The wrinkled prosecutor proceeds with confidence. He steps into a stripe of light. "That is when you decided to cut her open?"

"No, maître. That is when Mistress Putemonnoie ordered us to cut. That is, she ordered Bonne to cut. Bonne LaMère."

Another cheer behind us. The man proceeds, "But you made the cut, did you not?"

"I did not. Bonne cut her. Then the baby's head popped up and she wailed."

He rushes on, "Was it the accused who wailed?"

"No, she fainted."

"Did you think she was dying?"

"I was sure of it. I'd never seen a woman live through that before."

Triumphantly, the prosecutor addresses us all. "And yet you see," he says, with a gesture toward la Putemonnoie, "she lives." He turns back to the servant. "And did the child look healthy?"

"Very."

"Did it live, too?"

"As far as I know."

"And how was this witchcraft worked? What did you see?"

"Nothing," she replies. "Only Bonne. If Mistress Putemonnoie is a witch, then Bonne LaMère is one, too."

Godfridus's voice crackles, as if he hasn't used it in a long time. But I make out the words, and I understand. He never saw the Face, the face of the child he had carved and whose life he had once tried to emulate.

"Your statue is beautiful," I say. I try to think what he needs to hear, he who is thinking of his work. "People come from miles around to look—you can be very proud. And you must know God approves."

He shakes his head, as if trying to make sense of me. I'm afraid he might still see me as a stranger. If he looks red to me in this darkness, how must I look to him? Like painted marble, glowing white, holding a baby.

"But one thing is surprising," I continue gently. "Why did you put this figure on the altar, sign your name, and leave? Why haven't we seen you these weeks?"

The fiery eyes shift from side to side; he scratches nervously. He seems confused and about to bolt. I don't think he knows what I'm talking about.

Then I know: Of course he was not the one who brought the Virgin to the church. He didn't even sign the name that I rubbed out—the lettering was too clumsy for his hand. He went mad the night of the feast, mad from work and wine, and hasn't been right since. Someone played a trick on him. Someone removed him from this world.

It is up to me to bring him back.

"God loves you," I say. "Christ loves you."

The flaming face looks hunted.

I say, "You are God's child. I am not the Virgin you made, but she is worthy to be his bride."

The red loins tense. Only Rose's laughing coos hold him here. I approach very, very slowly, holding the baby so that he may see but not touch her. There is a strange light about him, and it is not only from pain and the sun.

"Please." Cautiously, careful of Rose, I lower myself to him. I touch his face with my hand. His flesh scorches mine. "Godfridus, you are ill."

GODFRIDUS

I have made false idols and found them good—
> *The Queen must die to ascend.*
> *I reach, and my hands fit her neck like gloves.*

THE BAKERWOMAN

The room is in an uproar. Almost every throat joins the cry, "We are grateful for miracles!" The people are shoving, surging, trying to catch the maid. She runs behind the judges and looks out over us. She seems smug.

Father Etienne, of the Little Church, jumps up. His voice thunders through the noise—"You are the people," he says, "of miracles!"

The judges bang on their table. They bang till it cracks down the middle, exposing the white wood within.

Paul screams, "Remove the accused! It is easier for a camel to pass through—"

His words are drowned as the guards stand. They grasp Radegonde Putemonnoie's elbows and pull. Then suddenly the guards vanish, but she stands on her own. Have they run away?

At this, the crowd explodes. "We are grateful! We are grateful!"

No, it seems the guards have slipped in a puddle. A thick red pool now seeping to the palace floor.

It comes from la Putemonnoie's feet. This is what the people say, and what I feel in my heart to be true.

Husband, I am burning, burning. Bring me forward.

"Godfridus!" I cough. "You're choking me!"

And he stares with those red eyes as his grip gets tighter, and tighter still. I struggle, but even with these weeks in sun and wood he's too strong for me. Rose begins to cry, but he doesn't hear. What will he do to *her?*

I know this: He is going to kill me. Already I hear a rushing in my ears, and my eyes and my tongue are bulging. Swooning, I force that tongue to move one last time—

I choke out, "Don't—do this . . . mortal sin . . . Not when you have— shown . . . the way to Christ . . ."

I will never know exactly why these words stop him. But I will be forever glad of their magic. All of a sudden his hands are gone and I can fall back, gulping sweet air. I shield Rose with my body and she falls quiet.

"Godfridus . . ." My throat is sore, and I can barely speak. I am edging away, trying to put safe distance between us. But I feel little Rose's head craning to look at the wild man, and I feel her little lips smile. "Godfridus, why?"

The red face has crumpled. He begins to weep, and his tears root him to the earth. They bring him back to us.

G ODFRIDUS

She says, "Don't weep, you'll burn yourself. You're starving, I will feed you."

So I am forgiven. I crawl forward and suck, with the infant between us. And I am grateful.

My tears splash that baby. A mortal baby. He puts out his tongue and drinks. Him they do not burn—him they nourish. Bonne gazes in wonder.

"Godfridus, Godfridus," she murmurs.

I close my eyes, as she closes hers. And I think that together we see a fig-ure clad in blue and white, her feet cradled in the crescent moon, rising toward the sky . . . Queen of Heaven.

His skin cools as if, drinking, he steps into a spring river. He becomes cool enough to bear a touch, and I run my fingers in his hair, combing out the tangles, easing out the leaves. He drinks and drinks, and Rose lets him.

We are at peace. I have that good feeling—not the feel of the second heart, but good enough for this world.

And that thought makes me remember.

I pull his head away from me; I'm nearly empty anyway. "We have to get back—as soon as we can."

"It is almost night," he says, his voice still crackling but regaining strength. "I know a place to sleep. I'll watch over you all night. We can stay as long as you like—"

"We can't stay even one night," I interrupt. "Radegonde Putemon-noie wants you. She sent me for you. Godfridus, she's dying."

"Dying?" I think I see his skin fade to white, and I feel a stab of my own special pain. "How? Why?"

"She's caught a womb fever," I say, perhaps harshly. "It is incur-able—her wound is rotting away, and she is going mad. She will die. I can't leave her alone."

THE BAKERWOMAN

"Take her!" Father Pierre shouts it. "Take her to prison! We will try her again in private!"

"No!" shouts Civis, equally loud, and Froisson and d'Orage are behind him. "Take her to my house—to my wife."

The guards hesitate. Where does their duty lie? It is three judges against three.

Whatever they do, they must face the crowd. We are slipping and slid-ing on one another but coming toward them. Where the words came from we don't know, but soon our whisper is a roar: "Father Pierre is a ruiner of saints! Pierre defiles the holy!"

Radegonde, Blanche, Bonne. It is for them we advance.

Radegonde Putemonnoie sways. She seems to be smiling, or perhaps that's because she can't hold any other look. She touches her hands to her belly, then her crown, and then there is blood on her cheeks.

The people bleat, "We are grateful for miracles!"

And so we are granted another. A flock of gray doves swoop through the windows and alight on Radegonde. They dig their claws in her shoulders, her arms, her hair, and they beat their wings.

"Husband, they will take her to heaven!" And saying this, I fall. The last taste in my mouth is the taste of Putemonnoie blood.

The sunset stains the land without the town; within, the shadows have begun their reign. At the Narbonne gate the guards know me. They're not used to seeing me with a crying baby and a wild man wearing my chemise, but they give way immediately.

"Mother." They bow respectfully, ask no questions.

So we enter this brown blot, this mottle of wood and smoke and painted churches. People are scarce, as the time is near curfew, or perhaps they are still tending their home gardens. Only the cats and stray dogs are still about, with the occasional pig, and they follow their business with no regard for us.

We pass the new church. Godfridus doesn't give it a look. We walk through the deserted marketplace, where I see half a rotten cauliflower and think how quickly times change. A few weeks ago people would have fought for this thing like dogs for a bitch.

And here is the prison.

GODFRIDUS

She will not believe till she sees it with her own eyes. She demands that the guards show her. She brings me and the baby so we must see it, too.

The cell is empty. Completely empty—no bed, no basins, not even a speck of straw remains.

"She is gone! She is gone!" keen the other prisoners.

Bonne comforts her child. "But where?"

"Mother"—a guard clears his throat—"we do not know."

Outside, the believers have assembled. They wait with the prison widows, a candlelight vigil. Their lips are praying. Do they wait for me or my mistress?

I step into their midst, Godfridus and Rose on either arm. "Who do you follow?" I ask them.

They answer, "We follow!"

They follow me, gray and obedient, to the great house, the one place I know to go. They give up their usual silence and ask to kiss my hands, kiss Rose. They even seem ready to embrace Godfridus, this strange wild man. I think they are drunk. And so they are, drunk with miracles—but not yet, thank God, surfeited.

As we walk together, the faithful tell me the story that is many stories. How Radegonde bled. How Pierre tried to make me a traitor. How Agnès tried to make me a witch. How Radegonde was surrounded by a cloud of pigeons and raised toward the rafters. How the crowd surged and slipped and lost sight of her, and how the people now think that Pierre is my father (though I know this cannot be). They tell Godfridus of a wonderful statue set on the altar at the new church. He says nothing.

We hear that the bakerwoman, my former hostess, died with blood on her lips. I hear she died exalting us, Radegonde and me. This I cannot believe.

379

Radegonde, I keep thinking. Radegonde is dead. The words make no sense.

As we approach the district of great houses, a light grows around us. It is the moon, bright for the second time this month. And it is the Putemonnoie house, with light in every room. Even the tower's lit like a star.

The keys are still at my belt. Useless in the wilderness, they will save us here. I let Godfridus in first, then swing the gate shut behind me and Rose. The doves wait without, ever patient. The ribbons on the bars stream in the breeze.

From Henri Putemonnoie's livre de raison
To enliven the corpse of a dead man, place a ring from the left hand of a bishop upon the hand or foot of the body and say the following charm: "Hare's blood, knight's brood, furrow in the moon." If it is well spoken, for

the next six days will six demons appear in turn, to inhabit the corpse and
make it sit, walk, and speak. If you do not anger the demons, the dead man
will do your bidding.

A woman's body is not recommended for this charm, as it is prone to de-
ceit and disappointment, and will often turn against the summoner.

For the purpose of prophesying, a spirit can be made to appear to a boy
who has not yet known the flesh of woman (or, rarely, to a virgin girl, if a
special purification is undergone). The charm to summon such a spirit is
this: "Nauta, reginae, cum cura dixit." The spirit will appear in the quick of
the boy's fingernail. When the image becomes clear, the boy must ask if the
spirit is hungry. If the answer is yes, provide the spirit with a shoulder of
mutton. It will tell you what you wish to know.

The uses of these charms are innumerable, but they must be applied
with caution.

The house is empty. The servants have deserted again, this time without
looting—the chests and tapestries, chairs and coffers stand or hang in
their accustomed places. And on every surface I see a prick of light.

At my side, Godfridus trembles. He hasn't been here since the place
drove him mad. I see he fears return to wildness.

"Come." I take his hand. I feel a sense of inevitability—there may be
something here for our lost souls. "We'll show Rose where she was conceived."

The baby nestles into me. I've never seen a child who smiled so soon.

I know the way now. Up the stairs and past the solar, up and down the
corridors we go, Godfridus's hand hot in my own. In good time, we reach
the room with its great velvet bed.

The door is closed. We push it open.

And there—surprise!—we find what we've been seeking.

GODFRIDUS
The lights are everywhere—resting on the floor and on chests, even on the
bed itself, where they are fixed in puddles of wax. The place could go up in
flames any heartbeat.

Bonne and I look, and look at each other in wonder. It seems we are see-
ing the same thing, it seems this is real.

This is the reason for the light. On the bed lies Radegonde Putemon-noie, stretched like a queen on a bier. On an altar. Naked, but draped with a fur.

Agnès, who once attended me, attends her now. She sits with the candles on the edge of the bed, weeping. She strokes the woman's shaven skull. She barely notices us.

So the astonishing Radegonde Putemonnoie has died, I think. She escaped prison and the stake in order to die in bed.

Sometime along the way, Bonne drops my hand. Now she lifts the baby, steps to the body, and whispers, "See? This is the woman who bore you."

And Agnès, I remember, is the one with whom I . . .

When I speak, Radegonde's eyelids flutter.

Before I can think, Maybe it's a trick of my breath, maybe the wind or the candles' heat—I see her bosom rise and I hear, ever so faintly, the soft outrush of a sigh. I stagger back.

"She's alive!" The heart pounds loud in my ears. "But how . . ." It is useless to ask. Agnès has no thought for me, only for her grief, and it's as if I'm not even here. I see that if Radegonde is living, it will be for the shortest of whiles.

In the bed my mistress sighs again; this is how she breathes, I realize. And her maid says nothing. So I think it must in fact be the doves, always Radegonde's enemies, who saved her. Not friends, not guards, but doves.

Godfridus's huge hand hovers over the maid's head, but he does not touch. "Will she die?"

As I begin to weep myself, Agnès's sobs renew. I see her lean into him, heedless of the chemise or his ruddy skin. She shows no surprise at seeing him, not even gladness.

"Then," he says, pulling himself together, "I must find my tools."

G*ODFRIDUS*

They warm to the hands, they sing to the touch. They were here all along, waiting. But I have become stiff.

I cannot give the woman what she wants, I cannot give her corruption—I can carve only what I see. Her perfect face, her strong, soft hands, unbroken.

While Agnès weeps, Bonne unpacks a chest that depicts the Wise and Foolish Virgins. With my hammer, she dismantles it. She presents me with a board from the bottom, rich cherrywood. I take up my gouger, walk to where Agnès is not, and carve.

Balancing that baby, Bonne pulls the fur from the mistress, and as I thought, she is nude. Her limbs are smooth, her fleece is long. Her belly bears the signs of struggle. It is still swollen—perhaps it doesn't think itself empty yet.

Or perhaps it is too empty. Bonne unwraps the baby, wipes it clean, and places the wriggling pink thing upon its mother, over her wound. Then Radegonde sighs again, and her belly seems to shrink, and she is the woman we have long known.

Bonne stands behind me as I work, taking my careful strokes.

"You know," Bonne says softly, "the baby is a girl."

"I know. I see." And I will show the world.

It is Agnès who suggests it—Agnès who surprises me, because until now she has not seemed to believe in me. Maybe she believes in Radegonde. Or maybe she thinks it is worth trying anything.

"Suckle her," she begs, as Radegonde's face takes shape under my friend's knife. They are the first words she's spoken since Godfridus and I arrived. "Give her the Miracle of the Milk."

My blood runs cold. What am I to do? I who in my day could command a whole town, could perhaps still command them, based on their claims for my milk. Their claims to a wonder that was not a miracle at all, no matter how I have hoped, just the result of my own good fortune and nature's resilience. When I see Death before me, I know I have no special powers.

"I don't think so," I say, feeling the milk shrink deep within me. "It would be foolish to expect . . . that . . . to work."

We hear Godfridus scraping, shaping woman and child. In sleep, Rose apes her mother.

When I look back, Agnès's ferrety eyes have gone soft. She understands my fears and my pain; she feels them, too, but she still has hope. "Christ gave her His heart," she says, stroking her own belly. "Can't you give a little blood?"

And so I do.

As I have said, it is our oldest instinct. To suck. And to give forth.

HERCULE

Stars, show me something real. Show me something else.

Good . . . Good . . . At last I see it. The only way to be with her.

Watch me—if you can! Drained limbs move fast—they have no weight to bear. Except the weight of what will hide them, will block them stonily— for my body slides like moonlight, then builds a wall against the moon.

One . . . two . . . three . . . four. I build and build.

And now you cannot see me. Because there's nothing left. Only rubble in a heap, a slit of sky to read by, and a flock of winging doves that shit upon the rooftops. I am the anchorite, and to her anchor will she return.

This at least I know.

Radegonde's lips work on me and I forget everything else—Agnès, Godfridus, the town, and the trial. I feel nothing but that good sensation spreading from her lips to my body—my whole body, all of me. She gives me that, and it is worth forgetting all else now.

All except the baby. Except Rose. As I lean over the bed, I attach her mouth to the other nipple, and the two of them suckle together, mouths in rhythm.

My heart, two hearts, dance.

THERE IS A CRASH. I'm pulled back into myself—surrounded by sputtering candles and wooden planks. My caliginous mistress lies beneath me, sucking no longer.

When I spring up, cloudy liquor runs down my ribs. "What happened?" The mouths in the bed close as one.

Godfridus has thrown the wood panel to the floor and is crouching on top of it, in his chemise, attacking the board with his chisel the way a carpenter would attack the looter of a temple. It lies in splinters.

"What are you doing?" I catch at his arms, and they're burning again.

With a wince of pain he stops, his head hung low and his eyes weeping once more.

"I can see it in my mind," he says. "I see it . . ."

Agnès appears not to hear. She still sits by Rose and Radegonde, the woman my milk failed to save.

"Then let *us* see," I plead. "Finish the statue of our mistress." By now I am begging as much for myself as for her. I add tenderly, "Don't destroy the gift you give us. God gave it to *you.*"

He groans, and I think he'd gouge his own flesh if his arms were free. "It isn't right. It isn't right."

"It's beautiful," I say, though I haven't seen the panel. "It's perfect."

He tears himself away and looks straight at me, red-eyed. "It is wrong. Wrong! And *you* are wrong. I have no gift—I will never carve again."

He bolts.

GODFRIDUS might do himself a great injury, perhaps even the greatest, if he isn't caught. How I will subdue him once I have him, I don't know. But I know I should try.

I search the hall, the warehouses, the room where Henri is kept. All their doors are unlocked; all their candles are lit. I go every place I know, and many I haven't seen before. I find the mirror with the carved ivory lady, showing then hiding my startled face.

I run farther, faster—I shout myself hoarse. "Godfridus! Godfridus!"

At last I stop and listen. I am lost, and the walls are repeating my name.

HERCULE

I hear it everywhere. In the blow of the wind, in the drift of the stars. And can only erase it with words of my own:

"Two moons in June quicken the womb—Two in July, someone will . . ."

When I finally give up and find myself again, as I do by climbing stairs and following the random dictates of my heart, the tapers have burned low. Some are dead. The smell of beeswax fills each room, and tendrils of smoke wisp in and out before my eyes. I have to palm my way to the bedroom again.

think they saw. I half-listen to their stories and consider my possibilities. A convent. The orphanage. To be a nun, to be a recluse, to journey to a foreign land and try my fortune there. I know I am too little a soul for any of these. Perhaps those who are greater will try.

The faithful shout, "We are grateful for miracles!"

GODFRIDUS

I run, and the streets are lit white. This time I know the glow's of the moon, not my creation—I am nothing, and He is everything, and my Lady must vanish.

The one thing I have made and loved, the one that sent me into wildness. My Lady . . . I imagine what it will be like to hold her body between my legs again, this time to smash her to dust. A pain and a pleasure. After this I will never hold a chisel. I will serve God some other way.

Humble, poor, and chaste. I've been only one of these.

The moon shows me people—a prostitute, a priest, a Jew. None of these is the work of my hands, but they deserve my love much more. "Bless you!" I cry, as if I possess the power to bless anyone.

And here is the new church, with the door standing open. I hear the sound of prayer, and I enter.

And I am saved. Moonlight floods through the windows, tempered by the stained glass. My Lady—my Queen—stands before me. So beautiful . . . Slowly, slowly her eyes open, and they are blue and red and green, every color that is lovely. She says, "You are forgiven."

I weep.

Of course, there is just one place for me: the place it all began, the place I know my life will end. Saint-Porchaire.

This has been a day of wonders, and here is another. When I reach the ruined wall, when I step over the stones and approach my scattered bone piles, my followers do not stop. They follow me and are not afraid. I don't have to tell them, "This is a holy place," because on this day of miracles they know it. They have walked through the fire to see, and now they walk over bones.

From the blackened hulk of Saint-Porchaire, a white pillar rises to the moon. The fire colors everything else, even the moon itself, but this

It is open. It is shuttered, dark. Only by groping my way forward across the floor and into the bed do I make the discovery.

Rose lies alone, naked, with wetness spreading beneath her.

"Radegonde," I whisper. "Where have you gone?"

WHERE HAS SHE GONE, where did she come from?

There are some who will tell me she was never here, that God gave me visions tonight. But there are others who will say that, just before the fire began, they watched a figure in black and a figure in brown lead two horses from the stables, mount them bareback, and ride across the court-yard to where the gates swung open of their own accord. Both figures gleamed with gold and jewels. Both had their hair down.

These are all believers. They just believe different things.

Very few of the flock are left by the time Rose and I fight our way free of the house and come running for the street. Those who are there have thought they would witness my martyrdom, for as the shadowy fig-ures ride away it seems that every room ignites at once, and inside, though I stumble choking from corridor to chamber, I can't find a way out. I end up at the solar window with flames at my back, staring down at the green things in the garden far below. And because Rose is in my arms, and be-cause she deserves a life, I am able to find my courage. I climb onto the sill and jump.

For a moment it feels as if we're floating in the air, buoyed up by the heat and smoke and maybe something else. Then we fall, hair and skirts streaming, Rose screaming. I manage to land on a bush, and we come up with a few scratches, nothing more—those, and the black tears pouring from our eyes. We are in the garden. No one sees this.

But I see—that Rose is in my arms, safe. That we squeeze through the garden gate and run across the courtyard into the bosom of my flock, that my feet are tired and sore, and that we must find a place to rest.

There may be some better story. I don't know.

Jewels pop like stars, and hands are scorched in catching them. Molten gold marries the flesh that grabs for it. I imagine Henri burning along with his fortune.

The believers, unscathed, dove my footsteps and tell of what they milky column is unstained. Drawing close, we cross the atrium where the wooden skulls stare, the Grim Reapers dance. The people look, and in the orange-red light the skeletons seem to smile.

Though I know the place is empty, I am comforted to hear a voice calling out from the shadows: "Blood on the moon, you'll be home soon."

It is a voice I know.

I wish I could have had one last kiss, one last look from the everycolor eyes. But perhaps this will be enough:

The doves keep coming, gathering with candles and tales of wonder. I see the town's midwives, in from the forest. I see nuns from the orphanage, shining-eyed, carrying nurselings. Some doves bear other burdens; Etienne arrives with an armload of ashes, Marguerite with a skirtful of stones, and they lead a flock who've rescued other bits of wealth from the flames. One by one they lay their smoking tokens at my feet—lumps of heavy grayness, feather-light flakes of ash. They bow and fall back.

It is only after some time, when the offerings have piled up to my knees, that I realize these stones are smoked gold and jewels, these ashes leaves of Henri's book. They're worthless to a Paris merchant, thus now Rose's—and mine—and we will be glad of every damaged treasure. The parchment surfaces have burned away, but the ink has stayed deep in them and seems to glow now, begging to be read. A few bear my own writing and must look precious to the doves who can't read.

Nestling together, sharing light from their candles, the people gaze at me from the bone field. It is as if they are witnessing life—not miracles—for the first time.

With Rose on my arm, I reach into my pocket and pull out the one object I brought from the flames. The mirror. I turn the glass outward and press the button so the carved woman falls away.

Now the faithful can see themselves, perhaps for the first time in their lives. They crowd around me, feet crushing bones to dust.

"My children . . ." I say, and I pause—because I know my next words will be written down, and I want them to be good.

BLESSED BONNE LaMÈRE, ALSO CALLED MIRABILIS

c. 1350–?

FEAST DAY, JULY 31

LOCAL SAINT OF THE FORMER VILLENEUVE (now Mondville), Bonne LaMère was the illegitimate daughter of a woman once believed to have participated in a miracle herself. Orphaned at age twelve, Bonne lived for some years as an urchin before 1367, when she turns up in the town records as a wet nurse. Her career was of little distinction until Villeneuve was besieged in 1372; then general famine became the rule until Bonne miraculously began to nurse virtually the entire town for some weeks. It was her first miracle. She is said thereafter to have cured several people of severe affliction, including a sick child who lived with her, and a madman who later became a monk. She is also associated with the miraculous appearance of a statue in her likeness, now unfortunately lost.

Bonne weathered a number of misfortunes, including the death of her former patroness, before founding an orphanage on the

From *L'Encyclopédie spirituelle du Haut Poitou médiéval*, edited by Enid Dardanelles (Paris: Presses Universitaires de France, 1965).